Don't brin

Ronald D Morgan

Printed by CreateSpace

events or localities is purely coincidental.

Ron Morgan was born in Shrewsbury and has lived and worked in the USA and Canada. Ron has travelled extensively, tour managing groups worldwide and running his own tour company Ron Morgan Travel until 2001. He was a teacher of travel, tourism and business for twenty years and a Green Badge guide to tourists around the medieval town of Shrewsbury. Since 1995 Ron and his wife Dianne have devoted time to the charitable fund they founded, Dreamcatcher Children, which brightens the lives of chronically and terminally ill children and their families. Ron and Dianne continue to live in Shrewsbury.

for Mum and Dad, who gave me a wonderful childhood and the path to opportunity.

1

Billy Williams brushed away the cobwebs from his face as he bent his tall frame into the musty world of his parents' low-beamed attic space. What treasures had his now departed parents left for him to discover, he wondered.

Following his flashlight beam he created a path as he moved the orderly stacks of cardboard boxes filled with long-forgotten household items. Stumbling on an old cricket bat he moved deeper under the eaves and there it was, a small brown suitcase with his father's initials T.J.W. stencilled on it. The handle came away on one side as Billy pulled it towards him. He felt there was some weight to it as he brushed the dust off its surface.

Climbing down the ladder to the landing he placed the sturdy but battered vintage piece of luggage, complete with corner protectors, onto the thick Wilton carpet. He felt like a child at Christmas.

Kneeling beside this special link to his father, Billy momentarily felt guilty at this intrusion into his father's private world. He drew a breath, then clicked on the brass clasps. They duly snapped back and Billy slowly raised the suitcase lid.

He was quite astonished to see a green canvas holster lying on top of a jumble of papers and artefacts. Cautiously Billy pulled out a black metal revolver. He held the gun gingerly, moving it between his large hands. He noticed the name "Webley" at the top of the Bakelite grip and the imprint "Mark IV .38" above the barrel. Placing the weapon back into the holster he lay it gently beside the suitcase, his attention turning to the other contents.

He extracted a black leather zipped pouch inside which he found a well-used, brown leather wallet with an old pound note, a bus ticket and a photograph of a familiar face. Billy felt he was opening a secret door into his parents' lives as he gazed dolefully at the picture of his mother Peggy.

She looked so young, maybe seventeen or eighteen years old, and so beautiful, her hair falling in smooth rolls.

Inside the wallet was a letter from Peggy to Tom, and a pre-printed postcard from a POW camp in the Far East, its ready-printed statements in lines, some crossed out, the signature illegible.

Also tucked into the folds of the wallet was an old, highly patinated, Japanese banknote in green ink strangely printed with The Japanese Government and one rupee, rather than yen. The note had a fruit-bearing tree at one end and temples at the other. Billy would learn this was "invasion money" that people used under the occupation of the Japanese.

Finally, he found some more old sepia photographs

of his father Tom in uniform. Billy inclined his head as he held one towards the light. It showed a group of soldiers, their ragged, dishevelled uniforms matching their weary looks as they led heavily burdened donkeys along a muddy track, through dense jungle. Billy was sure one of the men was his father, despite his beard and a hat turned up at the side partially covering his face.

Another photograph showed a group of eight soldiers, with Tom and another officer sitting centrally. It had been taken in front of what was possibly a single-storey barracks with the Union flag flying above it. Billy guessed the soldiers might be Chinese or Malay. Billy would really have loved to have known more about his dad's wartime experiences.

Billy's attention was drawn to an old moth-eaten army beret with a cracked leather-bound rim. Attached was a slightly tarnished bronze Royal Engineers badge complete with the inscription "Honi soit qui mal y pense", which Billy knew loosely translated as "May you be shamed for thinking something bad".

Amongst the ration book, old foreign coins and bank notes Billy spotted a framed photograph of his mum wearing a black-and-white waitress uniform. On the back was written "Nippy Peggy. Lyons Corner House 1939". It was wrapped in a faded newspaper cutting.

Finally, Billy carefully picked out a small, yellow, British and Foreign Bible Society New Testament, with a King George VI crest emblazoned on it. Being gentle with the fragile spine of the well-worn book, he opened the front cover. Inside was proof it had been issued to New South Wales members of the Second Australian Imperial force. There was no name in the space provided. Billy speculated that it must have been issued to a fellow soldier.

As Billy handled it he noticed the edge of a photograph sticking out. This showed his father and two fine-looking nurses. Tom was wearing a short-sleeved army shirt and shorts, his cap at a jaunty angle. He had an arm around each nurse's waist. On the back was written Singapore 1941 with the initials GP and VW.

Taking a break to gather his thoughts Billy boiled the Morphy Richards kettle and watched as the steam rose. Making tea was a ritual he had inherited from his mother Peggy, who loved her copious brews. He could almost hear her, "Ah! A nice cup of tea, son." Conversely, his father never drank tea or coffee or indeed milk, always drinking water.

Out of the corner of his eye, Billy noticed on the kitchen counter the attendance cards from his father's recent funeral service.

He started to sift through them. Most were neighbours past and present, and representatives of the hospice.

In the small collection, one unfamiliar name stood out. Billy could not place or recollect a Gwen Powell. He remembers seeing a lady sitting on her own at the back of the church, very primly dressed in a black skirt, white blouse and veiled black pillbox hat.

She was probably about his father's age, maybe younger. He could not recall her leaving as all the mourners filed out of the church. Why would he? He had been preoccupied in following the coffin as his father made his last journey. Billy wondered if this lady might be Gwen Powell and whether she had come to the cemetery. Curious, Billy saw that there was a telephone number on the card, but no address.

Billy spent most of that day bringing down boxes from the attic. He was quite ruthless discarding what he saw as obsolete and irrelevant household items. Tired, he decided on an early night but did not sleep well.

Next morning, after his restless sleep punctuated with dreams of his mother and father, he looked into the bathroom mirror and regarded his drawn face and the bags under his eyes.

Billy was fifty years old, and quite happy to be single. He was a good-looking man, six feet tall, broad shouldered and strong jawed. He had bushy eyebrows that stood guard over soft, cornflower-blue, film-star eyes, which beguiled many a lady. A very straight Greek nose and perfect ears complemented his visage. He was disappointed in his receding hairline, but his mousy-coloured hair, which he parted in the middle, was still quite thick. His appearance was of a younger Tom. His father was almost identical other than his wrinkles and a kink at the top of his nose where it had perhaps been broken.

Billy felt strange to be in his parents' house alone. However, the familiarity of his childhood home was comforting. This red-bricked, three-bedroomed semi-detached held many fond memories but the loss of his parents, Peggy two years ago and now his dad, made him melancholy as he made a cup of tea and sank into his father's faded brown leather armchair with its sagging upholstery. He stared into oblivion through the rain-spattered window.

He had retired to look after his folks as they became

infirm and then ill, but now he had time on his hands to think.

He was intrigued by the funeral attendance card he held in his hand and decided to call Gwen Powell.

The phone rang out for a minute or so. Billy was on the verge of hanging up as he started to have doubts about making the call at all.

"Hello."

"Oh! Good morning, sorry to bother you. Is that Gwen Powell?"

"Yes, it is. Who is this?"

"This is William Williams, Billy, I am Tom Williams' son. I hope you don't mind me contacting you. I found an attendance card in the funeral directors' collection of attendees at my father's recent funeral, and it had your name and telephone number on it."

"I see," said Gwen.

"Well, I hope you don't feel I'm being rude, but I don't know who you are."

"I am an old friend of your parents."

"Really, how well did you know them?"

"I suppose it's fair to say I knew them better years ago," said the softly spoken voice. Billy detected a Welsh accent.

"So, you're not related to Mum or Dad?" said Billy in the hope he had finally found a living relative.

"No!"

"How long have you known my parents?"

"Well, I suppose I've known your father for over fifty years and your mother almost the same amount of time."

"I see. How did you meet?"

"So many questions, Billy. May I call you Billy?

"Sure."

"I met your father in Singapore. Why don't you come down and visit me and we can spend some time chatting about your folks? I don't see many people nowadays and it would brighten my day."

"Okay, that sounds fine if you don't mind me intruding. In fact, you may be able to help. I've been sorting through some old photographs, and maybe you'll know some of the people."

"Well, that's settled then. Remember to bring any photographs with you. Do you like cake or bara brith?" said Gwen's kind dulcitone.

"Both, I have a very sweet tooth," confessed Billy.

"Shall I give you my address? It's Awel y Mor, Ralph Street, Borth-y-Gest, near Porthmadog. Shall we say Friday?"

"Yes, that would be just fine."

"Cheerio, until Friday." And the phone line went dead.

2

That Friday Billy fired up his trusty old MG Midget, its well-polished red body and chrome glinting in the spring sunlight. Soft top down, Billy took a familiar route into Wales, one he had enjoyed many times as a child for family holidays.

Billy felt free, the wind in his hair as he sped past the hedgerows of Shropshire bordered by pastures of grazing cows and occasional swaying fields of bright yellow rapeseed painting the land. Soon this landscape gave way to steep, Welsh, rain-soaked valleys, dotted with sheep.

In less than two hours Billy was driving down the bank into Borth-y-Gest, the brooding grey skies of the valleys having given way to the bright blue cumulus of coastal North Wales. An aircraft's vapour trail blazed a path to some land beyond the British Isles.

A delightful horseshoe-shaped bay shimmered in the midday sun. Small boats bobbed at their anchor. Along the seafront assorted-coloured houses stood sentinel over the bay, sky blue, pink and lemon forming an urban rainbow. Billy pulled into the narrow forecourt of

Glanaber Garage at the base of the hill.

After a minute or so a voice appeared from the darkness of the small garage. "Prynhawn Da," said the old chap as he came out of the maintenance area and headed towards the sole petrol pump, wiping oil from his hands and tucking a rag into his overalls.

"Hello," said Billy, "I wonder if you can help me? I'm trying to find Mrs Gwen Powell. I believe she is in Ralph Street. Do you know her?"

The diminutive, ruddy-faced chap took the tatty tweed cap off his head, furrowed his brow and scratched his thinning thatch of hair. He looked north along the harbour wall.

"Do you see those houses facing you? Well, Ralph Street is behind them. So, you need to go past the Seaview café on the right, turn first right, then first left into Ralph Street, isn't it. Now be sure to tell Gwen, Glyn the garage said hello." Before Billy could reply, Glyn had returned to the wheel-less Ford Granada he was working on in the garage.

Billy was full of trepidation, feeling like a child on their first day at school. He pulled up in front of the slate-roofed, pebble-dashed terraced house called Awel y Mor. Its bright, Chinese-red door stood out from the otherwise drab façade. A large model sailboat featured in the bay window.

A petite old lady watched through net curtains in the bedroom and smiled as she saw Billy raise his lanky frame from such a small contraption. Billy leaned into the back seat and extracted a brown leather briefcase that reminded Gwen of a school satchel she had once had.

As the doorbell rang, she carefully descended the steep carpeted staircase. She stopped in front of the hall mirror to adjust her cameo brooch, which held together a lilac cardigan over her white silk blouse. Her small veined hands patted a bun of grey hair, smoothed down her calf-length black woollen skirt and then opened the door. Looking up at a face she thought familiar, she smiled, and inclined her head in welcome.

"Billy?" she said enquiringly.

"Yes, you must be Gwen. So pleased to meet you." He held out his hand, but Gwen had already turned and was walking down the long hallway. Closing the door behind him, Billy removed his tan brogues and in his stockinged feet he padded along the narrow hallway in pursuit.

The print-lined hall opened into a spacious kitchen and dining area, its patio doors giving a most beautiful vista over the bay and towards the mountains of Snowdonia. In the distance, a steam train chugged along the causeway known as the Cob.

Through the open patio doors he could smell the sea and hear the guttural sounds of the well-fed seagulls as they glided, then landed on telegraph poles, adopting sentry postures.

Billy studied Gwen as she swilled the hot water around the small brown enamel teapot and prepared a plate of digestive biscuits. "Can I help?"

"I can manage, thank you, Billy" Gwen replied as she carried the tray to the coffee table by the open patio doors. She settled onto the cushions of her walnut rocking chair which was positioned overlooking the bay, gesturing Billy towards a comfortable chenille-covered armchair.

"Sorry, I'm staring," said Gwen. "You remind me so much of your father. I understand you have found some photographs of him."

Billy stood and reached for his briefcase. Gwen poured the tea, then Billy passed a small wartime snap to Gwen. She reached for her glasses, held the photograph towards the light, and smiled.

"Tom was such a handsome man and a real charmer." She seemed to drift off to another time.

"How did you know him?" asked Billy.

Not answering Billy's question, Gwen continued, "How wonderful. I remember this being taken." She paused. "Yes! As if it was yesterday." She looked out towards the distant peaks of Snowdonia and for a moment time stood still.

After a few moments, Billy interrupted her thoughts. "Who else is in the picture?"

Gwen looked at Billy and hesitated. Her dark brown watery eyes appeared to be assessing what to tell him. "Your father, of course, and that is me on the left and that's Vi, a good friend and nurse on the right."

"May I?" said Billy, taking another look at this precious bit of his family history. He studied it and looked at Gwen. "My word, you've hardly changed."

Gwen laughed out loud. "A charmer, just like your father. I'm afraid old age has slowed me up a little since then," she said wistfully. With a sparkle in her eye, Gwen added, "I was a young nurse back then, barely twenty-five years old."

"Were you posted out there?".

Without any encouragement Gwen started to tell her

story. "I was born in Malaya. My parents were Welsh, but my father was a plantation manager in Negeri Sembalan, South Western Malaya. I loved the life, it was so carefree. I just wanted to play with the local children and help out in the plantations as they and their families did. However, my parents insisted on a good education, so I was sent from my childhood jungle idyll to a boarding school in a major city in what seemed a different world to me, Darlinghurst, in Sydney, Australia.

"It was the Sydney Church of England Girls' Grammar School. That's where I met Vi for the first time. Violet was older than me and was designated to show me around and generally take care of me. We became great friends. I was around seven years old, so it was quite lonely for me, so far from home. Thanks to Vi I soon began to enjoy life and flourish. Our headmistress Miss Wilkinson was very stern, yet when I left to return to Malaya I was so sad to leave.

"I no longer walked around barefoot wearing very little. I learned to be part of a social system, which involved school uniforms and discipline.

"I missed the sounds of the parakeets and the cicadas at night when the land came alive. Kangaroos bounded around everywhere, and I was astonished one day when a baby kanga poked its head from the fold in the skin of its mother's belly, which I soon learned was a pouch. Koala bears seemed pretty sleepy creatures. The kookaburra call was quite distinctive, it was almost as if it was laughing when I located it in the tree. It looked to me like a kingfisher.

"So, sure, there was still some wildlife in Sydney, but

it was the ocean that I really loved. Every opportunity we could get a chaperone, Vi and I and some of the other girls would head down to the beach. Usually Bondi, but that became quite busy, so we occasionally headed for Tamarama beach, which was just a small beach between two headlands.

"Our school was cocooned from most civilisation as we were out towards Potts Point. Nearby Darlinghurst wasn't the most salubrious area, we even had the jail located there.

"The school motto was drilled into us and we were never allowed to forget it in everything we did: 'Strive to achieve'."

Billy listened intently.

"As much as I learned to love the city and going to the cinema and having candyfloss and riding the fairground attractions at an amusement park close to Tamarama beach, I had mixed feelings when the time came to return home. Strangely though, when I got home to Negeri Sembalan, I was restless. I missed the city and, well, if truth be told, I guess I had become more aware of boys.

"I was growing up, a young lady now. Both Vi and I were interested in nursing, so we kept in touch by letter. I did some St John's Ambulance training locally, then travelled to Penang and worked as a Voluntary Aid Detachment nurse, or VAD as we were known. Really this was an auxiliary nursing service back then, not like a fully trained nurse, but competent to deal with a lot, as we soon found out.

"Before long I moved south down the coast to Malacca. I loved working at Malacca General Hospital, which was set on top of a hill with fabulous views to the sea. I had been training for about two years when war in the Pacific broke out, and by pure coincidence, that is where Vi and I met up again.

"One day I was coming across the lawn in front of the hospital when I saw a bus arrive and some overseas nurses disembark, and to my great delight I recognised Vi. It was great to see one another. There was already a large contingent of Aussies in Malacca. It was a fine life, we had gramophones and records, and the Aussies even had their own amahs to take care of cleaning and cooking.

"Vi had joined the AANS, the Australian Army Nursing Service, and Malacca Hospital became the base of the 2/10th Australian general hospital early in 1941. Alas, our fun stopped almost as soon as it started.

"In November, a small detachment of Voluntary Aid Detachment nurses was sent to St Andrew's Mission Hospital in Singapore, and I was one of those chosen."

Gwen hesitated and seemed to close her eyes, then looked up at Billy. "Please, help yourself to more tea and biscuits."

"In Singapore," she continued, "we were working wherever we were needed. I was mostly at St Andrew's Hospital until December 1941, when it closed. Vi and her colleagues were still based in a large section of the Malacca British General Hospital.

"Strangely, even though we were at war with the Japanese, not a lot changed. Washing still hung on lines above the streets, wave after wave of them like prayer flags, and roads were still busy with traffic. The Singapore river was full of various craft, bum-boats and junks plying their trade. There is no doubt this mangrove-fringed island was an impressive fortification. There were over 100,000 Allied troops, and it was often said Singapore was impregnable."

Gwen shook her head, her expression quite clearly acknowledging that falsehood. "We were always busy, as many soldiers and civilians alike were brought in with tropical maladies like malaria.

"For many of us in Singapore, there was a continuing and active social life, especially for the civil service and the military wives.

"The wives of Forces personnel seemed a little bored with keeping up appearances and supporting their husbands at social gatherings. Their day appeared to consist of breakfast, reading the *Singapore Times*, and going to Raffles for afternoon tea, interspersed with shopping at the newly opened Robinsons, all followed by a rest before an evening cocktail party or dinner." Gwen frowned.

Billy was trying to be polite, so didn't interrupt, but he wondered where this was heading.

"When we first arrived, we thought that after a hectic day we would be relaxing on a verandah with ceiling fans gently whirring above us as we sipped a few gin slings and watched the sunset." Smiling, she continued: "Sadly, although we managed an occasional night out at the Cathay Cinema, we were just so exhausted from the work and the humidity that we were glad to just relax and rest. Besides, I missed Vi's vivaciousness and sense of humour. I felt I couldn't converse quite as freely with my other colleagues, whereas Vi and I could tell each other anything."

A clock chimed loudly in the front lounge.

"My word, it's 4 o'clock," said Billy, checking his fathers' Cyma watch.

"Now, Billy, will you stop for tea?"

Without hesitation Billy said, "I would love to continue our conversation over tea. That would be splendid."

After some delicious ham sandwiches and homemade Victoria sponge, Gwen rose slowly from her chair and approached a barometer on the wall behind Billy. Billy turned and watched her tap the glass.

"Looks like we may have some rain later. Shall we go for a short walk to get some fresh air before the evening starts to draw in?"

"Sounds great," said Billy.

They left the house and dropped the short distance to the coastal path by the chapel, stopping briefly by a wooden bench which overlooked an old wartime gun emplacement. In silence they shared the panoramic view over the estuary. Seagulls called overhead, circling and hovering on the brisk sea breeze. The bracing air made Gwen's eyes water and her nose run. Wavelets created white dots on the water and the occasional sailboat took advantage of the wind. Billy's mind drifted as he pondered his father's life in Singapore.

Gwen dabbed her eyes, then blew her nose on a delicate linen handkerchief she had retrieved from her sleeve cuff. "Do you still work?" said Gwen, breaking Billy's train of thought.

"No. I used to teach history, but it became too much trying to work and look after my ailing parents, and the amount of paperwork and reporting was becoming burdensome. The time was right to semi-retire. I just marked exam papers for a little extra cash and played the share market! I fortunately benefited from a good pension earlier this year and gained a little time for myself, too."

"I was so sorry to hear of your father's passing. I had not heard from him for a while and had surmised his health was deteriorating the last time I had been in touch. He did ask the hospice to let me know he was there, which was kind of him. They let me know of his death. Tom was such a nice man."

Billy was surprised that neither his father nor the hospice had mentioned Gwen. He so wanted to know what Gwen could tell him about his father but knew she would get to that in her own time.

They walked along the narrow path bordered by gorse and ferns on one side, then giving rise to houses which sat above the coastline, enjoying wonderful views. A protective man-made fence intertwined with thorny bushes guarded them from the steep drop to the sea and coves below. As they reached each cove she looked, then moved on. It was as if she was moving intently between patients checking they were all right. He imagined she would have been a very caring and determined nurse.

"Have you ever been here?" asked Gwen.

"When I was a child we used to go to Black Rock Sands and I recall the harbour at Porthmadog, and the smells and sound of the steam train. I can still remember my excitement when we chugged up the line past all the little stations, fast rivers running alongside, then high mountains emerging. Sadly, I can't remember ever coming here to Borth-y-Gest, Gwen."

They walked for almost half an hour.

"Billy, do you see that house on the rocks at the far part of this bay?" asked Gwen, pointing into the distance and shielding her eyes against the brightness.

Billy nodded as he saw the white building on the headland.

"That's called the Pilot House and immediately around the headland is Black Rock Sands."

"I wasn't too far from Borth-y-Gest, then, Gwen. How long have you lived here?" asked Billy, trying to glean some background to Gwen's life.

"Many years. It used to be my grandparents' home," she said wistfully.

"What of your parents, Gwen?"

"Unfortunately, they didn't make it through the war." Changing the subject, she asked, "So what are your plans for the future?"

"Who knows? *Que será*. What does Awel y Mor mean?" said Billy, interested in the house name.

"Sea Breeze," came the response.

It had become a little cloudy, and a light squall set in. The wind growing cooler, Gwen raised the collar on her grey-blue flecked woollen coat, took a paisley headscarf from her pocket and wrapped it over her head, tucking her ears and hair in, and they headed slowly for home.

"Well, what would you like for dinner this evening, Billy?" questioned Gwen as she removed her coat and headscarf.

"That is so kind of you, Gwen, but I had planned to head down the coast to Aberdovey for a night at the Penhelig Arms and then drive home tomorrow. I really should get going."

"Nonsense!" retorted Gwen. "You can stay here this evening. I have a small spare bedroom. Anyway, we still have lots to talk about. I haven't told you about your father and our first meeting. I want to know a lot more about you too."

Billy did not baulk at the opportunity in prospect, he was rather enjoying himself. He truly wanted to hear more from his engaging host.

Without waiting for a reply Gwen suggested, "How about fish and chips? The shop at the bottom of Snowdon Street in Porthmadog has some of the best around."

Before Billy knew it, armed with directions, he went hunting for their fish supper. He returned with the goods and a delicious aroma of fish and chips, liberally sprinkled with malt vinegar and sea salt, wafted into Awel y Mor. Gwen had made another pot of tea and they both reclined in their chairs by the window.

Replete, Gwen appeared to be dozing. Billy noticed that her skin was surprisingly smooth, with just the odd wrinkle from the corners of her mouth and eyes. Her frame was small, but there was a redoubtable quality that shone through, making him feel this lady should not be underestimated.

Without opening her eyes, Gwen tantalised Billy with "I first met your father in Singapore."

3

Gwen played her own home movie, as her mind's projector whirred away. She rocked mesmerically back and forward like a ticking clock.

"When we all heard that the Japanese houseboys had gone absent without leave from officers' homes, we just thought they were afraid of being persecuted by the Japanese, should the Imperial Japanese Military ever breach the perimeter of the Singapore defences, God forbid."

Gwen went on without hesitation, almost like a newsreader. "In general, no one seemed that worried. There was an air of nonchalance, confidence in our infallibility, which history now shows as complacency, but you had to be there, Billy, to understand the arrogance of the British leadership, which many of us bought into. All that changed during one December night.

"My room-mate, Betty, was lying awake struggling to sleep in the heat, wiping her face and neck with a flannel. She told us later, she'd heard an unfamiliar sound that night. A persistent drone, which became louder, then an explosion that lit up the skyline and the room. You see, Billy, all the street lights were blazing; there was no black-out, that's how naïve and arrogant our leaders were. Betty watched it all unfold from the bedroom window.

"The first I knew about it was a whoosh of air that seemed to fill the room with great force. It startled me awake. I didn't see Betty at first. She was lying dazed on the ground. I heard her first, through the darkness, full of dust and debris. I had my hand over my mouth trying to breathe. I stumbled over her, and she took a large intake of breath and started to cry.

She just kept repeating hysterically, "We're being bombed, we're being bombed." I held her by the shoulders as she sobbed her heart out. We held each other for what seemed an age but was probably about ten minutes. "Are you okay, Betty?" I said as she relaxed her head on my shoulder, overcome with emotion.

"I helped her back onto her bed, then I cautiously peered between the shattered shutters where the window had been. Now the dust had settled I saw it was a bright moonlit night diffused by the smoke from fires caused by the bombing. I heard the all-clear sirens and the cacophony of panic in the street below. Ambulance and fire engine sirens, shouting, fire and smoke filled the air. War had found us!

"The Kampong, which was the Chinese Quarter, was the worst hit. We nurses and everyone else who could help were out trying to rescue people from fallen debris and tend to the wounded.

"Unfortunately, someone had to deal with collecting the dead. It was horrible; stretchers being rushed into service everywhere. These carried the dead and wounded, some moaning and shrieking as the pain wracked their prostrate bodies, their arms hanging lifeless. Ambulances and any available trucks arrived to take them away. In some cases, stretcher bearers, uniformed and civilian, were carrying people all the way to a first aid post on anything from doors to prams.

"We arrived back at St Andrew's Mission Hospital, where the corridors were like rush hour on the London underground, with many people waiting for care and attention. We were overrun as the people kept coming. Every nook and cranny occupied, we quickly filled to bursting point with the blood-spattered and traumatised and severely wounded. We had two wards of thirty beds each normally, but we were overflowing into any room we had, even on to the pavement outside.

"A makeshift operating theatre was trying to save lives, and many were transferred to the Queen Alexandra Hospital to deal with amputations and burns victims; truly horrendous. I believe I came of age that night!

"It's strange, but in this intense and frightening aftermath we were all incredibly calm, just getting on with our job, dispensing care and comfort as best we could.

"I came out of the hospital to take a break. It was sunrise and exhausted military personnel, nurses and civilians were sitting dazed on the pavement. Our whole world as we knew it had been shattered.

"That's the first time I saw your father. He was with his friend Jimmy. Tom was leaning against an army truck outside the main entrance. Jimmy was crouching by the side of him. Both looked drained.

"A pall of smoke rose from a bombed nearby shophouse. This poured over the top of the three-storey hospital. St Andrew's was shaped like the stern of a ship, its once white façade was now pock-marked by shrapnel and smoke damaged. Its louvred window screens were open, to allow air to flow, but it was getting more foul by the minute.

"Standing, Jimmy said 'Hello', peering grimy faced from under his jungle hat. They both wore baggy army shorts and long socks, but Jimmy had one sock up and one rolled to his ankle. Your father was far more presentable and appeared stoic and reflective, if weary.

"I said, 'Hello, soldier', but Tom didn't utter a word, just gave a half smile, as if too exhausted to communicate. Jimmy tapped a packet of Woodbines on the side of the truck. I can hear him now saying, 'Fancy one, sister?' as he offered me a cigarette.

"I remember his voice so well. I at first declined, but he insisted, 'Smoke, sister, it's been a tough night.' I took one, even though I didn't smoke. It was strong. As I tried to inhale I coughed and spluttered.

"Jimmy chuckled in benevolent amusement and I joined in the mirth. I loved Jimmy's smile and his friendly demeanour. He brushed a loose strand of hair from my face. Embarrassed, I tucked it behind my ear and under my cap, smiling, but remaining rather coy.

"'My name is Jimmy, and this is my best pal, Tom. What's your name?' he said.

"'That's for me to know and you to find out,' I said, 'and I am not a sister, by the way, Jimmy!'

"Your father and Jimmy were chalk and cheese.

Jimmy was outgoing and flirtatious, whilst Tom was quiet, measured, almost lugubrious. As I got to know them both, I found Tom had a wicked sense of humour and both were very thoughtful and kind men. They obviously complemented each other, you could see why they had become good friends."

Billy had never heard his father talk much at all about the war, only in generalities, and he certainly had not mentioned any fellow soldiers.

Gwen looked at Billy's wrist. "That's Tom's watch, I believe."

Billy sheepishly nodded, confirming her observation.

"He was wearing that watch the last time I saw him in Singapore and again when I saw him about ten years ago. This might surprise you, but he won it from an officer in a game of cards," she said, knowing she had imparted something of interest.

Billy just inclined his head, ran his hand over the wristwatch, and in a low whisper acknowledged, "It's the one thing that reminds me of him."

"Anyway, from then on, a few weeks seemed a lifetime. That morning, just as the boys were leaving and I was going back into the hospital, Jimmy shouted, 'Union Jack Club, behind the Capitol Cinema, Saturday evening; a knees-up if you fancy.' My back to them now, I put my hand up and as I walked away Jimmy added, '1900 hrs. Bring a friend for my mate Tom.'

"At the hospital door I turned and shouted, 'Gwen. My name's Gwen!'

"'See you later, Gwen,' shouted Jimmy, trying to get his voice heard above the truck engine's deep growl and gear crunching. He hung out of the window waving as they pulled away.

"That week I was transferred and attached to the nurse's mess at St Patrick's Hospital, a former school in the Siglap district. I was seconded to support Australian nurses from the 2/13th Australian General Hospital.

"I cannot recall any other attacks for a while, so life returned somewhat to normal.

"I was surprised on the Friday following when Vi showed up. She had a weekend pass, which was perfect, I thought. Gaining confidence from her presence, I told her about the bombing raid and the terrible consequences and she confided things were getting busier in Malacca, as troops were coming in their droves, no longer just with tropical ailments, but conflict wounds, a direct result of the Japanese landing along the Malay peninsula.

"When I told Vi about meeting Jimmy and Tom, and the chance of going out the following evening, she was cock-a-hoop. I have to say she bolstered my courage to go."

Billy replenished the teacups and could see Gwen was animated and in her element.

"On Saturday night Vi and I showered to freshen up. But it was hopeless, the humidity immediately made our dresses stick to our backs. We took a rickshaw to the Capitol Cinema and wandered around to Northbridge Road. The moment we entered the Union Jack Club with its ceiling fans whirring and the melodies of Glenn Miller playing we forgot any discomfort from the heat.

"In a trice, even before we could scan the room, Tom and Jimmy were there to greet us. Before I knew it, Jimmy had whisked me on to the dance floor." Gwen paused and reflected. "I can still hear his voice and see his face, especially his smile. His black wavy hair, shorn at the sides and back, and his emerald eyes beguiled me, that's for sure." She removed her handkerchief from her cardigan sleeve and dabbed her eyes.

Billy knelt awkwardly beside her and held her hand as Gwen tilted her head and regarded Billy affectionately.

She shrugged her shoulders, struggling to compose herself. "Happy memories. It is all we old folk have in the winter of our lives, just recollections of bygone days.

"We had a fabulous evening, Billy. Later that night I could hardly sleep, but this time it was not the heat that was keeping me awake. Vi and I talked into the wee hours, we were both rather smitten with our newly found chaps.

"It seemed an age before we saw the boys again, things had heated up and there was less time for socialising. We were starting to receive injured troops and civilians from higher up the peninsula.

"Violet managed to secure a pass for New Year's Eve. I do not know to this day how she managed that." With a wink, Gwen continued. "Although she was a persuasive and determined lady! Little did she know, though, that she would never return to Malacca.

"We were planning to go to the New Year's Eve dance at the St Patrick's Hospital mess when who should turn up at our mess but Jimmy and Tom. It was wonderful to see them. My heart skipped a beat. Seeing Jimmy again left me breathless. We told them of our plans and they fell in with them, but first they wanted to take us for cocktails. From somewhere they had commandeered a jeep, and before we knew it, we were at the entrance of the Raffles Hotel. Without missing a step, the boys escorted us past the grandly attired doormen. 'Long Bar,' said Tom as we drifted into the elegant foyer. Vi and I were on cloud nine.

"Earlier in the day Vi insisted we shop for something special to wear, so we had headed to Orchard Road and eventually bought cocktail dresses from Robinsons. I wore a shawl-collared, black taffeta dress, dotted with tiny sequins, like stars in the night. I borrowed a fox stole from Betty Jones, and Vi did my hair. With a mass of curls piled high and forward on to my face, I thought I was Betty Grable. I felt like royalty.

"Vi always looked great. Her hair flounced in blonde ringlets over her shoulders. Her black heels made her look even taller, her smile lit up the room and her red lipstick highlighted her beautiful mouth. She looked fabulous.

"As we entered the Long Bar, someone wolf-whistled, and Tom appeared irritated. Our men pulled out chairs for us. I could see Tom was becoming protective, but he need not have worried, for he was tall with debonair looks, making him an ideal match for Vi. He was also deep, and to Vi that was a challenge."

It was strange for Billy to think of his father with a woman other than his mother, Peggy.

Gwen continued, "We had a wonderful New Year's Eve; we danced and danced, big band melodies transported us to a time of make-believe, when the war didn't exist. I still swoon when I hear that timeless tune 'In the Mood', and I remember that numbers like 'A Nightingale Sang in Berkeley Square' always made us a little melancholy and homesick.

"As the evening drew to a close we all held our partners close, and the orchestra played 'Who's Taking You Home Tonight after the Dance is Through?' We just wanted time to stand still. We were in seventh heaven; just for a moment or two we were taken to a land beyond the turmoil.

"Then as everyone linked arms in a huge circle to sing 'Auld Lang Syne', piercing air-raid sirens brought us back to reality. We headed out of the hotel quickly to report for duty, driven by the boys, but it turned out to be a false alarm.

"Vi and I hoped the boys were still outside the hospital, but they had vanished into the airless night.

"I saw Jimmy just once more, a time that remains very special and locked in my heart forever. We found out the Royal Engineers were based at Gordon Barracks, but by the time we tried to make contact with Jimmy and Tom, they had all moved on. Medical teams were operating from there, such was the state of flux Singapore was in.

"The bombing returned with a vengeance and such intensity it felt like Dante's inferno at times. January brought more confusion. Casualties from the war raging all around us arrived in ever-increasing numbers. It was difficult to cope. Our seemingly blasé days were over.

"Surreal Christmas celebrations of dressing trees at the nurses' mess and in the hospital, just as if we were back home, seemed a million miles away. I even went to a soirée where a string quartet played 'Walking in a Winter Wonderland'. All rather unbelievable, in the heat of Singapore; totally bizarre," said Gwen, chuckling out loud and sipping her lukewarm tea.

"More and more wounded troops were arriving from the Malay Peninsula, and refugees were clogging the roads. The railway station down at Keppel Street was heaving with people, disorientated, not knowing where to go.

"Some of the officers' wives and high society members set up shelters, opening their own homes and offering food, bed and clothing. War is a great leveller!

"Vi's General Hospital Group 2/10th evacuated from Malacca to Singapore before she could return, so she lost some of her possessions, left back in Malacca. Times of war soon educate you that life is far more important than material belongings.

"Vi and her colleagues took up residence in a boys' school at Manor House about two miles north of Singapore. I think it was called Oldham's but can't be sure. It was great to have Vi so near, we saw each other as often as we could.

"Fighting and shelling drew nearer, but we were emboldened by the arrival of more Australian troops. I remember talking to boys from a machine gun battalion who had just arrived from Melbourne. One of the guys was a Sydney native and lived in the same Sydney street as Vi.

"It was not just the fear of air raids now, but also of close combat taking place very near to us, the mayhem was all consuming. We just had to blank it out and focus on helping the injured and rescue the wounded as the Japanese advanced. Sometimes, even we nurses were pinned down by crossfire between the Japs and our forces. The situation was so fluid, we could quickly be behind enemy lines.

"Two of our colleagues, Joan and Dorothy, were such shining examples of bravery. Once, I saw them dash across an open area to reach a wounded sapper. Somehow none of us saw danger, just people's pain. Invariably it left us slumped and exhausted in a chair, or on a bed for an hour or so, physically and emotionally wrought, occasionally sobbing until we slept, before being woken to re-enter the fray.

"Jap planes had flown over and dropped leaflets imploring us to surrender and promising safe conduct. These were written in a number of languages, Chinese, Malay and English. The shower of white paper seemed like white blossom descending from heaven, but in reality, they were introducing hell on earth.

"By the first week in February we knew the end was near. We had no water, Billy. The Japs had overrun the city's reservoir. Also, our hospital had no power. Some of the British and other nurses left with some Australian Army Nursing sisters on a Chinese ship caring for the wounded on board.

"For those of us remaining, the wounded lay all around, on stretchers spread over the grounds and verandahs and anywhere there was space. Vi told me a large red cross made of material and sheets had been put on one of the hospital lawns, but the Japanese paid no heed to this, bombing indiscriminately until their final bombing raids. We felt helpless.

"We were called together by our Matron on 10 February. I remember the date well. We were told a ship was available to evacuate us. We protested, but the Matron was adamant. A small team would stay until the last moment, then join us, as the Japanese had almost surrounded us, and we had to leave post-haste. With a heavy heart we headed for St Andrew's Cathedral, which was a holding area for transport to the docks, and already full of army nurses. I looked hopefully for Vi; anyone in a red cape could be her. Finally, to my relief, there she was, sitting in a corner on the floor, nursing a small suitcase.

"'Vi, you look different,' I said.

"Vi gave a half-hearted, tired laugh tinged with irony. 'I feel I've changed inside too, Gwen.'

"Vi wore a tin hat that looked incongruous on her blonde tresses, now pinned up. A loose strand of hair fell to her cheek and her face was wan, as if she had seen a ghost or indeed many. Unwashed, she sat exhausted.

"The whole church floor was covered in stretchers with wounded and dying souls groaning and crying out. We felt terrible we wouldn't be able to take them with us. As we sat together feeling helpless, roll-call was taken. We waited for an all-clear siren then boarded transport to the wharf. We were forced back by bombing and Zero fighters strafing anything that moved. Vehicles were blocking roads, some burned out, some crashed into buildings.

"It took almost three days of false starts before we finally reached the go-down warehouses at the docks. I remember a bomb falling on a building as we passed it and the truck we were on seemed to rise off the road then bounce back down. We felt like the air had been sucked out of us, but we kept going. We did what we could for the injured and dying, lying on stretchers or propped up against the side of the warehouses, as we waited our turn to be evacuated.

"Fires and devastation were everywhere. Ack-ack guns still tried to fire on Japanese planes. My nostrils stung from the smell of smoke and burning fuel. Unburied corpses, like rag dolls, dotted the streets and hung out of cars."

Gwen took a deep breath and her lower jaw quivered. "Hundreds, maybe thousands, of people queued to board ships to take them to safety. Some folk became aggressive. We witnessed some soldiers threaten sailors with guns to let them on to the ship and succeeded. The acrid smell of smoke affected our breathing.

"Waves of bombers came again and again. We shuddered as the noisy defence guns rattled our bones with their returning fire. A small child screamed then wailed, frightened beyond belief at the noise and despair all around. The heat and humidity sucked the life out of you, too, it was a living nightmare.

"It was now Friday 13 February 1942. We shuffled up the gangplank on to a small tug, which took us to another part of the dock, where we boarded a foreboding, dark-grey ship called *SS Vyner Brooke*, flying the Royal ensign. We learned that, like many craft, it had been commandeered from private ownership, in this case the Rajah of Sarawak. It had once been his private yacht, all fine mahogany woodwork and brass fittings. What a life it must have been on board in peacetime.

"Most of my colleagues had boarded another ship, an old tub called the *Wah Sui*, but I was thankful to be with Vi and a contingent of more than sixty of her Aussie colleagues alongside lots of civilians and a few military personnel. We were told to stay on deck as space was limited.

"I remember standing at the ship's rail and surveying the devastation of this once-fine colonial outpost and felt I was witnessing the end of a great imperial era, Billy. I saw how beautiful cars had been abandoned in the harbour waters to stop the Japanese using them. One solitary black Ford sticks in my mind. It was stood up on its nose with just the boot showing above the water, as if paying a final salute to Singapore before disappearing below the debris-strewn surface.

"A deep, topaz-blue sea under a cloud-free sunny sky above belied the danger we were all in. As our ship moved slowly out of the harbour, dodging the various sunken craft, we all looked back at the Singapore skyline with its Union building, the Hong Kong and Shanghai Bank, the Post Office, the Supreme Court cupola, the spire of St George's Cathedral and the towering Cathay Building that watched over Singapore.

"A huge black pall of smoke hung fatefully over the whole island, as the immense supplies of oil had been destroyed by the allies as they retreated. The tragedy unfolding was nothing compared to the months and years ahead."

Gwen was exhausted. "I need to rest now," she smiled benevolently. "I'm so glad you're staying. Sleep well," she added as she took a glass of water with her up the stairs.

That night Billy lay on his pillow. His Victorian-style wrought-iron bed had a lovely duvet on it, but he was too warm. He just stared at the picture rail and the wallpaper of little pink roses, which made the room feel small and claustrophobic. He gazed at the night sky through the sash window and got up to let some cool night air circulate in the room.

Lying back on the bed he began running the events of the day through his mind. He had been on a rollercoaster of emotion. Gwen, Violet and his father had lived through troubled times, when the intensity of relationships reflected the scarcity of certainty. Unions quickly kindled could just as rapidly be cast asunder. "Carpe diem" was no doubt the order of the day!

4

Billy tossed and turned, dreaming heavily. He dreamt he was being chased down a narrow alley lined with bamboo huts in a far-off land, only to find it was a dead end. He turned to confront his pursuers, then awoke perspiring heavily, his heart racing. Casting his eyes around the room as it came into focus, unsure of where he was for a moment, he was relieved to know he was safe.

A splinter of morning light found its way through the curtains, like a finger of fate pointing directly at Billy's torso. He rose and drew back the curtains, allowing the spring sunshine to purge the demons of the night.

Looking out over the bay, he saw that Borth-y-Gest had not yet fully woken. He spotted a lone figure down by the harbour. It seemed familiar. A pair of binoculars on his bedside table, a prerequisite of most seaside retreats, brought the figure into view. It was Gwen.

It was just after 7.30 am. Billy donned a pair of grey tracksuit bottoms, a T-shirt and his recently bought down-filled jacket, preparing for the often-cool early morning sea breeze. As he stepped out of the house, he was pleasantly surprised by the mildness of the morning. Unzipping his jacket, he ambled down to the sea.

Gwen was on a seat, looking out across the bay. She appeared to be lost in thought.

"Good morning, Gwen."

"Oh, hello! Bore da, Billy," came the Anglo/Welsh reply, as he joined her on the green wooden bench.

"I enjoy this time of the day," mused Gwen. "I love the stillness and the peace before the village wakes up and the tourists arrive. I can hear the water lapping and the birds calling and sometimes I …" She broke off. "Shall we take a stroll?" she added. They took a slow walk around the headland to the right of the bay.

"Borthy is filling up with more and more second homeowners as time goes by," Gwen said, looking up at Ivy Terrace, which had a prime spot overlooking the bay.

"I can smell bacon and a cooked breakfast," said Billy.

"Making you hungry, is it, Billy?" asked Gwen, her hands tucked into the pockets of her rain jacket.

As they came alongside a low wall, she stood and looked across at the Cob causeway. A cloud of steam was rising from the railway station as the volunteers prepared the first train of the day, ready for the daily tourist influx.

"Do you speak Welsh fluently, Gwen?"

"No! Just the pleasantries, though over the years I have come to understand a lot of what is being said. Jimmy Roberts taught me a few words to help me appreciate some of the Welsh verse he would occasionally share with me in Singapore, though not all the words were … shall we say, what you would use in public." She flashed a mischievous grin.

"Jimmy was born and bred in this area," she offered, now looking at Billy. "He was a Tremadog boy, which is a little town, well, more of a village actually, a few minutes' drive from here. Same birthplace as T.E. Lawrence, as it happens, you know, Lawrence of Arabia."

"What a coincidence, your grandparents living so near Jimmy's home town," said Billy.

"Life has its way of giving you these common denominators," Gwen replied. "Jimmy used to recite poetry. He loved Hedd Wyn, a First World War poet, who was from Trawsfynnyd on the way to Dolgellau, not far from here either."

Returning to Awel y Mor, Billy showered. It was a lovely sunny morning, so they breakfasted on the outside deck, enjoying the warmth of the weak spring sunshine. On the wooden picnic table were a variety of jams and honey, and toast and cereal.

Billy mused to himself that it felt good to be alive and to talk to this amazing lady. His train of thought was punctuated by the sounds of the corpulent seagulls, who were keeping an eye on a possible feast of leftovers.

Billy cut to the chase. "Did my father and Violet ever see one another again?"

Gwen smiled. "Indeed they did, at every available opportunity, I'm sure. Tom had fallen for Vi." Looking Billy in the eye before taking a small bite of toast and honey, she added, "I know the feeling was mutual. However, with the battle for Singapore intensifying, it allowed little time for frivolity, Billy. It was all hands to the pump, so to speak."

Almost afraid to ask, Billy phrased his next question carefully. "Did Violet get back to Australia?"

"I believe she did. It was a massive relief when we were demobbed. But repatriation was disjointed and chaotic at times, you just wanted to leave the God-forsaken place you were in, no matter what. You wanted to be somewhere safe and sound."

"Did you go back home to Malaya?"

"No, I didn't. First of all, from Java I was taken back to Singapore. We were taken to St Andrew's Hospital to recuperate. On the short journey we passed the Padang, which before the Jap invasion had been the scene of something quintessentially English, a cricket field. Not far from St Andrew's cathedral. I saw Japanese prisoners of war filling in air-raid trenches, supervised by Indian troops. How the worm had turned. It was rather strange being back at St Andrew's Hospital as a patient.

"It was during this time that I managed to contact villagers up country, who knew of my parents. I learned they'd been killed, our plantation home was devastated, apparently, indeed destroyed. I knew no more details. I toyed with the idea of returning to start the plantation myself and pay respect to my parents' graves, if there were any. I was physically and emotionally exhausted, and I struggled to make a decision. On balance, there seemed no point in going back to that area. I had no real home to go to.

"Very soon, a berth on a hospital ship became available and as a British citizen I was shipped back to Blighty. I had given my next of kin as my father's

45

parents in Borth-y-Gest, you see. Nan and Granddad, or in Welsh, Nain and Taid, Powell were the only family I had left. It was a leap of faith as I had never met them.

"When I arrived here at this very house they made me so welcome. They wanted to hear all about how life had been before the war, of my childhood in Malaya and of course about my parents. But not for a long time did we broach the subject of the war and what happened. I found it a little difficult to settle and initially harboured thoughts of returning to Malaya.

"But fate intervened. Nain took ill and I nursed her for over two years. Taid could not have coped on his own, so my being here was a blessing for all of us. I found them to be lovely people, and it's strange, but when I came here I felt a certain 'hiraeth', as they say in Welsh, a belonging, a fondness for this area, as if I was coming home, and once I got over missing Malaya I was smitten.

"Taid was bereft when his beloved Lilian passed away. For me it was another great loss, after losing my parents and then Jimmy, and the many friends and colleagues I lost in the war. Nain was another in that long list of people I grieved for. It was not long before Taid joined Nain. He died of a broken heart. Childhood sweethearts, you see, they had been married for fifty-two years.

"My Taid, Elwyn, was a lovely man, softly spoken and kind, even though he had rough hands from his days as a quarryman. He must have been strong in his day, but he was gentle, always measured in his reactions. He adored Lilian, there was no world without her. Anyone could see he was rudderless when she died.

"With their only child, my father Joseph, gone, Nain and Taid left the house to me, and I have been here ever since. I am so grateful to them for nurturing and mending me after the war. Borth-y-Gest has been my sanctuary. Never did they pry or ask questions, almost as if they knew my pain inside."

"What of Jimmy's family?" enquired Billy. Gwen seemed to be getting cool. Billy noticed her raise her shoulders and make that little shrug you do when a sudden shiver envelops you. "Shall we go inside?"

"No, but could you fetch my grey and red cloak from the hall cupboard?"

Billy returned and draped the cape around Gwen's shoulders.

"Is this your old nursing cape, Gwen?"

"No! It was Violet's, actually."

Gwen picked up the thread of her tale before Billy could respond. "It was as if fate had conspired to bring me here, that's for sure. I had been deposited by some greater power than we can understand. I was now close to Jimmy's home and his parents.

"When I felt strong enough to cope, I went to Tremadog to find them. Overlooking Tremadog square was an ominous grey crag of rock some three hundred feet high.

"I enquired at the local Post Office and, as in all small communities, I soon established where Mr and Mrs Roberts lived. They had a small two-bedroomed terraced house, whose front door opened directly onto the market square. I hesitated to knock at the door, but I'm so glad I did.

"I could feel Jimmy's presence in the house. I told

them I was just a friend who had met Jimmy and Tom in Singapore. We drank tea and ate homemade Welsh cakes in front of the open fire. I lost a little concentration and missed some of what they said to me as I tried to imagine Jimmy there. He must have sat in front of that hearth many times.

"After a while Jimmy's father, a thick-set and quiet character, showed me the small cottage garden with its raspberry bushes and rows of potatoes. The scent from a flower border of lavender drifted towards me and ruffled my senses, reminding me of some scent Jimmy had given me. Perhaps it had reminded him of home too!

"Mrs Roberts came out to join us as we sat in the arbour at the end of the garden. We listened to the birdsong and struggled to converse as their accent was very guttural, used to speaking Welsh and little English, I suppose. I noticed Mrs Roberts had a letter in her hand. I recognised Jimmy's handwriting from a poem he had written for me.

"This was the last letter Jimmy sent to us," said Mrs Roberts as she handed it to me. In the letter Billy opened his heart, talking of a girl he planned to marry, a heaven-sent angel, his cariad. As I held this precious testimony, a teardrop fell onto the ink, smudging his sentiment as if trying to say this was never real, it was only ever a dream, a blurry fantasy.

"I didn't need to say anything. Mrs Roberts put her arm around me, they knew full well I was that girl.

"I saw the Roberts every week. I would call by and take them some eggs or some fresh fish from Joe the Fish in Porthmadog, his catch of the day, and they made me feel part of the family. Every day they hoped that there would be a knock at the door and that they would open it and see their handsome, fresh faced, tousle-haired boy standing there.

"Eventually they, like me, came to accept he was not coming home. It was almost as if I had been sent as a consolation prize to help them through their grief."

"And you?" asked Billy sympathetically.

"I think of him often, Billy. It seems crazy when I knew him for such a short time." Gwen fumbled with a gold band on her right index finger. Without looking up she explained, "He meant the world to me. We talked of coming back to his home in Wales, making a life together. It sounds like a fairytale now, but we were besotted with one another, we were in love."

"You didn't meet anyone else over the years?"

Gwen did not answer the question. Her eyes portrayed the melancholy, the pain, her broken heart. Changing the subject, she said, "I suppose you're wondering if Violet and your father ever tried to contact each other after the war. After all, I would want to know if it was my father. I can tell you they did!

"Years after the war and purely by chance, I met your father again in Porthmadog High Street. We were both a lot older but I recognised him almost straight away. We went into Williams cafe on the corner of Snowdon and High Street.

"He told me of his initial escape from Singapore, and I longed to hear the words of a miracle, that Jimmy had survived too, and that he was in some far-off place, but safe. But Tom appeared to know little, saying they had become separated.

"We kept in touch and he told me of his son, who had graduated from university and chosen to teach history, and how proud he was of him and of your mother and his job on the railway."

Billy's mind thought back. He knew his father would head off for days out on the railway using his employee rail pass. He liked being alone.

"I gave Tom the photograph you have with you. I was relieved to know that your father had escaped from Singapore but sadly his war was not over, indeed many of us became guests of the Emperor of Japan. Your father wrote to Violet, you know. She had given him her family home address and, just like your father, he had committed it to memory.

"Your father confided in me. I suppose he felt guilty and anxious about your Mum finding out. He thought she may not understand why he needed to see if Violet was safe.

"The reply he received months later was from Violet's father. He told your father that Vi had survived the war but had decided not to return to Sydney. She apparently informed her father to tell Tom she did not want him to contact her again. She said she was a different person now. Time had moved on, Singapore was then but this is now. Her father said Violet wished Tom well and a long and happy life.

"This left your father bemused and bereft, Billy. He couldn't quite understand what had happened for her to not even want him to contact her."

"So, when was that?"

"I don't recall exactly. Not long after the war, I suspect," Gwen said, shrugging, with uncertainty in her voice. "I found it strange at the time that Vi would say that and especially that she was not going back to Sydney, a place she loved, but her father had clearly spoken to her. But where was she and why?"

Billy sat cogitating how his father must have felt having that rejection. Billy was also quite aware that his father had met his mother Peggy by then. Indeed, he, William James Williams, had been born in late 1946, so why did Tom still write to Violet?

"Time for a cup of tea and some bara brith, Billy!"

Billy was curious as to what happened with his father in Singapore. When Billy was growing up, there had never been talk of his dad being in a POW camp.

"I'm sure you 've heard all you want to know about my war," sighed Gwen. "At least you now know the story of the photograph you came with."

Billy shook his head. He surveyed the matriarchal lady opposite. He could now appreciate that her slightly tanned smooth skin was because of her formative years in the hot and humid Malayan climate. He felt he had learned more about what made his father tick in twenty-four hours with this lady than he had ever gleaned growing up. Gwen reminded him of his childhood recollections of his grandmother, feeling welcomed, cared for, included. Gwen had transported him to a time he had never known but now was intrigued to learn more about.

"Gwen." He held out his hand and she took it. He felt her small, fragile hand in his large grip. "I cannot thank you enough. You have shared memories that were both distressing and painful alongside some fond ones too."

Gwen rested her chin on her chest for a moment.

Then, looking up into Billy's deep blue eyes she saw Tom again. She perceived that, like Tom, Billy was no garrulous individual, but she was happy to fill any voids in the conversation.

"What happened to Violet and yourself?" Billy was fascinated to be listening to this first-hand account of a calamitous time in the history of the British Empire, one his father and Gwen were inextricably linked with.

"It was just the beginning of more than three years of torment for us, Billy."

Gwen sipped her tea from her fine china cup and daintily nibbled at the bara brith. She looked at Billy then focused on the wall behind him, as if she was watching a replay of her life on a screen on the living room wall.

"The ship we were on was commanded by a chap called Borton. In spite of Captain Borton's protests that his ship was overloaded, and trust me, he protested strongly and passionately, we sailed out of Singapore. zig-zagging and often hiding in the lee of islands to avoid aerial attack. We constantly scanned the sky and the sea in fear of being caught by the Japanese.

"We made slow progress and we had a couple of scares when planes were sighted. It was so overcrowded and very hot below deck where we were often confined. The sanitation on board was really poor and the smell made us all want to retch.

"As we headed towards the Banka Strait, which is a narrow strip of sea between the islands of Bangka and Sumatra, all hell broke loose. The ship pitched this way and that, trying to avoid the bombing. As the ship manoeuvred, Japanese planes appeared and started strafing and bombing us. Some people just froze, I felt sick to my stomach, but our training kicked in. One bomb hit an ambulance on the back of the boat and when the dust settled people all around were covered in a yellowy orange-like substance. It transpired that someone had filled the truck with curry powder and other condiments and if we were not so scared it would have been funny.

"People were screaming, children yelling and crying. Even as the devastation unfolded around us we tried to help the best we could, but the bombardment was intense.

"A third bomb hit the ship. Glass and wooden debris flew everywhere, causing terrible wounds. By now people had come on deck as they couldn't stand the claustrophobic heat and stench below. Soon the ship shuddered. I felt it vibrate through my bones and held on to something to steady myself. The ship then just stopped and began to list. The order to abandon ship was given very soon afterwards. Two of the planes flew over us again, people dived off the ship. I noticed one of the planes do a victory roll and then they were gone.

"Surprisingly there was an orderly, but frenetic evacuation. Soon, a deathly quiet pervaded this corner of the world, in all the smoke and fear the human spirit came through. I heard a nurse as she held the rails before jumping into the tempestuous cauldron of the bubbling sea. She broke into song, 'We're off to see the wizard, the wonderful wizard of Oz', we joined in, and she finally let go, descending into the inky, burning, oil-covered water below. As we looked back we saw the *Vyner Brooke* disappearing below the surface and wondered if the captain had stayed with his ship.

"We took it in turns to help the crew members. Being a strong swimmer, I paddled and swam to direct the raft, trying to push towards the distant shore. The water was quite warm, our life vests helped us stay afloat but were cumbersome and did not make it easy to swim.

"Soon we felt the heat of the day start to take its toll. In the boat, faces became red and puffy and eyes glazed over. We had little drinking water between us. Our initial energies and efforts waned, the land seemed to be farther away than ever. I later learned we had been shipwrecked ten miles away from Bangka Island. I became very weary and started to feel a little chilled and feverish.

All the life rafts and lifeboats were dispersed but finally ours and a few others reached the mangrove-lined shore of Bangka Island. We had been in the water about eighteen hours. As we passed a lighthouse the waves swept us onto a sandy beach. I had been reciting the Lord's prayer to myself, 'Our Father who art in heaven'… and this beach was heaven sent, it was indeed as if we had been delivered from evil.

"Many were so exhausted they just lay on the shoreline, as I did. I felt delirious.

"Soon some local inhabitants came down to the shore and tried to help us. One native climbed a palm tree and brought us some coconuts, so we had some liquid. Coconut milk tasted wonderful, it was like the nectar of the gods. Our joy was short-lived, though. We had ingested a lot of sea water and oil and many of us vomited after this.

"On the way inland we thought we'd seen a camp

fire on the beach around the headland and recognised the lifeboats from the ship. We considered trying to reach our fellow survivors, but the mangrove was too thick and we were too tired. It was clear the native people were frightened and did not want to be seen aiding us. Gestures were made to us that we should surrender to the Japanese, who apparently were close by.

"We were a ragged-looking bunch, Billy. We helped each other and after a period of rest we decided to walk to a road and inevitable captivity. We were a motley collection of bedraggled nurses, women and children. We wished our colleague Sister Bulwinkel, who was so capable and resourceful, was with us, but we had not seen her since before the ship was bombed.

"We passed through a small stream and came across a road, which was steaming in the midday heat. A short way along this was a Japanese road block. We stopped in our tracks. We were very frightened, we had heard terrible stories of cruelty and rape. As soon as the Jap soldiers saw us, we could see they were agitated and all the more frightening for us because of it.

"Slowly we moved towards them, but they came to meet us with these long rifles and bayonets attached. Not for the last time we thought this might be the end. They jostled and pushed us with their rifle butts as they shouted, but we couldn't understand them. One blow caught me in the side and made me wince.

"In time, we developed an understanding of Japanese, and the meaning of words like 'speedo'. Forcing us into a clearing by the side of the road we were told to turn our backs. Petrified, we waited to meet our maker.

"Then we heard some trucks and we were loaded roughly on to them and taken to a place called Muntok. Exhausted and hungry we had not realised how long we had gone without food and drink. Our faces were a picture of blotchiness, and all of us had raw red chins where the life vests had rubbed us.

"We were herded into what turned out to be the local Muntok cinema. Other survivors were already in the custom house there and they joined us in due course. We were alive, but the nightmare had just begun." Gwen sighed. "That is a whole other story for another day, Billy."

5

Billy looked at Gwen. Her breathing was laboured, her eyes heavy, her initial exuberance in seeing him had faded. He could that see the last two days had taken a lot out of Gwen.

"May I use your bathroom, Gwen?" Gwen just smiled as she nodded.

He decided to collect his overnight bag and briefcase from his guest room. He looked around, making sure he had everything, and pondered for a moment.

He presumed this had been Gwen's room when she had first arrived and before her Nain and Taid had passed away. He wondered how she had managed to settle with the experiences and memories she brought back with her from the war, and which she quite clearly had kept to herself all these years.

As he returned to the kitchen, he stood for a moment in the doorway, looking at Gwen, her back to him, as she stood by the sink, rhythmically swilling the flowing tap water around a brown ceramic teapot whilst staring out of the window.

"Well, Gwen, it has been wonderful meeting you. But

I think I really should make tracks. Thank you so much for your hospitality. It really has been a great honour. I cannot thank you enough for taking me into your confidence and sharing your wartime experiences."

Looking rather forlorn, Gwen was clearly disappointed as she turned to face Billy. Her head to one side, she smiled a kindly smile, looking Billy in the eyes and taking in his presence, whilst drying her hands on a tea cloth.

"You look so much like your father, Billy, upright and so correct. Sorry, have I said that before?"

Billy was filling the kitchen doorway. "Do I? I suppose there are bound to be similarities, Gwen."

"The timbre in your voice and just your general demeanour are unmistakably Tom's. I'm so sorry you have to leave. Can you not join me for one more cup of tea? You've not told me much about yourself. What is so urgent that you have to leave immediately?"

Billy looked down and shuffled his feet like a small child with a dilemma. "I think I've worn you out and I don't want to outstay my welcome. I do need to … well, I have to tidy up some of my father's financial affairs."

"I understand," said Gwen, accepting his reasoning. She turned, warming the teapot with the steaming water from the kettle. "It looks like it'll be a fine evening to drive home." She spooned in the loose-leafed tea one more time, filled the pot and stirred it. Picking up the tray of tea and Welsh cakes she passed Billy before placing them on the coffee table and saying, "Just a little sustenance for your journey, then, before you depart, Billy bach."

With that, Billy removed his brown leather overnight

bag from his shoulder and joined Gwen in their by now familiar chairs. He could see she had a way with people that made you feel you just had to fall in line.

"So, Billy, what are your plans for life?"

Billy fumbled for the right words, for the story to tell Gwen.

Sensing his awkwardness, Gwen suggested, "Tell me about your former wife and your divorce."

Billy smiled. He loved Gwen's directness, but dodged the question. "It's been a strange last ten years or so, Gwen, since getting divorced and then losing Mum and now Dad," he said with a catch in his voice.

An uneasy silence of a few seconds felt like longer, as he rubbed the top of his left hand with his right. He could not hold out any longer from the emotions he had pent up inside him. Outside a cloud covered the sun, temporarily blocking out the bright spring sunshine and a dark shadow enveloped the room.

Clearing his throat, Billy continued, "I had a very good childhood with caring, if at times distant, parents."

Gwen interjected, "Why do you say distant parents?"

"Perhaps that's a little unfair," reflected Billy. "My father was often absent, first of all on the railway, where he was an engine driver. Mum said he was in charge of taking express trains to far-flung parts of the country and could not always come back the same day. At weekends he seemed to be working on engineering or building projects with a friend. Later in life he used to like simply tinkering with his beloved sports car."

"That's often the way with parents trying to provide for their family," commented Gwen. "The car you refer to wouldn't be the one parked outside, would it?"

"Yes, it was Dad's pride and joy and in fairness it was always a delight he shared with me, taking me on drives from time to time. In many ways when I drive it now, I sort of imagine I'm taking Dad. Does that sound silly?"

"No, not at all for a son, not at all, Billy."

"Growing up it always felt to me as if Dad wanted to be away. I can't really explain. Mum and Dad never seemed to do much together."

"Do you have brothers and sisters?"

"No, I always wanted them, though. I have to admit I have always been a bit of a loner."

Gwen continued to listen intently.

"I enjoyed watching sports but was never much of a sportsman. Dad enjoyed cricket and used to try and encourage me, but my hand–eye coordination did not seem to play ball, so to speak!"

Gwen chuckled at the unintended pun. Billy poured more tea.

"These Welsh cakes are delicious."

"Was your wife a childhood sweetheart?" probed Gwen.

"No. I didn't have many girlfriends when I was younger, or indeed when I went to university. I had always wanted to teach, so was rather studious. My great-grandmother on my maternal side was a headmistress. Often on weekends my mother would send me by bus to my aunt Doris, who was a primary school teacher, and perhaps that was a factor in my decision making, as I learned a lot about geography and places around the world when my aunt and uncle talked about their travels. We would look at the places in an atlas and she would test me on country capitals too.

"Aunt Doris enthused about history. She used to buy me the *Victor* comic and *Commando* story books, and their great tales of 'derring do' titillated my imagination.

"At school I loved history and my teacher Miss Vaughan was wonderful. She made everything so interesting and engaging. She used a textbook called *1066 and All That*, which was a sort of parody of historical tales or events and kings and so on. It added in some light-hearted overviews of a passage of history, which made our lessons fun."

"I see," said Gwen. "So that is why you chose to teach history."

"It made sense to go to university and study history. I went to Keele in Staffordshire. I loved the course but hated the discipline of study. So, when there was a national drive to recruit more teachers for the creaking educational system of the time, with ever-growing class sizes, I sort of morphed my thinking. I suppose I wanted to emulate my history teacher and do the same as her and inspire and enthuse a new generation of children."

"Commendable, Billy, I'm very proud of you!"

Billy smiled. "Thank you. I attended teacher-training college. Beyond that, when I started training, I was taken with a certain theorist, Friedrich Froebel, who was a German educationalist who had developed the philosophy of education known as the Kindergarten system.

"As you probably know, 'Kindergarten' is German for 'child's garden' and is based on the idea that children are like plants and flowers and that their various attributes are in different stages of development or growth.

"So, it needs a teacher to take the role of the gardener, to understand their needs and to nurture their mental, physical, moral and spiritual being. Of course, the wonderment was in seeing this provision help them grow as individuals. He concentrated on catching children young."

Billy stopped and looked at Gwen, who nodded a silent acknowledgement of his enthusiasm and passion for his calling. "Sorry, Gwen, I'm waffling."

"No! You're not, please go on, Billy."

"Well," continued Billy, "it soon became clear to me that I wanted to teach senior school children. I didn't care what type of school it was. At the time, the Labour government was rolling out comprehensive schools, but I taught at a grammar school to start with. That is where I met my wife Ann."

"How long were you married to ... sorry, did you say Ann?"

"Ann. Yes. We lived together for a few years, it was the heady days at the end of the sixties and into the seventies. Whilst Ann was a little more, shall we say, outgoing than myself, I think my serious and pragmatic approach to most things followed the pattern of opposites attracting.

"Ann was a very attractive girl, the quintessential blonde, blue-eyed 'dolly bird', to coin a sixties phrase. Mini skirt and long legs! But it was her humour and fun that attracted me beyond that. At first, she rebuffed me, even making fun of me to her friends. I was seen as a 'square', a little too serious for some. Slowly but surely, though, a chemistry developed between us, we just seemed to hit it off. Eventually we moved into a little bedsit together in Stafford. It was really bijou, more of a love nest for students."

"What did your parents think?" Gwen quizzed.

"At first Mum and Dad were disappointed with me leaving university, but how that all changed when I brought Ann home. My mum was friendly, but her usual reserved self. My father was quite taken with Ann and welcomed her wholeheartedly. In fact, I felt a bit miffed, almost jealous initially, at the attention Dad gave Ann, especially when I had felt starved of such affection from him.

"As time went by we married and moved back to be close to my parents. Oh! I should say that, by coincidence, Ann was from Shropshire too, her family farmed at Dorrington near Shrewsbury. To cut a long story short, Gwen, we were unable to have children and I think this hurt Ann a lot, and indeed both sets of parents.

"Gradually the inability to conceive became a wedge between us. Ann wanted to go for counselling and medical tests. I refused, preferring to leave it to fate. So, it was my fault Ann eventually had an affair and became pregnant and the rest is history!"

Billy stopped and gazed into his past. Gwen saw his pain.

"Parting in any way can be difficult, Billy."

Billy was biting his bottom lip and wringing his hands again. He continued, "I was more hurt by the fact that my parents blamed me for the break up and Ann's adultery, and especially by the way my father seemed so disappointed in me."

"I remember him saying to me. 'Billy, I cannot believe

you messed up your marriage with Ann'."

Gwen hated introspection and self-pity, life was too short. "So," she said, "what are you going to do with your life now?"

"No real plans," said Billy, shrugging his shoulders.

Before Billy could continue Gwen said imploringly, "I would like you to help me."

"What can I do to help you, Gwen?" asked Billy, interested and keen to fulfil her heartfelt request.

"Your arrival here has got me thinking. I would like to know what happened to Violet." She paused as if hatching a plan. "I'm not sure where to start. But you, being a bright, intelligent boy, can be of great assistance, I'm sure."

Billy almost laughed at being called a boy. "Where would I start?"

"Well how about with what we know?" she said, opening a book that was lying on the small oak table beside her chair. Gwen handed Billy an old discoloured and faded airmail letter. It had a printed *Par Avion* moniker in the top left-hand corner. A beautifully scripted address was detailed on the front. He was rather taken aback to see that it was addressed to his father. However, the location was an unfamiliar one to him, perhaps somewhere his mum and dad had lived before their current home. "Your father left this letter with me when we met shortly after the war."

Billy became a little confused, even upset, at this belated revelation, but wanted to know what the contents of this submission contained. "But I thought you had only met him years later by chance in Porthmadog?" said Billy quizzically.

Gwen stood and stiffly walked to a substantial walnut sideboard. She opened a drawer and took out an ornate silver photograph frame. Billy pored over the black and white image, scanning a large group of people, some servicemen, some women in nursing uniform.

Gwen explained, "Your father and I met another time just after the war. We were all part of a project to take testimonies of our wartime experiences and especially the debacle at Singapore. I think the armed forces and government wanted to try and understand how this capitulation of a so-called 'impregnable fortress'could have happened. Perhaps it was to avoid making the same mistakes in the future, or indeed, many thought at the time, it was also a witch hunt, with a view to apportioning blame. Some of our testimonies were used later in war crime trials against Japanese military personnel for the treatment we received in prisoner of war camps."

Billy's attention turned to the letter. He realised it was from Violet's father. It was the correspondence that Gwen had talked of, and just by reading the short but precise dismissal of the brief Singaporean romance that Tom had enjoyed, Billy for the first time in his life felt real compassion towards his father for the rejection Tom had suffered by Violet. How could he not help Gwen? How could he deny his father? He knew he now needed to know more about his father's life before Billy was born.

He stood and hugged Gwen. "Of course I'll help, Gwen. You are right, we need to put this to bed, so to speak. Let's find out what happened to Violet and what sort of a life she has led."

Billy thought *and why she did not want my father in her life.*

"So, Gwen, where do we start?"

Looking up into Billy's eyes her soft expression of gratitude and hope shone through. "You'll do it? Help me find Violet?"

"I will do my best, Gwen."

Gwen took the envelope from Billy, turned it over and showed him the address.

He smiled. "43 Caroline Street, Redfern, Sydney, NSW, it is, then."

Billy carried the tray of tea and Welsh cakes to the draining board and started to put the crockery in the sink.

"Now leave them, Tom, and get on the road, while you still have some light. Oh! I'm sorry, I called you Tom again, Billy, so difficult, when I look at you. I see your Dad every time. Forgive me."

Billy raised his hand, waving away her words as not a problem. Then, shouldering his bag and carrying his briefcase, he headed for the door. He put his belongings into the small car boot and returned to Gwen standing in her doorway.

A mackerel sky above them with tints of red greeted the early evening which was now upon them. Gwen held out her hand, but Billy's large frame awkwardly embraced her once more. Gwen playfully pushed Billy away and said, "Go on with you. Safe journey and I look forward to hearing from you very soon."

Sitting at the steering wheel of the coupe with the roof down, he mocked an army salute reminiscent of his father and drove away.

Gwen walked through to her back yard and stood on her weatherworn deck in the shade of the house. She watched as the red sports car cruised alongside the harbour wall and passed Glanaber garage, disappearing out of sight behind the newly foliaged trees which lined the incline up out of Borth-y-Gest.

Billy felt strangely invigorated and euphoric, he barely noticed the journey home. He ran all the stories of the last forty-eight hours through his mind and he felt his life now had an immediate focus, a purpose.

Of course, he wanted to find out about Violet to help Gwen and satisfy himself, but he also wanted to learn about his father's wartime exploits. It might go a long way to explaining many things.

6

Billy could not wait to get home. He was excited to start his search for Violet and find out more about his father. He opened the door and kicked aside the accumulated mail, then dropped his bags in the hall at the foot of the stairs.

He could not remember leaving that many dishes in the sink and set about boiling a kettle and washing them up, before making himself a cup of tea and heading upstairs to the small bedroom, which he had converted into his study. On the wall he had a huge world map, courtesy of the geography department of his former school.

Leaning over his desk, he ran his finger over Singapore, at the tip of what used to be Malaya. He looked at Sumatra to the south, recognising its close proximity to Singapore. Gwen and Violet had not been taken very far at all.

On his large wooden desk stood an old electronic typewriter, which he had once used to prepare his class notes and do other paperwork. He placed it on the floor before moving his desk diary and his pot of assorted pens and pencils to one side.

Switching on his desk lamp, he pulled its arm over the centre of his desk. He closed the wooden-slatted venetian blinds, and settled onto his comfortable black leather desk chair, its lumbar support relieving the backache from his two-hour drive.

Sipping at his Earl Grey tea, he looked around the room and thought he really must do something with the miscellaneous detritus that at one time or another he had deposited at random around his small operations room.

He looked at his education certificates on the wall, set alongside old photographs of graduation and family scenes. His father holding him in his arms above the waves in the sea at Tenby. Billy could remember how the rush of the wave took his breath away in excitement and remembered recovering and asking for "more, more!" Billy calculated he must have been about four years old.

Billy smiled to himself as he recalled the photo in which he sported a bucket and spade and a small black felt cowboy hat, reminiscent of the Milky Bar kid television commercials. This room, formerly his bedroom, had been his sanctuary for most of his life and it felt safe.

He scanned his bookcase, full of the historical fiction and history textbooks he had collected over the years. There was a stack of his father's books in an old cardboard box, recently retrieved from the attic.

A few hours later, he took off his reading glasses and rubbed his tired eyes. After trawling through all the relevant tomes, he had established that this was going to be a difficult search. None of the textbooks he had were any more than superficial in their account of the "Fall of Singapore". There were just a few paragraphs about prisoners of war and their fate. He concluded he needed to visit the library.

Turning his attention to Violet's whereabouts, his confident promise to Gwen now seemed daunting. How could he possibly find out anything about Violet's life in Australia?

He gently examined the brittle airmail letter that Gwen had bestowed on him earlier that day. He deftly opened it, taking pains to avoid damaging this special connection with his father's past. He re-read the letter and wrote out the address that Gwen had pointed out to him.

All these years on he wondered if the house even existed. If it did, would anyone there know of Violet or her whereabouts?

It was getting late. Billy was starting to flag, he could barely keep his eyes open. He decided that tomorrow he would to go through all his father's papers and belongings again, to make sure he had not missed anything that may be helpful to his search.

Frustrated and exhausted, he slumped onto the double bed his parents had once shared. He found it small and indeed a little too short for him. Its familiar wooden headboard with a carved leaf pattern had been with them all Billy's life.

The room itself had changed little, with a large plain dark oak dressing table, its three drawers sporting small round, metal filigree handles in the shape of flowers in bloom. A large vanity mirror reflected his tired face. His mother's scent bottles were still displayed on lace doilies, as if she would return to use them soon.

His head sunk into the pillow, his mind clouded, and he drifted off.

Next morning, making himself a piece of toast under the grill, his mind went back to Violet. He pondered how he could find out what had happened to her since the war.

Returning to his study, he opened the blinds and blinked as the sunshine warmed his being whilst dust motes danced in the air.

He decided to analyse what he knew: he had her name and an Australian address. Violet was in the Australian Army Nursing Service, last known of at her family home in Sydney in 1946 as acknowledged by her father. Looking at the airmail letter once more, he noted something he had overlooked yesterday. The letter was signed. Violet's father was A. Watkins.

*****

Gwen had enjoyed seeing Billy, but her sojourn down memory lane had opened old wounds which never seemed to heal in her mind. Though troubled that evening, she fell asleep in her chair, and only found her way to bed in the early hours of the morning. Before she had slept, she had written a letter.

Next morning dawned too soon. She was an early riser normally, so even with little sleep, she set out into the grey overcast day. The slate roofs had been darkened by a recent shower, puddles lay on the road. Gwen had on her arm her wicker shopping basket, which reminded her of trips to market with Nain Lilian. She strolled down to the car park to meet the morning bus.

"Bore da, Mrs Phillips," she said to the lady a couple of doors down.

"Bore da, Gwen. Not so nice today," she replied, barely leaving her task of sweeping the front path.

Gwen reached the car park just as the green Crosville bus pulled into the terminus.

"Perfect timing, Gwen," said Bryn the driver, who was used to seeing Gwen Powell over the years.

"How are the children, Bryn?"

"Dew … growing up now, Gwen. Little one is at primary school now, she'll be married before I know it." Smiling, Gwen took her ticket and found a seat, watching a man throw a stick for his dog in the small dry area of the bay left by low tide under the harbour wall.

The bus drifted steadily along the sea front and ascended the bank out of the village. Gwen's mind went back to yesterday and her time with Billy She fingered the envelope in her basket and nodded to herself.

Alighting from the bus in Porthmadog she passed the Australia pub in the High Street, appreciating the irony of its name, given her current preoccupation. Calling first at the Post Office, she was greeted with "Bore da. Sut mae? How are you, Mrs Powell?"

"Da iawn, very well, Gwyneth," responded Gwen.

"How can I help you today?"

Gwen handed over a white envelope under the security window. Gwyneth examined the address, smiled and weighed the letter.

"£2.40 please, Mrs Powell. It'll be a lot warmer where this envelope is heading."

Gwen nodded. "Yes, you're right there, and drier, I suspect! Even though it is the middle of Autumn in Australia."

*****

Billy decided on a plan of action. He wrote some letters. One was to the Royal Australian Army Nursing Corps, asking them to check their records regarding Violet Watkins for details such as when she was discharged, and if they had an address for her, or any other pertinent information.

A second letter was addressed to the National Archives of Australia, asking for help with locating a former Australian Army Nurse, and guidance on how he should go about it. He had read this was the equivalent of the General Register Office at Kew Gardens.

Billy took a shower. As he shaved he studied himself in the mirror, seeing his father more and more as he revealed his face scrape by scrape.

Picking up the letters he had written earlier, he grabbed his wallet, waterproof jacket and rucksack before catching a bus into town.

Alighting at Raven Meadows bus station, he looked up at the splendid seventeenth-century library built of Grinshill stone above him and decided that would be his last port of call today.

He crossed the road and enjoyed the walk alongside the River Severn and up into the town.

As Billy walked along, his attention was caught by a travel agent's window, beckoning to him with posters of the Sydney Opera House and Singapore. Accepting that fate has its ways, he stepped inside. *What could it hurt to enquire?*

An hour later Billy was sitting in the town square on a wooden bench feeling the spring sunshine warm his soul. He had enquired about flights to Australia, but making a decision would be huge to Billy, spontaneous was something he had never been.

He removed three letters from his jacket pocket. He thought he would still post them, as he was not sure he would actually go to Australia. It was not the money, but the distance that worried him and having to get visas, coupled with health concerns and the awful thought of huge spiders and snakes invading his personal space, as he started to talk himself out of the idea.

He studied one addressed envelope again and smiled. Billy had planned to mail all these to Australia and wait patiently for a reply.

He walked across to the bright red Victorian postbox, situated at the top of Gullet passage, where he posted two of the letters. But something made him retain the third envelope. He was not quite sure what stopped him posting his letter to 43 Caroline Street, Sydney.

On his return home Billy opened the creaking patio doors and stepped onto the poorly maintained patio, aware it needed a good scour with a power hose.

He dragged his dad's old candy-striped deckchair from the garden shed and dusted away the cobwebs as the mustiness of the shed's inner sanctum assaulted his nostrils. The shed was surprisingly orderly. Billy spotted the rusting manual Qualcast lawnmower and assorted pea sticks. It will soon be time to mow these lawns, he thought.

Relaxing in the deckchair Billy enjoyed the mid-afternoon rays of the surprisingly warm spring sunshine. He could not believe the run of good weather lately.

In his hands, he had a library book he had picked up that day, *White Coolies* by Betty Jeffrey. The foreword explained she had been a sister in the Australian Army Nursing Service and a former prisoner of war.

Billy had read a magazine whilst on his long vigil at his father's bedside and recalled an evocative mantra.

The Devil whispered in my ear

"You're not strong enough to withstand the storm."

Today I whispered in the Devil's ear

"I am the storm."

He wondered if it was words like this that had kept the nurses defiant as prisoners of war. The more he read, he was sure their faith played a huge part in their survival and tolerance of their living conditions.

As Billy read his book he felt a growing desire to get to the bottom of where Violet was, as well as how her life had turned out. He thought by speaking to her he could learn about his father.

The question remained: was she still alive?

Billy's attention had been drawn to a passage in the book. It talked about the *SS Vyner Brooke*, the very ship Gwen had mentioned, on which she and Violet had escaped Singapore.

He read: "the Australian Army Nursing Service

volunteers were mostly in their mid to late-twenties and recently qualified from small hospitals in rural towns".

Billy started to ponder, his mind going on safari to another time. Billy's calculating logic went to work. Violet had obviously survived the war. Did she marry? Did she have children? If she had been, let's say, mid-twenties, as per the book he was reading, that would make her close to seventy-five years old today.

Immersed in his book, making notes as he went, the day gave way to evening without him noticing. He finished the last page of the thin wartime biography, collected his mug and enjoyed the last of the surprisingly warm evening sun. His back garden was mottled with a profusion of mayfly as they danced away their short life above the rampant shrubbery and daisy-covered lawn.

He then recalled Gwen saying Violet was older than her. He figured Gwen was about seventy-nine, so that put Violet in her eighties. Reality dawned on Billy, his chances of finding Violet alive may be slim … but, he thought, he may well be able to find her relatives. Maybe, just maybe, she had children or grandchildren still living in Australia or somewhere in the world.

7

Next morning Billy was sifting through the ever-growing stack of notes and reference materials with one hand as he spooned his cereal with the other, when there was a knock at the door.

Unshaven, looking as if he had enjoyed a night on the town, Billy opened the front door, which only the postman and uninvited callers used.

It was the postman with a recorded delivery.

A long, narrow, stiff manila envelope, with the printed moniker of Brierley, Davies and Jones of Talbot Chambers, Shrewsbury upon it, was presented to Billy. It was addressed rather formally to William James Williams Esq.

The envelope contained just one piece of A4 headed paper. It requested that Billy contact them as soon as possible, regarding a will and other papers and documents that his father had deposited with this firm of solicitors.

Billy was rather puzzled. He had not given any thought to the possibility his father would have made a will. He immediately felt guilty he had spent little time on sorting out his father's affairs, having been distracted by the funeral and then the visit to Gwen Powell. He dutifully called the law firm and arranged an appointment for the following Monday with the senior partner, a Mr Brierley.

He wondered what his father might have planned without any mention or consultation with him. Billy had rather presumed anything left by his father would be his. A slight fear overcame him. "Who knows?" thought Billy, "he may have left everything to an animal charity."

*****

Monday soon came.

"Good morning," said Billy as the intercom at the solicitors' door burst into life in response to the pressed button. "Mr Williams to see Mr Brierley."

A buzz was followed by a click, and Billy pushed the large door, which opened into a reception area with a worn maroon carpet. Three doors led off the vestibule and a stairway with an ornate metal bannister ascended to his right. A middle-aged woman stood framed in the entrance to a room on the left. "Please come in and take a seat. Mr Brierley will be with you shortly."

Adjusting her large, black-rimmed, thick-lensed spectacles on her nose, she returned to her typewriter. The hypnotic clickety-clack of the keys distracted Billy from an old copy of *Country Living*. Before long the phone rang, which she answered with "Brierley, Davies and Jones. How may I help you?"

Billy looked around. He deduced this was evidently

once the front parlour of a very grand Georgian townhouse, in what was then deemed a very select part of the town off Town Walls, the former defensive battlements of medieval Shrewsbury. A fireplace, long unused, sported a dried flower arrangement in need of attention. The elaborate and ornate rose around the ceiling light above gave a nod to grander days.

A bearded fellow peered around the door, interrupting Billy's observations. "Ah! Mr Williams, I presume?"

Billy stood and shook Mr Brierley's large skeletal hand as he looked up at a slim giant of a man.

"Follow me, it's a bit of a climb, I'm afraid, my office is on the top floor. Are you fine with a few stairs?" said the breathy voice, not waiting for a reply.

Billy acknowledged how unfit he was as he puffed his way up the winding stairwell with its well-trodden carpet to the top landing. He was aware of a heat and strain in his quadriceps that told him he needed to get out over the hills more.

He followed Mr Brierley into an irregularly shaped attic room. His host cleared piles of files from his desk onto the floor.

"Sorry about the mess, Mr Williams, it's been a rather busy time lately."

Billy, thankful there were no more stairs to climb, sank onto a rather uncomfortable but ornate wooden-backed chair, whose upholstery was a little threadbare and had seen better days.

A picture of Hogarth's "Gin Lane" decorated the wall behind Mr Brierley, complemented by a landscape print of Shrewsbury on the wall to Billy's left.

A small panelled window, which overlooked the street like an eagle's eyrie, offered some brightness and a skylight gave some natural light to supplement the ceiling's single suspended light bulb. A desk lamp with its jade-green glass shade was obviously positioned for poring over documents on darker winter days.

From behind the desk, Mr Brierley appeared to be on all fours, frantically searching an array of haphazardly placed files on the floor. "Now, Mr Williams," said a muffled voice. Popping up like a pantomime character Mr Brierley gave out a large sigh. "Thank you for coming in. Now, I presume you have come about your father's will?" He dropped some files on the desk and sank into his modern, black synthetic leather chair.

Billy blew heavily through his nostrils, trying to temper his frustration.

"Well, it was actually your company who asked me to come in with regard to the will, which my recently deceased father has apparently made."

"Ah. Yes. Can you please confirm your father's full name?"

Billy shuffled disgruntled as he witnessed the continued performance, which reminded him of a mad professor. "Thomas Joseph Williams," he said with an air of impatience.

Mr Brierley sifted the files and produced what appeared to be a rather thin beige file.

"I do apologise. I have been away and my secretary is ill at the moment. So, it's taking me a little while to sort things out." With another sigh Mr Brierley sat back and continued, "Now! Your father's will!" Leaning forward, he sorted through the contents of the folder, appearing to put one or two papers in order.

"Ah yes!" he said to himself and nodding, making a sort of sucking noise with his pursed lips, as if cogitating how to share the information.

Billy mused that the solicitor's height must cause him problems at times. It must be painful for his back, sitting and leaning over documents all day. His suit seemed short in the arms and he observed below the desk that his shoes must be size twelve or more.

Looking down at the papers on his desk, Mr Brierley finally started his submission.

"First of all, my sincere condolences on your father's passing. He was a very pleasant man and I am sure he is a great loss to you and your family."

Billy raised his hand, palm facing Mr Brierley in thanks, as if it to say, fine, now get on with it.

"Now, your father first came to me not long after your mother died, which I believe was a number of years ago." Without waiting for a reply, he continued, "Mr Williams wanted to make a will and he wanted to share certain information with you after he had passed away." Mr Brierley paused and looked over his glasses at Billy.

Billy was bemused as to what this information could be. He was distracted by a grease spot on the solicitor's navy-and-gold striped Shropshire Cricket Club tie. Mr Brierley looked down at himself following Billy's gaze.

Sensing the awkwardness of the moment Billy spoke. "So, will you read the will or should I have a look though it?"

Mr Brierley continued, "Mr Williams, your father, has left everything to you, the house and contents, the proceeds of his bank account and so on."

Billy sensed the but that was coming.

"But Mr Williams has stipulated that certain conditions are to be fulfilled in order for this to come to pass." Some more shuffling of papers and two envelopes were produced from the folder.

Holding them both up, Mr Brierley said, "Your father requires you to deliver these two envelopes in person to the addressees and once this has been accomplished and confirmed, the estate can be closed."

Billy took the two envelopes. He recognised his father's handwriting on both. One was addressed to Gwen Powell, Awel y Mor, Ralph Street, Borth-y-Gest, and the other to Violet Watkins, 43 Caroline Street, Sydney, New South Wales, Australia.

Mr Brierley was surprised that Billy appeared nonchalant. "Do you have any questions?"

"Only one. What if either or both of these ladies is no longer living?"

"Ah!" said Mr Brierley as he remembered another envelope and produced a letter from the folder like a magician producing a rabbit from a hat. "This is addressed to you. I believe it will explain every eventuality to you."

8

Billy left the solicitors, feeling a little disconcerted. He had always believed that he would inherit his parents' estate, because … well, after all, there was only him, all his relatives having died years ago. So why attach all this drama?

Instead of clarity and closure, Billy was none the wiser. He felt rather affronted. His nature was pragmatic, to say the least, he liked order and simplicity. He was not one for surprises, but they kept coming. Standing outside the law practice, he considered the envelopes in the legal folder he had been given.

The day was dry and mild with little breeze. He thought he would clear his head by dropping down the short, steep bank towards the river. He passed by the tennis courts, where players were hitting bright yellow tennis balls back and forth, a little like the thoughts that were bouncing around his head.

He strolled alongside the churned-up, brown-coloured River Severn, which had been disturbed by the overnight rainfall. He followed the tree-lined avenue. Joggers, cyclists and dog walkers passed by taking their exercise. In a world of his own, Billy barely noticed them as he tried to make sense of his father's will.

Passing under Kingsland Bridge, he stopped briefly to watch two rowing crews of coxswain and fours from Shrewsbury School, as they raced one another in preparation for the next regatta. The rhythmic coordination of the sculls' blades propelled the narrow craft through the muddied river, like knives through molten chocolate. The rowing coaches on cycles at the water's edge shouted instructions into hand-held megaphones to the boat crews. Occasionally their intensity was interrupted as they tried to avoid pedestrians out for a stroll.

Billy continued his walk alongside the groves of bright yellow daffodils that brightened the verges and river banks, lightening spirits with the message that spring was here.

Turning up past the Victorian bandstand, Billy reached the Dingle, a former stone quarry, now a horticultural explosion of floral colour. A lily-pad-strewn pond surrounded by shrubs and willow trees was the focal point and centrepiece for people sitting on the numerous sturdy wooden benches that were dotted around. Ducks moved frantically, churning up the expanse of enclosed water, as they moved towards a small child and his mother, the child throwing pieces of bread for them to consume. The little lad squealed and giggled as he witnessed the frenzy.

Billy found a bench to himself and extracted his father's letter. Full of trepidation he started to read, hoping the contents could assuage his hurt feelings and allay his fears.

Dear Billy

You are reading this letter because I am no longer around.

When we set out on life's adventure we are young and fearless and do not realise how fragile our mortality is, but life can change in the blink of an eye.

At the outset, I want you to know how much I love you and always have. I cared very much for your mother and have missed her immensely since her passing. Peggy was a good wife and mother.

No doubt there are many things I should have shared with you when I was alive, so you could have asked questions, but I will do my best in this letter.

The war has had a lasting effect on many people, not least your mother and I, who lost our remaining parents in the conflict, as well as good friends and other family members.

However, the unexpected joy of your arrival after the war's end gave us a new beginning and hope for the future. When you came along you brought us renewed energy, vigour and a reason for living.

It was tough in post-war Britain with rationing right up to 1954. We would have loved to have given you a brother or sister, but it was not to be.

Your mother and I met quite by chance at the Empire in Shrewsbury, not long after the war in Japan had finished.

I had just arrived home by train, on leave, and was exhausted. I did not want to go home to my sister's straight away. I had been away so long. It was pouring with rain, so I ducked into the Kings Head for a beer.

A little later the rain stopped, so I walked up past the Empire. I was in uniform and had my kit bag on my shoulder.

That's when I first saw your mother. She was waiting on the cinema steps, shifting from foot to foot and looking at her watch. I asked her the time. It soon became clear she had been stood up by a friend. I said I planned to go in and see the film, and would she like to join me. Much to my surprise she agreed.

Your mother was a petite lady with what they called a Marcel wave in her long auburn hair that fell to her shoulders. She was wearing a red coat and black skirt with a white blouse buttoned up to the collar and adorned with a cameo brooch. I can see her now. As the Yanks would say, she looked swell.

It was not until the film started that I realised we were watching *Brief Encounter*, a film about a woman meeting a stranger and being tempted to cheat on her husband.

Peggy appeared to enjoy the film. I offered to walk her home. She was unsure at first, but we began strolling and I walked her to her gate in the Belle Vue area of Shrewsbury.

We said our goodbyes and I felt comfortable and relaxed for the first time in ages, as though I had come home. A new dawn of hope allowed us to believe there was life after the horrors of the war. I carried on home to my sister's. She was living where we all grew up, the only place I could call home, even if I was made to feel like a lodger.

Eventually your mother and I saw each other again,

then as often as we could. Your mother was a fun-loving, sensitive lady, but she was quite comfortable with her own company. As soon as I could get a pass, during each leave, I made a beeline for Shrewsbury.

One such time we had been dancing at Morris's Ballroom on Pride Hill. As I walked your mother home, your mum dropped a bombshell on me. She was pregnant!

We were very happy and married post haste! Unfortunately, whilst I was back on duty, your Mum was out helping a neighbour move some logs one day into the out-house and the effort resulted in her miscarrying, so it was not to be. Your Mum was dreadfully bereft, but then you came along, and made life all worthwhile again.

We used to go for walks along the river with you in the pram, and as you grew we took you into the Dingle to feed the ducks. We had little money for going out, but we were happy and had one another.

We found a little terraced house to live together in Frankwell. The house was very damp, being close to the river, and you developed a bad chest quite often. Eventually we managed to get on the council housing list and moved to our lovely house in Berwick Avenue that you know so well.

Like all relationships we had our ups and downs. Do I have any regrets? No, not really. Perhaps I wish I had spent more time with you, instead of constantly working overtime, but we needed the money.

Billy, your mother was very good for me.

When I came back from the war, I had my demons to contend with. I was emotionally and physically scarred. I witnessed some awful sights, dreadful scenes which gave me nightmares throughout my life. I would wake up shouting and sweating, but your mother comforted me and tried to understand, even though I refused to talk about some of the terrible actions I took and was responsible for, and the atrocities I witnessed.

However, in that dark period of war there were some lighter moments. I spent a particularly joyful time in Singapore for a short period before we were embroiled in the sharp end of the war. I never felt more alive, before or since. I met many friends, but many of their lives were cut too short.

Along with this letter to you are two more, one for Gwen Powell and the other for Violet Watkins. Know that I treasure the friendship of both of them.

War, especially in Singapore, was at a time when senses were heightened! I can still feel the humidity and take in the aromas of the flowers and trees like the frangipani.

Gwen, I am sure, can tell you a lot more about our times together in Singapore. If you wanted to know more about my time in the services, I suggest you contact Captain David Tulloch at the Royal Engineers Museum in Gillingham. I knew his father.

Please deliver these letters in person, that is most important. I have my reasons. Both letters contain information and explanations I have never been able to share before.

Thank you so much, son, for blessing me with your existence and now your understanding and loyalty.

God bless you

Love Dad X

The sun appeared from behind a cloud and warmed him through. A small child came by. Pushing, then coasting on a bright red Triang scooter, the small boy wore a short-sleeved indigo and burgundy striped T-shirt and blue shorts, white sports socks and red Nike trainers. He stopped and studied Billy, said nothing and scooted on. For a moment, Billy saw himself as a child.

He considered the content of the other letters in his possession and knew he must return to see Gwen.

9

Billy decided to contact the Royal Engineers by telephone. People there were very helpful and, following a few security questions, agreed to send him details of his father's war record.

A few days later he received a short precis of his father's service record. It showed he had enlisted and been trained in Aldershot and sent to STS Lochailort, Scotland, before transferring to Singapore in August 1941.

Other places that he had never heard of or understood followed: GTU Kharakvasla India, SEI Alam Bazaar India, Jessore India. Dec 1944 Horana Ceylon Operation. Operation Hyena Burma.

Billy called the Royal Engineers once more to make sure he had the right service record for his father and ask for information on a fellow soldier James Roberts, explaining he was a great friend of his father. He mentioned that his father had told him to ask for a David Tulloch and the adjutant agreed to look into it and write to Billy again.

A week or so later as he was mowing the lawn the

postman arrived with another bundle of mail. One letter stood out, its Royal Engineers emblem emblazoned on the envelope.

Billy reached for the wooden letter opener from the letter rack that his father used. Billy considered the opener's provenance. Had it perhaps been brought back by his father from the Far East?

Billy toyed with the letter, examining it on both sides, a little like savouring the thought of the cream and jam in the middle of a piece of Victoria sponge cake, which as a child he would save until last, whilst nibbling the sponge around it. He opened it up.

Dear Mr Williams

I have been handed your enquiry regarding the wartime service records of your father Thomas Williams and his colleague James Roberts.

I believe as historian for the Royal Engineers, I may be able to answer a question or two which may be puzzling you and your family, i.e., how your father came to serve in Burma. Thomas Williams was an exemplary soldier and his various skills came to the attention of the Special Operations Executive.

Your father's main task was initially as a wireless operator. He would have been inserted or landed in some secluded jungle clearing behind enemy lines, to assist with communication but also to help train the Karen tribe. The Karenni were loyal to the Allies and especially to the Brits. In time they were armed with a view to harassing the Japanese. The less than one hundred NCOs who were spirited into Burma did a great job in training them in covert operations with the goal of disrupting Japanese activities.

You mention a James Roberts, who was also parachuted into Burma with your father. He did sterling work but was unfortunately injured and captured in an ambush whilst he and some of the Karenni fought a rearguard action allowing your father and many of the men to escape. This was indeed a very brave and selfless act.

Although Roberts survived the ambush, he spent some time on the death railway, fifteen kilometres south of Thanbyuzazat, where, for some reason, he was eventually taken to hospital. Ironically, perhaps even fortuitously, we understand he was killed in an RAF bombing raid and he was eventually interred, alongside many other Allied troops who were gathered from their trackside burial sites, in a cemetery run by the Commonwealth Graves Commission at Thanbyuzazat, which was actually the Burmese terminus of the death railway.

Lieutenant Roberts and your father made a very important contribution to the allied success in Burma and the Far East. They were well thought of among their superiors and colleagues and were especially revered by the Karenni who fought with them.

If you have any questions, please call the number below.

Yours sincerely

Captain David Tulloch (Retired)

Billy sat on his doorstep, a tear in his eye. He felt very proud of his father and very grateful for Jimmy Roberts' sacrifice and wished he were able to thank him personally for saving his father's life.

10

Gwen had been very interested to hear that Billy had new information to share with her. Greeting him at her door like a long-lost friend, she sensed a certain awkwardness from Billy.

"Come in, come in," she said. Billy followed her into the familiar setting of the room with its splendid mountain and sea outlook from the patio doors, which he felt he could never tire of. A newspaper lay open on the coffee table, announcing the upcoming celebrations of the fiftieth anniversary of Victory in Europe Day.

"Tea is in the pot and I have made some nice Welsh cakes, Billy. Would you bring them over?" Gwen sat back in her rocking chair as she gazed over the bay.

Billy, placing the tray on the coffee table, removed the newspaper. "Big celebrations coming up, especially in London. I believe they're going to have a fly-past along the Mall and over Buckingham Palace, all the old warplanes. I suspect Spitfires will be prominent."

"Indeed," said Gwen.

"I read somewhere they are going to have bonfires up and down the country to celebrate the event, and of course Dame Vera Lynn is going to sing some of the wartime favourites," enthused Billy.

Gwen nodded. "The Forces' sweetheart, yes, she was an earthy lass, she had a great voice and it wasn't just her voice, it was the intonation, she really meant those lyrics, you know, and I'm sure her songs made many folk think of home."

Billy saw the pensiveness in Gwen's face as she thought back to those tough wartime days, never knowing what the next day would bring, if indeed the next day ever came. Always one for facts, he said, "I didn't know that she went overseas to sing. She didn't just perform in a studio. She went to Burma of all places, even close to the front line near India in a place called Kohima. She must have been very brave."

Gwen thought for a minute. "People did extraordinary things during the war, it's surprising what being in a difficult position can do to you, it can bring out the best and indeed the worst in you. No doubt Vera's selflessness and bravery meant a lot to the lads. Words in her songs, especially 'We'll meet again, don't know where, don't know when, but I know we'll meet again some sunny day', well, those words kept people going, gave them hope. I wonder if they'll have a celebration for VJ Day, Victory in Japan?"

"I think I read there is to be a celebration parade on 15 August." Billy could see this whole episode of his father dying and his last visit had stirred up a lot of emotions in Gwen. He imagined many would be painful, but hopefully there were a few good memories too.

He had planned to just breeze in, tell Gwen about his

father's will, hand the letter over as his father requested and leave as soon as he could. But he felt a duty, no, not just a duty, but heartfelt concern that he should stay with Gwen and comfort her and support her and learn more in the process. He had really taken to her.

"I will be celebrating, if that is the right word, on 24 August, as that is the day in 1945 I learned the war was over. I was struggling with malaria, but the news made my spirits soar." Gwen looked at Billy and added, "People do things in wartime that in peacetime would be thought of as criminal, immoral and just plain wrong."

Billy nodded. He could see the tears in her eyes.

Gwen looked at the distant mountains and watched as the peak of Cnicht emerged from the cloud, much like her life had emerged from the fog of war. "My time as a prisoner of war taught me a lot about people and indeed myself, Billy."

"How long were you a prisoner?"

"Physically, for the rest of the war after the fall of Singapore. Emotionally, I have never escaped. I am still incarcerated in the memories of those days. However, like everything in life, there are some who had it worse than others, take Violet for instance …" With that Gwen's voice trailed off. "I suspect the Americans will be having their parades on 2 September, the day they took the surrender from the Japanese on that big fancy ship of theirs."

Billy felt uncomfortable. Gwen did not seem in a good place. "Please don't distress yourself Gwen, let's talk about better times, your time living here, for example."

"Billy, I have found it quite cathartic to share these thoughts. It may sound a little depressing to you, but it may eventually help me purge the dreadful fears and trembling I have every night I go to bed. It helps if I get these things off my chest, it eases my burden if I can talk." She fixed him with a mournful, almost painful gaze. "Can you bear hearing what this old lady has to say? After all, I don't know how much longer I'll be around, and I feel this experience should be shared and passed on to generations to come."

Before Billy knew it, he was transported back to 1942 as Gwen remembered her incarceration on Bangka Island again.

"After a couple of days, we were forced to march out of town to a sort of native jail. We wore a mishmash of clothing to keep us decent. Some of us in sarongs, some in the remnants of uniform. This jail was very basic, with concrete floors. The dormitories had tin roofs and were set in a quadrangle. It was tough sleeping on concrete slabs, and we were crammed in, around forty of us per hut.

"Each hut had a drain at the end, which was our toilet. It was basic to say the least, and any pride you had went out the window, if you had to go, you went. That was, if you could make it in time, which was not always the case. We all used one tap to draw water from, and there was only a small amount of it. We used a sort of old stone trough as a large sink, which we all bathed at in turn.

"We were about five hundred or more people, I would say, civilians, service personnel and all sorts of ages, shapes and sizes. Men, women and children. It soon became clear with the sick and injured we had that we needed to create a separate area to nurse and care for them. Soon, a hospital ward developed. We nurses were gainfully employed, our reward being to help people to survive.

"Lack of facilities, soap and other necessities meant hygiene was compromised and ultimately disease was a problem. We were lucky enough to have three doctors, who were in charge.

"Food was almost non-existent, just a bit of rice, which was awful, and probably the scrapings from the Jap leftovers. Occasionally it had a bit of vegetable in it or a sliver of meat. We eventually became very resourceful in adding protein as the diet was so meagre.

"Our days were governed by the rising and setting of the sun, as there was little light in our control that we could live our lives in. You know, the Japs used this as mental torture, putting on searchlights or general lights to disorientate us at night to stop us sleeping. Individual guards would do this too, with flashlights.

"A few days after arriving at this jail, much to our elation, Sister Vivien Bulwinkel was brought into camp to re-join us. I think I may have mentioned her before. Anyway, just the sight of her raised our spirits. I didn't know her well, but Vi and the others held her in high regard. She was a tall, slim lady, with short, straight fair hair and blue eyes and, boy, she had some presence, although her manner was reserved, some might consider stern. I recall she had a great sense of humour, which helped all of us through each day. Billy, humour was a prerequisite for survival. Without it life would have been intolerable.

"Our happiness at being reunited was short-lived when she told us of how she and around twenty nurses were found on the beach by the Japanese. Apparently, they were herded back into the sea. She said they were standing almost in a line when the Japanese opened fire on them killing all but Sister Bulwinkel. Sister said she only survived by playing dead and floating and keeping still in the shallow water until the Japs had gone. She also said a lifeboat had arrived with men in, and they had been marched into the jungle and later she heard shooting.

"After this small moment of triumph and joy, we soon got used to routines and the constant haranguing by the guards. One of the worst things initially was the primitive latrines, which we had to dig ourselves, as well as the trench toilets. The hastily erected bamboo huts had mud floors and every rainstorm they leaked. Sometimes, even now, I can smell those latrines, it makes me feel sick thinking about them.

"After about two weeks we were transferred by a really old steamer across the twenty miles of Bangka Strait. It was about three in the morning, as I recall, we were given a small bowl of rice, we wrapped some of the rice in a banana leaf and took it with us. Some women brought some minuscule biscuits they had managed to bake the day before, how I do not know.

"You recall the most random of things, Billy. I have just thought, I was sitting on a pile of timber, there was hardly any conversation, children asleep on mothers' laps, it was almost eerie. Then I saw the most wonderful sunrise and a double rainbow, it was the sort of moment that uplifted your spirits and in a funny sort of way gave you hope and a reason for living.

"Our only sanitation on board was an old fruit box with a panel missing, which was suspended over the back of the boat, under the watch of the Japanese guards. Only the most desperate availed themselves of it. We felt they stood watching more to humiliate us than to prevent escape.

"Once we entered the mouth of the hot and steamy Musi River, the heat became even more oppressive. The sun was up now, we had no shade, many of us didn't even have a hat. I could hardly breathe and was dripping in perspiration. It even rained heavily, such were the joys of this land. We were soaked, then the sun came out and it was even more stifling.

"One of the sisters, it may have been Vivien Bulwinkel, I don't rightly remember, led a small deputation to see if we could get some water and cover to shade us, and after a bit of debate some grime-covered tarpaulins were erected, but by the time we reached Palembang in Sumatra, it was 4.30 pm and we were all suffering badly. I remember the date quite well, it was 2 March 1942, Agatha's birthday. Agatha was a Q.A. nurse who hailed from Kent, she had been suffering with dysentery and malaria. We had taken it in turns to mop her brow and keep an eye on her as we placed her in the shadiest area we could. We had made her a little rice cake and gathered around to sing Happy Birthday to her. Agatha had become so emaciated, her eyes shrunk back into her skull. I remember her smiling weakly then closing her eyes. She never opened them again.

"We all realised how evil these people could be, Billy.

In all honesty each day was a bonus, yet sometimes in our deepest, darkest hours we did not want the morning to come. That might sound an awful thing to say, as life is precious. But I can't tell you how tough life in those years was, no words could do it justice."

Gwen calmly continued to recollect the drama and despair of the awful years in captivity. There were no histrionics, just descriptions of doleful, abject misery and hopelessness. As Gwen spoke, Billy tried to imagine the horror and deprivation these people were subjected to. He had never been in tropical heat like that but knew even the civility of a gym steam room was too much for him, so what it must have been like for Gwen and Violet and the others in an insect-ridden, disease-bearing, humid climate like Sumatra, whilst being incarcerated and frightened, he could not get near to comprehending. Monsoons sounded merciless and miserable.

"When we did disembark, it was along a precariously wobbly, narrow plank. I can tell you, Billy, in our weak state, it took some negotiating. We waited for what seemed an age on the dock before trucks arrived and loaded us all.

"We were standing, holding on to what we could, as the trucks swayed and braked and bumped, all being driven erratically, as if the drivers were in some sort of jungle rally! We passed through Palembang, where locals jeered at us, finally getting their own back on the colonisers, as they saw us, as if we had subjected them to some awful ordeal under European occupation.

"Much to our surprise, our destination was a school and, even more astonishing, we were met by a group of Allied servicemen who served us a wonderful hot meal.

It was like manna from heaven, quite the best we had consumed in ages, it was like a stew and tasted fabulous.

"It was so good to see our fellow comrades and male ones at that. Alas, things didn't last, we were soon separated from them and moved yet again. Eventually we were put in a hut. The building next door to our new home was a Japanese Officers' Club. We often heard them in high spirits.

"You might be wondering how I remember all this. Well, one or two of us kept a diary, which, if the Japs had found them, would have led to big trouble for us! Frankly, apart from the dates, and even most of those I remember, the rest is indelibly printed on my mind, times I can never forget. Faces of people I worked with, cared for, shared tough times with, many of whom did not make it through. That is why I must tell this story to someone, it must not die with me."

"How did you manage to keep a diary secret?" asked Billy with a furrowed brow.

"It was probably foolish in many ways, as if I had been caught, I would probably have faced execution. Not only that, the rest of the prisoners would have faced more hardship as a penalty, the Japanese were that horrible, especially the Kempeitai, the secret police, who made the German Gestapo look like choir boys." Gwen shrugged her shoulders. "But I needed to keep a record of all that was happening, so people could understand what we were enduring. Little did I know it would be a forty-two-month diary!

"I had to hide the diary not just from the Japanese, but from informers amongst the prisoners. Some would be that desperate for extra rations or privileges or simply to survive, that they would perform this act of treachery and turn you in to the Japanese."

Billy shook his head in disbelief. "How did you keep up the practice of writing your diary, then, and where did you keep it?"

"It varied from camp to camp, it was a mixture of scraps of paper and backs of cigarette packets and anything I could get my hands on, plus a pencil, of course. After a stolen few minutes under the shade of a tree or the hut, I would put them in my underwear, then hide them wherever possible. Sometimes in bamboo pipes, sometimes I just dug a hole and buried them. I told no one, although I'm sure some of my closest friends knew.

"Each day we followed the same routine. We dreaded 'Tenko', which was roll-call. It was worse when it was called at random times, and we had to bow deeply to the Japanese and then stand in the unforgiving heat of the sun.

"Rarely did a day pass without someone else becoming ill with dysentery or malaria, tropical ulcers and worse. But life went on. We felt we had to do the cooking, washing and cleaning to keep us sane and focused, and as disease-free as possible.

"We created our own entertainment, putting on little plays, singing as a choir, lots of things. At first the Japanese were touchy about too many of us being together, until they understood why, and I think they eventually enjoyed listening to the fruits of our work.

"Most of the Japs couldn't speak English, but you had to be careful what you said, as the odd one or two soldiers could understand us.

"Our faith was the main thing that kept us going and, in spite of our predicament, mixed denomination services were held and enjoyed. They renewed our hope on a regular basis.

"The mosquitoes were awful, especially at night and we had no mosquito nets. We knew the Japs had quinine tablets, most of which were from Red Cross parcels, which they kept from us. We resorted to bartering with natives, be it through the perimeter fences or when we went on working parties to repair roads or some other menial task. Sometimes we collected water from creeks. We would give the natives anything we had of value for quinine tablets and other medication. Any little luxury, even soap, was a bonus.

"Vegetables, including Chinese cabbages, most of them already rotting, used to be dumped onto the ground from a truck and there was a melee amongst us to collect it all and take it to what passed for a kitchen for us. Occasionally we had a bit of meat, but there was very little to go around and added little taste to the watery soup.

"After a while some more people joined us, a few British nurses and some Dutch colonial women and children and nuns. The good thing about this was they brought news that over sixty Aussie nurses from Singapore had managed to get back to Australia safely on one of the evacuation ships.

"Occasionally, a local trader was allowed in with an oxen cart, full of goods to buy. It was mostly food on offer, but occasionally some sandal-type shoes appeared. Few of us had any shoes by now. The main joy of this cart was fruit, though the downside was if you had nothing to barter you were just an onlooker or occasionally resorted to stealing.

"And so, life went on. There were occasional beatings and sad times as we lost people to disease or just malnourishment and the little cemetery started to grow. Disease would peak at times, typhus was a killer, and we did the best we could to combat it with hygiene and the basic medicine we could beg or barter. Sometimes some of us were so ill we were taken to Palembang Hospital, and many did not return.

"We had all tried to ease our sleeping arrangements by getting dry grass and stuffing rice sacks we appropriated. How we longed for a bed with a real mattress, Billy.

"We tried to earn some money doing chores for others, such as cutting hair or chopping some wood, so that we had money or goods for bartering. Our clothes would fall apart, so we scavenged any sort of remnants from rubbish tips and devised implements to sew things together. It's surprising how resourceful you become when you have too! That is what disappoints me at times today, how people can think it is their right to demand so much is beyond me. Especially some children, instead of being thankful for what they have.

"We formed a library with a few books that had been retained or found when we moved camps. We used to have talks by individuals telling us about their lives or occupations or anything they felt they wanted to talk about. It all kept us focused on life rather than despair.

"We had moments of optimism, such as when we were instructed to have an air-raid drill. We thought this could only mean one thing, that the Allies must be nearer, but we ended up being disappointed.

"Regular searches for contraband and diaries and anything written were stepped up. Each day became more intense and difficult. Then with little warning we were told we were moving! It turned out not to be very far, but it was heartbreaking. We had to start again as we entered filthy huts, located in a mosquito-ridden, low-lying, swampy area. It was early 1944 and we were on our last legs, some emotionally as well as physically."

At that moment the telephone rang and startled both Billy and Gwen back to 1995.

Gwen made her way steadily to the phone and picked up the receiver. "Lovely to hear from you," she concluded. "I have the son of a good friend visiting me at the moment. That would be best. Certainly, yes, that would be lovely, it will be good to see you, Mair."

Gwen checked her watch. "That was a friend who calls now and then. She's coming to visit on Saturday. My word, Billy, I have talked a lot. Shall we have some sustenance? How about a little walk to the harbour and a snack in the Seaview cafe? Now, where are my glasses?"

Billy and Gwen dined on cheese toasties and a pot of tea, followed by a splendid Welsh ice cream cornet, whilst sitting at the little patio table in front of the Seaview cafe.

"That ice cream tasted so good, it can't be good for you, Gwen."

Time seemed to stand still for them. They were almost oblivious to the constant ebb and flow of tourists visiting Borth-y-Gest. Wading birds enjoyed their pickings from the mud around the marooned hulls of small sailing vessels and rowing boats, which had been left high and dry by the outgoing tide. A dog chased a stick thrown by his owner, barking as he bounded into the recently revealed silt and mud. The sun was shining brightly and everyone was at one with the world.

A far cry, thought Billy, from the times Gwen had been describing to him earlier. *How had she survived?*

11

As they walked back to Awel y Mor, Billy puffed his way up the incline that was Mersey Street. He was amazed at the fitness of Gwen, who carried on talking to him about various neighbours and local happenings. Ahead of them, they saw an old black Labrador that could barely walk. Turning into Ralph Street they followed and soon reached the dog plodding along with its grey snout and tottery gait.

Gwen patted him. "Good boy! Where's your master today? Not far behind, I'm sure."

Billy turned and saw no one. Entering the front door of Awel y Mor, Gwen headed upstairs, and Billy peeked around the door into the lounge. It was a room he had not explored before. It was a cosy room, with a well-worn rose-pink velvet couch with deep-seated cushions. Two matching armchairs, all bedecked in crocheted throws and sprinkled with brightly coloured cushions completed the suite. A surprisingly modern flat-screen television was positioned to one side of the bay window, through which Billy's attention was drawn to a rather frail old man with a stick, who was barely moving forward.

"That's the dog's master," said Gwen, startling Billy slightly, as he had not heard her return down the stairs. "I'm not sure who will go first, they're both getting on, but devoted to one another."

"I can see what you mean, Gwen. The fellow is barely able to shuffle. How does he manage these inclines, I wonder?"

"Somehow! It's just determination and bloody-mindedness, they pass by twice a day. One of these days it will only be one of them. Although, I rather think when one goes, so will the other.

"Before you leave, I would just like to finish my story as best I can. I know it must be tedious to you, but it may help you in your research and pursuit of Vi's whereabouts."

Billy shook his head. "Gwen, it is so good of you to share what must be most painful memories. I am intrigued and saddened in equal measure."

Gwen put her hand up, gesturing as if there was no need to feel sad. "It was a difficult time for many and some did not make it. They were perhaps the lucky ones, as those of us who did make it out alive are scarred forever."

Sitting back into her favourite chair, Gwen adjusted the cushion and gently rocked her story into life again.

"Exhausted as we were, we had to get this new camp ship-shape. So we set about trying to clean things up."

"How big was the camp, Gwen?"

"Let me see. It was about the size of a football pitch. Mostly dirt. The few remaining blades of grass testified to a once fertile area, but the flow of human traffic and monsoonal muddy weather had ruined it. Fortunately, it was dry when we arrived, but very hot.

"Work was dreadfully difficult in the humidity. The mosquitoes and indeed other mites, like fleas and bugs, along with various vermin added to our woes. It was a God-awful existence, Billy, but we had no choice, survival was the name of the game.

"As more people arrived, the one side of the camp was designated for the Dutch and the other side for us. We even had our own kitchens and had a rota for the showers, basic as they were.

"Rain provided a water supply for the showers but when the rains did come, so did the terrible mud which made our daily drudge even more miserable. Violent winds, at least a couple of times a week, used to whip the rains into a terrible tempest and the inadequately roofed and walled tree-fronded *attap* huts, well … they just didn't pass muster for keeping the elements out. It made our lives desperate at times.

"But when the rain stopped, the wells in and around the camp soon became dry, so we really needed any rain, it was just a vicious circle.

"Birds called in the trees around the settlement, reminding us of our jungle isolation. It sounded like they were laughing at us sometimes, a raucous 'caw caw', like a cackle.

"We had some children in the camp, brought mostly by the Dutch families.

"Toilets were a joy as always," said Gwen, grimacing. "Just a long trench, which drained away, and had to be cleared out from time to time. We used whatever was to hand, and indeed sometimes it was our hands. Needless to say, we had a rota for that. You needed to have a strong constitution to cope, and by now we were all a little kettle-stomached as our physical condition had deteriorated because of disease and poor nutrition."

"Gwen, did they ever hurt you or try to molest you in any way?" Billy said, not quite knowing why he had asked the question.

Gwen seemed to wince. She lowered her head as if concentrating on the right hand twisting the fingers of the left, trying to squeeze the anguished memory out. For what seemed an age, she did not look at Billy and stayed quiet. She looked up with tears in her eyes.

"One day at 'Tenko', as we all stood to attention, an officer and his adjutant arrived in a very smart staff car. We were all lined up in the heat, bowing, as was expected by the Japs, under fear of reprisal if you failed to. Both disappeared into the prison commandant's quarters for ages, while we were left to stand in the unforgiving heat.

"Some folks were wavering and swaying a little, sweat pouring off us. Eventually the officer appeared. He slowly walked up the line and touched some of the prisoners on the shoulders, notably younger girls in the Dutch lines. Then he came to us. We could see the girls were distressed. He touched me and then Vi on the shoulder and a good friend Mavis, then he left.

"We were dismissed, except the guards made all those who the officer had singled out carry on standing. We were scared. We thought we were going to be executed, but why us? I thought they must have found out about my diary, someone must have told.

"Before long a truck arrived, we were all loaded on to

it. We bounced around on the back of the truck. The breeze was a pleasant respite from the heat of the camp, but it still beat down oppressively upon us in the open back of the lorry. The Dutch girls were still crying, we tried to comfort them. We headed back towards Palembang.

"After a while we turned off the road. We followed a lovely manicured drive, bordered by exotic plants and bushes, and came to a circular turning area which surrounded a lush green lawn. In the middle of this verdant circle there was a flagpole sporting the Rising Sun flag. One of the girls jested that the national emblem looked like a fried egg."

Billy smiled.

"We had arrived at a grand-looking colonial building with a 'widows walk' around the top, and an attractive verandah below. We were escorted from the car onto the cream-coloured wooden terrace, where ceiling fans whirred above. We were invited to sit on the comfortable cushioned bamboo couches and given refreshing drinks.

"We were left to languish full of trepidation for a few minutes, which seemed like an age. Nothing was said, we just looked at one another, which said it all! Like a whirlwind in came an officer and what turned out to be a doctor and some other soldiers. All jabbered away in Japanese and nodding ensued. An officer looking at us directly as if surveying a cattle auction ready to bid, suddenly grunted 'jugunianfu', then he grinned broadly.

"Next a soldier came in and we were taken one by one to stand against the plain background of the clapperboard side of the house and photographs were taken of us. As quickly as they came the phalanx of officers left. We were firmly herded up the teak wooden stairs and separated into different rooms, a flower emblem on each door.

"My room was airy with a dressing table and stool, and a bed with a large rattan headboard and a mosquito net draped over it. Through a shuttered window was the garden below, and suddenly it dawned on me why we were there.

"Before I could gather my senses the door was swung open and a short, portly Japanese officer in cap and uniform entered. He sported a long sword which jangled at his side. His face was pock-marked. As he removed his cap, he ran his hand over his thinly covered pate and smiled smugly.

"'You English?' I didn't reply. 'You English?' he shouted, startling me.

"'No … No,' I stuttered. 'I'm a nurse and under the Geneva Convention …' Before I could finish he strode towards me and slapped my face so hard I could barely stand. I slumped on to the bed. I regained my composure and stood again. I was angry. I tried to speak again, but no words came out.

"What followed was horrendous. When he had finished I heard the door slam. It seemed an age as I lay there shaking, afraid to move.

"After a while as quietly as possible, I opened the bedroom door and stepped into the hallway, I was joined in the corridors by other girls as they too staggered around in a daze. An officer passed me, put his cap on and smirked.

"I stumbled towards the communal bathroom and tried to cleanse myself of the shame of being defiled by such a brute. I looked into the mirror and saw my shame and despair.

"Other girls came in, all as distressed as myself, some very young, just children. I soon learned that the words I'd heard on arrival, 'jugun ianfu', meant comfort girls or more accurately prostitutes. I had become 'Kuchinashi' or as we know it 'Gardenia', the picture that was on my door.

"On the entrance hall wall was a board with all our photographs on, positioned alongside our flower designation, so we could be selected by those coming in for gratification.

"For months Mavis, myself and others were raped and beaten, sometimes many times a day, yet we enjoyed better rations and conditions than the others in the camp. That was the trade-off. Billy, you become numb and accept this as just another form of torture. You just try and survive.

"Every day my door handle turned my body shivered. I became deadened, insensitive to their actions. I hate to admit I even stooped to playing the part of a demi-monde as I found that way, they were more gentle and responsive. The experience rarely lasted more than a few minutes, and as time went by they would often bring gifts, which I kept to barter with. This was now my life. During the act, I would just focus my mind on survival, whilst keeping my eyes on the wall.

"Often, they would whisper sweet nothings, as if I was their girlfriend and I soon found that that was exactly what I was to many. A replacement for their loved one, miles away. They even used a name sometimes, which I'm sure was that of their sweetheart. I had learned to play the game.

"Then one day, with no warning, we were told to pack the few belongings we had accumulated there. We were taken from the house and returned to our comrades. We were threatened not to discuss what had happened to us under fear of death. I swore I would never talk of those terrible, shameful experiences as a 'comfort woman'.

"To this day I have never enjoyed flowers in the house or as a gift. As beautiful as they are as nature's bounty to most people, their connotation to me is far too painful to contemplate."

Billy was visibly shocked and angry. Gwen was shaking. He moved to her and held her.

Taking a handkerchief from the sleeve of her cardigan, she dried her tears. "Sorry, Billy, it's so painful just recalling that awful time, what must you think of me?"

Billy, now kneeling by Gwen's chair, shook his head, still speechless. Finally, almost whispering, "I do not have the words to help console you enough, Gwen. I just didn't realise ..." He broke off, stood and made a pot of tea.

When Billy was settled in his chair once more, Gwen continued. "Life went on, but almost every day someone passed away, be it of beri-beri, malaria or a local jungle fever. Finally, we were brought a small bottle of quinine tablets. These helped but were too few. Over time the supply increased.

"We women had to carry the corpses to a small local Chinese cemetery and bury the dead. We had to dig the graves with any implement we could find, like bowls and tins. A spade would have made the unenviable task a bit easier.

"Water was the main problem. There was a standpipe we used, a fair walk away, but even that pipe ran dry as the rains ceased. Many were suffering from malnutrition and disease.

"Eventually we were moved again, it took days before we reached another camp, this time on Sumatra. Before we could settle, we were moved again. We could not figure out what was going on. On each journey people died, but these were not just 'people'." Gwen hesitated. "Billy, they had become our friends, our fellow sufferers, it was like losing a member of your family. We tried to dig a shallow grave for them. Those poor people, their families will never know where they are buried. Finally, about a hundred of us ended up at a new camp. It was by a shallow stream of cool water, and what a blessing that was."

"What pulled you through all this, Gwen?" asked Billy with a pained expression on his face.

Gwen did not hesitate. "My faith in God, Billy, and the thought that one day I would see Jimmy again, and we would grow old together! Often, I would lie at night, tormented by mosquitoes and wracked with stomach pain, followed by regular urgent visits to the toilet. All the time I was determined to get through it.

"Some still nights, I could make out the stars in the sky above, twinkling through a split in the *attap* roof of our hut. They reminded me of glow worms. I had seen a tree by a river once when I was growing up. I was with my parents paddling along a river, out later than we expected. but the blessing was the sight of this magical illumination. The tree was alive with glow worms or as the Americans call them 'lightning bugs'. It was so wondrous, like I imagined the large Christmas tree in Trafalgar Square would look. I can remember the beautiful moons we had, too, a beacon of hope against a dark blue sky, illuminating my future. Jimmy and I always said that, wherever we were, we would look at the moon and know we were thinking of one another. It gave me hope, Billy, a reason for living.

"We were short of wood and saw all the dead rubber trees close to the perimeter fence. We were not allowed to go outside and get some, which was crazy and harsh. Work details still continued, with lots of chores just made up and repeated day after day like a punishment. We would move rocks, for no purpose, then were sent back the next day and had to move the rocks back to the same place they came from.

"Eventually, we realised things were beginning to thaw in our relationship with the Japanese, who were becoming rather helpful. Some women were allowed to meet their men folk for a visit in a nearby camp.

"We received a huge backlog of letters. Some of us learned of the deaths of family members, others of new family members being born. News could be cruel and wonderful, but the best thing was contact from loved ones. It helped us survive, too, gave us a reason for living.

"Then, after three-and-a half long, weary years, where every day you survived was a bonus, a miracle happened.

"All of us were in a poor state. Not for the first time I was laid low with a bout of malaria and so could not fully appreciate the day. The date is etched on my mind, though, 24 August 1945. Do you know, I think of our liberation every year on this date?

"Apparently the camp commandant made a speech formally telling us war was over and that 'Americano and English' would be with us in a few days. He added, much to our ire, that we were now all friends!

"We noticed they had opened the gates and some people dared to walk in and out, just because they could, but then those that could carried on daily life. Our morale rocketed. We liberated the stores, full of Red Cross parcels. We found mosquito nets and quinine, other medical supplies, butter and powdered milk and a little chocolate. That made us angry, to think of the lives these supplies could have saved.

"Soon the men from the nearby camp found their way to our camp, some hobbling on crutches, all in ragged clothing like ourselves. We used new sheets in the store to make new garments.

"Finally, at the beginning of September the Allies arrived, firstly some Dutch and Chinese troops. About a week later some Aussies came. We sat and talked with them and learned a lot of what had been happening.

"We were beside ourselves, somewhat mesmerised by our sudden freedom, we didn't know what to do. The fact there was no more 'Tenko' or rationing was difficult to adapt to, after all those 7 am and 5 pm roll calls, let alone the deprivation, cruelty, sickness and death.

"We learned that President Roosevelt had died, Hitler had committed suicide, and we became strangely sad when we heard how some huge bombs dropped on Japan had ended the war, with great loss of life.

"One day a plane flew low over the trees and we could see a uniformed fellow throwing out packages. For the first time in ages we had bread, sweets, powdered egg, cheese and cocoa with sugar. The Aussies loved their Vegemite, which is like Marmite. To this day, I have some on toast, almost like a liberation meal, Billy.

"Eventually we were trucked to a rail station about ten or more miles away, a good few hours' journey. Then we joined a train full of all sorts of waifs and strays, male and female. Strange thing was, there were still Japs around, but this time they were trying to be overly kind to us, giving us food and other sustenance. From the station at Tahat, we went to a small airfield and waited for a plane. It was delayed, but I will never forget the joy of seeing that Australian plane landing, its huge green and brown camouflaged frame lumbering along the runway to stop in front of us.

The doors opened and there was Sister Patterson. I had not seen her since Singapore and the evacuation from there. Sister Patterson had been in the same Australian General Hospital as Vi.

"I can't remember a lot about that flight to Singapore. I believe I fell asleep, emotionally exhausted. I vaguely remember arriving at St Andrew's Hospital. Some went to St Patrick's Hospital where I had worked a little before the evacuation.

"Oh, to see and then lie in proper beds with pristine

white sheets! Not one but two pillows, we were in heaven. In truth, I was too tired, worn out and indeed sick, to really appreciate it. On arrival we were given a few assorted items, which were luxuries to us, like soap, toothbrush and toothpaste and cigarettes.

"We washed and were given pyjamas and slippers and dressing gowns, then we managed to get off to sleep. We slept spasmodically, waking up fearing it was all a dream.

"You may laugh at this, Billy, but we were so unused to such comfort, we often struggled to sleep at all. So, we would get out of bed and sleep on the floor. It took us quite a while to adapt to lots of things, and my digestive system found a lot of things too rich to eat. I was full quickly and physically sick sometimes. In fact, even to this day my system has never recovered fully.

"Over the next few days we were given new clothes and all sorts of gifts and food. We were interviewed and some even took part in a television broadcast to the folk back home. It was about another month before we headed home by ship. It was called the *Tairea*. A large, old-fashioned vessel with three tall grey funnels, it had vivid red crosses painted down each side of the hull. A crew member told me it had been built in Glasgow in 1924, which made the Scots on board very proud, a fitting vessel to take them home. Ironically, it had been used in peacetime before the war to travel between Britain and Japan.

"On board, there were teams of doctors and nursing sisters and of course a Matron. There were over 500 of us being taken home. Our beds were fixed to the sides of the ship in two tiers. It was basic but heaven compared to the POW camps. Nurses were in tropical uniform, white dresses, veils and white canvas shoes.

"Some of the sights were pitiful. Emaciated bodies, where you could clearly make out the skeleton below a stretched, thin skin. Eyes sunken in sockets. Most were quiet, still somewhat cowed and frightened, not quite believing they might be heading home to loved ones. Many did not get home, they were too weak to survive the journey in spite of good nursing care. They were buried at sea.

"We were fed puréed foods and fluids to get our strength up and let our stomachs get used to working properly again. Our bowels struggled badly, which made the latrines a challenge once more. I saw some poor souls who had hook-worms. These worms had to be removed before they burrowed in and became parasites on our bodies. Nurses would get small pieces of wood and wrap the hook-worm tails around it and pull ever so gently, so as not to leave the head behind under the skin. This was a difficult task. Many days we heard of people going a bit 'doolally' and jumping overboard.

"We arrived back at Portsmouth to a tumultuous welcome on the docks. How wonderful it was to feel as though normal life had begun to return. In reality, of course, life could never be normal for us again. We spent a week or so in a hospital recuperating and being debriefed, and then my grandparents came to fetch me, and, as you know, I am still here!"

"Gwen that is one amazing and humbling story."

"Now," said Gwen, "you told me you have some news."

Billy for whatever reason decided he did not want to share the news that he had found out about Jimmy in Burma. Not just yet.

Gwen watched expectantly as he fumbled in his briefcase and produced an envelope. "Gwen, a lot has happened in the time since we last spoke together here. Not least of which my father had made a will, which in all honesty I was not expecting. There were certain requests in that will." He hesitated and turned the envelope around in his hands. I'm afraid I have not made any headway in finding Violet, but I will redouble my efforts and keep you informed."

Billy gave a brief overview of his conversation with the solicitor and a short account of where his father Jimmy went after Singapore and said he was trying to find out more.

"So, Gwen, I was asked to give you this correspondence, which Dad wanted you to have after he had passed away."

Gwen held the Basildon Bond, pale blue vellum envelope and saw the writing so familiar to her. But she was afraid she would not like the contents.

12

Gwen stood and propped the envelope from Tom against the colourful pottery jug showing an old Welsh spinning maid resplendent in traditional costume against a blue sky, a symbolic if kitsch contrast to the dark oak Welsh dresser on which it stood. Gwen straightened the ruck of cream crocheted lace protecting the fine antique furniture. Turning to Billy she said "Well, I believe I have told you all I can now, Billy."

"Well, I guess I'll make tracks."

Gwen smiled and walked down the dim narrow hallway towards the front door. Billy followed. Opening the door, Gwen stood aside, her arms folded, head slightly bowed, to let Billy out.

"Thank you once again for helping me understand more about those very difficult dark days of war, Gwen," said Billy, as he stooped to hug her gently.

Gwen nodded. "It was a long time ago. Yet still so clear in my mind, Billy. Thank you for bringing me the letter from your father. Look after yourself, Billy and good luck."

Billy drove off and Gwen was alone with her

memories and back to the anchorite existence she was used to and preferred. A weak evening sun was casting shadows on the front of the house.

Gwen collected her old Barbour jacket, then fetched the envelope, tucking it into her pocket. On her way out, she looked into the hall mirror and relocated strands of her hair behind her ears.

Ambling down Ralph Street, towards the sea, she passed by the chapel and sat on a bench above the former wartime gun emplacement. She looked out across the estuary, towards Harlech castle, which was bathing in the glow of the evening sun in that lovely time just before sunset. Her hands rested on her lap, holding the envelope.

For a short while, she thought back to the happy days in Singapore. Times before the war caught up with them. She could see Tom, Jimmy and Violet in the kaleidoscope of her mind's eye.

Turning her attention to the sky-blue envelope, she peeled open the seal. With trepidation she pulled out the writing paper. Tom's exquisite handwriting in fountain pen was so unusual for a man.

A seagull made a shrill call overhead, like a warning. She followed its flight and watched it land on top of the former gun emplacement. A black Labrador deviated from the path and sniffed at the end of her bench, before returning to its owners. Gwen started to read.

Dear Gwen,
If you are reading this I am no longer alive. I just wanted to say thank you for being such a good friend, confidante and special person in my life.

I want to apologise for not being in contact with you as much as I would have liked over the years.

I know how much you loved Jimmy, and trust me, I loved him dearly too. He was everything you could hope for in a man and a friend.

I have asked Billy to bring this letter to you.

I treasured our times in Singapore and often wonder what would have happened if the war had not intervened. I could have been living in Australia with Violet and you could well be married with lots of little Jimmys. But then, as we know, peacetime brought changes to our lives which were unexpected.

I have taken a dreadful secret to my grave and I sincerely hope you can forgive me for this. You asked me what happened to Jimmy and to my shame I told you I didn't really know. I just didn't want to hurt you. I misguidedly wanted you to still have hope.

In the early days I felt this was right and proper. I now know I was desperately wrong in this calculation, but the more time went on the more I felt I could not admit to you what had occurred and that I knew Jimmy was never coming home.

Gwen could feel herself getting upset, her stomach started to churn. How could Tom have misled her like this? Tom, who she cared for and who always seemed so straightforward and matter-of-fact and trustworthy. Her eyes filled with tears, her face reddened, she read on through her misted vision.

Jimmy and I were seconded to a special unit which was trained for subversive counter-invasion tactics. The powers that be had realised we were going to lose Malaya and probably Singapore and wanted to leave troops to organise the local resistance to harass the Japanese as well as keep eyes and ears on the ground for a future effort to retake Malaya. After the fall of Burma, we were extracted from Malaya. We spent a bit of time recuperating, re-arming and training in India before being dropped into Burma, to do the same there.

For the most part we were successful and built up a good relationship with the Karen tribe, but many awful things happened too. The Japanese, as you know, were vicious in their treatment of and reprisals on any collaborators or indeed anyone suspected of giving us assistance or sustenance.

Our unit, though, continued to be a thorn in the Japs' side. I led my unit on many raids alongside Jimmy, but we were targeted more and more.

Their pursuit of us was relentless, and to try and erode our support they persecuted the local people mercilessly.

One day we were out on a mission and we were ambushed. Jimmy and some of the brave Karenni fought the Japanese off while the main body of our patrol escaped. Jimmy was shot and captured, local informants brought us news he was okay and had been taken to a prisoner of war camp in northern Thailand, but we later learned he had been killed.

To my shame I felt I could never share this with you. I cannot explain, perhaps it was because we had survived and Jimmy had not because of me. Jimmy was like a brother to me and I have thought about him every day.

I am taking this guilt to my Maker and will ask

forgiveness from him as I ask the same of you now.

Please find enclosed something of Jimmy's which was amongst his possessions in our camp and I am sure he would have wanted you to have.

I am so sorry.

Love Tom

Gwen was not just disappointed, she felt betrayed and angry. She wiped her eyes with her handkerchief and tipped the envelope, out of which slid an old cigarette packet with a poem written upon it, a poem by Hedd Wyn, which read:

> For Gwen
> We have no claim to the stars
> Nor the sad-faced moon of night
> Nor the golden cloud that immerses
> Itself in celestial light.
> We only have a right to exist
> On earth in its vast devastation,
> And it's only man's strife that destroys
> The glory of God's creation.

For days, a deep melancholia came over Gwen, she struggled to leave her bed, she just sobbed. Finally, she was able to grieve for Jimmy. Even though she knew in her heart he had been dead all this time, the mind is a strange entity, it kept Jimmy alive. There was always hope he was there in some corner of the world looking at the moon each night and remembering her.

At first Gwen was in a silent rage, an inertia. She felt maddened by Tom's deceit. Gwen felt meeting Billy had just raked up all these hidden fears and emotions, to which she had cultivated a tolerance over the years. Now everything was raw again.

Gwen heard her phone ring a number of times and heard knocking at her door, as the days blended into nights and back to day.

It was Saturday afternoon before she found herself wrapping her dressing gown around herself, weakly holding the staircase bannister and descending towards the kitchen. She had lost track of time and forgotten the friend who had rung her earlier last week and who was calling by. Gwen was mortified to think she had let her down.

Her long grey hair in a ponytail draped over her left shoulder, she gazed at the mass of mail that had accumulated, and then saw herself in the hall mirror, her eyes red, her face blotchy. "I really must get a grip," she said to herself.

Picking up the mail, she immediately rang her friend to apologise. "Hello, Mair, I'm so sorry I missed you earlier."

Clouds hung low over the distant mountains, but the sun was starting to peep through. Gwen wanted to forgive Tom and understand how war had affected him badly, too, especially knowing that it was not just her that Jimmy meant so much to. Gwen was very proud of Jimmy for his gallantry and selflessness and bravery. *How could you show your love for fellow man better than sacrificing yourself for them?* she thought.

Gwen reflected on her initial emotions of feeling betrayed and cheated of closure all this time. Then her mind turned to Violet and she nodded silently to herself.

She thought about the last time she had seen Violet.

Violet had been her best friend as Jimmy had been Tom's. It's strange what war and emotion does to you!

She twisted the gold band on her right-hand index finger and cried once more.

13

Billy had been back home a few days and had been consumed by sorting out household affairs and putting all his father's financial matters in order.

He felt a calling not only to go to Australia, but to visit Burma on the way. He was intrigued to go and see where his father had served, and indeed pay his respects to Jimmy Roberts.

His father's will and the condition his father had imposed was a factor, but he truly wanted to find Violet and establish if she was still alive and learn a little more about his father and his past too.

He had tried to call Gwen but there had been no reply. He wanted to tell her more about his findings regarding Burma and to see if she was coping. He assumed she would have opened his father's letter to her by now.

It was Saturday. Like a flower searching for sunlight on a beautiful day, he positioned his well-used Lloyd Loom garden chair in the warm late morning sun on his back patio. He sipped a steaming hot coffee from his favourite Shrewsbury Town football club mug. He felt content.

He placed his coffee on the uneven paving slabs. Billy was full of anticipation as he opened a letter received that very morning. It sported an Australian stamp depicting a kangaroo.

Dear Mr Williams,

Thank you for your enquiry regarding a former Australian Army Nursing Service nurse serving during the Second World War. As you may know we are now referred to as the Royal Australian Army Nursing Corps.

We can tell you that Nurse Watkins did indeed join the Service, which was staffed by volunteer civilian nurses. Before the war the understanding was that they were available for duty during times of national emergency, unlike today when we are now part of the army.

Violet May Watkins enlisted in the Australian Army Nursing Service on 13 December 1939. Attached to the 2/10 Australian General Hospital after training, she was posted to Malacca in Malaya during 1941.

On 14 February 1942, Nurse Watkins was one of the 65 nurses aboard the ship *Vyner Brooke* when it was sunk by Japanese bombing. She was captured along with others by the Japanese and became a prisoner of war for the next three-and-a-half years before being liberated.

Nurse Watkins was discharged from the nursing service on 20 September 1946. Her file shows that she married British serviceman Ronald Duncan in Singapore in 1946 at the Garrison church. We understand the couple then relocated to the United Kingdom.

We do hope this helps in your pursuit of your relative Nurse Watkins.

Yours sincerely

Nursing Officer Sarah Gregson

Archives Dept

Royal Australian Army Nursing Corps

Billy felt a fleeting twinge of guilt at the little white lie he had offered in his enquiry, whereby he had claimed Violet as a relative.

He was amazed to find out that Violet may have been a lot closer to home than Gwen, Tom or indeed he, could ever have imagined.

His first reaction was to ring Gwen, but he hesitated. What if Violet was dead? He would be giving her false hope. He also cogitated on what his father might have disclosed to Gwen in the letter. *So where to start?* he pondered. Then it occurred to him as he re-read the letter from Australia, he had another name to investigate: Ronald Duncan.

Billy spoke to the local library who informed him that the General Registry Office was now at Kew Gardens in London. He immediately rang the number the library had provided. He checked opening times and how he might go about finding a Second World War serviceman, Ronald Duncan. The staff at Kew were most helpful, suggesting something he had never considered. For a small fee they would be prepared to research this for him. He just needed to send the fee, along with all the details he had on Ronald Duncan and any other information he may require.

Billy could now put his journey to South East Asia and Australia on hold, or indeed maybe not even go at all. He sent off his letter, money and questions to Kew Gardens and waited.

Meanwhile Billy set about getting his house shipshape.

14

Ten days passed before Billy received the much-anticipated delivery from Kew Gardens. He sat in his father's armchair and eagerly opened the large A4 manila envelope, producing a sheaf of paper held together with a large pink paper clip. Sure enough, it was the research results he had been waiting for. He was astonished at what he read.

*****

Later that week Gwen was pleased to see the handwritten letter from Billy. Sitting in her rocking chair, she adjusted her glasses and read what Billy had to say.

Dear Gwen,

It was great to see you recently and I hope all is well with you.

I have been trying to call you but without any joy. You must be very busy out and about.

Following some letters I sent to Australia and enquiries I made with our national records office at Kew Gardens I finally have some news for you regarding Violet.

The most amazing news was from Violet's service record sent from Australia, in which they tell us and I quote: "Nurse Watkins was discharged from the nursing service on 20 September 1946. Her file shows that she married British serviceman Ronald Duncan in Singapore in 1946 at the Garrison church. We understand the couple then relocated to the United Kingdom."

This came as a big and welcome surprise, so from there I tried to track her down in this country by first of all tracing Ronald Duncan, her husband. I had a reply today.

It confirmed that Ronald Duncan and Violet May Watkins were married at the Garrison church in Singapore in 1946.

Later that year they travelled back to the United Kingdom on the *Empress of Australia* ship and, it would appear, settled in Lamlash, on the Isle of Arran in Scotland, which is where they were registered as voters according to the 1947 electoral register.

Of course, they may well have passed through various demobilisation camps when returning to the UK before heading home. I suspect certain immigration formalities needed to be sorted out on behalf of Violet too.

Apparently, they have a reference to them in notes on Ronald Duncan's war record, but no concrete evidence.

Ronald Duncan was born on 21 April 1905 in the small hamlet of Lamlash, Isle of Arran, Scotland. His father, Reginald Duncan, was a local fisherman and his wife Lizzie Duncan née Macgregor, a housewife, at the time of his birth. It would appear Mr Duncan had two siblings, a brother Stuart and a sister Mary Elizabeth.

Mr Ronald Duncan enlisted and rose to the rank of Lieutenant in the Royal Army Medical Corps. He was a prisoner of war on the Thai–Burma railway having survived the massacre at the British Medical Hospital at Singapore in 1942.

They found the death certificates for all of the family, Ronald Duncan having died on 21 June 1979 of heart failure.

Unfortunately, they have had trouble finding information on Violet, who is now Mrs Violet May Duncan, of course, but following consultation with their counterparts in Sydney for background information they advise she was born on 13 March 1913 in the family home at 43 Caroline Street, Sydney. Her father Albert Watkins was a schoolteacher and her mother a housewife at the time of her birth. This tallies with the letter to Dad that you showed me, Gwen, as it was signed by A Watkins and the address is the same.

With regard to siblings, they found just one, Thomas Watkins, born 4 April 1915. Both of Violet's parents have passed away. They have no record of Thomas passing, so he may still be alive, but they cannot find him on an electoral register in Australia.

Other names shown in the past at 43 Caroline Street, Sydney, New South Wales, Australia were Eric and Vaughan Watkins, but they do not know if they are siblings or other relatives, and they are not registered there now. Head of household is now Danny Brady.

Crucially, though, they cannot find a current address for Violet May Duncan, nor indeed a death certificate. So they cannot confirm her whereabouts. The good news, Gwen, is that it's possible that Violet could still be alive and here in this country.

Look forward to seeing you again before too long.

Warmest wishes

Billy

*****

A few minutes later Billy's phone rang.

"Hello," said Billy.

"Why don't we just go to Scotland and try and find her?" came the reply.

"Hello, Gwen, you received the letter then. How are you? I have been trying to ring you on and off."

"I'm fine, just been a little busy. Thank you so much for all your efforts in tracking down Vi. I am so excited I may get to see her again."

"Being optimistic I am sure that will be possible. To answer your original question, we could of course head north. The logical place to start our search would be in Lamlash on the Isle of Arran. I can't believe it's a very big place. Someone may have some information and at least have known Ronald and Violet." Billy hesitated a moment. "Looking at the facts, Ronald Duncan has been dead sixteen years, and there is no trace of Violet at the moment. Well, I wonder …" Billy's voice trailed off.

"What do you wonder, Billy?" said Gwen half-expectantly.

"Well, as Violet would not have had much family here, and Ronald's family are all gone, would she have stayed in that locality or indeed in the country? What if she has gone back to Australia?"

"Billy, there is only one way to find out, we need to go to Scotland, or rather you do!" retorted Gwen, more with a command rather than a request.

Billy smiled to himself. "I see," he said, acknowledging Gwen's order. "Why not? I have nothing else too pressing right now," he added facetiously. "But I need to tell you something, Gwen. I did some research into what happened to Dad and Jimmy after they last saw you in Singapore in 1942"

"I know, Billy. Jimmy never made it back. Your father had never told me all this until I read his letter. I just wish he had talked to me about it. I understand his guilt but not his rationale for keeping this from me."

Billy was relieved he didn't have to break the bad news to Gwen.

"I have another favour to ask. If you ever get to Burma, will you go to the cemetery and take a photo of Jimmy's grave and lay some flowers for me?"

"Of course, Gwen," said Billy solemnly.

"Thank you. Keep me informed. Cheerio for now," said Gwen as she hung up the phone.

Scotland it is, then, mused Billy.

Next morning, he set about preparing for the journey ahead, packing an overnight bag. He collected all the paperwork, photographs and anything relevant he could find. He checked the road atlas for a route to Lamlash. He checked the oil and tyre pressures and refuelled before calling the ferry company who operated over to the Isle of Arran from Ardrossan on the mainland.

Just lately every day seemed to bring something new and he was quite excited by this adventure into the unknown. He imagined himself as the fictional detective, Hercule Poirot, tracking down the person who had committed the crime.

It was going to be a long journey, over 300 miles, he figured, and he estimated it would take him the best part of the day. Other Scottish names came to mind. Where were Lochailort and Arisaig, where Jimmy and his father trained? Maybe he would go there too!

The following day, a bright sunny morning greeted Billy as he headed towards the M6. He was up before the larks, it was not even 7.30 am, but he wanted to beat the rush hour. He had to find accommodation when he arrived, so did not want to get there in the dark. As he crossed the border at Gretna Green he cogitated on how many lovers had eloped to get married there.

He had made good time and it was not quite 2 pm when he saw the ferry terminal at Ardrossan, the jumping-off point for his trip to Arran. He could not help bursting into song, *Speed, bonnie boat, like a bird on the wing, over the sea to Skye, well, Arran anyway.*

He had not made a reservation but fortunately was able to get a car and passenger space and before he knew it, he was standing at the prow of the ship, the cool breeze toying gently with wisps of his hair as he watched Arran bring his fascinating search closer to fruition.

Disembarking at Brodick, he drove south along the coast. About four miles later he dropped down the black ribbon of asphalt into the beautiful small village of Lamlash, with its bay protected by an island, which Billy learned in due course was called Holy Isle, used as a religious retreat for Buddhists and nuns. Small boats were anchored in the blue-green water, a light breeze rippling the surface of the sheltered bay.

Seaweed fringed the narrow, soft sand beach and seagulls called to one another overhead. A small boat was trying to tie up at a small jetty, bobbing up and down as the sea toyed with it. It was a bright sunny afternoon. Billy looked up to a fine, craggy fell which brooded over the island with a hat of white cloud.

Billy decided a pub would be as good a place as any to ask about somewhere to stay. He had already driven past the aptly named Drift Inn. He parked and, setting out on foot, he came first to the nearby Pierhead Tavern.

15

"Can I help you?" asked the strong Scottish accent as Billy approached the barman busy drying a pint glass with a cloth.

"Please," said Billy. "I'm looking for a room for a night. Is there a bed and breakfast or guest house you can recommend here locally?"

"Aye! There are a few, try the Lilybank. I saw the owner Colin this morning, I ken they have vacancies." The barman lifted the flap in the bar and walked to the door of the pub and Billy followed. Standing on the steps the local Scot pointed. "Just head down there, and you will find it a little-ways on the right, ye cannae miss it."

Billy thanked him and strolled down to the characterful old stone seafront cottage, divided from the bay road by a low white wall and narrow, low-maintenance front garden of coloured stone chippings. Opening the squeaky wrought iron gate, he rang the bell before turning to look at the splendid vista once more.

The door opened. Billy looked around to be greeted by a diminutive red-faced lady, brushing her hair from her eyes with the back of her flour-covered hands. Her sleeves rolled up, she was wearing a blue and white paisley pinafore.

"Hello," said Billy. "I wondered if you had a single room for the night, preferably with its own bathroom?"

"Aye. Come on in. I'm Sarah Macgregor. I would shake your hand only ..." She brandished her flour-covered hands palm up. Billy smiled and followed Sarah into her kitchen.

"Let me just wipe my hands. Youse'll have to excuse me. I'm a little warm from the heat of the kitchen. I'm in the middle of baking a few pies and a bit of soda bread," she explained in her strong Scottish brogue.

"Not a problem."

"Right, follow me, laddie." They walked up the stairs to a front bedroom, which had a superb view of the bay out to Holy Island. It was a large room with a double bed sporting a bright floral duvet, or was it an old-fashioned eiderdown? wondered Billy. A comfortable armchair was positioned at the window and a pair of binoculars sat on the window sill beside it.

"Would this suit you?"

Billy nodded. "Absolutely."

"One night, you say. Well, that will be £50, which includes a full Scottish breakfast. Let me know if you want kippers as I dinnae have any in and will have to go and buy them for you," she said as she fussed, straightening the bedding.

"Shall I pay you now?"

"No, when ya leave will be just fine, cash though, as we dinnae take cheques."

"That will be splendid. It's a beautiful place you

have, in a wonderful setting, on the bay with the mountain behind and the view of the island. You are very lucky to have such a lovely place to live in."

Sarah nodded. "Aye, that we are. It's home. Mind, the weather can be a bit bleak in the winter and Goat Fell has had its share of casualties. Walkers just dinnae give it the respect it deserves," she warned. "Are you just visiting on holiday and travelling around?"

"Well, er … no. I'm trying to trace somebody."

With that the phone went, and Sarah scurried off to answer it. Billy looked out of the window once more at the view. A vista that once upon a time would have been familiar to Violet, he thought.

Heading down the stairs he went and collected his overnight bag and his briefcase from the car. Sarah greeted him again. "Now make yourself comfortable. If there is anything you want, please let us know. My husband Colin will be back from Brodick soon. Please feel free to use the lounge," she said, opening the door to the pleasant and homely room.

It was furnished with a well-stocked dark wood bookshelf, which stood floor to ceiling, and a coffee table made of driftwood, shaped uncannily like the Isle of Arran itself. A large black leather sofa was positioned on the back wall facing the window that looked out across the bay. The sofa was flanked by two matching chairs.

Two of the walls had centrally positioned, framed pictures. All of them appeared to be prints of times gone by, including a very old-looking one, of what appeared to be the Lilybank guest house. Other, smaller pictures seemed to be of local characters or perhaps family members, some in Highland dress.

143

"Would you like a coffee or tea?" asked Sarah interrupting Billy's observations.

"That would be lovely. Coffee, please, no sugar, no milk."

Sarah frowned and disappeared, returning ten minutes later with a tray of coffee and Scottish shortbread. "Now if you'll excuse me, I must get on with my baking, I dinnae want to burn anything," she said with a mischievous yet purposeful grin.

"Before you go, Mrs Macgregor," Billy interjected. "Do you know a Mr and Mrs Duncan, Ronald and Violet?"

Something in Sarah's demeanour changed, her head lowered as she frowned. "You'll need to speak to my husband, he knows most about folk around here," and with that Sarah was gone.

Billy sat and drank his coffee and snapped one of the Scottish shortbread, which melted in his mouth. He browsed the bookshelf, which was full of local walking guides and books on flora, fauna, wildlife, birds and Scottish history.

Later Billy went to his room, and settled in. Then, though tired after his drive, he headed out for some fresh air whilst the pleasant weather allowed.

Looking around, Mrs Macgregor was nowhere to be seen. He realised he had no key, but decided to go for a stroll anyway. A stiff breeze soon picked up. Feeling hungry he ducked into a little tearoom close to the pier.

Billy had just caught the local cafe before it closed for the day. His late arrival didn't seem to faze them. He sat by a window at a small table for two and thought about Violet and what she would have made of Lamlash when she arrived.

Billy returned to Lilybank. This time a man answered the door.

"You must be Colin?" said Billy. "Sorry, I failed to take a key with me."

"Aye, you're right there, I am Colin. It's nae bother at all, I will find you a key. Sorry, I dinnae know your name, my wife said we had a visitor. Come on in," he said, proferring his hand.

Colin was a tall, thick-set man. Billy gauged he was in his mid-sixties. His face was rugged, like the fells beyond. He wore a flat cap, which he removed to reveal a thinning ginger thatch of hair.

"I'm Billy Williams, I met your wife earlier."

"Ah yes! Come on in. Can I get you some tea?"

Billy liked Colin instantly, he was open and friendly with a beaming, sincere ruddy-faced smile. He declined the tea, but before he could ask anything, Colin spoke.

"Now, Sarah said you were looking for the Duncans, have I got that right?"

"Aye," said Billy unwittingly dropping into the vernacular and immediately hoping he was not causing offence by doing so.

Colin did not seem to notice Billy's lapse into colloquialism, and Billy followed him through to a cosy little lounge at the back of the house. Colin stopped to collect a glass of water en route. A sloping back garden led Billy's eyes to the hills beyond.

"It's a lovely house you have here, Colin, in a perfect position. Have you lived here long?"

"Aye, we've lived here many years. We only recently decided to let a room. So, I built a separate toilet and bathroom, as that is what folk seem to want now. We couldn't do that whilst we had my mother here."

"Oh!" said Billy nervously. "Was she, has she …?"

"Aye, she has passed on now, that's her room you have."

Billy just nodded, not sure of his feelings about that revelation. "Did she live to a good age?"

"Och aye. She was a doughty, feisty lady. She was ninety-three and if she had not fallen she would probably still be here."

Billy suddenly remembered the notes from Kew gardens said that Ronald Duncan's mother was also a Macgregor

"So, which Duncans do ye need to know about, are they relatives to you?" questioned Colin.

"Well, it's a long story why I'm trying to find them, but it's Ronald and Violet Duncan."

Colin pursed his lips and moved his mouth a little like Popeye chewing spinach. "I see, well they're not here any more, I'm afraid. Ronald Duncan died a while back and … well, Mrs Duncan had nae been well."

Billy sat straighter in the chair, then leaned forward. "Are you saying Mrs Duncan is still alive?"

"Well, I think she might be, she went a little doolally, and as far as I know she was in a home for the elderly, last I heard."

Billy's shoulders slumped. "Did you know them well?"

Colin seemed to be slow in answering, as if he was considering what to say. "Well. Ron Duncan had a lot of demons, he was in the war, you know? He was a nice chap when he was sober, but he liked a wee dram, if you

146

get my drift."

"What about Mrs Duncan?" quizzed Billy, anxious to build up a picture of Violet and her life here.

"Aye, now she was a gem. She was nae from around here, she was a sassenach, but no' an Englander, she was a Kiwi or something, came home with Duncan after the war, with their bairn. She was a really friendly and helpful soul, but she suffered with Ron, he … well, he didn't treat her very well."

Billy was astonished to hear Colin mention a "bairn", he had not given family a thought. "Colin, you mention they had a child," said Billy said raising his eyebrows.

"Oh, that's for sure, but she never really settled here, they sent her away to school. I don't think Ron liked children, they didn't have any more."

Acknowledging he had now learned Violet had a daughter, Billy bombarded Colin with questions.

"Is she still alive? Do you know where she lives?"

"I cannae tell you, Billy. She moved away down south somewhere, a long time ago. I dinnae think she even came back for her father's funeral, she was a strange one."

"What makes you say that, Colin?"

"Och. It's not for me to say, she just never fitted in, and kept herself to herself. She had nothing much to do with the other children, she was a loner."

"So, you have no idea where she went. Would anyone else know, presumably her mother?"

"I cannae help you there much either, not sure her mother can tell you anything, not the state she was in, and that's if she's still alive."

Billy was excited and frustrated in equal measure.

"Youse may want to check with Mrs Macleod at the Post Office, she knows most things that are going on."

"Well, thank you, Colin, I'll do that first thing tomorrow, that has been most helpful."

Billy briefly explained why he was trying to track down Violet as he felt he owed that to Colin in the hope of further help from him. He didn't go into too much detail, just mentioning that the Duncans had been through a tough time in Singapore and as prisoners of war. Colin took it all in.

"Well," said Colin, "that explains quite a lot. So, she's an Aussie." He nodded, feeling he now understood a little more background to the Duncans' lives.

"Did Violet have any friends here? Did she have a job?"

"She kept herself to herself mostly. Ron didn't like her mixing much, I guess that's where the daughter got it from. Ron worked at various trades, but he could not seem to settle when he came back from the war. I think it was probably the bottle that did for him in the end. No one really cared for his company, he could be a bit fractious. So, no. Violet was just a timorous housewife."

Colin stood and added "My ma knew her, took her under her wing, you could say, she had a soft spot for Violet, used to go up and see her. You see, my mother was Ron's sister."

"Where did the Duncans live?" said Billy nodding, acknowledging confirmation of the Macgregor connection.

"Just in this row of houses along the front here, to the right, Hamilton Terrace, in the middle, I would check the number with the postmistress just to make sure.

Well, I have to get washed up. It's dominoes tonight."

Next morning Billy was up bright and early. He decided he would not have kippers but enjoyed a fabulous Scottish breakfast with local produce of bacon, eggs, tomatoes, mushrooms, black pudding and fried bread. A steaming hot mug of tea complemented his meal. His appetite satiated, he sat staring out of the window, contemplating the day ahead and hoping beyond hope he would find Violet alive.

16

Billy headed out for the Post Office just after 9 am. A stiff, cool breeze barrelled in off the sea. The blue-and-white Saltire flag of Scotland flew on the flagpole of a nearby building, the noise when it cracked like a whip catching Billy's attention. It was cooler today, with odd wisps of white cloud scudding above Holy Isle, but Billy took consolation that the day had started off without any rain and the sky appeared relatively clear.

The Post Office bell announced his arrival as the heavy wood and glass panelled door opened. The room was made small by the form-filled shelves either side and a counter with security glass facing him. Incongruously, an honesty box with eggs in cartons and stacked jars of honey nestled on the corner of the counter.

"Good morning," said Billy, having patiently waited behind the only other customer, "Mrs Macleod, is it?"

Mrs Macleod weighed him up cautiously. She adjusted her large tortoiseshell-rimmed spectacles to the end of her nose, surveyed Billy without speaking, then carried on filling in some sort of form. "What can I do for you?" she said, not looking up.

"I wonder if you recall Ronald and Violet Duncan and which house they lived in?"

"Aye, number 11 just along the terrace from us here, but they're nae there now. Ronald Duncan is long gone, and Mrs Duncan, well, the unfortunate soul went to a nursing home a few years back, she was never the same after her daughter left."

"Do you know where the daughter and Violet are now?"

The bell went on the Post Office door and Billy stepped aside and let the new arrival be served.

"Susan Duncan went to Australia, I believe," said Mrs Macleod, carrying on where she left off after her customer had been served.

Billy was disappointed to hear that, but at least he now knew her name. "And Mrs Duncan?"

"A care home on the mainland. What is your connection to the Duncans?" asked Mrs Macleod.

Billy gave a quick precis of his father's story and connection with Violet.

"Pity," said Mrs Macleod. "I suspect Mrs Duncan would have been far better off with your father!"

"Do you know where the care home is and the name and address?"

Mrs Macleod disappeared into the back room and returned with a name and address scribbled on a piece of Post Office notepaper.

An old lady in sou'wester and oilskin coat arrived, followed by another customer, as the Lamlash Post Office rush hour gained pace. Billy thanked Mrs Macleod and turned to leave. As he opened the door,

Mrs Macleod added, "She was no gomeral, no fool, that is. We all felt sorry for her."

Billy nodded, held up the piece of paper in thanks and walked along the row of terraced houses, stopping in front of number eleven and trying to imagine the blonde-tressed Violet arriving here for the first time.

Collecting his bags from the guest house, Billy thanked Mrs Macgregor very much, and returned to his vehicle. As he sat in the car surveying the road map, a tap came at his window, which startled him. Winding down the window, he was surprised to see Colin leaning towards him.

"My wife reminded me, the Duncan girl had one friend. I think she still works at the Arran Memorial Hospital up the hill here in Lamlash. A Mary Anderson, she might be able to help. You take the lower road, you will see the hospital and the drive up to it. Safe journey, and good luck."

Billy followed the coast road for less than a mile, then ascended steeply through landscaped grounds to the small hospital. Its red-brick, solid building with a Tudor influence evidenced by its apexed roof had an imposing location, with beautiful views across Lamlash bay towards the mainland.

Entering the hospital foyer, the immediately familiar smell of hospital cleanliness greeted him. Billy approached the reception desk. "Hello! Sorry to disturb you, I wonder if you could tell me if Mary Anderson is working today?"

"That'll be Sister Mary Anderson you'll be wanting. Let me see," said the receptionist, looking at the clock on the wall behind her. "She will likely be on the wards. Is there anything I can help with?"

"No! But thank you. What time does Sister Anderson finish today?"

"Let me see. She started at 7 am and her shift finishes at 3 pm today, but she often stays longer."

Billy looked at his watch. He wanted to get on his way, as he wanted to find the address Mrs Macleod had provided and stop off on the long drive home to Shropshire. "Could I perhaps interrupt Sister, for just five minutes?"

The receptionist frowned and disappeared, returning a few minutes later with a tall, slim, well-groomed nurse.

"Can I help you?" said Sister Anderson.

"Oh, hello, sorry to disturb you. Thank you. My name is Billy Williams. Could I possibly have a few minutes of your time. I promise I will not keep you?"

"Well I am very busy, what is it about?"

"I'm trying to track down Susan Duncan and her mother."

If Sister Anderson was surprised by the enquiry she did not show it. Without hesitation, Sister Anderson said, "You had better follow me."

Mary Anderson took off at a gallop, down the bland, sterile, hospital-smell-infused corridor. Scurrying through double doors adorned with brass push plates. Billy found it hard to keep up with her as they passed wards, which seemed to be rather quiet, containing few patients. A maroon-coloured door opened into a very small room, which was evidently Sister Anderson's office.

"Take a seat," she said sharply.

They sat at a wooden desk that had a rather splendid inlaid leather top, quite grand for a hospital, thought Billy. The large desk made the room feel even smaller. There was an in-tray and an out-tray and a container of pens and pencils. Everything was very orderly. A multi-paned window allowed the daylight to brighten the otherwise austere room, which sported a framed photograph of a class of nurses, which Billy presumed was Sister Anderson's graduation class.

"Mr Williams."

"Billy, please."

"It's a long time since I've seen Susan."

Billy listened intently. "How well did you know her?"

Mary Anderson sat primly, her jewellery-free hands interlocked in front of her, resting on the desk. At times, she held them open, as if channelling the sentences towards Billy. "We were young girls together in Lamlash, we both became friends out of a common cause."

Billy shrugged his shoulders, tilted his head to one side and gave Mary Anderson a quizzical look.

"Bullying, Mr Williams. Bullying!"

"Why was that?" queried Billy.

"In a nutshell, I wore glasses and, as you can see, was not the prettiest girl around and was very studious. On the other hand, Susan was just different, she was not from around these parts and was treated as an outsider from her first day at school."

Billy shook his head.

"Of course, for Susan it was also a difficult home life, so she was never very happy, and longed to get away. I am sure she was relieved to go to boarding school."

"Did you go to boarding school too?" Billy interjected.

"No, I didn't. My parents couldn't afford it. But I didn't lose touch with Susan. We wrote to one another through all the years she was away. I only recall seeing her come home once, maybe twice, in that time. Finally, she did return briefly, but by then we had both grown up.

"When she came home she had blossomed into a young woman, as I suppose we both had. We seemed quite different people, yet strangely we were both interested in nursing."

"Did Susan nurse?"

"Yes! She did. It was a way of getting away from here, I always thought she would work for Dr Barnado's homes or something child-focused as, in spite of her childhood or perhaps because of it, she loved children. As much as I could see, Susan loved her mother, she just wanted to get away from Lamlash, indeed needed to.

"One day I called by, as by then I knew Susan had planned to leave and go to a mainland hospital in Glasgow, as a student nurse. I wanted to say goodbye. I had knocked on the door and found it was on the latch, but before I could shout 'Is anyone in?' I could hear a clamour coming from the kitchen.

"It was Susan. I remember her words: *Please, Mum, come with me to Glasgow, you don't have to put up with his constant tirades*. She was so worried something dreadful might happen if she stayed."

Mary Anderson looked across at Billy. "He abused her, Mr Williams. Not so much physically but emotionally, Mrs Duncan was a virtual prisoner. Ronald Duncan was a jealous, controlling, chauvinistic man. My parents did not like me even going near the house. But, alas, Mrs Duncan stayed whilst Susan went nursing. She qualified and nursed in Glasgow, then I believe she went to London."

"Did you keep in touch?" asked Billy.

"We did sporadically. I too trained on the mainland but when a post came up back here in Lamlash, well, frankly, I'm a bit of a home bird and needed to look after my mother. I jumped at the chance. I wasn't one for cities."

Mary Anderson paused, stood and looked out of the window. "I have not seen Susan since that day when she asked her mother to leave with her. Her father died perhaps ten years or so later, but she did not come home for his funeral, because by then she had emigrated."

"Emigrated … I see," said Billy. "So! Do you know where she might be now?"

"Susan emigrated to her mother's birth country, Australia. A new life, I suppose. Australia was crying out for nurses. Susan tried to encourage me to go in some of the letters she sent. I'm afraid to say I have lost touch with her over the years."

"Do you have an address for Susan now?"

"It was many years ago. I'm not sure if she will still be living in Sydney, but I suggest you might want to contact the hospital she was working in, that may help you. I remember it was the Prince of Wales Hospital in Sydney."

"I hope you don't mind me asking, but about how old is Susan?"

"Same age as me, fifty or thereabouts," she said removing her glasses.

"Me too or thereabouts," responded Billy, smiling back at Mary Anderson's beguiling grin.

"I really must get back to work," said Sister Anderson, blushing slightly.

"Oh, of course, I'm so sorry to take up your time." Billy stood, scraping back his incongruous, blue plastic chair on the highly polished wooden marquetry floor.

As Sister Anderson came around the desk, Billy proffered his hand to thank her for her information and said, "I wonder if I could take you to dinner tonight? I would like to learn more about Susan and her mother."

Mary Anderson's cheeks felt like they were on fire and was quite stuck for words. She tried to think of an excuse, as she always did when out of her comfort zone.

"Well, I can't …" Before she knew it, she had agreed. "Shall we say around 6 pm, as I have an early shift again tomorrow and I need my beauty sleep. Where are you staying?"

"I'm at the Lilybank guesthouse."

"Ah! A nice place, Mr and Mrs Macgregor's," she said, approving his choice. I live with my mother at 4 Hamilton Terrace."

"I know it," said Billy. "I walked by it this morning."

Billy felt Mary's firm yet delicate hand in his. Momentarily he caught a vague scent of lavender.

"I will see myself out, see you later," chirped Billy as he departed with a new spring in his step.

Sister Anderson, still a little warm faced, re-entered a ward, full of the joys of spring. Billy returned to Lilybank and booked in for another night.

That evening, Mary opened the door before Billy could even knock.

"I saw you coming, you're very punctual," she said, smiling and turning the key in the door as she spoke. She wore a white blouse and a red and green tartan skirt and carried a black cardigan over her arm. She was even taller than he remembered now she was wearing heels.

Sitting across the table from Mary in the Glen Isle Hotel restaurant, which Sarah Macgregor had kindly booked for him, he could not believe it was the same person he had met earlier. Mary inclined her head, as if waiting for Billy to say something, instead of just staring and smiling awkwardly at her. Mary's auburn hair was now down in a bob, which framed her heart-shaped face. Her hazel eyes seemed to be full of mirth and care all at once.

"I hardly recognise you with your hair down and without your uniform on and not wearing glasses … well."

Mary raised her eyebrows, her wide smile and beautiful teeth enhancing her looks even more. Billy realised his words could be taken out of context, and started to flounder, searching for words, but the waitress arrived, saving his embarrassment.

"Sorry to keep youse all. Oh! Hello, Mary, how's your mother?"

"Very well, thank you, Cait."

"Now, can I get you some drinks, folks?" said the waitress cheerily.

A bottle of red wine was duly delivered and meals ordered.

"So, tell me about yourself," probed Mary.

"Nothing much to tell, I live alone in Shropshire and my parents have passed away. I have no children and no siblings. I'm a retired history teacher and, well, that's about it. How about you?"

"Well, as you know, I'm a nurse and have been for over thirty years. My father died, I live with my mother who's eighty. I have a brother who is older than me, he lives in Edinburgh."

"Is there anyone, perhaps a significant other in your life?" said Billy, probing.

"My mother!" replied Mary with an impudent grin. "She has always provided for me and now it's my turn, although she is quite an independent woman. And you?" she asked, turning the tables.

"No. I've been busy looking after my parents for a number of years. They became a little infirm and that's why I retired eventually. There was no time for relationships, really." Billy hesitated, turning the long-stemmed wine glass in his hand as he spoke. "I was married but divorced many years ago." Billy felt relieved getting this off his chest.

"What do you find to do in all this spare time you have now, apart from looking for the Duncans?" teased Mary.

"I enjoy walking, especially over the hills. I run too when the energy allows me. Reading historical fiction …" Billy started to laugh, Mary joined in. "This is sounding more like a television game show with every minute," said Billy with a wide grin.

"Yes! Or *This is your Life*," added Mary.

"Now, who used to be the presenter, a Scottish chap, I remember … ummm …"

"I do believe you mean Eamonn Andrews," said Mary. "I think you'll find he was Irish. He died a while back and I guess that's when he finished being the presenter." Both laughed and clinked their glasses just as the soup arrived.

Following a pleasant meal, they retired to the hotel lounge for coffee. Mary and Billy sat side by side on a large leather settee. Mary poured the coffee.

"Sugar, milk?" she asked.

"Neither, thanks," replied Billy.

She leaned back with her coffee cup and saucer in hand. Turning towards Mary, Billy awkwardly rested his arm across the back of the settee. Mary seemed to stiffen a little

"Billy, we never talked about Mrs Duncan."

Billy changed his seating position, reaching over to the table for his coffee and offering an After Eight mint to Mary before taking one himself. "What happened to her?"

"As you know, Mr Duncan died and Susan wasn't around. I am sure she wrote to her mother. But Violet Duncan struggled more and more with life. We saw her occasionally, going out shopping for essentials. But she kept herself to herself. We always thought when Mr Duncan passed away she might start to feel free and start to mingle more in the local community, but no, by then she was almost reclusive.

"As time went by, she had become more and more arthritic. One day, in 1991, I think it was, she fell and was brought to Arran War Memorial Hospital. This is when I managed to get to know her quite well. I found her to be a lovely, gentle woman, with a good sense of humour. She loved Susan, or Susie as she called her, so much.

"Mrs Duncan missed Susan dreadfully, it soon became clear her constant talking about Susan and Australia and occasionally the war, that she was not just being melancholy or reminiscing, but she was starting to show early signs of dementia.

"She went home but not long afterwards she fell again, this time breaking her hip. She had been struggling for some time with mobility and with the arthritis, which meant she could barely hold a cup. Her constant muttering and lack of awareness as to where she was became worse as time passed.

"She could have lucid moments, and she remembered my name for the most part. But it was clear she couldn't go home. Social Services became involved and she was transferred to Arran View Care Home in Saltcoates on the mainland."

"Is that where she is now or has she …?" Billy hated to finish the sentence.

"Yes! I visit her once a month, usually when I take my mother shopping in Ayr and we call on Violet."

"Well, that is marvellous," enthused Billy. "I was hoping beyond hope that Violet might still be alive, but I am sad to hear about her dementia."

"Sadly, she barely recognises even me now," said Mary.

Billy reached for his inside pocket and produced the photograph of his father with Violet and Gwen in Singapore. He had made a copy for Gwen and one for Violet, too.

Mary looked hard at the photograph, then opened

her small evening bag and produced her glasses. Holding up the picture towards the somewhat subdued, artificial light, she nodded. "I can certainly tell which one is Violet. Apart from her almost white hair now, her features are much the same today, just older."

"I would love to meet Violet. Do you think that possible? I have a letter to give her that my father wanted to share with her."

Mary dropped her head towards her right shoulder and gave him a doleful look. "I don't think she would be able to read the letter or respond, she is too confused. I would be happy to go with you. We could go after my shift tomorrow, but she might be tired when we get there. If you could wait until Friday, I have a day off and we could go in the morning if you are prepared to wait another day."

Billy did not hesitate. "Friday works for me."

As they walked slowly back to Hamilton Terrace Billy scanned the skies above Lamlash. "It's a beautiful evening."'

Mary stealthily put the key in the door, turned and thanked Billy for a lovely evening.

"It was my pleasure, thank you for all your help with the Duncans and …" whispered Billy.

"I really enjoyed your company, Billy."

Billy smiled, leaned forward and gave Mary a kiss on the cheek, her eyes holding his for just a moment.

"Goodnight. Friday morning, then, shall we say 9 am sharp?"

"I'll be here," said Billy. "Sweet dreams."

With that Mary closed the door. Billy felt strangely like a schoolboy on his first date. He crossed the road and looked back at the terraced house. A light went on in the bedroom behind the closed curtains.

Mary watched Billy across the road through the chink in the curtains, butterflies fluttering, her emotions stirred. She did not sleep well that night.

17

Billy's extended stay was noted and appreciated by the Macgregors. Another fine but cool morning greeted Lamlash as Billy polished off a full Scottish breakfast.

"So where will you be heading today, or do you love the place so much youse have decided to move here?" said Mrs Macgregor, jibing Billy.

"Well, I'm being taken to the mainland by Mary Anderson, as it transpires Violet Duncan is still alive, albeit she has severe dementia."

"Och, such a shame. Well, you be having a good day, Mary is a nice lass," said Mrs Macgregor, looking over her glasses as she held Billy's empty plate in one hand and the teapot in the other.

Fifteen minutes later Billy headed over to Hamilton Terrace and knocked on Mary's door.

"Good morning, Mary, sleep well?"

"Once I managed to drop off," said Mary, closing the door behind her.

"That's a lovely dress, Mary, it suits you."

"Thank you." Mary nodded her appreciation, smoothing down her knee-length emerald green linen dress. It had a high square neckline and hugged her slim, long-legged figure.

Taking the short drive to Brodick, they were soon clambering up the internal stairs from the car deck of the ferry to Ardrossan. Opening the heavy door to the outside, a gush of cool maritime air greeted their arrival on deck. Mary was thankful for her green paisley-patterned headscarf, tucking in strands of her hair that the wind was blowing across her eyes. As Mary and Billy stood on deck side by side, looking over the stern, seagulls called with piercing screeches overhead as they followed the boat out of the port. The smell of the briny sea assaulted the deck passengers' senses.

"It's bracing." commented Billy, barely able to draw breath and speak as the ferry picked up speed.

Mary laughed. "Bracing indeed," she replied. She was glad she had brought her tweed jacket too, which she wrapped tightly around herself.

The short crossing and drive soon passed and before long they arrived at the care home in Saltcoates. As they pulled into the car park, Billy was full of trepidation.

"Mary, how come you do not have as strong a Scottish accent as many in these parts have?"

Mary tilted her head right and left. "You're right, I guess it's partially having worked away, when training, especially as I spent some time in London too. But, actually, when I first met Susan, I used to mimic her rather strange Australian accent, as it was foreign to us all, much like the Scottish accent may be to you. I guess spending so much time with Susan influenced my way of speaking. I know you might think this sounds silly, but I wanted to be like Susan, so my accent is a hybrid of

Australian, English and Scottish."

"Well, I think your accent is perfect!"

With that he stepped out of the car, walked around and offered a hand to Mary, who declined as she raised herself from the sporty motor's low seat in as lady-like a fashion as possible.

Billy followed Mary through the double doors in the relatively modern building. The entrance portico had a clock above it on the brickwork, which did not seem to have worked for a while. Inside, Mary nodded to a passing staff member who smiled back, as Mary led Billy down a short corridor. Stopping at a doorway, they noticed the door was slightly ajar. Mary softly tapped on the light-coloured pine door as she entered.

"Hello, Violet, it's Mary," she said, breezing into the light and airy bedroom. A single bed with sky-blue bed linen and a cream duvet was tucked up against the wall immediately to the left of the door. On a bedside cabinet beside it was a blue lamp with a rose-red shade beside a photo frame.

A white-haired figure was slouched uncomfortably in a high-backed cream linen chair that overlooked the garden. Violet seemed to be watching two sparrows dancing beside a small fountain, which was positioned in the middle of connecting paths, bordered by lush green shrubbery.

Mary knelt beside Violet and took her hand. Violet slowly turned her head, looked at Mary, then back at the birds by the fountain.

"Violet, I have brought you a visitor," said Mary with an excited tone she might have used to a child.

Mary looked towards Billy who was standing just

166

inside the doorway. With her hand, she motioned him towards the matching armchair, beside Violet.

He settled awkwardly, unsure of how Violet might react. Looking at Violet, he could see that she had once been a very beautiful woman. She was wearing a mauve thin cardigan over a dress decorated with pink roses. Her sleepy eyelids could not cloak the beauty of her cornflower-blue eyes, which shone from her time-worn porcelain-like features. He wondered what his father would say of Violet's predicament now.

"Hello, Violet, I'm Billy. You knew my father Tom, Tom Williams."

There was no response.

Billy was aware of Mary kneeling somewhat uncomfortably beside Violet. "Mary, please take this chair."

"It's okay," said Mary, half-smiling but looking forlorn. "I can get another if I need it. I just want to keep Violet calm. She enjoys me holding her hand. Show her the photograph you showed me."

Billy reached into his inside jacket pocket and produced the small, square, black-and-white photograph. He handed it to Mary. Violet looked at the picture in Mary's hand, looked at the garden then back again at the picture. A few moments passed.

"Gwen," said Violet. "I would like a cup of tea."

Billy could still pick out her Australian accent, slightly tempered with a Scottish lilt.

"Shall we go along to the lounge and get one, Violet?" offered Mary.

Looking at the picture again, Violet continued, "I'm sorry, Gwen." Tears misted her vision. Violet reached inside her cardigan sleeve for a handkerchief. She looked at Billy. "Where have you been, Tom?" she said full of admonishment.

Billy and Mary were taken aback. Billy so wanted to reply with the words *I … I have missed you, Violet, so I thought I would come and see you!*

Violet continued to look at him intently. Billy, slightly unnerved, decided to produce the letter. He figured that now was as good a time as any.

"Violet … Tom has passed away, but I have a letter from him for you." He placed it on her lap.

Violet turned it over and over in her hands, staring at it, then into space. Violet adjusted a hair grip which was keeping the hair off her eyes, then ran her small, delicate, liver-spotted hands through her hair, in turn adjusting her wedding band and engagement ring as she inspected them.

"Is my tea here yet?" she queried.

Mary looked at Billy. "May I open this and read it to Violet?"

Billy shrugged his shoulders. "If you don't mind? I think that might be best."

Mary deftly extracted the letter. There was an air of anticipation for Billy and Mary, but Violet did not seem to be engaged.

Looking at Violet, Mary read …

Dear Violet

I am not sure I have the right words to express my true feelings, but here goes.

A lot of water has passed under the bridge since our days together in Singapore, Vi. For me it was a wonderful time of heady feelings and love, during a terrible time, with war and death all around us.

I just wanted you to know I have never forgotten you. I tried to contact you but received a letter from your father saying you had moved on with your life. I was so happy that you were alive, but so despondent that I would never see you again.

Indeed, I too moved on. I married and had a wonderful son, Billy. I am hoping you are reading this now because of him.

Alas, if that is the case I will no longer be here, but rest assured I will take my love for you to the grave.

I hope you have had a wonderful life and enjoyed a peaceful, happy existence in good health and want to thank you for the short time of bliss we had together.

Your ever loving

Tom

Violet squinted as if she was sitting in bright sunlight, then relaxed, accentuating the crow's feet around her eyes.

"I'm tired now, I think I will have a nap." With that she raised herself slowly and stiffly from the chair. Aided by Mary she shuffled towards the bed, sat on the edge, raised her legs and lay her head on the soft down-filled pillow before closing her eyes.

Mary nodded towards Billy and they left the room quietly.

As she heard the door click shut, Violet reached under her pillow and retrieved a pocket-sized British Army issue bible. She opened it and retrieved a torn photograph showing a man in British Army uniform.

She held the picture to her heart, a mournful smile lightened her face, tears fell onto the pillow, like the poppies dropping from the ceiling of the Royal Albert Hall on Remembrance Day, when they commemorate the fallen.

One of his father's rare moments alone with Billy came back to him as they drove away from the nursing home. Billy recalled one November day being with his father, standing by the war memorial in the Quarry Park, Shrewsbury. He had watched the long procession of dignitaries, soldiers and the military band marching through the town, then a bugler played what he learned was "The Last Post".

As the crowd dispersed his father with tears in his eyes turned to him and gave him a sage piece of advice: "Son, never accept your fate. Always challenge it. Only that way will you find your true self." Those words always resonated, and now they kept going around and around in Billy's head, as he ran a kaleidoscope of memories through his mind from his childhood. He recollected his mother and father and the picture show in his mind, culminating in the recurring vision of Violet sitting in her chair facing the garden. He wondered what faraway thoughts she had as she gazed through the window.

"Penny for them?" interrupted Mary.

"Sorry, Mary. I was miles away … I guess we will never know anything more from Violet about the war or indeed her feelings generally about my father and so on. But I did feel we triggered some memories even if Violet was not able to engage with us about them."

"So, what are your plans now?" Mary asked

hopefully.

"I'm not too sure, Mary, I had wanted to go to a place called Lock-a-lot … or something like that."

Mary smiled benevolently.

"What?" He smiled back at her patronising, silent smirk, before returning his concentration to the road.

"Lochailort," she corrected.

"Aye, that's the one!" he said, using a poor Scottish accent as he gunned the accelerator, making Mary hold her hair as it whipped back in the airstream of the open-top Midget. Like a television commercial, the little sports car headed along the coast road back to Ardrossan.

"What's at Lochailort?" she enquired.

"That's where my father and his best friend Jimmy trained. A castle there, Inver fort, or something like that."

"It's about four hours' drive from here, Billy," cautioned Mary. "Actually, I was thinking more about what you plan to do with your life after leaving Scotland." Mary could not believe how forward she had been.

Billy considered this for a moment. A minute or so passed, which seemed ages. "I still plan to go to Australia. I would like to find Susan, Violet's daughter. Maybe, just maybe, she can tell me more about Violet and whether or not she ever mentioned my father, and perhaps she knows about what happened to her mother in the prisoner of war camps. Plus, I feel I should make her aware of my father's letter too.

Mary looked at Billy incredulously. "Hold on, hold on … Violet a prisoner of war?"

Billy nodded.

"I didn't know that. I figured Mr Duncan had been, but never even gave a thought as to where Violet had been in the war. Perhaps that explains the deterioration in her mental condition," Mary softly muttered to herself. "Alongside her time and experiences with Mr Duncan, of course."

Billy's mind was shooting from one thing to another. Should he tell Gwen he had found Violet? After all, it was not the Violet she would remember, but then Violet had mentioned Gwen and said she was sorry. That could mean an awful lot to Gwen. His thinking was a maelstrom of indecision.

The strong smell of diesel assaulted their nostrils on the car deck of the returning ferry. They ascended from the depths of the black-and-white hulled ship to clear their minds. Mary saw Billy was deep in thought; he had said little on the drive to Ardrossan. Walking around the deck they braved the invasive rush of sea air at the prow where the Saltire flag blew strongly, snapping in the gusts of wind as the ferry ploughed the waves towards Brodick on Arran. Mary donned her headscarf for protection once more. Passing the familiar red-and-black smoke stack with rampant yellow lion of the Caledonian Macbrayne logo, they edged towards a more sheltered space for the one-hour crossing.

Sitting on fixed plastic seats at the stern of the vessel, they watched the wake of the ferry form a watery path back to Ardrossan and the road to Violet. Seagulls performed effortlessly, pumping their wings then gliding as they followed the boat, making their customary excited, shrill call, as if goading one another in a race with the Caledonian Macbrayne lifeline as it headed towards Arran.

Mary put her arm through Billy's, catching him off guard. He turned his head, and through her bright hazel eyes he looked into her soul.

"Take me to Australia with you!" said Mary as the sun appeared from behind a cloud.

Billy smiled, then turned to look out to sea. There was a long silence. A passing plane in the blue sky above left a vapour trail and invaded Billy's consciousness.

He turned to Mary. "How soon can you leave?"

18

It was July and Mary had managed to get four weeks leave. She had rarely taken holidays and was owed plenty. Her colleagues were somewhat taken aback at this rapid decision, and plenty of gossip made its way through the hospital and the small tight-knit community of Lamlash.

Billy had explained to Mary he wanted to visit Myanmar, so they had booked flights via Singapore and Myanmar to Sydney, Australia, courtesy of his friendly local travel agent Claire in Shrewsbury. Billy took care of the visas and Mary the health advice on vaccinations and medication. What an adventure, thought Billy.

*****

Borth-y-Gest was busy now. The better weather encouraged the tourists, arriving in droves in camper vans and caravans and renting houses. Families with their dogs and children smothered the beaches like wasps around a jam jar. It wasn't even school summer holidays yet, thought Gwen, as she headed back, a little hot and bothered, from her usually deserted beach to her own favourite resting place, a seat bearing a dedication plaque that read: "Many a day spent enjoying this view. Take a weight off and you can too. In memory of John Glyn Jones." It was set amongst the brambles and gorse high above the coastal footpath, looking out across the estuary towards Harlech Castle. This vantage point was blessed with solitude away from the main tourist path.

Extracting a letter from her anorak pocket, she again looked across the smooth sheet of water and watched as pleasure craft came in and out of Porthmadog harbour, her peace interrupted for a minute or so by the sound of the noisy engine whine of a jet ski as it bounced across the water's surface below her, following the narrow channel of water from the harbour and no doubt heading for Black Rock Sands up the coast. Gwen could never understand why people preferred Black Rock Sands over Borth-y-Gest, but she was glad they did.

The letter that had arrived an hour or so back was from Billy.

Dear Gwen

Sorry I've not been in touch recently, but I have been so busy. Anyway, I hope you're well.

Lots of news, Gwen. I have found Violet.

Gwen's heart skipped and started to beat faster. She could feel herself getting a little hot and she loosened her collar. Brushing her forehead as if her hand might cool her, she fanned herself briefly, with the correspondence, then continued reading.

I travelled up to Lamlash on the Isle of Arran and, to cut a long story short, she does not live there any more. But I met a lovely lady called Mary, a nurse like yourself, and she knew Violet and indeed had nursed her.

Sadly, Violet, it would appear, had a tough life. It's a long story that I will share with you in full when we are next together.

A number of years ago, Violet had fallen and broken her hip. She had been in hospital at Lamlash, where Mary nursed her. Mary and her family knew her anyway, as it is a small community and, actually, they lived a few doors from one another. Gradually Violet deteriorated mentally. The good news is she is still alive and living in a nursing home on the mainland at Saltcoates.

We went to visit her, Gwen. I am sorry to say Violet has dementia quite badly. She barely recognises anyone. It was very sad to see someone in such a confused state of existence. I can tell, even now, Violet was a very attractive lady.

Gwen, I showed her the photograph of you, my father and her in Singapore, and she said, "Sorry, Gwen" and became upset. She also called me Tom. Then she seemed confused and just wanted a cup of tea.

Anyway, I wanted to share that with you and hope it helps you in some way.

I've learned that Violet has a daughter, named Susan, who lives in Australia. As luck would have it, Mary turns out to have been Susan's best childhood friend.

You will love Mary, she is sweet, sensitive, yet measured and driven. We have both decided to travel together to Australia to find Susan and see what else we can learn.

Mary cannot wait to see her long-time friend again. We will head to Sydney, but as promised to you we will go to Myanmar en route and I will find out what I can about where Jimmy was, and hopefully go to where he is buried and pay our respects.

I am so sorry to tell you all this in a letter, but things have moved apace, spontaneity has taken over. We travel next week. "Carpe Diem", Gwen.

I promise you when we come back I will bring Mary to see you and deluge you with stories and photographs. You will adore Mary. What is more, if you would like to and feel up to it, we will take you to see Violet.

Warmest regards

Billy

*****

On the plane to Singapore, Mary and Billy both talked of having lonely childhoods. Relaxed, they settled in for a long journey, occasionally disturbed by cabin service.

Billy recalled, "I remember playing in the fields by the brook, fishing for minnows and tadpoles using a jam jar held by a piece of string."

Mary said, "Most of my time was spent in rock pools with a net finding what had been left by the tide. We used to go with my uncle on fishing trips and walks with Mum and Dad on hillsides filtered by burns, their ice-cool water babbling its way to the sea."

Billy beguiled Mary with tales. "Summers were idyllic miles of hedgerows along country lanes strewn with cow parsley, horse-drawn hay carts, picnics at the end of the harvest, occasionally hiding under the hay cart with a half-full flagon of cider and some cheese we hoped our parents or grandparents would not miss.

"I remember picking blackberries and wincing from the acid of the nettle leaf that left a raised rash on our skin, which was joined by scratches from the brambles and briars. All this from running amok through the wilderness near my home. I used to rub the dock leaf juice onto the nettle rash by splitting the leaf.

"Avoiding the odious hard-skinned cow pats was tricky if you ran full tilt down the meadows, let me tell you."

Both recalled buttercups and celandines in great profusion.

"Did you hold the buttercup under your chin to see whether or not you liked butter?" said Mary.

"We did. We used to search for a four-leafed clover so we could be blessed with good fortune, but we never found one."

Billy continued, "Near our home there were groves of bluebells in the woods and the smell of wild garlic. Song thrushes, sparrows, chaffinches and blackbirds with their beautiful song juxtaposed against the coarse sound of cawing crows, whilst sheep bleated and baahed on the Shropshire hillsides of the Church Stretton area known as 'Little Switzerland'. The summer breezes carried the cacophony of the rural soundtrack to families picnicking in valleys beside streams in the valleys.

"Dad taught me how to tickle stickleback under the bank of the rushing water where they rested. The rhythmic tickle of the fingers mesmerised the small fish before the stickleback was plucked from the water." Mary listened intently to the anecdotes and recollections and assimilated them all, totally enthralled by her companion.

"Sorry," said Billy, "I am going on! Tell me more about your childhood!"

Every now and then, their bare arms would touch on the arm rest between their narrow plane seats, and both felt a frisson of warmth and desire. The hum of the plane's engines, the announcements, the occasional interruptions for meals and drinks, the chatter and movement of other passengers seemed to be in a different orbit, as Billy and Mary were engrossed with each other and time flew by.

The Captain announced their descent into Singapore was imminent and advised the arrangements for connections to other flights.

"My word," said Mary as she clipped and tightened her seat belt. "Where have fifteen hours gone?"

Before long after a smooth connection Billy and Mary were sitting on board their flight to Yangon, formerly Rangoon.

Both of them felt a real trepidation as they entered the pariah state of Myanmar. Whilst they had managed to get visas, Billy wondered if they were doing the right thing, bearing in mind what he had read in the press and seen on the news over the years. Opposition to the regime in the British press often commented that anyone visiting as tourists gave credence to the military rulers.

He feared getting arrested too, as many stories of imprisonment without trial were bandied around the media, and of course the subjection of its own people including the Buddhist monks was well known in the West.

It had been a long day since leaving Heathrow Airport. They had changed planes in Singapore that morning having flown overnight, the jetlag in itself was disorientating, let alone the hubbub of people speaking in a language totally foreign to them. Like a pool of spilt mercury, the mass of disembarking passengers from a plethora of plane arrivals pressed all around them, beneath the creaking whirr of the ineffective ceiling fans above. Moving as one, Billy and Mary felt hemmed in on all sides.

Billy was carrying a lot of American dollars, as he had been told this was the currency of choice and that they had to be in pristine condition. This meant no marks, tears, or bends, almost as if they were hot off the printing press. He was worried that he would be searched and the dollars confiscated. Credit cards were not acceptable, thanks to the non-cooperation of the big Western banks with Myanmar. He would be in big trouble without the cash, he thought. He protected his legitimate funds nervously, feeling like a drug mule must feel, fearing discovery. All these thoughts went through his mind.

Mary was paranoic, too, but her fears were about mosquitoes and the malaria she might contract. She was hot and bothered and wiping her brow. Scottish midges were one thing, but tropical diseases posed a far bigger threat.

Billy wondered for just a second whether all this was worth it.

Fortunately, they passed through passport and customs control without any trouble whatsoever. Wheeling their suitcases, they entered the arrivals hall. Billy had made transfer arrangements through an ex-work colleague, who had a Burmese friend he had met at university. The plan was they would be met by a former history teacher who used to study in the United Kingdom.

"Keep your eyes open, Mary, for a sign with our name on."

At that moment, they were approached by an attractive, petite young woman, perhaps in her thirties. She held a sign that said "Mr Williams".

Billy and Mary must have looked bewildered, and obviously Western, as there were very few other Europeans in the arrivals hall. Bowing and smiling profusely the woman repeated, "Mingalaba, mingalaba". It had a lovely ring to it, and they presumed meant welcome. Billy bowed too, Mary smiled and nodded.

"Hello," said Billy with hesitation.

"My name is Jenny. Please follow me," she said in very good English as she took his bag but not Mary's.

In a typical Far Eastern gait, Jenny shuffled along at a rather rapid pace, Billy and Mary struggling to keep up with her as she surged through the throng of people. As they exited the terminal building, a cacophony of sound and an appearance of chaos greeted them. They witnessed a noisy, bustling phalanx of taxi cabs and minibuses, all somewhat dented, none very new. The humidity and heat of the morning hit them, the heavy air sapping them immediately. This is going to be intolerable, Billy thought as he immediately felt his shirt damp and sticking to his back.

Mary thought how attractive Jenny was, in her gold blouse, her long silky black hair draped in a side ponytail over her right shoulder. Her blouse buttoned on the left from a neckline bouquet of embroidered pink roses brocaded above her small chest. Her black htamein, a Burmese long folded skirt, was tightly wound over her slim waist and tucked in at the side

For Billy it was Jenny's deep-brown, almond-shaped eyes that allured him, their warmth genuinely welcoming him to her land.

Escaping the amoeba of humanity, they reached their transport. Zaw, the driver, took the luggage with a big smile that presented them with their first glimpse of what the results of betel nut chewing can do to your teeth.

Billy held the door for Mary as she slid onto the cherry-coloured, faded and cracked leather rear seat. Clutching a shoulder bag, Billy bent his tall frame into the seat beside her. The vehicle was an old but comfortable, dust-covered but air-conditioned car. Soon they were watching the buildings pass by, Jenny turning every now and again to talk to them.

"'Mingalabar' literally means 'it's a blessing' but is accepted as an everyday 'Hello'," she explained. Billy and Mary smiled in unison. "It is a holiday today in Yangon. It commemorates the assassination of General Aung San, Aung San Suu Kyi's father and Myanmar's independence hero."

"Aah, that's why it's so busy," said Mary languidly. Jenny, sensing her guests were tired, decided to say no more.

Yangon, or Rangoon, as Billy preferred to think of it, was greener than he had expected, the traffic not as congested as a capital city might be. Passing numerous temples on their way, with their gold exteriors reflecting the waning evening sun, they soon arrived at the Summit View Hotel. Jenny helped check them in.

"I will meet you tomorrow at 9 am ready for your journey south. Is that okay?"

"Yes, sure, that's just fine," said Billy, looking at Mary in case of disapproval, but none came.

Jenny wished them a good night's rest. A round of bowing ensued before she departed.

Exhausted, Billy and Mary were shown to their single rooms on the fifth floor, both within a few doors of each other. "Good night," said Billy.

"Sweet dreams," replied Mary.

It was approaching dusk. Billy turned and pushed a dollar bill into the hand of the bellboy as he placed Billy's bag in the narrow hallway of the room.

The bell boy refused his tip politely, but Billy insisted "Jaay Zu," said the young fellow in grateful thanks, as with a beaming white-toothed grin he pulled the door to with a clunk.

Billy took a cursory glance at the basic but adequate bathroom facilities as he passed them on his left before gazing across the spacious room with its queen-sized bed, which reminded him of an American motel room he had once stayed in during the eighties. He was drawn to the window, where beyond, the once sun-filled blue sky darkened and a veil of crimson cloud reflected the last rays of the Burmese sun, which was sinking fast.

In the distance, he saw a magnificent illuminated pagoda. He at once knew it to be the fabled and stunning Shwedagon Paya, a gleaming golden stupa visible from all over the city. It had a mesmeric effect on Billy. He wondered if his father had thought the same when he first encountered this fabulous jewel-encrusted vision.

After a fitful sleep, Billy awoke and at first could not get his bearings. He wondered momentarily where he was, his jetlag affecting his senses. From his bed, through the still-open curtains, he could see the early morning mist shrouding the golden stupa and he felt good, this was not a dream but reality.

It was still early. He thought of waking Mary, until he looked at his watch on the bedside cabinet. It was only 5.30 am, so he poured himself a cup of green tea from the flask provided by the hotel, which slaked his thirst.

He showered, dressed and answered the knock on the door.

"Shall we go for some breakfast?" beamed an excited Mary, suitably attired in a cool sleeveless cream-coloured cotton dress. Her hair was pulled back into a bunch, exposing her heart-shaped face.

Billy was at one with the world.

19

After a very enjoyable leisurely breakfast, and with their cases packed, Billy and Mary stood outside and took in the morning air as it warmed their souls after the air-conditioned dining room. Cars came and went and then they saw Jenny and their driver arrive, a little early and smiling as ever, Zaw's broad red-toothed grin brightening the day, like the sun rising at dawn illuminating the earth, as he put the bags in the boot of the battered old Toyota.

Jenny made sure they had everything and soon they were heading south. Warm air streamed in the open windows, as did the sounds of car and truck horns and the smell of the sea of humanity going about its everyday activities in Yangon.

The pungency of sewage and drainage mixed with stale sweat from cyclists and pedestrians wafted into the vehicle as they passed by slowly in the traffic melee, becoming even stronger as the humidity intensified. Local people went about their chores dressed in colourful longyi, a large piece of colourful cloth wrapped over and tucked in at the waist, different patterns and colours distinguishing tribal affiliations. Even though the longyi invariably was worn to their ankles it kept them cool during the daily grind in the already unbearable heat. A cocktail of jasmine and spice aromas from stalls lining the roadside teased the senses. Mary wound up her window, but Billy was assimilating everything.

Cars and mopeds buzzed around each side of their vehicle. Old bull-nosed Chinese-built trucks laden with consumer goods and fresh produce crunched through gears heading for some distant market destination. All clamoured for space on the inadequate highways.

Finally, the peace of the countryside brought harmony to their day and they were able to relax a little, as the sight of paddy fields and open spaces allowed the soul to unwind.

Jenny half turned in her seat to face back towards Billy and Mary. "It is going to be a long drive today, it is monsoon season and …" Before she could finish her sentence, almost on cue, a band of torrential rain doused the vehicle.

The Toyota's high-speed windscreen wipers were barely able to cope with the deluge. Zaw slowed the Toyota to a crawl, muttering his frustration as he struggled for visibility. Car windows were rapidly raised to stop the flood that threatened to turn their car into a mobile bathtub.

All smiles and giggles, Jenny continued unfazed. "I was about to say … During the day we will make a few welcome stops, at roadside tea houses for refreshment and the necessary ablutions. Please let us know if you need to stop or have any questions. Here is a bottle of water each, we have plenty."

Zaw ploughed on through puddles and potholes. Roads at times resembled streams. Billy had never witnessed such a downpour; it was constant. Stopping briefly at Pegu for a visit to a pagoda, they continued south, heading down towards Moulmein.

Everyone except the driver had dozed off. Zaw nudged Jenny who had just closed her eyes. "Mawlaymine," he grunted.

"This is Mawlaymine, we will take a short stop here, and visit the pagoda, which gives you wonderful views," she advised in a weary voice.

Billy remembered reading about the military significance of Moulmein during the Burma campaign. "Is Moulmein the same place as Mawlaymine?" asked Billy

"Yes!" replied Jenny. "We now say both, depending on who you speak too. Now spelt M-A-W-L-A-Y-M-I-N-E."

Zaw dropped them at the bottom of a flight of steps. They ascended between two fierce-looking golden lion-like effigies guarding the entrance, reached the golden stupa, and looked over the ramparts across the Thanlwin river, once called the Salween.

A flight of pigeons, disturbed by their arrival, took off and circled the stupa. Jenny looked back at the stupa as Billy took a photograph. "Shall I take one of you both in front of the stupa?" she suggested.

"Please, that would be great," said Mary.

"The pagoda here was the inspiration for one of your famous poets and writers. It is mentioned in Rudyard Kipling's *Mandalay*, a poem he is reputed to have written here, when he lived in this locality."

Billy could not resist. He launched into the poem:

> By the old Moulmein Pagoda, lookin' eastward to the sea,
> There's a Burma girl a-settin', and I know she thinks o' me;
> For the wind is in the palm-trees, and the temple-bells they say:
> "Come you back, you British soldier; come you back to Mandalay!"
> Come you back to Mandalay,
> Where the old Flotilla lay;
> Can't you 'ear their paddles chunkin' from Rangoon to Mandalay,
> On the road to Mandalay,
> Where the flyin'-fishes play,
> An' the dawn comes up like thunder outer China 'crost the Bay!

"Bravo," said Mary and both Jenny and Mary gave due applause. Zaw, who had strained up the steps to be with them, beamed without truly understanding.

*****

After a very long wearisome day they reached their destination. Driving into the settlement of Thanbuyazat, its main road lined with bazaars and tea houses, they reached a small traffic island with a model-size clock tower set in the centre, which seemed strangely out of place. They continued for a few hundred metres to what seemed like an abandoned steam engine. As the car came to a halt Jenny did not need to encourage them to get out and stretch.

"I believe as you're interested in the Second World War, this steam engine has importance. This was the end of the Thailand to Burma railway, where many of your Allied prisoners and indeed Burmese prisoners died whilst constructing it for the Japanese. It is now all run down and the museum that once existed is closed."

Billy and Mary could not imagine what horrors these men had to endure and stood in silence. Billy said a prayer in his head and thanked the Lord for his father's deliverance. He fanned himself with his Tilley sun hat before returning it to his head to protect him from the oppressive sun, which was back out with a vengeance now the storm clouds had passed.

It was late and they decided to check in to the small hotel Jenny had arranged. As soon as Billy and Mary were registered, Jenny wished them a pleasant evening and disappeared with Zaw. Billy and Mary were exhausted and turned in for an early night.

Next day, Jenny and Zaw returned to collect them as pre-arranged. They retraced their steps, stopping at a local market to buy flowers and, turning right at the roundabout before the steam engine, they soon came to the Commonwealth Grave site.

Billy was impressed with the immaculate state of the whole site, a great tribute to the men. It was a Saturday and already hot and humid at 10 am.

"My word, Jenny, this heat is so strength sapping. The air is so heavy, do you think there is a threat of rain again?" asked Billy.

"Always at this time of year," said Jenny. They left Zaw with the car and meandered along the paths between graves.

They appeared to be alone in the cemetery. "It is so still and quiet," said Billy, "as if the spirits are co-mingling and at rest in an after-world of calm after leaving this world in such turmoil. It is eerily quiet, not even any birdsong."

No one replied. The only shade came from the small trees dotted here and there. Billy and Mary stood a while under a thin-trunked, sinewy tree, out of direct sunlight. The welcome respite was immediate. Sipping on bottled water, they surveyed the graves of seven Gurkhas they were stood by.

Jenny had left them briefly. She caught up with them and had thoughtfully been back to the car and brought along parasols to shield them from the intensity of the Burmese sun.

They took the time to read the inscriptions on each grave as they passed. Mary stopped to look at the grave of a young man from the Manchester Regiment aged just twenty-two, who had died in 1943 on the so-called "Death Railway". She shook her head. "So many young men whose lives were tragically ended too soon."

Billy had walked ahead searching. Finally, after almost half an hour, he was stood in front of a tombstone which made him shiver even in this heat. He read and re-read the inscription on James Roberts' headstone. It was only really now he truly realised the enormity of the sacrifice this man James Roberts had made for his father.

Mary caught up with him. Seeing the grave, she put

her arm around him. A bunch of wilted flowers lay on the front ledge of the white marble stone.

Billy took a step forward and knelt by the headstone. He opened his shoulder bag and placed his father's Royal Engineers cap badge and his own flowers on behalf of Gwen by the floral tribute.

Mary and Jenny watched in silence as Billy paid his respects and thanked him for saving his father's life. In the stillness, a few minutes of mindfulness and a glance around the cemetery brought Mary to tears. The question on her lips was "Why?"

Billy took out his camera and took a photograph of the grave and then asked Jenny to take one of him kneeling by it too. Returning to the car without a word being spoken, Billy trailed behind until he saw a gardener, who was watering the lush, well-maintained grass.

"Hello, Mingalabar," said Billy nervously. Very slowly he continued, "You do a wonderful job looking after this cemetery. Can you tell me who puts the flowers on Jimmy Roberts' grave?" It was clear the gardener spoke no English, just nodding and smiling in response. Beckoning to the small man in his plain khaki brown uniform, Billy retraced his steps to Jimmy's grave, with the gardener not far behind.

Jenny and Mary, who had walked on ahead back towards the car, turned to see Billy disappearing in the other direction. Leaving Mary fanning herself under the thick canopy of a gnarled old tree, Jenny rejoined Billy.

"Who puts the flowers on this grave?" Billy tried again, pointing to the flowers. But again, all the gardener did was nod and smile until Jenny arrived and acted as interpreter. She established the gardener knew nothing much, but at the gardener's behest, they followed him to see the Cemetery Superintendent.

The gardener knocked on the door of a seemingly locked and redundant white one-storey building, the only one on site. Shortly, a small old man peered around the door frame. His weathered face reminded Billy of a walnut casing.

"Hello, Superintendent," said Jenny in the local patois. "Do you know who puts the flowers on the grave of …" she hesitated and looked to the gardener asking him which grave and in turn he spoke to the Superintendent. All of a sudden, the Superintendent's face lit up and his arms became animated. He gushed with explanation.

Jenny thanked him very much and all shook hands, with Billy none the wiser. Jenny turned and nodded, her face aglow. "He says an old lady used to put flowers on the grave every week, ever since he can remember, then she stopped coming."

Billy frowned his disappointment.

"He says a younger lady comes now, usually on a Sunday. He does not know her by name, he has said hello but nothing more. He does not think she lives locally."

Billy was both ecstatic and bemused at this information. "I wonder if she will come tomorrow, Jenny, as luck has it, it will be Sunday. I would like to stay another night, Jenny, I have come all this way and it would be remiss of me to miss an opportunity to glean more information. Is this possible?"

Twenty minutes later, they were sitting in a roadside

tea house, awkwardly adjusting their bodies to perch at low tables, which were covered in colourful tablecloths. Billy was uncomfortable on the little blue plastic stools, which were barely big enough for school children.

However, the refreshing and much needed drink of milky sweet tea soon revived them. Jenny rejoined them after a few minutes. She confirmed that the hotel they were staying in could take them for another night.

"Thank you, Jenny, you are very efficient," said Mary. Billy nodded too, putting up his thumb to acknowledge his agreement.

*****

Billy and Mary were up early on Sunday morning full of anticipation. They had not asked what time the lady came to the grave but did not want to miss her. After breakfast they returned to the cemetery. Mary had brought a sketch pad with her, and spent her time making sketches of the panorama of white headstones looking like rows of perfect teeth in a giant's mouth.

Midday came and went. Billy could feel his shirt sticking to his back. He brushed away some flies with his hat, but they just resettled on him and he gave up.

Jenny had packed some refreshment and spread a blanket on the grass under the trees by the "Cross of Sacrifice" at the rear of the cemetery. Mary sat eating a banana, her long legs stretched in front of her as she rested on one arm. She contemplated the once vibrant sea of humanity before her, once so full of ambition and hope, who no longer enjoyed life. Australians, British and Dutch, Nepalese and some who had no names or designated nationality.

Billy lay back and relaxed, closing his eyes, the dappled sunlight finding its way through the trees' canopy and playing on his prostrate body, as the light welcome breeze made the tree branches shiver. He thought of his dad. What sort of life had he led here? He must have been constantly on his guard, never able to relax. Grasshoppers and other insects played a symphony in the background of his thoughts.

An hour or so later Jenny became excited. A woman had arrived and gone over to a grave. As they quickly left their picnic debris, all strewn by the memorial like a mini tornado had hit the area, they could all see the figure of a woman knelt beside the tombstone of Jimmy Roberts. As the small group approached, the figure stood, still looking at the newly placed flowers, her head bent in respect.

Billy thought she might be in her thirties. She wore a scarlet htamein wrapped tightly around her narrow abdomen, complemented by a matching blouse and white chiffon scarf, draped around her shoulders. Aware of their arrival she turned, her dark eyes looked up at them, gleaming like onyx jewels in the sunlight as they stood out from her thanaka-marked face.

"Mingalabar," said Jenny. "Jimmy Roberts was a close friend of Billy's father," she explained as she gestured towards Billy.

This beautiful and elegant young woman seemed a little stunned. In Burmese she said, "Hello, I am Zoya, granddaughter of Bway Paw." Then in perfect English she added, "I am so sorry for your loss."

Billy and Mary were dumbfounded. Jenny was

194

surprised to hear English spoken so well, too. "Can you help us?" said Billy, full of hope and anticipation.

Jenny saw the trepidation and almost fear the young lady exuded. She looked around anxiously. Jenny explained to Billy and Mary that Burmese people are so gracious and this request is almost like a command to them, as they always want to help. Equally, it is very difficult for them to ask for help, even if they desperately need it. They might be almost completely out of food, yet they would give you the last food they had if you came to visit. The woman might also be concerned about the authorities watching her.

Billy and Mary acknowledged the regime had a lot to answer for.

Zoya nodded. "I am happy to help. If I can."

"We can go somewhere more comfortable out of the hot sun and talk?" Jenny suggested.

"That would be fine," said Zoya, following them.

All four walked together and rejoined the driver, who drove to a nearby tea house. Jenny ordered some refreshment. Billy regarded Zoya, quite taken by her presence, intrigued by the thanaka on her smooth caramel-coloured skin.

"Zoya, what a pretty name," said Mary.

Embarrassed, Zoya lowered her head. "Thank you."

Sitting with their drinks of hot tea, somewhat incongruous given the weather, Billy started to tell Zoya about where they lived. "I come for a small town in England. It's cool and wet a lot of the year." Mary added her comments on her island life.

"What about you?" said Mary.

"I enjoyed geography at school and learning about

195

Britain. I was at the University in Yangon and studied Contemporary Europe and earned my degree," replied Zoya.

"Are your family from around here? Did you mind living in Yangon away from your family?"

"I was born in the Karenni hills, but we moved. I had relatives in Yangon, I lived with them whilst at University."

"Was it expensive to go to University?" asked Mary.

"My expenses were covered by a special payment I received from the United Kingdom each year, a sort of trust, my mother told me. My mother had saved some of the trust money. Before she passed away she gave it to me, for my education."

"I am sorry to hear about your mother. When did she pass?" said Mary inquisitively.

"Last year, she was very old and not well at all."

Billy just listened, enthralled by Zoya's clipped and soft educated accent.

Mary nodded. "So that's why it is you who comes and tends the grave of James Roberts." She let the statement hang in the air.

"Yes. My mother always used to come, and she asked me to promise that I would continue to do so. I used to come with her sometimes and she used to spend some time here whilst I would often walk around or play."

"Did you know James Roberts?" said Mary, who then smiled and said, "Of course you wouldn't have, you are too young."

Zoya smiled. "No, you are right, I was not born."

Billy interjected. "So how did your mother know James Roberts and why do you come and put flowers on his grave?"

"I am sorry," said Zoya hesitantly. "I don't know much about soldier Roberts. All I know is he was very good to my family during the Second World War."

Billy let out a sigh.

Zoya added, "But my grandmother might be able to tell you more."

"Wow, your grandmother is still alive," said Billy and Mary in chorus. "Where does she live?" quizzed Billy.

"Bway Paw lives with my husband and me and my children in Yangon. It is quite far from here, she used to live in Loikaw, but Grandfather died, and she was alone and frail."

"Gosh," said Mary, "that's a long journey for you to come here."

"I cannot do it too often now, because of my work and money and the children and, of course, Bway Paw, Grandma. I come with my friend when he delivers goods to Thanbyuzazat and sees his family. So, if he is coming, I sometimes come with him. Sunday is a good day for me, but it is not always for him."

"How old is your grandmother, Zoya?" asked Billy, his mathematical brain ticking.

"She is ninety years old. She is frail but still very sharp in her mind."

Billy could not help himself. "We are so pleased to hear that. Do you think we might be able to meet her?"

"I could ask if she would be happy to do so," replied Zoya.

*****

Rather than get her normal lift back to Yangon, Zoya was thankful to take the ride with Zaw and her new-found acquaintances. On the long journey, they learned a little more of life in Burma and how difficult it was at times for many under the current government.

Billy had been trying to pick the right moment but could wait no longer. "You mentioned, Zoya, that your mother received money from the UK. Do you know who sent that money?"

"I am sorry, I don't, other than it was someone who wanted to help," replied Zoya with a sad expression.

It was late when they arrived in Yangon and dropped off Zoya. They said their farewells and arranged to see her and her grandmother the following day.

Jenny had booked rooms for them at the Hotel Orchid, near the iconic Sule Pagoda. A mustiness hung in the air throughout the hotel but especially in the bedrooms, which were bestowed with 1970s-type furniture and huge monstrosities of Chinese-made televisions with twenty-inch screens, spluttering into life with barely audible and viewable Chinese and Burmese programmes. The beds were lumpy and basic, bathroom fittings were rusty. There was a mini-bar fridge in Billy's room, but it was not working, he noticed, even though it was stocked with canned drinks and bottles of water.

Breakfast was another interesting surprise. The options were either fried rice or fried noodles with fried eggs, or some bread, butter and jam.

It was a bit of a disappointment but cheap, and the best and most important thing about the hotel was its central location, sitting behind the City Hall, and near to

Sule Pagoda. A lovely park surrounded Independence Monument and nearby was Emmanuel Church. Fine colonial buildings looked over the park. It was a fair trek to Bogyoke market, or Scott's, as Billy's father would have known it.

Lots of questions ran through Billy's mind and he shared his thoughts with Mary as they sat in a terraced cafe near the hotel.

"I wonder if Zoya knows more than she is letting on?"

"You're a suspicious fellow, Billy, but I'm intrigued to find out how Jimmy Roberts is connected with Zoya's family," agreed Mary.

That afternoon, escorted by Jenny, they walked over to the impressive gold Sule Pagoda, which was located in the middle of what was essentially a traffic roundabout on a very busy road. Throwing caution to the wind, they walked into the congested road. It took a leap of faith to walk into the continuous flow of vehicles, but miraculously the traffic parted. Billy felt like Moses walking through the Dead Sea. But the charge of mechanised vehicles did not stop; they just avoided Billy and Mary, and the sense of achievement for the two of them was palpable, or, wondered Billy, was that just their blood pressure?

Mary felt a sense of both power and wonder as they reached the pagoda unscathed, even if her mind did jump ahead with trepidation to the return journey.

Jenny smiled at the clear relief her guests felt. She walked them into the pagoda and explained, "The prayers are simple and you can offer flowers. If it was your birthday, you should offer water on the shrine where the birth date will be written. This brings you good luck and it is said your wishes are fulfilled."

Even though it was not his birthday Billy used his bottled water, indispensable in this climate, and silently prayed to the gods.

Looking back across the road, Mary focused on an array of colourful washing that hung on a line above the dirty flow of traffic below. It looked so bizarre against the cracked facade of the once pristine white building it hung from, almost like bunting put out to welcome home long-lost travellers.

That night Mary and Billy found it very difficult to sleep. Mary was hot. She stripped off the T-shirt she was sleeping in and sat up in bed looking out through the faded, jade green shuttered windows. From her bed, Sule Paya was framed perfectly, illuminated in all its majesty. She walked to the window and looked out at the pagoda, static in the spin-dryer of ever-constant traffic circumnavigating its glory.

She made a cup of tea thanks to her trusty travel kettle, which she never failed to pack, and contemplated what revelations might be forthcoming tomorrow. She feared a little for Billy.

20

Next morning in the foyer Jenny was waiting for them, trusty and dependable as ever.

They gazed out of the car window looking at nothing in particular, just the sea of humanity, rickshaws, bicycles, motorcycles, huge, fume-exuding bull-nosed trucks and a variety of old cars, all surrounded and intermingled with decaying buildings. Many of the people looked weary and forlorn.

After a short drive Zaw pulled over at the end of a shabby-looking terrace of deteriorating shops, offices and apartments. They walked a short way along a narrow street of stalls bedecked with colourful, exotic fruit and vegetables, many foreign to them. Taking a left turn, they strolled up a narrow alley with crumbling buildings either side.

Following Jenny, they left the street and walked up a flight of concrete steps of a rather austere building, each step announcing their ascent as it echoed up the staircase. The eye-watering odour of sewage, exacerbated by the morning's rising temperature, assaulted their nostrils. Mary covered her mouth.

Reaching the first floor, a door opened and Zoya greeted them. They entered a surprisingly large room, a real contrast to the world outside its door. On its dark teak floor lay a large emerald green carpet, around which were placed a couch and a few chairs and floor cushions. A small bookcase with a few books on one shelf also displayed two framed photographs and a bowl of fruit. A wall hanging of the Shwedagon Paya enlivened the wall above the couch.

Zoya proudly presented their host. "This is my ah pwa (my grandmother) Bway Paw." A wizened old lady sat pensively on a chair in the corner of the room, nervously holding a small tattered book, turning it in her hands. She just nodded, without expression.

Mary and Billy said "Hello" and looked at Zoya for a lead. "Can you thank your grandmother for seeing us and explain who we are, please?" said Billy.

Zoya nodded, smiled and said "Ah Pwa does understand some English, but please speak slowly. I have told her of our meeting. I spoke at length with Ah Pwa last night. She told me of a man called 'Uncle Myint Saw', or at least that was his name to all the tribe, it meant tall. His real name, she told me, was 'Williams'."

A young man entered the room and nodded. "Tommy Williams," he added.

A chill ran down Billy's spine and the hairs on his neck raised as he heard his father's name mentioned.

Zoya looked up and introduced her brother, Khin Naw, a history scholar. He sat at the back of the room and listened.

Mary pondered the novelty of meeting a Burmese family. Zoya disappeared as all in the room continued to smile and nod at each other awkwardly until she returned with some soft drinks.

Khin Naw proceeded to give them a history lesson, spoken in Burmese and translated slowly by Zoya with occasional clarification by Jenny. Constantly using inflection and stopping for Zoya to translate, he began: "In 1942, the Japanese were supporting the Burmese army, instructing and encouraging them to harass and take arms from the Karen tribe people. Many Karenni had soldiered in the Burma Rifles and generally supported the Allied British forces, not so much around Burma but mostly in the delta region of the Aerawaddy. This caused the Japanese to really hate them.

"Many of the Karenni lived in the forested mountain areas, the Karenni mountains near Thailand. With a view to harassing the Japanese, many had been given a rifle and ammunition and a few months' pay when the British had retreated.

"A few British army officers had also been left behind in the Karenni to try and organise resistance amongst any pro-British tribes.

"In 1943 and 1944, the Japanese made big efforts to attack and destabilise the communities and people of the Karenni, where they knew a British unit was operating under the command of 'Uncle Myint Saw', Tom Williams.

"Many massacres, much crop burning and other devastation and persecution took place, and many Karen and some British soldiers were killed. Many villagers were tortured, women were raped."

Billy added his newly learned knowledge "Force 136, which was a British clandestine band of guerillas supporting the Karenni to cause upheaval in the Japanese way of life continued to supply the Karenni, and from late 1944 they mounted Operation Character, which organised large-scale resistance in the Karenni.

"In April 1945," Billy continued, "Force 136 organised a major uprising with all sorts of clandestine operations to weaken the Japanese 15th Army while the Allies advanced on Rangoon. After the capture of Rangoon, Karen resistance fighters continued to harass Japanese units and stragglers as they retreated, causing major disruption. There were thousands of Karen, all led and supported by British officers who coordinated supplies and provided medical assistance with their orderlies. My father, Tom Williams, and his good friend Jimmy Roberts were two of those officers."

Zoya's grandmother opened the book she had been holding and gave Zoya a photograph to show Billy and Mary. Billy was taken aback. A tear came in his eye. The photograph showed his father and Jimmy Roberts with a family and was very similar to the one Billy had discovered in his father's possessions. He now began to understand.

Zoya confirmed his thoughts. "My grandmother Bway Paw, my mother in her arms, and my grandfather with Soldier Williams and Jimmy Roberts!"

Zoya's grandmother was wiping a tear from her eye and said something in Burmese to Zoya, who smiled and comforted her grandmother with an arm around her.

Looking at Billy and Mary, Zoya started to speak and faltered. "Bway Paw says … these brave men saved them from the Kalagong Massacre."

Billy was dumbfounded. His father was not only a mystery soldier behind enemy lines, he was a revered war hero. He wondered if his mother ever knew …

Jenny and Zoya went on to translate the grandmother's story.

"The Kalagong Massacre was committed against my villagers by the Japanese Army and the Kempeitai, the evil military police, ordered by Major General Seiei Yamamoto, because we were believed to have been helping the British.

"The Japanese occupied the village and rounded up all the villagers and questioned mostly the men. Then women and children were raped and beaten, all to force information from us, but we did not give them anything … many did not have information to give. The Kempeitai were feared and hated in equal measure, as they were known to be massacring everyone in revenge.

"It was not only the Japanese but Burmese Army regulars. Villagers were taken in groups to village wells close by, some blindfolded, and were bayoneted, their bodies dumped in the wells. Very few escaped. But Uncle Myint Saw and Soldier Roberts had heard of the Japanese advance and just before the Japanese arrival insisted we come with them, as my husband was one of the resistance fighters. Others were implored to come but they wanted to remain as they did not foresee what might happen."

Billy and Mary were spellbound by this revelation and full of growing admiration.

Zoya stood. "Grandmother is very tired now, but she was so pleased to meet you and talk about your father and his best friend Soldier Roberts."

"Please thank her so much." Billy approached her and knelt before her. Bway Paw's tired hooded eyes looked at Billy benevolently. She took Billy's hands. "Your father never forgot us!" As she spoke a tear fell down her cheek and onto Billy's hand. He raised her hand and kissed it. Turning to Zoya, he asked, "Would you mind if I had a photograph taken with you and your grandmother?"

Photographs taken, Bway Paw held out in front of her the book she had been nursing. "This is for you," she said to Billy.

Billy saw it was a battered journal. As he opened it the pages of writing and sketches were loose and fragile. He looked at Bway Paw and then Zoya. He was speechless, this was the wartime diary of Jimmy Roberts. Billy contemplated the journal's contents while they retraced their steps to the Orchid Hotel. Jenny was smiling as indeed she always did. Little was said as they all reflected on the powerful story they had just heard.

That evening in the comfort of his hotel room Billy made himself a cup of tea and settled down with Jimmy Roberts' diary. Jimmy wrote in an easy-to-read script with occasional words of Welsh reflecting his upbringing on the Mid-Wales coast. Jimmy was with the Royal Engineers and like Tom had served in Singapore before being selected to join what he thought was a commando unit which would operate behind enemy lines as and when needed. He wrote:

> Today we were told to report to the Cathay Building in Singapore, which we did, and to ask for a chap called Warren. It soon became clear, he was

206

putting together a force for clandestine operations.

He was very convivial and relaxed and said we had been recommended to him as he was looking for brave men who could think for themselves and if necessary be resilient and operate alone but also be able to lead and be creative.

Tom and I don't know quite what to think of it all. We are having a good time in Singapore despite the bombing by the Japs and I personally have met a lovely girl called Gwen, who I am very fond of. Today was not so much an invitation, as a command, and both of us along with a few others were driven out to Tanjong Balai, a headland connected to Singapore on the Jurong River.

We were greeted by a Captain Cumming.

Command was based in a grand, colonial, white-painted wooden property. It had wide verandahs at ground level. An elevated and attractive outside walkway on the second-floor added elegance to the property. We noticed two officers were chatting there. One smoking a pipe caught my attention.

Lush tropical plants and shrubbery cocooned the property from the outside world, yet the river was nearby, so secure and secret to the outside world and perfect for manoeuvres and escape by water. We trained a lot more with explosives and developed the craft of sabotage.

It was great to meet up again with Major Gavin too. We first knew him when he trained with us in Scotland.

Billy read on and learned that Jimmy and Tom had been

inserted behind enemy lines and spent some time, like other clandestine raiding parties, trying to hold up the Japs in Malaya, blowing up airfields, bridges and the like. Somehow, they had managed to get back towards Singapore.

Jimmy had so hoped he would see Gwen once more. Jimmy and Tom gave up an opportunity to be evacuated by boat to Trincomalee on 5 February. But by now it was murderous trying to get back into Singapore. They had heard that many nurses had already left. Under intense fire they reached RAF Seletar after two days to be evacuated by plane, all the time being bombed and strafed from the air. The chaps there told them the air base was where in 1930 Amy Johnson, the famous aviator, had dropped down to refuel her Gypsy Moth on the way to Australia.

Billy read on …

It's a hell hole here, we can barely fight back. The ack-ack guns seem inadequate, and any Allied planes have either been blown up on the ground or never return after scrambling. Craters are everywhere, in the runway and landing area, and all buildings are destroyed. We spend most of our time in foxholes close to the remaining trees.

Last night some Nips came as far as the perimeter of the airfield. We managed to repel them, Jones was injured in the shoulder and an RAF maintenance lad took a hit in the chest and died shortly afterwards. I feel awful, exhausted and hungry. We have little in the way of food. I look around at the grimy and stubbled faces of weary men, eyes barely open under tin helmets.

Billy felt like this could have been the last diary entry, until he turned the page.

Thank you, Lord, we have been plucked from this insanity. We are being flown from Seletar tonight, thanks to Major Goodfellow.

We were crammed into a camouflaged B14 Hudson bomber. Our Australian pilot called it "Old Boomerang". (His nickname was "Nutty", very apt if you ask me!) We have managed to evade the flak and groundfire and head into the British Empire's "jewel in the crown", India.

Crikey, Calcutta is a hectic port. I kept saying to myself on the plane I hope we make it. My tired old bones were vibrating so much during the plane ride, I felt like my body was on a huge fairground ride to hell!

I feel terrible I haven't been able to say goodbye to Gwen. I have really fallen head over heels for her. I hold the conviction that one day we will meet again in peacetime and walk along the beaches around home on the Welsh Coast.

Billy took a sip of his cold tea. He was so engrossed, as if he were reading an adventure story, but this was real and involved his father. Like a great novel, it was a page turner. He could not put the journal down.

We touched down in Ceylon on the way to India, which was a hive of activity. In Calcutta we have been joined by about another forty or fifty chaps who had been seconded from various regiments. We were met by a fellow called Yates, who along with his officers and trainers are shaping us into quite a potent force.

This involves jungle and forest training AGAIN! We have been told that we will soon be moved to Manipur State near the border with Burma to accomplish this.

Billy noticed for the first time none of the entries was dated. He just assumed it was the following day and of course in chronological order.

Briefing at 1400hrs today. Looks like something pretty important is going down. Only two of us at the briefing, Tom and myself. We are told we will be taking our agreed limited kit and flying out at 1800hrs.

Our destination was a clearing in the jungle in Burma where we were to make contact with local guerillas, who would escort us further south west, to join up with other officers and men. Our mission is to give them instructions from GSI headquarters here in India. Our brief is to lead and train local Karenni in the skills of espionage and guerilla warfare, so we are now part of a fight-back. Looks like the show is on.

Tom and I were full of trepidation. The first problem was the little Lysander Mark One we were travelling in. It could only take us just into Burma because of its range. It's very small inside, originally meant for one, but now two good-sized fellows were being squeezed in … and we knew we were going to be behind enemy lines, a vicious, unforgiving enemy at that … I hope this works out, Gwen!

Billy took a break as there seemed to be a gap in the journal and he was in need of something to eat He called down to room service for a sandwich and a cold drink. Catching sight of himself in the bathroom mirror he thought he looked tired.

Billy spent most of the night reading the book and became emotional at every mention of his father, comments like "Tom is very quiet, but when he says something it is measured and meaningful and he has a wicked sense of humour, and he loves life". This was some commendation from a fellow soldier, thought Billy.

I am really missing Gwen. How I would love to marry her and raise a family back in Wales. We could have a boy. Thomas for a boy and Daisy after my grandmother if it's a girl, if that's fine with Gwen, of course. Perhaps Daisy Gwen Roberts. I often think about our time together in Singapore, Gwen. I promise we'll meet up after the war and we'll have a home in Borth-y-Gest on the coast not far from my parents.

A light knock on the door brought Billy back to 1995 Myanmar.

"Hello," said Mary, as Billy held the door slightly ajar. "I couldn't sleep. I wondered if you might be awake."

Billy returned to his chair and Mary closed the door behind her.

"I've been reading Jimmy's journal …"

Billy felt a light hand on his neck. "Are you not going

211

to bed, Billy, you must be exhausted."

"This is fascinating, Mary." He proceeded to excitedly tell Mary what Jimmy and Tom had endured and achieved.

Mary sat opposite him, in a thin silk dressing gown she had bought on a whim when passing a stall in Scott's market. As she leaned forward and crossed her legs, her dressing gown opened to reveal her smooth legs, her knees just covered by a cream silk nightdress.

"There seem to be gaps, Mary. Then Jimmy appears to catch up with the lost weeks when he finally starts his entries again. Look at the smudges of dirty fingermarks that add to the patina on the old journal. It was obviously a harrowing and dangerous transit avoiding the Japanese patrols and booby traps, but his guides were excellent and passionate in their hatred of not just the Japanese but the Burmese National Army under Aung San … It's clear they much preferred their life under British colonial rule, although there were those who wanted their own autonomous region for the Karenni. Whilst the safer zones were well up in the forested mountains they needed to be constantly on the move and within striking distance of the Japanese activities.

"Invariably a mission led by Jimmy and Tom would mean a platoon-size group of Karenni guerillas and a radio operator officer infiltrating Japanese lines, trying to establish what the Japanese were up to and work out their strength and movements.

"Given the opportunity, they would destroy installations or, more often than not, ambush the Japs. Jimmy showed they could be on the move for weeks on end and constantly contacted operational bases in India to ask for supplies at agreed drop zones, where big C47 transport planes would drop munitions and medical and other supplies.

"But for a long time, the radio sets were either inadequate and breaking down or for the most part useless in trying to communicate in such difficult terrain over such long distances. Let me read you some of this." Billy dipped in and out, reading passages of script. Mary listened and studied Billy's intent expression and concentration. She noticed how his large hands turned the pages rather delicately for a big fellow.

October 1943. We have finally received hermetically sealed wireless/Morse sets designed to avoid the problems we encountered with our original transmitters, which were almost useless in the humidity. Thanks to this and the radio operators' use of complicated codes, which they change daily to avoid detection, we are at last in regular contact with Operations Command.

Every day at prearranged times, the radio operator climbs to a high point with a support team to assist with reception and transmission. It's a tough climb up through forest or jungle. Leeches attach to their legs and bodies, but it's so important to tell headquarters what's happening on the ground and also to receive our orders. The radio operators are crucial to our mission. If we lose them or the radio sets, HQ would be working blind and so would we.

Billy commented, "Often in his notes, Jimmy mentions

213

that, if he was captured he was not sure he could bring himself to use his cyanide pill, knowing he would never see Gwen again."

He continued reading:

Of course, the Japanese have their patrols and we have to be so wary of them, we can't be sure whether they are trying to listen into our communications, but more than that, they would love to seize the radio sets and our operators … it's a constant game of cat and mouse.

One day we had a near miss. We'd paused to take some refreshment when all of a sudden, a Japanese patrol stumbled on us while we were waiting for the radio operator and his bodyguard to return. After a quick firefight we managed to kill about seven of them and were lucky to only receive one flesh wound in our squad. Other Japanese hightailed it, so we knew we had to extract the radio operator and get out of there. We trekked for two days knowing they were in pursuit and reinforced, but fortunately shook them off after leaving a booby trap or two to hold them up.

God! I thought it was tough being attacked by Jap Zeros at Seletar airbase. But nothing can prepare you for living rough in the jungle. Whether it's travelling up-river or overland it's a living hell. Especially in the impenetrable jungle, where you can't see more than five yards in front of you.

I fully expect a prehistoric creature to appear from the tangle of trees and bushes. Some of the animals and creepy insects defy description, thinking of them makes my skin crawl. You can hardly get any air when you breathe, the atmosphere saps the life from you. Darn mosquitoes are the bane of our lives. Malaria is rife. It's a welcome change when we're on patrol to come across a more civilised area that has been cultivated, either for coconuts or other crops. Although crops are starting to fail, as the plantation owners and workers have either disappeared to avoid capture, been imprisoned or killed.

Bamboo thickets are the worst, they are like nature's wall, and you have to try and circumvent them. On the plus side the bamboo comes in handy for lots of things from making stretchers to blowpipes.

This darn heat. I look up at the jungle canopy sometimes and hear all sorts of animal sounds. No plane could see us down in the thick of this, that's for sure. The birds and animals with their alarm calls soon put us on our guard with their cacophony of shrill panic!

We occasionally see monkeys swinging from tree to tree. If we can catch them they supplement our meagre diet, which consists of a bit of fish we might catch, or plants the Karen bring in. Last week I tasted snake for the first time. One of the lads thought it tasted like chicken but I reckon rabbit is nearer the mark.

One plus point of the thick jungle is it protects us from the sun, I suppose. I have got quite used to its sounds. Sometimes I drift off to sleep at night to the rhythmic sound of the cicadas. You almost feel the jungle is alive when their steady thrum begins. One of the natives told me they make the noise by rubbing their legs together.

We have learned a lot, trapping our own food, eating roots of plants, identifying trees like rambutan and lambong, which we can eat from. We are adept at finding drinking water. I am quite accomplished at starting a fire without matches now, simply by rubbing sticks together over some dry moss or kindling. Finding dry wood is an art in the rainforest and jungle, let me tell you. Tom and I made a raft today, no mean feat, again bamboo is excellent for this. But I still get frightened, especially when the malaria kicks in.

Like most of the boys, Tom and I have both had fevers. We fear dengue fever, but it's probably malaria most of the time. It's dreadful. We have medication called mepacrine and atabrine, but it just seems to hold back the symptoms, it doesn't get rid of it. It's not just us pale faces, but the Karen struggle at times too.

I also hate the leeches. The darn things suck your blood. After each patrol we have to get them off. Mostly off our legs but often our necks and anything exposed. I usually find burning them with a cigarette-end does the trick. Well, I'm tired now, God knows how much sleep I will get …

We have succeeded in stirring up a hornet's nest, the Japanese are everywhere. Today we rescued a family from a massacre in the village of Kalagong. It was pointless engaging the enemy as we were outnumbered. They were persecuting the villagers, trying to find out where a British officer called Williams was. How did they find out Tom's name?

Presumably they have mine too. It can only be through fear and torture. What shall we do? These people are suffering intolerably under the Nips. They are led by an evil officer of the much-feared Kempeitai called Major Muruji, sent by Yamamoto, no doubt.

Life is being made pretty difficult for us right now. The Japs are determined to catch us and wipe us all out.

This was the last entry in Jimmy Roberts' diary.

At breakfast Billy poured Mary a cup of tea, then poured himself a coffee. "So, what do you think we should do now, Mary?"

"I suppose a little more shopping at Scott's market would be out of the question?" she said reaching for a piece of toast.

Billy frowned, feigning disapproval. "I was thinking more of whether we might bring forward our flight to Singapore and extend our stay there, as I would love to see the places Jimmy mentions in his diary."

Mary passed Billy the marmalade. "I really like it here, Billy. Jenny said there is a super beach at a place called Ngapali, it's a long drive to the west but we could get a cheap flight."

"Our trip's not really long enough for a beach break, Mary. Anyway, I hope we will get some beach time in Australia. Let's keep the same itinerary, then. We can still explore a few of the places in Singapore that would have been familiar to Jimmy, Tom, Violet and Gwen, and I suppose that gives us a day or so for shopping here." Billy raised his eyebrows and nodded towards a beaming Mary.

*****

Two days later they were sitting on the Silk Air plane for the relatively short flight to Singapore. Mary and Billy talked of their Burma adventures and the treasures they had unearthed, not least of which was Jimmy's journal.

"I'm still astonished that we have in our possession the last words of Jimmy Roberts. This is a historic artefact, Mary."

"You are certainly not wrong, Billy, but I take a lot more from this wonderful country. The people are so kind and chivalrous, and honest … I mean that in the most endearing way. I have been enthralled and intrigued by all the people and places we've encountered."

"You're right there," agreed Billy as the cabin staff called for tables up and seat backs in an upright position ready for landing. "I'm kicking myself for not finding out how the diary actually ended in Bway Paw's possession, but I guess that matters little now."

Soon they touched down and wandered through the modern terminal building, so sanitised and full of modern technology and modern conveniences.

Billy felt bewildered, as it was juxtaposed against his mind's eye view of a colonial Singapore under the British of which he was hoping there was some semblance remaining. This modern and spacious airport in Singapore was called "Changi", the very same name as the notorious prison camp in which many Allied troops were incarcerated and indeed which many never left alive.

Stepping outside the air-conditioned micro-climate, they were once more hit with the humid wall of tropical air. "Peninsula Excelsior Hotel, please," said Billy to the taxi driver.

21

Mary and Billy got out of the taxi and stared up at the modern high-rise buildings that created concrete valleys on the once marshy land.

Settled into his hotel room, Billy went in search of Mary and was soon knocking on her door. A few seconds later Mary opened the door. "Well, are you all unpacked?" said Billy with an air of mischief.

"Billy, a lady takes a lot longer than you men. Come and look at this view," she said, turning and walking towards the lofty picture window, with its vista across the Singapore skyscape towards the bay. The building opposite seemed to have a lower tier where cars were parked in the open above the road, and beyond the next road was a white church set in lawned grounds, incongruous in modern Singapore.

Billy stood slightly behind Mary. She could feel his warm breath on her neck. He almost kissed her bare shoulder, but as he contemplated this, she turned, looking into his eyes. He averted his gaze and looked out to the city's modern revolution.

"I don't know about you, Mary, but I can't begin to

envisage 1942 Singapore, although that church looks like it's been around a while. Shall we check it out?"

Without much more ado they ventured out to explore. For the next few hours they took the wonderfully easy hop-on hop-off bus that Singapore Airlines passengers benefit from to take in Singapore's sights. It was perfect to familiarise them with the city.

Before they had left the hotel that afternoon, with the help of the concierge they had made a telephone call and were quite surprised to be allowed special dispensation at such short notice to visit Alexandra Hospital, which was the Queen Alexandra Military Hospital in 1942. It was one of the last areas to fall to the Japanese and was the site of the violation of nurses and the murder of patients, including those on operating theatre tables, and medical staff.

Hopping off the bus and walking a short way, the fine hospital soon came into sight at 378 Alexandra Road. The area around it, once farms and post-war cemeteries, was now a mass of accommodation, shops and roads, but the building itself was externally much the same as Billy had imagined having seen library photographs. It had been a modern building in the 1940s and it was still used as a hospital, part of the University Faculty of Medicine.

Set on a hill above the city, it benefited from any breeze and had been specifically designed to take advantage of natural ventilation. The building had high ceilings, large windows, overhanging eaves and shaded, wide corridors. Set in its own grounds it was a perfect environment for rest and recuperation.

A Eurasian woman, small, fine-boned and very

221

efficient in her manner was waiting at the entrance of the hospital. "Hello, Mr and Mrs Williams, my name is Carol Cheng."

"Hello," said Mary on their behalf. "Thank you so much for seeing us at such short notice."

"Not a problem, although I must explain because of the time of day it will be a rather truncated tour. I understand your interest is in the hospital as it was in the forties, but a lot of changes have taken place since then. Some areas of the hospital are naturally difficult to visit because of everyday working activities."

Billy explained, "I was hoping to get a feel for the hospital as it was in 1940. So, it would be great to see any parts that are still used and possible to view."

"Certainly, I have a personal interest too, my late grandmother worked here as a Voluntary Aid Detachment Nurse during the Second World War."

An hour later Billy thanked Ms Cheng for her kind help and guidance. But he had not got a real sense of what his father or the wartime nurses endured with the advancing Japanese army, as the building had changed so much inside.

As they stood on the steps at the hospital entrance looking out across Singapore, Billy looked at Mary. "I'm trying to imagine what the commotion of casualties and warfare going on all around must have been like and what Gwen and Violet must have witnessed." A tear came into Billy's eye as he thought once more of what he had read in Jimmy's diary. "Perhaps tomorrow we can look for St Patrick's, the hospital where Gwen served, and also see if Manor House Hospital still exists, where Gwen first met Tom and Jimmy.

"Did you hear Carol Cheng mention that we might like to visit the Alexandra Garrison Church, which has the Reredos Memorial Chapel dedicated to the memory of the Queen Alexandra Nursing Corps and VAD nurses who were killed in Singapore?" Billy looked at his watch. "Shall we do that now?"

Mary nodded and took his arm and they walked down the inclined drive, once bordered by lush lawns.

Fortunately, the church was open, but they were surprised to find the building empty. Sitting in a pew towards the back, Billy was thankful for the serenity. Here he could feel the history of the place and imagine the anguish that once would have filled its wartime congregation. He said a quiet prayer for all the souls who did not make it through the war and for his father, Jimmy, Gwen and Violet, who he wished were with him today.

Mary had carried Jimmy's diary in her shoulder bag at Billy's request and started turning the pages. Bright shafts of light filtered through the stained-glass windows, illuminating Billy and Mary in their pew. She started to read about the days in Singapore. "Billy, look … Jimmy mentions the Shackle Club in Raffles Place. He describes it as a sort of recreational club-cum-fleet canteen of the NAAFI. It's opposite the Raffles Hotel on Beach Road. He talks of trips to the Pavilion Cinema on Orchard Road." Mary pondered how it all must have seemed such fun until the reality of war struck.

Just then the door creaked open and two women entered, one much older than the other. They smiled and nodded and headed for the front of the church and the reredos screen behind the altar. Billy and Mary watched them as they settled on the wooden pew at the front of the church and paid their respects. A bright beam of sunshine flowed through the stained glass as if energising the nave.

Billy followed their every movement as they said a prayer, then approached the memorial and started reading the names. The older lady seemed to falter and was helped back to the pew by the younger woman, where they sat in silence.

Approaching them, Mary, closely followed by Billy, just could not help but ask. "Sorry to disturb you, but I … er, well, we could not help but notice your interest in the memorial. Were any of these relatives?"

The older lady looked up, red eyed, handkerchief in hand and said in a distinct Australian accent, "No dear, but many were friends and colleagues."

Billy's interest was piqued. "Did you serve with them?" he said hopefully, adding, "My father also served here in Singapore during the war, he was a Royal Engineer. He was friends with a British nurse, Gwen Powell and an Australian nurse, Violet."

"Was she with the Australian contingent, then?" asked the younger lady.

"Indeed! Violet was with the 2/10th Australian General Hospital. I believe she may have worked at Alexandra Hospital, of course, as well as St Patrick's."

"My mother's name is Gloria, Gloria Pilcher, she was with the Australian 10th General Hospital, weren't you, Mum?"

Gloria nodded and, keen to speak for herself, stated, "We had a lot of good friends in the Australian Nursing Service and the QA's. We were sisters in arms," she said with a melancholy smile.

"In fact, when we were evacuating Singapore a number of us volunteered to stay behind, as long as we could." Her eyes wandered, around the empty pews of the church as if doing a roll call. "There was Dorothy and Win and Mary, and, yes, there was a Violet, but then there were probably lots of that name. When we knew the game was up, we were ordered to go to St Andrew's Cathedral to be evacuated, as by then a number of us were working at St Patrick's Hospital. Do you know Violet's surname?"

"Duncan, well, actually, it would have been Watkins before she was married," said Mary excitedly.

Gloria smiled. "Really? Well, goodness gracious me. If it's the Vi Watkins I'm thinking of, she was a pretty little thing. All the boys had an eye for her, long blonde hair and a waist like a wasp. She was not really 'little', actually quite leggy, if I have the right one. elegant, yet mischievous. I'm sure the war changed all that for her, as it did for us all," said Gloria, her voice cracking.

Billy fumbled in Mary's jute bag emblazoned with the national flower of Singapore, a vivid purple orchid. He produced a few photographs, handing them to Gloria.

"Well, my word," said Gloria, her swollen red eyes now adjusting to the spectacles she donned to view the snaps. Focusing on the photograph of Gwen and Violet with Tom in the centre she exclaimed, "Vi for vibrant, we used to say, such an easy-going, fun-loving girl, I never knew what happened to her … Did she survive the war and get back to Australia, then?"

"So this is definitely the Violet you knew?" said Billy,

very intently.

"No doubt," said the now smiling former nurse.

"Vi eventually did find freedom, but not before being a prisoner of war and having a pretty tough time. She moved to Scotland, after marrying a British army officer. She is in a home now and suffering from dementia," lamented Billy.

Gloria lowered her head, then gazed at Billy and said, "I'm so sorry to hear of her torment, then and now. It would have been so good to see her and speak to her!"

Gloria's daughter put her arm around her. "Let's get back now, Mum, you're tired." She looked disapprovingly at Billy and Mary as if they had purposefully upset her mother.

"I'm sure Violet, too, would have loved that," said Mary, patting Gloria on the shoulder.

Billy and Mary said their good-byes and watched as Gloria's frail figure shuffled out of the church.

Billy looked at the list of names on the memorial, trying to imagine the horrors and fears they had suffered.

Mary and Billy said little as they reached the bus stop. As they left the bus and headed back to their hotel, they were both deep in thought. "Shall we meet in Reception around 7 pm and perhaps walk down to Clarke Quay and grab a bite to eat by the riverside?" said Billy.

"Sure."

*****

Mary was dressed in a white cotton dress.

"That dress looks wonderful on you, Mary, it highlights your sun-tanned skin."

Mary blushed. Billy felt it made her even more alluring. Her dark auburn hair was gathered in a bun, leaving her shoulders exposed.

Together they walked slowly down to the river. The evening was hot, humid and stifling. Finding a restaurant with an outside terrace, they sat beneath the stars, settling themselves into bamboo chairs at an intimate table for two overlooking the river.

"We really must visit Raffles tomorrow as it's our last day," said Mary. "After all, that is the main reason for coming to Singapore."

"I'd also like to visit the Cathay Building and one or two of the places Dad and Gwen have mentioned, too, especially St Patrick's Hospital and St Andrew's Cathedral ..." Billy was distracted. Mary's slender neck was draped with a jade heart suspended on a silver chain. Her hazel eyes seemed to sparkle in the evening light.

"Shall we throw caution to the wind and have an exotic cocktail?" suggested Billy as he perused the drinks menu and leaned over and touched Mary's hand.

An electric-like charge consumed Mary's body. She struggled to answer. Breathless, she just looked into Billy's eyes.

The drink flowed, they relaxed and laughed and told tales, chortling at almost anything.

A rather short man and his much taller Asian escort promenaded by. "I wonder where they met?" said Billy.

"Perhaps they're from a touring circus, just out for a stroll discussing high wire act combinations?"

227

"I wonder if they plan an intimate culmination to the evening?" said Billy.

"No, is the long and the short of it!" said Mary. They both laughed out loud, attracting the attention of the imagined circus performers, who shook their heads and walked on as Billy and Mary clasped hands over the table, rather embarrassed at their audible faux pas.

"It's been a perfect evening. Eating, drinking and chatting, all beside the romantic Singapore river with those little tourist bumboats plying up and down. Thank you, Billy," said Mary.

"Let's get the bill and head back to the hotel, we have a busy day ahead tomorrow," said Billy.

As they left the table Mary's heel caught and she stumbled but Billy caught her arm. "What was in those cocktails?" she giggled. "I just don't drink much normally."

"Take my arm," said Billy.

Slowly wending their way back to the Peninsula Excelsior, the night could not last long enough for either of them. Holding hands in the lift, something had changed that night.

Billy helped Mary with the key to her room and opened the door, the light chiffon-like curtains rippling in the evening air of the open window, diffusing the bright lights of the city beyond.

Billy followed Mary into the shadows of her room. He put his hand on the back of her neck and brought her towards him, his full lips touching hers, tenderly expressing his desire for her. She gave no resistance as he unzipped her dress and it fell to the floor. Picking her up in his strong arms, he lay her softly, like a feather descending gently, on to the bed's white cotton sheets.

Billy caressed her face. She looked into those deep blue eyes of his and wanted him more than she had wanted anything in her life.

22

Billy coyly kissed Mary on the forehead as she lay sleeping. He pulled on his clothes, carefully opened the door and studied the corridor left and right. He listened for a moment before closing the door quietly and returning to his own room to shower.

Mary awoke with a start. A fire alarm was going off in the little hospital in Lamlash, until she realised where she was and recognised the ring tone of her room telephone. Searching for the phone, she found it beneath her underwear on the bedside cabinet. "Hello?" she said, a little out of breath by now.

"Is that Mary Queen of Scots? Would you like room service, your majesty, or would you like to meet in the 22nd floor Sky Lounge restaurant at 9.30 am for breakfast?" jested Billy.

"Room service sounds interesting. What time is it?" she said, stretching as she spoke.

"It's already 8.15. Did you sleep in, perchance?" teased Billy.

"Give me time to shower. I'll meet you upstairs shortly!" Putting the receiver down she scurried to the bathroom to behold a dishevelled but glowing reflection in the mirror.

Billy looked out of his window two floors higher and on the other side of the hotel to Mary. He could see the sky looked ominously dark, but he felt on top of the world.

After breakfast, they strolled together, arm in arm under the protection of Billy's umbrella as the heavy rain greeted their short walk to St Andrew's Cathedral. Rain was bouncing off the hot pavements creating an ethereal steaming effect. Soon the gutters were filled with torrents of rainwater, irrigating the city streets. Billy silently questioned his choice of shorts and sandals, but Mary was quite comfortable in her white cotton dress and flat shoes.

The white stone building of St Andrew's looked incongruous, dwarfed by the skyscrapers above, a grove of green acacia trees protecting it and softening its presence. They approached the exquisitely arched neo-gothic entrance.

As they entered the huge nave, Billy imagined the cavernous building when it was briefly an emergency hospital, just before Singapore fell to the Japanese in February 1942, full of wounded service personnel and civilians being tended by their nurses and doctors. He had read that its pews were removed to the Padang to leave more room for all the stretchers.

Now, its colossal white pillars and dark wood pews channelled Billy's eyes towards the white and Wedgewood-blue surrounds of the altar. Stained-glass windows commemorating the founder of Singapore, Stamford Raffles, drew the eye with a kaleidoscope of vibrant colour.

"Wow! This is an amazing monument to history and the stories we have of Violet and Gwen. Bring it alive for me, Billy."

Billy began reading a leaflet he had picked up. "According to this, there is a Memorial Hall dedicated to World War II." He scanned around for signage or someone to ask. A few other visitors ambled aimlessly through the cathedral, drifting silently, looking half-interested, as if they were just keeping out of the morning downpour.

"You can feel a real connection here to the hostilities of the war, Mary," said Billy as he remembered the stories Gwen had told him. Those wartime scenes seem a bit of a paradox in a place of holy worship and peace."

Mary took Billy's hand. Billy stroked her soft and lustrous auburn hair and said. "It's hard to believe that such atrocities took place in Singapore and Asia during the war, and that this wonderful building was a sanctuary from air raids and a makeshift hospital as well as a place of worship. Come on, we have a lot to do."

Leaving St Andrew's Mary looked around. "It is amazing that this green oasis has survived in such a go-ahead, avant-garde city."

"Yes, it is," concurred Billy, as he unfolded the city map. Donning his sunglasses to avoid the glare of the strengthening morning sun, he quickly located their next destination.

"Shall we walk or take a taxi?" he asked, showing Mary the Cathay Building on the map.

"Oh, let's walk," said Mary. "The rain seems to have stopped for now." Splashing across the intersection through steaming puddles, weaving through the throng of people rising from a subway station and the hustle and bustle of the sidewalks, they headed back past the Peninsula Excelsior, ascended the street called Canning Rise and walked through Canning Park.

As they climbed, holding hands through the lush greenery and well-kept lawns, wet from the recent downpour, Billy stopped, turned towards Mary and slowly lowered his head to kiss her tenderly on the lips. Her eyes closed. She felt so happy!

Walking on, Billy could not help but become the tour guide based on what he had studied. "During the war, there were underground bunkers in this park and they became the headquarters of the Allies during the Japanese invasion. There is apparently a small hidden door where you can still enter the bunkers. Shame we don't have enough time for that. Maybe next time we're in Singapore."

Mary hugged Billy's arm like a childhood sweetheart, moved that he had mentioned a future and a next time.

"Oh, look," said Billy as he stopped. They turned to look back at the cityscape spread out below them. Hugging, they looked into one another's eyes. Nothing needed to be said.

It was a steep walk, but before long they left the park and made their way across Canning Road to Orchard Road and eventually they stood in front of the Cathay Cinema.

Billy was visibly disappointed. The Cathay Building that had once been the hub of the controlling powers, be it British or Japanese, was not as it was when his father and Jimmy Roberts would have been recruited for their eventual clandestine Special Operations work.

"What's wrong?" asked Mary, seeing his shoulders drop.

"I'm just disappointed, Mary. All that's left of the original building is this Art Deco façade, look at the modern glass architecture behind. The Cathay was a modern building in 1941, solid, and it used to be Malaya's tallest building, would you believe. It was the first skyscraper and the first air-conditioned cinema in Singapore and a very important building.

"But that's life, time moves on. At least there's a cinema here again! It just doesn't help me create a picture in my mind of Dad and Jimmy standing outside it, as they wondered what the future held in 1941."

"Time stands still for no man, or woman, for that matter," said Mary.

Still entranced at the building's façade, as if trying to take himself back in time, Billy studied the vertical sign of the Cathay, wondering what films his father had watched here.

"What are you thinking?" interjected Mary.

"Did you know that on 15 February 1942 the British were instructed to fly a Japanese flag and a white flag at the top of the Cathay Building for ten minutes as one of the conditions of surrender," said Billy, reverting to history teacher mode.

Mary smiled and raised her eyebrows as she shook her head in fun mockery, before extracting her old black Kodak instamatic camera from her bag, Mary stopped a passer-by and asked if they would take a photograph of Billy and herself outside the Cathay. A young Singaporean man duly obliged.

"Thanks, Mary," said Billy, "I always forget to take photographs. Let's head down to Raffles. I will treat you to lunch if we can get a reservation."

"That sounds splendid, Mr Williams," said Mary in the best British officer's voice she could muster. So off they strode downhill on to busy Orchard Road, long famed as a shopping mecca. Billy hastened Mary along, as a bigger temptation, selfishly, loomed in his mind. Soon Orchard Road became Bras Basah Road. It was busy both on the sidewalks and the highway as it headed towards the sea. Neither Billy nor Mary cared for this hustle and bustle.

Passing a characterful old building that was being remodelled and brought back to life, Billy and Mary stepped into the sanctuary of its grounds, taking in the Palladian grandeur. A large hoarding said, "Singapore Art Museum due to open October 1995".

"So, it's not all high-rise modern buildings, Billy. It is nice to see them restoring such venerable old properties and another reason to return one day," Mary commented, squeezing his hand.

Billy looked up at the newly restored front of the building. It still proclaimed its original title: St Joseph's Institution founded 1862.

They re-entered the pulsating, busy throng of everyday Singapore life, passing subway stations which momentarily disgorged a stream of commuters and shoppers before they dispersed to their various appointments, jobs and destinations. Soon they approached Beach Road and Raffles Hotel came into sight. An excitement enveloped both of them, an anticipation that history was coming full circle in Billy's family.

They found their way alongside the colossal iconic structure. "Here it is! I bet this has been much changed since 1942," quipped Billy. They smiled at the bearded Sikh doormen in full costume, as if in a time warp, proud of their uniform of white turban and tunic, with red and gold collar and cuffs and hem with a black sash, epaulettes and gold braids with a broad leather belt. They certainly looked the part and made a great first impression.

A surprisingly small semi-circle of drive, lined with tropical plants, was frequented by limousines as they dropped off their important passengers. A rather swish silver Bentley eased up to the terracotta-tiled, cast-iron portico. A doorman stepped forward as the car door opened and a rather well-dressed Asian man stepped out followed in his wake by two more men both with briefcases.

It was not as big an entrance as Billy had imagined, but still grand nevertheless. He looked up at the name "Raffles Hotel", the tall black painted letters just below the apex of the building standing out on the impressive white façade of the hotel.

Mary waylaid a passing couple to take a photograph of Billy and herself alongside the splendid-looking Sikh doorman and returned the favour. The jewellery-laden fingers of the woman underlined their ability to afford the high cost of the rooms at this hotel.

Stepping in to the main building of the hotel, Billy and Mary felt like they had been transported back in time to 1941, history repeating itself. Here was where

Tom with his nurse, exhilarated, excited and amused, had stood all those years back. Now here was his son, with his nurse and lover too!

The magnificence of the lobby seemed as if it had not changed since then and Mary's breath was taken away.

"Gosh, Billy! Look at the white marble colonnades." Billy and Mary's eyes followed them three floors up to grand chandeliers that hung in wait, ready to brighten the darkening evenings.

A discreetly located reception desk lay between two of the pillars, a floral display and baby grand piano were a central focal point, but the visitors' attention was drawn to the dual Raffles staircases beyond.

"Just think," said Billy. "Over the years, some of the most famous people have walked through this lobby and up those stairs. Somerset Maugham, Rudyard Kipling, Ernest Hemingway ... Tom Williams and Violet Watkins, not forgetting Gwen Powell and Jimmy Roberts." Looking at Mary he added, "Now us." He crooked his arm for Mary to hold. "Shall we?"

Mary beamed.

"Perhaps we can stay here next time we're in Singapore," said Billy.

"Oh, it would be far too expensive here, Billy."

"Oh, I don't know, probably not much different if we had a double room instead of two singles," he said with a glint in his eye.

Tugging his arm, she retorted, "Billy Williams, will you behave?" She smiled that wicked smile that Billy loved.

They walked through to a courtyard, a green oasis of tall palm trees surrounded by white accommodation wings with terracotta roof tiles. Slowly they walked up a flight of stairs to the first-floor corridor where sunlight poured through, illuminating polished teak floorboards.

Billy said, "You can almost hear its colonial guests, 'Chin, chin'… 'Tally ho!' … 'What oh, old chap!'" Mary giggled.

As they strolled on along the historic high-ceilinged verandahs heading for the Long Bar, they passed guests reclined in rattan chairs appreciating the solitude to read, as they enjoyed the afternoon breeze. A different world, thought Billy. "Shall we go and have some lunch?" he said. "I'm famished."

"Yes, let's, we didn't eat too much for breakfast, did we?"

"No. I think we were living off the fruits of love," said Billy, playing the teaser once more.

Mary had an ability to admonish with one look of exaggerated and false displeasure, followed by a smile, which Billy was starting to understand.

"Table for two?" said Billy to the young man who greeted them in the Tiffin restaurant. The maître d' came over and looked Billy and Mary up and down before advising in a quiet and professional manner, "I am sorry, sir, madam." He looked from one to the other. "But there is a code of dress in the Tiffin restaurant. Closed toe shoes and long trousers are required for diners. But please come back for lunch or dinner, as the curry buffet is a hot favourite, both with tourists and locals alike. North Indian specialities, including vegetarian curries if you don't eat meat." He could see he was not engaging his potential diners, but he persisted enthusiastically making eye contact with Mary making her blush.

"In the afternoon, we have a classic English tradition when we serve high tea with cucumber sandwiches," he said with a smile, as his head wiggled back and forth.

Rather disappointed, Billy felt he had let Mary down but hid his blushes by reverting to humour as they walked away. Moving his head from side to side, Billy mimicked the maître d': "There is a code of dress and it's not shorts and sandals!!" They both burst out laughing and decided on a plan B.

"What does tiffin mean? Didn't there used to be a chocolate bar called that back home?" asked Mary.

"Yes, that's right," recalled Billy. "There was a Cadbury's chocolate bar full of raisins and bits of biscuit, as I remember. Tiffin is an Indian phrase meaning 'light midday meal'!"

Mary nodded, pursing her lips and smiling, quite impressed with Billy's knowledge.

Eventually, walking through a labyrinth of stairs and corridors they found the Long Bar and were immediately taken back in time.

"You can really imagine soldiers in full dress uniform sat on stools at the bar, and ladies in evening dresses, sedately sipping cocktails while fans whirred above, stirring the warm air," said Mary swooning.

But today, they were confronted with casually dressed tourists, like themselves, sipping overpriced Singapore Slings and crunching over monkey nut shells on the floor as they walked. They were shown to a glass-topped table in the corner of the bar. The steward pulled out the dark brown rattan chairs for them.

"It's smaller than I'd expected," said Billy. "Sure, it still has the fans and teak floorboards, but there is something of a commercial reproduction feel about it, rather than historical," mused Billy.

A pleasant young man took their order and returned with the obligatory Singapore Slings, which came with a bent straw, a piece of pineapple and a cherry sitting on the side of the glass, supplemented by the ubiquitous monkey nuts.

Both were disappointed by the rather tacky sign on the glasses, which stated "Singapore Sling Raffles Hotel", accompanied by some 1920s characters as a motif.

"So why are the Singapore Slings so famous?" Mary asked the waiter.

"Ah, madam, Nigiam Tong Boon, a barman here, invented this drink in this very bar in 1915. Gin, pineapple, Benedictine, cherry liqueur and Cointreau."

Interrupting, Mary asked, "What makes it pink, the cherry liqueur?"

"Ah! That is the secret ingredient I was coming to, it is Grenadine, madam!"

"Thank you," said Mary.

"You are welcome, madam, sir."

Billy had been distracted, listening to a rather loud American customer at a nearby table, telling his attendant party that this was not the original Long Bar, which was "lonnnnnng gone" and they all guffawed and carried on drinking.

"My word, it's pretty warm and humid today. I could do with a swim this afternoon," said Mary.

"But there's one more place I want to take you to this afternoon," said Billy.

Mary inclined her head to one side and looked into Billy's eyes, grinning mischievously.

"St Patrick's School, where Tom, Violet and Gwen used to meet at the mess after it was turned into a hospital."

Mary faked being disappointed, then gave Billy her most winning smile. "I will go wherever you want to go, Mr Williams!"

A short taxi ride later they stood on Marine Parade outside what was now the sea-facing St Patrick's School complex, sandwiched between Marine Parade and the East Coast Road. But because of land reclamation, it was now positioned away from the sea.

Apart from the central façade of the school building, being somewhat art deco in style, neither Billy nor Mary could imagine how it must have been in the forties for Gwen and the other nurses here. Although by the sea, the buildings did look more like dormitories, so they could see how the school lent itself to being commandeered as a hospital.

"Other hospitals where Gwen served and met Jimmy and Tom, like the St Andrew's Mission Hospital's original forties-era building, no longer exist," commented Billy.

"I'm feeling a little weary after all this sightseeing," said Mary. "Shall we go back to the hotel?"

"Yes. I'm tired and ready for a swim to refresh me," agreed Billy.

Following their swim, they showered and had a leisurely dinner before hot-footing it to the airport.

It was close, but they managed to get to Changi airport in time for the 23.30 Singapore Airlines flight to Sydney.

Billy looked fondly at Mary as she sat at the departure gate perusing a magazine. How he wished he had met her when he was younger, but the time was now!

Mary was appreciating the freedom from family responsibility. Looking at Billy she could not believe she had become so besotted.

23

It had been a long day since leaving Osaka that morning. Fifty-five-year-old Akihiko Kuroki was tired and bowed wearily to the tour guide holding up a welcome board with his name on it.

The guide responded accordingly, bowing and smiling, resplendent in national dress. "Mingalaba, mingalaba," she said excitedly, and Akihiko bowed once more followed by the predictable reciprocation from Thuzar, his excitable and animated guide. Thuzar was her Karen Tribe name, but like many, she had anglicised her name, calling herself "Judy". "Mingalabar," she effused again. "My name is Judy", her greeting enhanced warmly by her shining brown eyes and welcoming smile. He thought of his wife Miho.

Judy beckoned him to follow her as she shuffled along, whilst endeavouring to usher Akihiko, who was pulling his wheeled suitcase behind him having refused Judy's assistance. Judy smiled as she walked, looking back occasionally, just to make sure Akihiko was still in tow.

She led Akihiko through the busy arrivals hall of

Yangon airport out into the waiting hubbub of minibuses and taxi cabs. The heat and humidity of the afternoon hit them, sucking the air from their lungs. Immediately Akihiko's shirt felt damp, like a second skin on his back.

Akihiko admired Judy's long, silky black hair that fell over her gold coloured blouse, which was buttoned up the back. Her blouse overlapped the top of her mustard-yellow longyii, which in turn hugged her hips and legs down to her ankles.

Aung the driver greeted him with his cartoon-like toothy grin as he nodded and smiled, taking Akihiko's case.

Clutching his shoulder bag, Akihiko slid his small frame into the well-worn but comfortable rear seat of the old saloon car.

Yangon was busy, but nothing like Tokyo. It was drab in comparison, thought Akihiko, some would say it was in a time warp. After a short journey they checked in at the Kandawgyi Lake Hotel. Judy knew her client was tired, so she gave him his room key and arranged for the staff to help him with his bags.

"Thank you so much for visiting Myanmar. I know you are weary, so I will meet you here at 9 am tomorrow, ready for your tour of Yangon. Is that okay?"

"Yes, thank you very much, Judy. Sayonara." Akihiko bowed slightly; Judy bowed lower out of respect.

Akihiko had contemplated this journey ever since he was at university in Nagasaki. Recently retired, he mused to himself, "this has been a long time coming". Now fatigued from his journey and the excitement of his first visit to Myanmar he longed to take a hot shower and to rest.

It was approaching dusk as he turned and thanked the hotel bellboy who had brought him and his bag to his room. The young boy held the ten-dollar gratuity as if he had been given the crown jewels. The boy was transfixed, in a temporary state of inertia, before departing, bowing and thanking Akihiko effusively.

Akihiko barely assimilated the luxury of the large Governor suite. Its elegance and space, exquisite teak flooring and Burmese woodwork were lost on him. He moved to the sitting area and picked up an apple from the fruit bowl which was set in the middle of the coffee table. He sat on the end of the bed, lay back, gave out a big sigh and fell asleep.

It was first light before he awoke. He adjusted his mind to his location before visiting the bathroom, which was so large you could have fitted in three baths, thought Akihiko. He languished in the walk-in shower, relieving his aching bones under the jet of hot water which brought him back to life.

Wrapping himself in the complimentary fluffy robe, which was far too big for his small stature, he re-entered his suite and finally noticed the superb panoramic view he had of the famous Shwedagon Pagoda as it rose from the early dawn mist. The first tendrils of sunlight were bringing it to life. It had a calming effect on Akihiko, almost mesmeric, as the sun illuminated this iconic paya, as if renewing its magical aura.

He had wanted to share this adventure with his wife Miho, but she politely and firmly reminded him of the cost that would entail and encouraged him to embark alone on this pilgrimage, which she knew meant so much to him.

He had booked a suite to impress and treat her. When she had declined, he had seen no reason to change his plans.

Akihiko had met Miho at university and fallen in love almost immediately. Miho was a beautiful girl. But it was not just that, it was her caring nature, her thoughtfulness and her quick wit as she flirted with him between classes that had beguiled him.

As soon as they left university they were married, and Akihiko followed his father and his grandfather before him to become an interpreter for the foreign trade missions and companies who came to do business in Yokohama and Nagasaki. Finally, Akihiko owned his own company before selling up and retiring.

Judy was waiting in the lobby as Akihiko came down for breakfast. He saw her lovely smile and it brightened his morning. She bowed and greeted him with the already familiar "Mingalabar" and asked him if he had slept well. Nodding, Akihiko said, "I need to change some money."

"Sure," Judy replied. "There is a good foreign exchange here in the hotel, let me show you."

Akihiko followed Judy to a small room at the end of a corridor. Within was a simple desk stacked with banknotes in Kyat, the local currency, and a calculator, all supervised by an attendant cashier, whilst behind a partition, the counting of money could be seen and heard through a glass screen.

After changing his US dollars, Akihiko had his own large pile of Kyats. He smiled to himself. Judy smiled back and acknowledged his quandary as he juggled the huge stack of paper currency.

Judy courteously advised, "You can use the safety deposit box behind reception if you need to."

Akihiko gave a small look of amusement and took her advice. "Come and join me for breakfast, please," said Akihiko.

"Thank you, but I have already eaten, Uncle."

"Please just have some tea, then. I would appreciate the company." Judy graciously complied.

"Are you from Yangon?" said Akihiko, sipping Miso soup.

"I am from the south-west, from the Karen tribe, up in the Karenni Hills."

"What brought you to Yangon? Work? You speak very good English!"

"Thank you. I studied at the university in Yangon. I wanted to be a doctor but soon found languages, and in particular Japanese and English, could be put to good use, earning some tourist dollars. Maybe in the future it will be even better, right now we do not have many tourists. But life has been pretty busy."

Akihiko smiled. "Your easy, outgoing and always smiling personality is a wonderful complement to your linguistic abilities. Thank you for being my guide."

"Thank you, Uncle," said Judy coyly.

Akihiko weighed her up as he ate. Like most Burmese women she was small in stature with dark hair and beautiful walnut-coloured eyes, with their exotic, single eyelids. Judy wore a touch of thanaka on her high cheekbones and her distinctive nose, and her full lips sported a subtle light pink lipstick. Akihiko thought of

Miho, his wife, and her perfect Japanese oriental look. Then his mind became preoccupied as his thoughts diverted to his children and their futures, even though they had left home years ago.

"So," said Akihiko as he finished his coffee and brushed his mouth with his napkin, "what is this?" He pointed to her cheek.

"Ah, the use of thanaka. It is more for my guests, if I am honest. I do like to use Western cosmetics when I can, it is just far easier. It is true many of the children and ladies in Myanmar still wear thanaka, but most often to aid as a sunscreen.

"Just this morning I have ground thanaka bark with a sprinkle of water on a stone slab. I called my two children, who had just finished bathing, and they stood dutifully in front of me as I applied the watery thanaka sparingly on the exposed parts of their bodies. On each cheek I daub much thicker layers and use decorative stencils in the shape of leaves and circles on my daughter to give her individuality and style. It is a ritual performed still in many households here each day."

Akihiko inclined his head fascinated. "Is this too for the tourists?" he said, pointing to her clothes.

"This is a traditional dress, called a 'htamein', a sort of wrap-around skirt."

Akihiko admired the colours of the emerald skirt and her distinctive gold yinzi top with a detailed fastening of embroidered flowers below the padded shoulders.

After breakfast Aung the driver was waiting by the trusty old Toyota Camry and off they headed to explore Yangon.

"Are you feeling cooler with the thanaka? Maybe I

should use some?"

Judy smiled as ever and replied. "Would you like me to bring some tomorrow for you?" He just smiled and returned to viewing the passing cityscape as they approached the fabled Shwedagon Pagoda, the jewel in Yangon's crown.

"This is very impressive," said Akihiko climbing out of the car to walk up the steps to the Shwedagon reception area.

"Thank you, Uncle,' replied Judy.

Akihiko smiled. He had heard that they used the term uncle to older men. Taking off his shoes he followed Judy to explore the Golden Temple.

Finding a little shade, Judy informed Akihiko, "Shwedagon Pagoda has over 8,000 gold plates covering the monument and in excess of 5,000 diamonds and 2,000 other semi-precious stones, which create an awesome sight." Akihiko listened intently for a while, but his mind strayed to what his father may have thought when he first set eyes on this famous landmark above what was then Rangoon.

The day moved along with visits to Yangon's colonial-style city centre. Driving around the busy Sule Pagoda, dating back over 2,000 years, which appeared to be a rather elaborate traffic island today, he mused, he gazed at Independence Monument set in a park, as he passed a plethora of decaying former colonial edifices.

After a visit to the magnificent reclining Buddha at Chauk Htat Gyi, Akihiko's enthusiasm for temples and statues was dissipating and he said, "Judy, I am a little tired now. Could we have some lunch?"

"Certainly, Uncle. We shall head to the waterside. I

have a really good restaurant in mind, very restful for you." Aung guided the car through the streets until they arrived at the Nanthidar ferry terminal. Once the main arrival place for any visitor to Rangoon, it was now the Junior Duck restaurant.

"Locals refer to this as the 'Be Le'. Many famous people have passed through this building, George Orwell and Rudyard Kipling and King Thibaw with his Queen Supalayat." Akihiko was sure his father may have been one of them, but no mention came of Captain Satoshi Kuroki, but then, why would there be?

Akihiko felt the place lacked ambience as a restaurant. It still felt like a cavernous warehouse.

Meal completed, Judy asked, "How did you enjoy lunch?"

"Fine, fine," said a less-than-enthused Akihiko. As he left the restaurant he mopped his brow and his eyes were drawn to the Strand Hotel across the road.

Judy caught his gaze and proceeded to educate him with the history of this venerable establishment. "A very fine hotel, Uncle. You may be interested to know that after the Japanese occupation of Burma, this hotel was used to quarter Japanese troops. The following year, the Strand's ownership was transferred to the Imperial Hotel in Tokyo …"

Akihiko nodded but seemed irritated. He did not know if his father had been billeted here, but perhaps he had to come here to see his superior officers.

Judy continued her patter: "This hotel has been renovated and refurbished to reflect its former colonial grandeur of the 1920s." Crossing the busy road, they entered the hotel. Akihiko looked around the relatively small reception area and tried to conjure up a vision of his father standing here sixty-five years ago.

"We can come here for afternoon high tea, if you would like," said Judy.

Akihiko smiled. "I think I would like to go back to the hotel for a rest now, please." He bowed, as if wanting to accentuate his need for a break.

Judy bowed and they headed for the car. Aung drove them steadily back to the Kawdawgyi Palace, the creaking in-car air conditioning barely relieving the humidity, which was draining Akihiko's energy levels.

"Tell me," said Akihiko as he stared out of the window in contemplation. "Does the old Rangoon Jail still exist?"

There was a pause before Judy turned from the front seat to face him.

"Do you mean Insein Prison?"

"Yes," said Akihiko.

Judy shivered at the thought of the prison, which had held her father and uncles in the past, accused of crimes against the state. "I am afraid we cannot visit it, as it is a working prison. Insein has an interesting layout," she continued. "It is a wheel-shaped design, built by the British. Even now it strikes fear into most Myanmar people at the mere mention of the name. Its long blocks are like the spokes of a wheel. They fill people's minds with terror at the thought of incarceration there."

"Can we go and see it, is there a viewpoint of the prison?" said Akihiko.

"You know most of the prisoners have been political dissidents," said Judy, trying to stay on track as a tour guide without betraying her inner feelings and fear.

Insein meant such terrible conditions and consequences for some of her family and friends.

She wanted to say that the prison was notorious worldwide for its inhumane and dirty conditions, abusive techniques, and use of mental and physical torture, but felt this was best left unsaid. A certain irony, she thought, that the pronunciation is as the English would say "insane".

Akihiko nodded. "I think I must explain, my father Captain Satoshi Kuroki served in the Imperial Japanese Army, which once fought here after liberating Burma from the yolk of colonial oppression." As he did so he lowered his head and gazed directly into Judy's eyes, as if correcting her earlier statement on the Japanese arrival being an "occupation". "I am not sure if my father was billeted at the Strand Hotel, but he told stories in letters he sent to my mother about his work at Rangoon Jail, Insein Prison, which became a prisoner of war camp."

Judy forced a smile. "Sure, sure. I will show you," she said, trying to mask her lack of enthusiasm.

She knew her grandparents had suffered under the Japanese, and her own parents despised them. However, today was today and she had a job to do. She remembered a story of her grandfather helping to bury British POWs. All the men were buried by fellow prisoners of war, laid to rest in the Rangoon Cantonment Cemetery, approximately one mile from the jail. She also remembered her father saying the Japanese were very cruel, to the point of being inhuman.

Changing the subject, Akihiko turned to Judy and said, "I see Aung is chewing something. It's very common here, yes?"

Judy nodded, appreciating the diversion. "It's a national pastime. Small street stalls sell the palm-sized green leaves everywhere you go. The leaves are filled with hard squares of betel nut, spices and sometimes a pinch of tobacco and then folded up and popped in the mouth and chewed. You have to chew a while before you feel the mild narcotic effect of the betel nut."

"How much does it cost?"

"About six cents a wrap. How do you say? It's a cheap score. But there are bad side effects too. Not only does betel nut stain your teeth a reddish-brown, the little packages are spat out on the floor when finished, making for messy sidewalks." Akihiko acknowledged with a nod, barely listening, his mind elsewhere again. He sensed Judy was uncomfortable with going to Insein Prison, but why?

"It's also highly addictive," added Judy.

"So why do people chew it, especially when driving? Is that not dangerous?" Akihiko said, puzzled.

Judy merely opened her hands, as if to say that is how it is.

24

Following a fitful night's sleep, Judy rose to the occasion and looked resplendent in her traditional Karen tribe black longyii and loose-fitting lilac blouse embroidered with white flowers. She was waiting in reception for Akihiko. Nervously, she checked her jet-black lustrous hair adorned with a bright pink floral bloom. She wanted to look presentable. She smiled at her reflection in the glass door of the lobby. Outside, Aung fussed around his pride and joy, polishing his car, making sure the windows were smear free for his guest.

It was a pleasant morning as they walked down the hotel steps to the car. A flight of birds took off from a nearby tall building and circled around, then flew away to the horizon, in perfect formation against the clear blue sky, like an oil painting. Aung drove around Kandawgyi Lake and headed towards the Yangon River.

Akihiko felt Yangon in 1995 was not so very different from how it may have been during his father's time here.

Captain Satoshi Kuroki appeared to have enjoyed his time in Rangoon. He talked of the pleasant Burmese people and the wonderful stupas and sunsets. He had been surprised by the rapid victory of the mighty Imperial Army, and how proud he was to bring freedom to the Burmese. But then his father did not say too much about his time at Insein Prison.

Akihiko had a flashback at that moment to his childhood. It was of his father's benevolent smile as Akihiko would run towards him when he returned home, just before the end of the war. His father with his awkward, limping gait, was picking him up and holding him above his head and calling him "bright boy, bright boy".

Akihiko often recalled the last time his father spent time with his family at Aoshima-jinja, a Shinto shrine located in Miyazaki. A very happy time when all was at one with the world. His mother and father lived in Nagasaki, where his father worked in the huge naval yards before the war, his interpreter skills invaluable in completing deals with overseas companies but also in the day-to-day activities of the yards as different ships under different flags came and went.

Akihiko remembered that Satoshi was not the same on his last return home before going back to war. He seemed morose and taciturn and barely smiled. It was as if he was far away in his thoughts. He often snapped at Akihiko if he was playing loudly with his toys, or if he interrupted his father without warning, as children do. Then he would pick Akihiko up to mollify him and stop him crying.

Akihiko remembers asking his mother about why his father now limped, to be told he had been shot in the leg during the war. His letters home talked of being transferred to prison camp duty in Sumatra in 1943.

Akihiko felt the car slow. As the battered old Toyota reached the environs of Insein Prison, Judy felt a chill come over her. Akihiko could sense the unease in his guide and in the driver, Aung.

"We are here, Uncle," said Judy, jolting Akihiko back to the here and now from his reminiscing. "We have travelled down Bayint Naung Road," she added. "It is difficult to really appreciate the size and design of the prison. I am told it looks like a giant cartwheel from the air, but I fear with all the tree coverage around the prison, we will not be able to see much of the prison exterior, and if we drive to the main gate, we will not be allowed near, not without an invitation or arranged meeting. We have to give our reasons for visiting."

Akihiko understood. "Just get me as near as possible and that will be fine." He knew he did not have enough time to arrange a special visit, and was starting to wonder, given his motivation for visiting, whether he would have been approved or welcome, as the son of a former officer of the Japanese. An army who had once controlled the city!

Aung slowly approached the prison checkpoint.

A short verbal exchange with the guards followed as he asked if it was possible for their Japanese visitor to have a closer look at the prison. The guards appeared nervous and very hostile. Akihiko could not understand what was being said.

"Papers, papers, out, get out of your vehicle." Judy and Aung left the car quickly leaving their doors open before Judy leaned back into the car.

"Sorry, Uncle, the guards want you out of the car. Do

you have your passport with you?"

Akihiko joined them. He was asked for his passport once more, but he explained it was in the hotel safe. One of the guards leaned into Judy, almost touching her face, and growled something. Judy lowered her head.

Before long a more senior officer came along, with a wave of his hand he commanded the soldiers to step back. His smile was both intimidating and smug at the same time, making them feel as if they were all caught in a spider's web. "Why would you want to visit a prison in Yangon?" he enquired of Akihiko in good English. He raised his sunglasses, and his stare seemed to penetrate and frighten Akihiko. He was without doubt a calculating, potentially vicious adversary.

Straightening up, Akihiko smiled and said, "It was just an older building of Yangon which was interesting and novel in design, I felt it should be on my tourist journey." Akihiko had made the decision not to mention his father and the Japanese army. He felt it might only make things worse.

The officer put his sunglasses down, smiled and said something to the soldiers and disappeared. Once he was out of sight the soldiers ushered them all to the car and barked out a command. Aung quickly turned the car around and they left.

Judy apologised profusely for the reception they had witnessed, saying "This is not the normal way of Myanmar people."

Akihiko nodded and said, "No problem. I fully understand. Sorry to put you in that predicament."

Judy nodded with her hands clasped together in front of her showing her appreciation of his graciousness.

Akihiko sank back into the seat and pondered how his father may have dealt with this officer and the soldiers, but no matter.

Judy enthusiastically tried to regain the momentum of better offerings from Yangon. "Uncle, would you like to visit a Burmese tea house?"

Akihiko nodded, but said nothing. "I know just the place," added Judy.

"Can we walk a little too? I would like some exercise and, indeed, I would like to buy some sandals somewhere. It is far too hot to be wearing my office shoes."

"Most certainly. We will visit Thone Pan Hia tea house. Then we can have a leisurely walk to Bogyoke Aung San market. You can buy almost anything there, and at very good prices," beamed Judy.

Judy settled back to allow Akihiko time to reflect on the morning and instructed Aung of the plans. Placid as ever, his wide betel-nut-stained grin acknowledged the day's closing itinerary. Judy had become increasingly uncomfortable with Akihiko, or more so with the concept that her father may still, even fifty years later, consider her to be consorting with the enemy. Judy decided in that moment to go and see her mother when she had finished for the day. Her mother was now in her seventies, but she was sharp as a whip and her memory was excellent.

Judy felt that she needed to know more regarding the Second World War and the Japanese occupation of Burma. This might help her put things in perspective regarding Akihiko and his father. She did not like feeling the way she did.

Her father was now in his eighties. He said little about the war. He had been particularly bitter regarding the Japanese when they had been mentioned in the past, so she felt she should not tell him of her current assignment with a Japanese tourist, Akihiko Kuroki.

Later that day, feeling tired and relieved her morning was over, Judy entered the small, humble dwelling of her parents. It stood in a poorer area of Yangon, its shabby, flaking walls belying the tidiness within.

As she entered she stopped for a moment and watched her mother. Judy admired her finely lined face, partly covered by her wispy greying hair. She was leaning forward over the table, cutting vegetables for their evening meal.

Hearing the door Judy's mother looked up. A broad grin revealed it was already too late for remedial dental work. Drying her hands, she affectionately hugged Judy and excitedly asked her, "So, daughter, to what do we owe this visit, are you all right? How is your work?"

Judy looked over her mother's shoulder as they hugged, spying her father, who was sitting crossed-legged on the small verandah at the back of their bijou dwelling.

"Hello, father," Judy said awkwardly, fearing she was interrupting his train of thought. Her father inhaled on his cigarette and smiled at Judy and motioned for her to join him.

Judy's father refused to call her Judy. "How are you, Thuzar?" He loved the name and from the time she was born she was his "angel", the meaning of the word Thuzar.

Soon her mother joined them as they talked

pleasantries, catching up on health and neighbours' whereabouts and thoughts on the latest government decree.

Judy's father had the look of a tormented man and Judy could see he was not well again. He was rubbing a coin on his leg, especially around his knee, where he had poured some heated oil. He closed his eyes, rubbing until a red mark appeared. This was an ancient, some would say old wives' tale, that this would release the "bad" from his painful leg. No doubt something that his parents and others had done for generations before.

Judy had tried to say in the past that it may be arthritis, encouraging him to visit the doctor for some medication. He always refused to go, partly because of his old-fashioned belief and partly because of the cost of medicine.

"How are you, Father?"

"Fine, fine," he said dismissively.

Judy knew she needed to broach the subject of the Japanese and their occupation during the Second World War. Her inquisitive nature was too strong to hold back. "Father, I wonder if you can help me? I have a Japanese tourist I am showing around Yangon." There, she had said it.

Her father immediately raised his hand as if to stop any further conversation. He stood awkwardly and walked inside.

Judy's mother apologised and said, "He had a hard time with the Japanese, or at least his parents did.

"Your grandfather had been one of the 3,500 or more volunteers who were armed by the Japanese in the Burma Independence Army, which entered the Karen hills from Thailand at the end of 1941 to support the invading Japanese 15th Army.

"They wanted independence and came after the formation of the 'Thirty comrades' under Aung San and other senior agitators who were the catalyst for this force."

Judy's father reappeared, interrupting, "You know little about this, *may-may*." Judy's father continued the story. "Despite a lot of hard effort, and loss of good friends, Burma's 'independence' was not declared until August 1943. It was never a true independence. Many young people immediately went back to more undercover activities when we realised the Japanese were just another occupying master. A cruel people.

"We disappeared from the towns. In the countryside we met people of all persuasions, such as the Communist Party, Burma's oldest political party, led by Thakin Soe. We knew they had refused to join our Burma Independence movement and continued to oppose what they saw as the main problem, fascism. Thein Pe Myint was a communist. He and others made their way to India through Arakan, to join the British as allies, and to get arms and support."

"Where was Grandfather at this time?" asked Judy.

"I will come to that," said her father as he lit up another cigarette, coughing as he inhaled. His red, tired eyes watered. He held his knee once more, then continued. Judy's mother fanned him to alleviate the humid heat, but he waved her away, irritated by the interruption.

"An important meeting of Communist, Socialist and Burma Independence Army leaders took place in Pegu in August 1944 unbeknown to the Japanese. Your grandfather was at this meeting as an aide to Aung San. It transpired they agreed to join forces together, in a united front, headed by Aung San, calling themselves the 'Anti-Fascist People's Freedom League', and the result was a plan for a second nationalist revolt.

"It took a while to get everything agreed and arranged and supported by the British, who had some men here, still hidden after their earlier defeats. The British were working against the Japanese mostly with our tribe of people in the Karenni mountains and all over, down to the Sittang Delta.

"We commenced our offensive on 27 March. I remember it well. It was your grandfather's birthday.

"As the British attacked from India, Aung San ordered his units to surprise the Japanese and attack their positions. This caught out the mighty Imperial Army totally." Judy's father smiled proudly. "Our army, now called the Burmese National Army, fought hard. My father lost many friends, but we the Karen," he said, banging his chest, "alongside other Burmese army elements, were first back into Rangoon. We had liberated our capital." He nodded defiantly before continuing.

"Grandfather, your Ah-Poh and grandmother had been arrested as enemies of the Japanese regime by the Kempeitai. This meant they were taken to Insein Prison. After interrogation they were executed. They refused to give information about me and my fellow fighters' whereabouts. Before they were executed they were tortured cruelly, then after execution their heads were severed and put on public display.

"I will never forgive the Japanese. If only I could have got my hands on those evil Kempeitai!"

Judy's father bowed his head and started to shake a little. It was the first time Judy could ever remember him being so emotional.

He composed himself quickly, continuing, "But forcing the Japanese out of Rangoon and Burma was not the end of our troubles as a nation.

"That was just the start of things. Everyone wanted their say to force their own ideas on the others. Aung San still held sway but many of the Thirty Comrades would struggle to agree a way forward, so much so that in July 1947 Aung San was assassinated right here in Rangoon, at the Secretariat building." With that her father stuttered, hesitated and then started to cry.

"Dad," said Judy. Her father held up his hand, regaining his composure. "Two of your aunties were also taken and used as sex slaves for the Kempeitai. They were bayoneted as the Japanese retreated, being of no further use to these animals."

A silence descended on the room

Judy's father kept going, reliving the whole scenario that he had kept to himself for so long. "Ne Win plotted and eventually seized power in 1962, the Burmese Army, or Tatmadaw, took control and many of the Thirty Comrades disappeared to set up counter-activities in secret locations around Burma, which is why there is so much time spent by the current government trying to seek out these people and destroy them. Only Aung San Suu Kyi can bring unity, but I fear she is too weak, just a woman, against the generals."

Judy and her mother hugged each other and saw the

pain her father was feeling.

"I was young, the excitement of independence soon changed back to fear. It has been a long life of subjection, not least by our own people!"

Now Judy felt a mixture of emotions: anger, strength from the knowledge she now possessed and admiration for her grandfather and indeed her father for the pain he had borne all these years without sharing.

*****

The next morning Akihiko packed his belongings. His sojourn in Myanmar had come to an end. His mind was full of memories of his father and perhaps even though many questions were unanswered, he felt closer to his father having walked in his footsteps.

Judy, professional as ever, greeted him and Aung collected them. Together they took Akihiko to the airport. Judy helped with his bags and escorted him to the check-in desk for his flight on Silk Air to Singapore.

"Thank you so much for visiting my country. I hope you have enjoyed your stay." She bowed to her waist.

Akihiko said, "I remember you saying you were from the Karen tribe. I thought the women from that tribe wore a lot of gold bands around their neck, making them long necked?"

"You are right and you are wrong," responded Judy. "It is a sub-tribe of the Karen called 'Padaung' you may be thinking of."

Akihiko sensed a sudden terseness in her reply, but he thought no more of it. "Thank you for your benevolence and knowledge," he said as he handed her an envelope, before disappearing to passport control. He did not turn or wave; he was gone.

Judy turned and did not look back either. As she sat in the car from the airport she decided whatever money was in the envelope she would give to her father but not tell him where it came from.

Akihiko planned for a few days' stopover in Singapore. Here he would rendezvous with his family before returning to Japan. As he sat on the plane for the relatively short flight, he read a letter which he had found in his father's diary. It was headed with the address "Cathay Building, Syonan-to". Following some earlier research, he understood Syonan-to to be the old Japanese name given to Singapore following the defeat of the British. It meant "Light of the South".

In the letter addressed to his wife, his father said, "How happy the people were to have been liberated from the British yolk of oppression and how happy the children were learning Japanese. The children faced Japan every morning and sang the Japanese national anthem. It made me proud."

Satoshi had written that the people loved Japanese films and were really taking to Japanese culture. He went on to say how much he missed Akihiko and his mother and that soon he would return with gifts and one day he would take them both to Syonan-to.

His father talked of the plan for a "Syonan Jinja", a shrine to commemorate Japanese soldiers who had died in Singapore.

Akihiko really wanted to see this shrine. The Singapore tourist board were not very helpful. They told him that it was inaccessible, consumed by jungle or forest somewhere. This had made Akihiko angry. *Why had it not been respected like the Western memorials were?*

He understood Singapore was a developing nation and had changed greatly, becoming very modern and forward-thinking. He did not expect too much to reflect his father's time in Singapore from 1942, which was the date on his father's letter.

After collecting his bags, he decided to greet his family rather than meet them at the hotel, so he waited the two hours for their flight arrival. As his family came through the Arrivals Hall Akihiko was so pleased to see his son Kin, which meant "golden" and his daughter Cho, meaning "butterfly". Looking a little tired and bewildered, Miho's eyes lit up when she saw Akihiko.

Akihiko's children were grown up now, in their thirties, but he still thought of them as his responsibility. Kin was tall compared to his parents, who were barely up to his shoulder. Conversely, Cho was petite, like her mother, but there was a vibrancy about her. Within the parameter of her typically Japanese black bob of shaped hair, her long Roman nose led to a sweet mouth of perfectly shaped, pale pink full lips. But it was her eyes that gave you a clue to her soul, dark brown, almost ebony, and mournful, tear-drop shaped.

His children's partners were unable to make the journey, but Akihiko was glad of time with his family alone, back together again. He looked forward to telling them of his father's life in Burma and Singapore during the war.

He was disappointed he had no grandchildren. He put this down to the effects of the nuclear bomb fallout in Nagasaki skipping a generation, although there was no proof of this. It fuelled a deep-down anger and bitterness that surfaced now and again for Akihiko and many of his generation.

Staying at the Goodwood Hotel on Orchard Road, they enjoyed a welcome dinner together and an early night. Akihiko had missed Miho and watched as she ironed his clothes for the following day. He had offered to send them to the laundry, but she thought this unnecessary.

Studying a recently purchased guidebook, Akihiko had planned an itinerary for the family.

"So, what is the plan, Aki?" said Miho as she watched Akihiko poring over a map of Singapore.

"Well, we will first of all visit the botanical gardens, with its tranquil, tropical walkways. It has many of your favourite orchids, and so many other species too." Miho smiled; she loved her plants.

"Next, we will take a tour out to the zoo on Mandai Lake, which has Asian elephants, white tigers, orangutans, long-nosed proboscis monkeys and pygmy hippos."

Throughout the following day they took many photographs, the children raising "v" signs with their fingers in most that included them, a custom Akihiko puzzled at.

As dusk approached they headed for Raffles Hotel. Akihiko settled down around a table with his family in the Long Bar. Akihiko looked at his wife Miho and their children, and he let out a huge sigh of contentment.

"It's so good to have you all here. If only my father could be here, too. He would be as proud as I am. He was certainly a visitor to Raffles Hotel during the war, you know," said Akihiko proudly.

"He was a great man and would have loved to have met you all. He was a fine man, a warrior, and very loyal to the emperor."

Kin and Cho nodded, but inside felt uneasy, as the bar was so full of Western tourists. But they accepted that their father was proud of their grandfather.

Soon the drinks came. Akihiko insisted that he and Miho indulged themselves by ordering Singapore Slings.

"Kampai," said their father as they all raised their glasses and held them there. "To my honourable father, Captain Satoshi Kuroki."

Akihiko became louder as he had another drink, followed by another. He bemoaned how the Western world was still making up terrible things about his father and other esteemed Japanese soldiers of the Imperial Army. "How could they be asking us to own up to scurrilous war crime claims and demanding reparations? It was war, not a board game like 'Monopoly' with rules! Anyway, none of it is true."

With that his son stood and said "Father, we cannot live in the past." He turned and walked away. His sister Cho stood too, bowed to her mother and father and followed her brother Kin.

Shocked, Akihiko shouted across the bar "Come back here at once." But they were gone.

People around them were showing their dissatisfaction. A wave of muttering swept through the bar.

Akihiko grunted and muttered and then belligerently summoned the waiting staff for another drink. Miho just sat there saying nothing.

"Can I help, sir?" asked the bar manager as he approached the table, leaning into Akihiko and quietly adding, "Please can you perhaps be a little quieter, as you are disturbing some of our customers."

Rising from his seat, Akihiko scowled. He fixed the manager with a withering look. Growling, "You have no respect," and oblivious to the stares from other tables, he stormed out of the Long Bar followed by Miho shuffling along in his wake. She bowed in apology to the manager as she left.

Next morning Akihiko did not see his children at breakfast. "So where are Cho and Kin this morning?" said Akihiko.

"I believe they decided to go out early," Miho explained. "They were visiting the Peranakan Museum to learn about some of the original indigenous people."

Akihiko said nothing and just ate his breakfast in silence.

That evening the family came together for a farewell dinner at the Goodwood Hotel. Unabashed and unapologetic for the previous day's outburst, Akihiko shared his experiences of his recent visit to Myanmar with his family, as if nothing had taken place the day before. Reverently and politely, they listened, but before long Akihiko mentioned the war again.

Staying impartial and distant from his feelings and experience of their grandfather, Kin spoke up. "Father, it was so long ago, and the world has changed, views have changed."

Akihiko tried not to show his anger this time. He was proud of his father and felt the lack of acknowledgement from his children of his father's achievements and war service was disrespectful.

Cho, thoughtful as ever, played the peacemaker. "Mother and father, do you remember when as a child I travelled with my school to the Peace Park in Hiroshima? We learned how this awful war should never visit our country ever again and that the world should be at peace."

Miho smiled and nodded. Akihiko merely looked across the restaurant and said nothing. Akihiko's memories of the terrible destruction on the day the bomb was dropped on his home city came flooding back. As far as he was concerned the younger generation knew nothing of this pain and would never understand.

He felt this act was barbaric and the devil's work and blamed the British for their colonialism and support for the Americans, whilst the Japanese were trying to free the people of Asia from their colonial oppressors. Even though he and his mother had miraculously escaped the blast, he remembered the resultant devastation of the Nagasaki bomb.

"I remember the 'black rain' full of dirt and debris. The abiding memory I have is of telegraph poles that stood at odd angles, and landmarks I once knew were gone, obliterated. Buildings destroyed completely, others gutted by fire. It was as if a huge wind had blown through Nagasaki and flattened everything for miles around.

"I heard stories of survivors, known as 'hibakusha', who had terrible injuries. But it was later when people had symptoms such as nausea, burns, a susceptibility to leukemia, cataracts and tumours from the radiation that the true toll was counted.

"Many people had died instantly, some vaporised. Others with burns tried to soothe themselves in the river. The awful disfigurement I witnessed in the days and weeks and months that followed left a huge impression on me as a child. You, my children, could never understand, but don't ever forget."

Nothing more was said.

Next morning, they all headed back to the airport, but Kin and Cho had disappointed their father again. Not just because of last night or in the Long Bar at Raffles and what he saw as a lack of respect and loyalty.

"Sorry, father, that we are travelling onwards into Asia, not returning with you to Japan right now," said Kin.

"We are travelling to Siem Reap to visit the amazing temples of Angkor Wat and then plan to travel around Cambodia and Laos. It's a chance to explore and see different cultures. If we get the chance we may get to Myanmar and see where Grandfather was during the war."

Akihiko knew this was just to allay his disaffection. As they said their goodbyes, Miho, tears in her eyes, turned to Akihiko. "At least we can have time together, Akihiko, now you are retired. Something we have not had much of in all the years you have worked so hard."

He scowled, nodded and they headed off to their gate to join their flight to Osaka.

25

It was early morning when they arrived in Sydney. Mary was dressed in a light cotton dress and Billy in T-shirt and shorts and they shivered a little as they made their way quickly from the taxi to the reception desk of the Renaissance Hotel.

It was winter in Sydney and the cool morning air had rather surprised them.

"G'day. Welcome to the Renaissance Hotel," said the receptionist. "Fa' too cold for me today," she announced, revealing her strong Australian accent. She observed the lightly clothed couple standing in front of her. "Been somewhere warm, have we?"

"Indeed," replied Billy. "Is it always this cold in July here in Sydney?"

"Pretty much. I had to clear ice off my windscreen this morning. I reckon it's usually the coldest month of the year for us!"

Billy handed over his reservation voucher for two single rooms. "I wonder if you have a double room available?" asked Billy in a soft tone.

The receptionist looked up to see Mary drifting off

into the lobby. "I am so sorry, er … Mr Williams," she said, looking down at the voucher details. "We only have an executive suite available for the three nights you plan to be with us. It is beautiful, though, with fabulous views."

"I'll take it," said Billy, proffering his Visa card and anxious to conclude the transaction.

Like two children on an adventure, they held hands without talking. The fast elevator sped them to the 32nd floor. Opening the suite door, Billy watched as Mary's eyes were agog and immediately drawn to the picture window.

"Oh, my Goodness, look at the view, Billy." She dropped her bag and, open-mouthed, took in the panoramic vista.

Billy put his arm around her waist. She turned, he felt her soft warm lips inflame his desire. He picked her up and carried her through the sitting area to the king-size bed, their lips not parting. Billy's shorts and Mary's underwear flew away from the bed like grass cuttings from a mower.

Slipping out of bed Mary headed for the bathroom. "Welcome to Sydney, Mr Williams," she called without turning around.

Billy, revived by his shower, came into the large lounge area of the suite to see Mary holding her towel in front of her leaving the curve of her back open to his gaze. He could see she was transfixed by the view over Sydney Harbour and Circular Quay and in awe of the iconic Opera House beyond.

The harbour was a hive of activity, ferry boats coming and going to Manly and other destinations, smaller craft dodging between the shipping lanes.

Crossing the carpeted room, his white fluffy bath towel wrapped around his waist, he kissed her neck just behind the ear. She reached back with her right arm, bringing his head forward with its hair still damp. She swivelled and looked into his eyes. "Thank you."

It was still only midday when they walked hand in hand the short distance down Pitt Street to Circular Quay. Now in jeans and with a few thin layers to ward off the autumnal feel of Sydney, Billy said, "I don't think we'll need our extra layers for long. I understand the temperature is going to be warming up, as Sydney does at this time of year. It will soon reach a balmy 13 degrees centigrade."

"Darn," said Mary, chuckling. "You had my hopes up there."

Billy had initially planned to head for the area known as the Rocks, an old part of Sydney with its terraced houses and old cafes and pubs but figured it would be good to get up close and personal with the harbour area first. Mary was just happy to be there.

"Let's check out the Opera House," said Billy, leading Mary by the hand along the quayside. They mingled with tourists and locals heading about their business, coming to and from the port gates on their ferry commute in and out of the city.

Their attention was drawn to a young aboriginal man, his body painted with inexplicable patterns. Soon they were enthralled by his musical dexterity as he played the didgeridoo. It gave the illusion of vibration, his mouth sideways on as he blew into the long, light wooden tube. It was decorated with what appeared to be a large lizard, its body drawn in a white, maroon and gold chequered pattern, as if it had sieved its prey once eaten. At the top and bottom of the drawing the same colour combination was painted around in bands.

The haunting, rising and falling bass sound of the instrument was mesmeric. Mary stood beside the performer as Billy took their picture and dropped a few coins in his collection box. Then the guy stopped playing.

Mary couldn't help but say, "Hello. That was really good, how long have you played the …"

"Didgeridoo, miss, since I was a kid," and before long this enterprising young fellow educated Billy and Mary.

Mary was fascinated by the young man's dark cocoa-toned skin and his firm body, with its alternate white and gold markings and then the angled white stripes that resembled feathers.

"My name is Wakijima, and the colours all mean something. The white being for my ancestors and the maroon red for their spirits. The didgeridoo itself is made of eucalyptus wood. The painting was done by hand, using a piece of grass as a brush."

He was proud to tell them the didgeridoo was made by his grandfather who lived in Katherine in the Northern Territories. Mary and Billy were spellbound.

Billy asked, "What is the meaning of the lizard?"

Wakajima smiled, his rough black hair rising with his raised forehead and the white marks on his face moving in unison. "This is a 'Wardapi' or you may hear it called a 'Goanna', a large lizard, for sure. It represents our heritage, the Goanna dreaming of our ancestral spirits."

He invited Billy to have a go, but Billy failed miserably. He looked at Mary, who laughed and put her arm around him. "Billy, that was like a sassenach trying to play the bagpipes." Both laughed, the young man joining in, even though the analogy had left him nonplussed and somewhat confused.

Their aboriginal friend explained the technique. "You have to breathe through the nose while pushing the stored air out of the mouth with the tongue and cheeks, whilst continuously vibrating the lips to produce the sound. Ladies did not play the didgeridoo in Aboriginal culture, but they were allowed to dance." Mary frowned.

Billy nodded without truly understanding the methodology of creating the didgeridoo sound. "Go on, then, Mary, give us a jig."

"Not a chance, Billy boy," she said laughing.

Billy and Mary strolled away, leaving the young man to draw other tourists into his mystical world. Moving around the harbour quay, they looked across to the fabulous Sydney Harbour Bridge. They had seen it many times on television, especially on New Year's Eve, when the BBC News showed the fireworks display and celebrations.

Mary leaned against the rail, scanning the view as she tried to keep the hair out of her eyes as the breeze picked up, making her eyes water and slightly smudging her mascara. "I can't believe we're here, Billy!"

Billy took a photograph of Mary and managed to get the bridge in the background with its three flags atop whipping in the wind. Wavelets appeared in the bay, accentuating the cool breeze and encouraging them to move on and head the short distance to the Opera House, in the hope of some respite from the cooler air.

"I feel like I should pinch myself," said Mary. As they stood marvelling at the distinctive concertina shell of its exterior, which they had seen in so many pictures, Billy once more was about to take a photograph when a passing couple offered to photograph them together.

Billy put his arm around Mary's waist, pulling her closer. Mary raised her shoulders, loving the moment and their first picture together in Sydney.

Billy and Mary put on their extra sweaters to keep out the wind blowing off the harbour.

"Now," said Billy. "I am sure we are both hungry, and there is so much to see and do, but we need to focus on the main reason we are here." He raised his eyebrows.

"Spoken like a true teacher," said Mary.

Ignoring Mary's jibe, Billy continued, "We need to establish if Susan is here in Sydney or indeed, dare I say it, see if she is still alive."

"Yes, you're right, Billy. But I'm so excited. I just can't believe we're here," she said, holding and squeezing his arm whilst taking in the Harbour Bridge, Opera House and the north shore. "Isn't this fabulous?"

"It certainly is. Let's head for the tourist information office and see how far Caroline Street is and where we can get some food, as I'm starting to feel peckish. Is that okay?"

Mary took stock of all the posters in the tourist information office at The Rocks, covering the Great Barrier Reef, Great Ocean Drive and Ayers Rock, while

Billy made enquiries.

Billy returned to Mary, map and leaflets in hand.

Mary looked at Billy, then the poster on the wall. "Can we visit the Blue Mountains while we're here?" she asked, pointing to a picture of rock pinnacles called the Three Sisters. "They look fabulous."

"At the risk of making you blue," he said with a smile, "let's see how we go."

"Please!"

"Let's see how things pan out," he repeated. "We need to eat first, then take a taxi to a district called Redfern, which is where Caroline Street is. Apparently, if we go a short way from here there's a pub called The Australian. I'm told it has some fair dinkum tucker," he said, mimicking a very bad Australian accent.

The Australian was easy to find. A two-storey, flat-iron-shaped building, on a slight camber as the harbour road ascended. It was juxtaposed with high-rise modern buildings nearby.

"It looks like a typical old coastal harbour pub that could have been in Plymouth or Portsmouth," Billy said as they approached. "Except it has a distinct Aussie flavour with those large glass windows stencilled with 'draught beer being served'."

Although there was a canopy outside, covering pavement dining, Billy figured it would be warmer and cosier inside. Pushing through the throng of lunchtime clientele to the side of the pub they settled a table with red leather chairs, the upholstery sturdily secured with studs. Sure, there were some Aussies in there, but Billy and Mary could make out Japanese, English and many other accents and languages.

Neither of them was ready for the emu and kangaroo pizza with bush tomato on the menu, so they settled on Aussie beef burgers swashed down with draught beer.

Replete and ready to investigate, they took the cab the publican had kindly called for them. Rising from Darling harbour, they seemed to be heading towards the university according to the road signs and followed train tracks for some of the way. It took twenty minutes to reach Redfern, an area that seemed to be up and coming, with warehouses and Victorian terraces appearing to be enjoying a new lease of life.

Finally, they turned into Caroline Street and parked outside an ornate two-storey terraced house full of character, its red door covered by a metal-grilled exterior door beckoning Billy and Mary forward.

As the cab pulled away they stood full of trepidation on the other side of the tree-lined road and looked at the wrought-iron second-floor balcony above the street. They could see the door was open, presumably to a bedroom, meaning someone was almost certainly at home.

A garret window, unusual in the terrace, stood out from the corrugated tin roof. It looked well-kept compared to the rusting covering next door.

Mary looked at Billy. It had been many years since Mary had seen Susan. If she was there, would she recognise her? Billy just could not think straight now he was here, he was not even sure what the plan was, other than he was fulfilling his father's wishes.

Holding hands, more for support this time than anything else, they crossed the road to 43 Caroline Street, as the breeze gusted and lulled almost as if to announce or warn of them. Billy knocked at the door tentatively, almost as if they did not want anyone to answer.

For a few moments nothing, then the door opened slightly. A young man peered around the door frame. Billy estimated he was early to mid-twenties, not very tall and with a smooth fair complexion. His eyes squinted below his short fair hair, yet there was no sun in his cornflower-blue eyes.

"How you going, mate, can I help?"

Mary was the first to respond. "So sorry to bother you, but we wonder if a Susan Duncan lives here?"

"Hang on …" He called over his shoulder, "Mum, somebody here for you."

Their excitement rose. A minute or so passed, which seemed an age, then the door opened further.

For a moment Mary was not sure, then she could see the indisputable, albeit slightly laughter-lined, face of her childhood friend. She was smaller than she remembered and looked older than she'd imagined.

"Susan …?" said Mary, in an exploratory, tentative tone.

Susan stepped nearer, bringing her visitors into focus. "Mary … Mary Anderson, is that you?"

The grille door opened and Mary stepped forward. She hugged her friend tightly and tears came from them both. The young man was bemused, Billy just stood back as they observed the emotion and power of the girls' reunion.

Susan, holding Mary away from her said, "You haven't changed."

"And you haven't grown," Mary retorted and they all

laughed.

"Come on in. Danny, put the kettle on, this is a very old friend of mine from Britain," said Susan.

They went into the narrow hallway of the house with its light varnished wooden floorboards. With a brick wall to their left they passed a small study to the right before following the attractive traditional flooring into the bijou living room made smaller by the ascending staircase.

A long white linen couch seemed to stretch the length of the wall, looking towards a Victorian fireplace, which had a solid iron grate, brown ceramic tiles either side and a wooden mantelpiece above, bedecked with two small ornaments, all set below a large mirror, which, aided by the high ceiling, gave an airiness to the room.

Susan brought a small coffee table from its resting place under the open staircase and placed it in front of Billy and Mary who had settled on the settee.

"Oh, this is my good friend, Billy," Mary said in belated introduction.

Billy held Susan's small hand in his and thought of Violet. Her daughter did not look a lot like Violet, except perhaps around the mouth. Her nose was long but cute, her light green eyes peeked from tanned smooth skin.

Her white cheesecloth shirt contrasted with her silky, long black hair, which had hints of grey, as it fell like a waterfall down her back to her waist, finishing just above her blue jeans. It made her stature look even more petite. Her comfortable persona did not give any clues of the resolve this woman must have had. To leave home and come across the world to the former home of her mother … It was this thought he held and tried to fathom.

Before long the young man returned with a tray and teapot and a plate of cakes.

"My word, you have this young man trained," said Mary. "Is this…?"

"This is my son Danny." Susan stood proudly clutching his waist, Danny draping his arm around his mother's shoulder.

"Wow, I can't believe it," said Susan, sitting by Mary and hugging her some more. How did you find me? Why are you here?" A deluge of questions cascaded out.

26

"It's a long story," said Mary. "But Billy, here," she said, patting his leg, "was given an envelope which was once sent from your grandfather to Billy's father and that is where we had this address from."

Susan inclined her head and gave a bemused glance at Billy, waiting for an explanation.

Mary, also looking at Billy, added, "When Billy came into my life ... well, before I tell you how Billy and I met, I will let Billy take over."

Billy studied Susan. Her high cheekbones made it seem as if she was constantly smiling. "It would appear that your mother and my father ..." he hesitated. "Well, shall we say, had a bit of a fling, many years ago in wartime Singapore," he went on.

Susan gave a winsome smile.

Billy produced the now well-fingered photograph of Gwen, Tom and Violet.

Susan held it with both hands, her elbows resting on her knees, peering in astonishment. She drank in the scene of her mother looking so happy. Her eyes watered, Mary put her arm around Susan's shoulders.

"I really have missed her," said Susan. "Wasn't she beautiful? I have missed her dreadfully and I know I've been very selfish," she continued, wiping a tear from her eye. "Mum has never met Danny, and for all I know, she doesn't even know he exists."

Full of remorse, she sobbed, her body convulsing as the years of pain flowed out. "I feel so guilty, leaving her alone with that man," she said with a cracked voice.

Billy passed Susan a handkerchief, which she gratefully accepted.

"Did you know that Ronald Duncan, your father, had died?" asked Mary.

"He wasn't my father," said Susan firmly as she turned red-eyed towards Mary. "When did he die?"

"At least fifteen years ago. I suspected you didn't know, as you weren't at the funeral and …"

"I'm almost afraid to ask, but how is Mum? Is she still alive …?"

There was a momentary silence. Mary looked apprehensively at Billy, then at Susan, seeing the hope and fear on her face. "Yes, she is still alive …" Mary held Susan's hand. "But, Susan, she has dementia, rather badly, I'm afraid. She doesn't recognise people very well now."

"Is she still at home?"

"No, she's in a nursing home, on the Scottish mainland." Striking an upbeat tone Mary continued, "But your Mum is in good health otherwise, and well looked after. I try and call on her when I can.

"I actually nursed your mum for a while at Lamlash hospital, over five years ago now. She had fallen at home and broken a hip."

Susan looked so forlorn as she learned of her mother's slow but sure deterioration.

"Your mum did go home, but she seemed to go downhill in many ways after that. It's difficult to explain. It was as if she didn't have the will to go on. Yet she is still with us."

"I wish I could see her, just for a moment. I need to hold her and tell her I love her," said Susan. She looked up at Danny, who was standing by the fireplace. Shifting from foot to foot, he looked uncomfortable seeing his mother so bereft. "I would love for her and Danny to meet." Susan took a deep breath and tried to compose herself.

"You said earlier that Ronald Duncan was not your father. Do you know who your father was?" questioned Billy.

Mary gave Billy an agitated look, annoyed he was badgering her friend at such a time. Before Susan had the chance to respond to Billy Mary proceeded to fill in the blanks in the years since she had last seen Susan, telling her about her rise to the post of Sister at the hospital in Lamlash and apologising for losing touch.

Billy had sat quietly and watched Susan and Mary get reacquainted. He could see that even after all this time there was still a real affinity between them. The joy in their eyes as they remembered and laughed about their childhood memories, inconsequential to others, but treasure to them, was wonderful to behold.

"Other than that, not a lot has changed. Mrs Macleod is older but still runs the Post Office. The tide still comes in and goes out, and the winter is darn miserable, I bet you don't miss that, Susan," beamed Mary.

"I bet the midges are still as bad in the summer, too," said Susan with a weak smile.

"You're right there. Susan, do you still nurse?"

"I do a couple of days a week at the local children's hospital. Mum gave me this address when I said I planned to come out here nursing. She told me not to say anything to my father. Ron, that is.

"When I arrived, the family weren't really expecting me. Mum said she would write to my grandfather, but I suppose the letter took a while to come, or maybe she never did write.

"But after getting over the initial shock grandfather was so pleased to see me and could not have been more welcoming. What I didn't know at the time was that he was ill, in fact he was slowly dying.

"He was a lovely man and we clicked straight away, we got on really well. I felt he loved me like a daughter, it was such a change to being in that house in Lamlash.

"I looked after Pops as he deteriorated. He thought he had bronchitis and used to take all sorts of medication. Finally, after some tests, he was diagnosed with lung cancer. He battled away for over a year.

"He had left the house to Mum, as she was the only one of his children still alive. But when he learned from me how things were in Lamlash, he changed his mind. He altered his will and left this house to me.

"Perhaps he also did this because I was pregnant and he wanted me to have a future for myself and the bairn, I don't know. I'm not sure if he tried to contact Mum again. He said he had written in the past, but he had received no reply.

"When I first arrived, my cousin Vaughan was living

here with Granddad, but we didn't get on. He was abusing Grandad's good nature and I told him so. He called me names, he referred to me as a 'Pommie bastard' and constantly belittled me and after a few months he left in a huff. I don't know where he is now, I haven't heard from him for many years.

"Not many months after I came to Sydney, I actually met a nice guy, a doctor. We got on very well, as friends and colleagues. Then … well, our relationship flourished. I had Danny a year or so later, we planned to marry, but Danny's father, Gerry … Gerry Brady, was tragically killed in a car crash," she said, her voice breaking.

"Oh, Susan! I am so sorry," said Mary, hugging Susan again.

"It was devastating. Just when I thought my life was on the up, and we were going to have a real-life stable family, full of love, something I had always wanted and admired in other families, it was snatched away from me." Holding both Mary's hands and looking into her eyes, she added, "I am happy, Mary." She looked up at Danny. "I am so lucky to have Danny. I think of what I have in my life, not what I have lost! Danny is my best friend, at least we have each other.

"Do you know Mary, I wrote for two years after coming out here in 1969. But my letters were returned unopened. I used to enclose a note for Mum to give to you, too. I thought Mum didn't reply because she was upset that I'd left. I understood, I had left her alone, trapped in a dreadful relationship.

"My mother never replied. I kept sending Christmas cards and birthday cards to Mum for years afterwards.

Then I just stopped, when Danny was about five years old. I became resigned to the fact that I had lost my mother and never knew my father. I swore then that I would always be there for Danny."

Mary and Billy both felt so much compassion for Susan; it was hard not to.

Then Danny chimed in, his Aussie accent vehement and almost aggressive, "I bet your old goat of a stepfather intercepted the letters and your Mum never even saw them."

"We don't know that," said Susan, "but I wouldn't put it past him!"

"Maybe one day you will find your real father," said Billy softly.

Susan looked at Billy. "I wouldn't know where to start. If I ever asked Mum the question, I was shut down quickly. Mum just said it was a wartime liaison and she would not want to rake up the past. She said, 'What's done is done. Ronald is your father now!'" Susan's tone was tinged with bitterness.

Mary looked at Susan. "Did your mother have any photographs of your real father or any letters from him?"

"I'm not sure. If she did, she never shared them with me."

"Well, how about I take you all out to dinner?" said Billy trying to lighten the moment. "I suspect you know some good places to eat around here."

"And I would love to see where you work," said Mary. "I seem to recall you used to write to me from the Prince of Wales hospital."

"So sorry we lost touch," said Susan, hugging Mary

once more.

"What sort of food would you like to eat?" asked Danny.

"Danny is the food expert. He's also a trained chef but tends to write articles for magazines rather than chef right now," said Susan proudly as she stood and ran her hand lovingly down his face. "What do you think, Billy?"

"Well, I do like a good steak," replied Billy, almost salivating at the thought.

"But we are on the ocean here," said Mary. "We really should go for seafood, I think."

"Where are you staying?" asked Danny.

"The Renaissance on Pitt Street."

"Only one place we ought to be heading for seafood and tradition is Doyles on the Beach. We'll need to take a cab. Do you guys need to freshen up? We could head back to your hotel and then get out to Doyle's in time for a sundowner! It's tricky to get a table but I know the owners, so fingers crossed," said Danny confidently.

Before they knew it, the taxi was arriving at the small and delightfully situated Doyles on the foreshore of Watson Bay.

Danny was greeted with gusto by the maître d', who seemed to know him well and was pleased to see him. The party were shown to a beachside table bedecked in white tablecloth and blue napkins.

"Boy, look at that panorama," said Mary.

"Wow! Is that the Sydney skyline and the top of the Harbour Bridge I can make out?"

"It sure is," said Danny, pleased with his recommendation.

The restaurant was surrounded by lush vegetation, a perfect position when it started in 1885 and just as relevant 110 years later. Norfolk Pines stood like weathermen reading the sea breezes. The building's cream clapperboard façade with cream and green structural supports and canopies helped it blend into the landscape.

A blue table umbrella rippled above them in the light warm breeze giving them perfect shade from the bright early evening sun. The scraping of chairs could be heard on the wooden verandah above as new people arrived for an early dinner. The ladies ordered exotic cocktails, Billy a glass of red wine and Danny a pint of Fosters, just in time to watch the sun go down.

Boats were bobbing in the semi-circular bay, the water almost lapping at their feet. There were rowing boats upturned on the narrow strip of sand and promenade. It reminded Mary a little of Lamlash and home. She stirred her mango, lemon and cherry fruit liqueur-filled extravaganza. As she sucked on the straw, the elixir found her taste buds and her eyes watered as she did so.

"Cheers," said Billy. The cacophony of response echoed his salute.

"This is a wonderful place," said Mary. "Thank you so much, Danny, for organising this."

"My pleasure," said Danny, raising his glass once more. "It's a special occasion."

Susan patted Danny's hand. "Well done, son."

The menu was a cornucopia of seafood. The choice of dishes was superb, and a smorgasbord of marine life descended on the table throughout the evening. From seafood chowder to oysters Kilpatrick, mussels, whiting fillets in a deliciously light batter and, much to Mary's delight, a whole, locally caught snapper.

"The co-founder, Alice Doyle, created recipes that still survive and are served here today. She certainly had a winning formula," said Danny.

Their feast was complemented by a vibrant, citrusy and crisp Semillon from the Hunter Valley.

The sun set over the Sydney Harbour Bridge and lights started to twinkle in the distant cityscape. The party were relaxed and replete.

Susan had been thinking of their conversation earlier that day. "How would I go about finding who my father is, Billy?"

"Ummm. That's a good question. I'm not quite sure where to start, Susan. What does it say on your birth certificate?" replied Billy as he sipped his wine.

"It shows Ronald Duncan as my father. I recall Mum telling me when I needed the birth certificate for my passport application. He had registered the birth with his army administration department in 1945/46 sort of time as he was still in the Royal Army Medical Corps. Then a British birth certificate was issued by the Registrar of Births and Deaths later.

"I did look into it many years ago, when I needed this birth certificate for my passport," continued Susan. "But I didn't think any more of it until now. I really owe it to Danny to find out who his grandfather really is and Mum is unlikely to supply the answers."

"Well, we need to find out for you and Danny," said Mary. "Don't we, Billy?" Billy responded with a nod.

"Perhaps we need to find out more about your Mum

Violet's release from the POW camp and her time in Singapore. That might help us. Also, I wonder if anyone is still living, and perhaps even in Australia, who knew your mum in the camps?" said Billy.

Susan swallowed and looked sheepishly at Mary. "So, you know about Mum being a prisoner of war?"

"Yes, Susan, but only recently from a friend of Billy's father. Did your mum tell you?"

"No, Mary, it was a sort of family secret, my Grandfather told me before he died and when I wrote to Mum to ask her about her experiences I had no reply, so figured that was not something she wanted to talk about. Pops didn't say much. He seemed … well, it was clear he was upset by the thought of Mum being subjected to jail, it must have been tough for him and Nan to deal with. I guess the not knowing if she was alive during the war and then her going to live in Britain must have hurt them. But he still loved Mum so much he would often talk about her childhood and playing games with her and going for walks and picnics."

Billy interjected. "I can understand that, Susan. I have met a lady called Gwen, who was a good friend of Violet before and during the war. She was the other nurse in the photo I showed you earlier, but she was as surprised as me when she heard about the fact that Violet had a daughter. She also longs to find out more about you and indeed what happened to your mother.

"I think we need to go back to the Australian Army Nursing Corps and see if they have a list of other nurses who served with Violet. Hopefully they may still have a contact for some."

A chill breeze blew off the harbour, and Susan pulled

her wrap around her shoulders. Danny suggested they return to Sydney on the ferry as a novelty and once the *Susie O'Neill* arrived they boarded for Circular Quay, content with their evening and company, and their new mission.

27

Next day, a bright morning came into focus as Billy opened his eyes and squinted at the clock, showing 7.30 am. He shuffled half asleep across to the window, with its fabulous vista high over Sydney Harbour. He just felt he had to keep drinking it in and savouring the moment. It was a view he could never get tired of.

He looked back at Mary, who was still sleeping. She was lying on her back, arms above her head. Her hair spread like a flame over the pillow. Her slender neck and elegant shoulders visible above the white cotton sheet, her covered chest rose and fell with her shallow rhythmic breathing. Billy found her slumber soothing to watch.

Settling himself in the chair by the window, Billy extracted a letter from his document folder and looked at the number he needed to call Nurse Gregson. He checked the address, which was in Canberra. Perhaps, Billy pondered, if they could travel to the national archive they could find out more about the circumstances and predicament in which Gwen and Violet found themselves. Maybe learn something of the time when they both left Sumatra and arrived in Singapore and what happened then.

Mary was awoken by a rapping at the door. Billy answered, annoyed Mary had been disturbed.

"Thank you so much," said Billy as the waiter delivered the breakfast tray, depositing it on the table by the window. He rearranged the orchid in the vase between the plates as he did so.

"Anything else I can help you with?" asked the young waiter.

Billy shook his head, tucking a tip into his hand.

"Thank you, sir. Have a good day!" said the young man, nodding towards Mary as he left the room. She was now sitting up in bed, the sheets hiding her modesty.

"Wow! This is a treat," she said, stepping out of bed, as Billy held out a white fluffy bathrobe for her to slip into.

Mary freed her hair from the neck of the robe and shook it loose. Kissing Billy on the cheek, she followed him to their window table.

"Sleep well?"

"Pretty well," said Mary, as she speared some mango.

Billy smiled and looked out across the bay. "Coffee or tea? I took the liberty of ordering both."

"Coffee. As it comes please," said Mary.

"I've been thinking. I was going to ring the Royal Australian Army Nursing Corps. They're in Canberra. We could fly or drive there to see them and have a good look though the archive. But I still feel the best bet is finding someone still alive from the forties. Somebody who knew Violet on Sumatra, or indeed recalls anything from when Violet got back to Singapore after the war. What do you think?"

Mary thought for a moment as she scraped butter on to a piece of well-toasted bread. "I agree, but how do we go about finding someone?"

"Well, I propose we go to the main Sydney newspaper and tell our story, and even perhaps the local radio. I'm sure the fact we're trying to find someone who knew Violet, to fill in the blanks of the story, would be of interest to one or both of them.

"We could tell them a little about Violet. If Susan is in agreement, she could be the local interest, telling them she knows nothing of her mother's wartime experience. Also, as it's the fifty-year anniversary of the war ending, and there are lots of celebrations and commemorations going on, it has to be newsworthy!"

Mary concurred. "That's quite true, the subject is topical, and it could be a lot faster than doing document searches that potentially take a lot of time and throw up nothing new. It's worth a shot, Billy."

After showering they headed down to reception and checked with the desk staff the name of the main newspaper, and where the local radio station was.

They made a quick telephone call to Susan, who thought it was a great idea to involve the local media and agreed to their plan, albeit with some trepidation. They arranged to meet downtown that afternoon to discuss it further.

Two hours later, Susan and Danny joined Mary and Billy in the reception of ABC Radio Sydney, waiting to see programme presenter David Oliver, who had been intrigued enough to see them at short notice.

"Well done, guys, you work fast," said Susan.

"If you don't ask you don't get!" said Billy.

"Can I get you both a coffee?"

"Yes, please," said Susan, "just black for me."

Billy and Danny headed off to find coffee for them all.

"So," said Susan, "how long have you known this guy, did you say?"

Mary smiled. "I suppose it's been a couple of months."

"Wow. Well, I guess that's what you might call a whirlwind romance."

"He's a great guy, Susan. He treats me so well and makes me feel good!"

"I bet he does," said Susan, tapping her friend's hand and smiling mischievously, as Billy and Danny returned with four coffees.

"Sorry to keep you," said a young lady arriving at the same time. "Mr Oliver is ready to see you now. Please follow me."

David Oliver sat in his small, somewhat untidy office, papers everywhere on his desk. As Mary and Susan sat in the only available chairs Billy and Danny stood behind them. Billy assessed David Oliver as middle-aged, with long, unruly hair and a goatee beard, both with a hint of grey. His shirt buttons strained under his well-fed form as he leaned back in his seat.

"Look, I would like to help," said David Oliver after listening to their story, mostly from Billy.

"I think it would be great if we could find someone who knew your mum, Susan. May I call you Susan?"

Susan nodded enthusiastically.

Tugging at his beard in contemplation he said, "I think the angle should be … well, to start with anyway … Childhood friends meet after over thirty years apart, to try and find out what happened to Susan's mother in World War II. We can focus on the fact that both friends are nurses, too, we could emphasise that as your mother, Susan, was also a nurse. But, of course, Susan's mother nursed under very different circumstances during the war," he said, looking around at them all.

Susan and Mary looked at one another and agreed excitedly.

Billy said, "What about my father's part in all this?"

"Sure, of course. We can mention that your father's letter is what brought them together again but of course the main story has to be linked to Violet Watkins, a Sydney girl, and what she went through during the war for her country and how she survived. It fits in well with our current story patterns, with VJ Day coming up.

"We of course need to focus on and find out how Violet survived the surrender to the Japanese and her incarceration, with a view to telling them what we know, and asking if anyone knows her and can add to the story.

"Now, I will get my researcher on this. I realise you are only here on vacation," said David looking at Billy and Mary. "Shall we say a little spot on the radio this coming Sunday morning? That should give us a little time to work out an interview and pitch and get some background done."

"Yes! That sounds great," said Mary excitedly. Susan nodded her approval.

"Billy?" said Mary.

"I guess I could go up to Canberra while you both do that," said Billy somewhat sulkily.

"That's great, then. 9 am Sunday morning we'll go on air. Can you be here for 8.30?"

"Yes," confirmed Susan. "That'll be just fine. I don't work again until Tuesday."

Billy said nothing as they all walked out into the bright Sydney afternoon sunlight. It was warmer today.

"You seem quiet," said Mary to Billy, as they all stood on the sidewalk. "You aren't really going to go all the way to Canberra, are you?"

"I was thinking, while you both get better acquainted this morning, I could go and have a word with the *Sydney Herald*. I believe there is a reporter there called Felicity McIntosh who we've been advised might be the person to see."

"Shouldn't we all go together?" asked Mary.

"I think it would be good for you both to have some time together." Without more ado, he pecked Mary on the cheek. "I'll catch you back at the hotel later, Mary," said Billy, waving his hand to them both before heading across the street.

"Is Billy okay?" said Susan.

"Sure, I think he's just a little tired after all the travelling and being with us ladies all the time," she said with a little giggle. "Probably needs some time on his own, to clear his head and think straight on how we can best find someone who knew your mum."

"Well, shall we get some lunch?" said Susan, shrugging her shoulders in mischievous invitation.

As they walked down the street arm in arm towards

the harbour area, it was just like being schoolgirls all over again. That afternoon Susan and Mary had fun talking about something and nothing.

When Mary returned to the hotel Billy was lying on the bed reading a paper. He didn't look up.

Mary shut the door a little harder than she would normally, but still he didn't greet her.

"Look, I hate silences, what's the matter, Billy?"

"What do you mean?" said Billy, folding the newspaper and swinging his legs off the bed. He sat pensively staring at her. He saw Mary was not in the mood for games. He walked over to Mary and tried to kiss her, but she leaned back, crossing her arms.

"Okay! Okay! I'm sorry, you're right. I threw my toys out of the pram. I have been so invested in this whole search, in finding information about Violet Watkins, but that presenter chap just cut me out."

"That's the fault of Susan and myself, is it?" Billy was about to reply but Mary continued. "For what it's worth, I thought the presenter was right in his approach to our search for more information, both about Susan's mother's wartime experiences, and staying topical with this being the fiftieth anniversary of the war finishing. As indeed you said yourself earlier today."

Billy tried to hug Mary, but she turned and walked towards the window, keeping her back to him. "Of course it's not your fault, I guess I'm just a little tired and I was disappointed and … look, I'm sorry I overreacted," said Billy as he approached her, wrapping his strong arms around her and kissing her on the back of her head.

She turned, he kissed her lips. They were soft and

tasted sweet, her breath smelt of coffee.

She pushed him away playfully. "Apology accepted. I need to shower. We're going to take a harbour cruise this evening, you need to get ready too."

"That's great. What time is the boat booked for?"

"Danny and Susan are picking us up at six."

Mary did not see the frown on Billy's face as she walked to the bathroom.

A couple of hours later they were cruising the Sydney Harbour with Captain Cook Cruises. Billy soon warmed to the fabulous experience of watching the sun set over the water. He watched the lights of Sydney twinkle as the light faded to dark and the evening cityscape took on a different persona. He breathed a sigh of contentment as they dined on steak and lobster. *What is there not to like about this?* he said silently to himself.

"So, Billy, how did your visit to the *Sydney Herald* go?" asked Susan.

"Pretty well, thank you. I managed to have a brief word with Flick McIntosh, who said she would be happy to write an article based on the information I gave her. She suggested it would be better, though, if I wrote an open letter to anyone who may have served with, or known, Violet Watkins in Singapore or Sumatra during the war."

"That's great," said Danny.

Billy continued, "… and they would print it this Sunday. She then said that if someone comes forward she is happy to interview them. With us, of course, and hopefully have a feature in the coming week's paper."

"Did you write a letter?"

"I did indeed, with the help of Flick's assistant, a

lovely girl called Sasha, who was very helpful and good fun."

Mary bristled. "Do you have a copy of the letter?"

"No, but it will be in the paper soon!" said Billy, taking another sip of a very palatable Penfold red wine called Rawsons Retreat.

"So, what did you say?" prompted Susan.

"I love this Penfold wine," said Billy.

"You ought to try a bottle of their 'Grange', it's likely to win an award this year, that's for sure," said Danny.

"Billy …" said Susan.

Billy cut his steak purposefully and held it on the end of his fork before looking up at Susan. "In a nutshell, I just said that your mother served with the Australian Army Nursing Service in Malaya and Singapore, and that she was captured by the Japanese and held in Sumatra, and is there anyone out there who may have served with her or known her during the war. Is that all right?" asked Billy defensively.

Susan raised her eyebrows, then carried on eating.

The boat hit the wake of a larger vessel coming into the harbour and moved gently with the swell like a plastic duck on bath water. Susan looked at Mary, and then through the window beyond to the Opera House, which for some reason, at that moment, reminded her of an armadillo with its hackles up.

28

Sunday soon came. Billy and Mary met Susan and Danny down at the ABC radio station.

Danny and Billy watched behind a glass screen as Susan and Mary were shown into the studio. "Right," said the assistant, "let's just check these headsets are working." Mary and Susan adjusted the earphones, making sure their hair was tucked behind their ears.

"G'day again, ladies," greeted David Oliver, as he bounced into the room. "How are you? All okay with the headsets? Good," he said, without waiting for a reply.

Mary and Susan nodded, smiling. "We're just fine, thank you, David," said Susan, resplendent in bright red lipstick.

"Right, we'll be on air in about ten minutes. Let me just run you through a few things. Firstly, I will introduce you both, then give a bit of background to your relationship and the reason you're here today. Then we'll head into the question-and-answer scenario. I ask you a question and point at you to answer. Please relax and take your time to reply. Let's have a little practice.

"Good morning, listeners, this is David Oliver. Today we have two ladies here, who have just met again after over forty years apart. Now, as you know, it is the fiftieth anniversary of the end of World War II and next month we will celebrate VJ Day for the fiftieth time.

"Good morning, ladies."

"Good morning," replied Mary and Susan in unison.

"Now the reason we are speaking to Susan and Mary today is we're hoping that you wonderful people out there may be able to help us find out what happened to Susan's mother, Violet. So, cast your minds back all those years to the forties and World War II.

"We do know that Violet Watkins joined the Australian Army Nursing Service and served in Malaya before escaping Singapore in 1942, but she was then captured by the Japanese and imprisoned in awful conditions on Sumatra, until at least 1945.

"We are going to talk a little about Violet, and of course about these lovely ladies here with me, who were childhood friends. But first, does anyone know or remember Violet Watkins? She was a Sydney-born girl, who served with the Australian Army Nursing Service."

Overall the interview probably took about twenty minutes. David Oliver was very accommodating at one or two moments when Susan became a little emotional.

"Well done, ladies. I think that went pretty well. Let's see what response we get now!"

After thanking David for his help, Mary and Susan were shown along to a small reception suite where there were some easy chairs and a low wooden table with magazines on it. A pot of coffee simmered on a hob. A large window afforded views out across the Central Business District of Sydney.

"So, what happens now?" Susan asked the fresh-faced young woman who had escorted them from the studio.

"Mr Oliver needs to finish his show. But don't fret, one of his assistants will be with you shortly. Feel free to help yourselves to coffee."

A few minutes later Danny entered the room full of gusto and enthusiasm. "That sounded great, you did really well, Mum!"

Billy arrived in Danny's wake, adding to the plaudits. The aroma of strong coffee filled the air as Danny poured them all a cup, whilst they talked over what was said on air and relived the whole experience.

About twenty minutes later the door opened and an excitable young fellow swept in. He brushed his flaxen hair from his eyes with one hand, holding a clipboard in the other.

"Hi, everyone. My name is Jake. We have had a few calls already, many talking about the war and Singapore in particular. Plus, one or two prisoner of war experiences too. Unfortunately, no calls from anyone who knew Violet Watkins as yet, but there is still time."

"Well, I guess we just wait and see then," said Billy. "Meanwhile, Mary, I have a surprise for you. Guess where you and I are off to tomorrow?" he exclaimed with an air of excitement.

Sipping her coffee, Mary looked intrigued. "I have no idea."

"The Blue Mountains."

"Wow! That's fantastic! Thank you!" beamed Mary.

"That's great," said Susan. "You will love them."

Nothing more came of the interview that day, but they remained hopeful. The open letter Billy and the *Sydney Herald* assistant had concocted appeared in the newspaper that same day.

Next morning Billy and Mary set off for the Blue Mountains, escorted by a private guide. It was a fine day as they headed out west from the city through Paramatta and followed the ascending Great Western Highway. It took them just over an hour, passing through the little town of Katoomba.

"Wow, this place looks as though it's stuck in the fifties," commented Billy.

Their guide Bruce smiled and nodded. "You're right there, sir. They don't like a lot of change around here," he chortled.

Soon they arrived at Echo Point and the Three Sisters landmark. Three strangely shaped freestanding rock forms towered as sentinels above the forest of eucalyptus. The traces of early morning mountain mist, which hung ethereally above and around the trees, reminded Billy of areas of Wales.

"So why are they called the Blue Mountains?" asked Billy.

"Ah! That is from the eucalyptus trees, whose dispersed oil droplets, combined with dust particles and light refraction, give an illusion of blue air and thus create the name 'Blue Mountains'."

Billy looked at Mary, then back at their guide. "It's not very blue this morning."

"No, conditions are not so good today. Maybe later," said Bruce, shrugging. He was proving to be very knowledgeable, and had a dry wit tinged with sarcasm that resonated with Billy and Mary's sense of humour.

It was a lot cooler up here in the mountains and Mary drew her pashmina tightly around her. "So why are they called the Three Sisters?" she enquired, her arm locked in Billy's.

"Well, there are a number of versions of the legend, but this is mine," winked Bruce.

"The Aborigines believe that three sisters, Meehni, Wimlah and Gunnedoo of the Katoomba tribe lived in the Jamison Valley.

"These beautiful young ladies fell in love with three brothers from the Nepean tribe, yet tribal law forbade them to marry. The brothers were not happy with this so decided to capture the three sisters by force. Well, this caused a big conflict between the tribes.

"As the lives of the three sisters were in big danger, a witch doctor from the Katoomba tribe turned the three sisters into stone to protect them from any harm.

"He intended to reverse the spell when the battle was over, but the witch doctor himself was killed. As only he could reverse the spell to return the ladies to their former beauty, the sisters remain in their magnificent rock formation as a reminder of this battle for generations to come."

"Wow, that's a neat story," said Mary.

It had been a long day. Arriving back at the Renaissance Hotel, they parted company. Bruce thanked Billy for his tip and implored them to contact him if they wanted to visit anywhere else, suggesting the Hunter Valley to enjoy some wine tasting.

Entering the lobby, they went to collect their key

from reception.

"Oh! Mr Williams," said the receptionist, looking up and recognising Billy. "Have you had a good day?"

"Yes. A 'bonzer' day, as you guys like to say."

With a smirk the receptionist continued. "You have a visitor. She has been waiting quite some time. I did say that I didn't know when you'd be back from your little excursion. But she insisted she would wait."

The receptionist pointed over Billy's shoulder towards an older woman, who was sat on a couch reading the *Sydney Herald*. A teapot and empty cup sat on a low table in front of her. She was smartly dressed in a sky-blue trouser suit. As they approached her, Mary noticed a brooch of red and blue stones shaped like a leaf on her right lapel.

"Hello! How can I help you? I'm Billy Williams and this is Mary Anderson, I believe you have been waiting for us."

"Hello," she said. As she rose a little unsteadily, she folded the copy of the *Sydney Herald* and responded. "I'm Mavis Walker. I have come about your letter in this paper. I knew Violet!"

Billy had mentioned he was staying at the Renaissance Hotel in his published letter but had presumed anybody with information would contact the newspaper.

Mavis was surprisingly erect when she stood, her shoulders back as if standing to attention. Her small light-blue eyes sat deep in their sockets, but there was a keenness about them. Her handshake was firm and committed.

"So good to meet you," said Billy.

308

"Can we go somewhere to talk?" asked Mavis in a commanding tone.

"Certainly," said Billy, escorting her to the elevator and the eleventh floor.

"My word," exclaimed Mavis as she entered their room, immediately spellbound by the space and opulence of the Opera Suite in its elevated location and the splendid view before her. Even though Mavis had lived in Sydney for most of her life, she never failed to marvel at the beautiful harbour of her home city.

"Please make yourself comfortable," said Billy.

"Can I order you some fresh coffee or tea?" asked Mary.

"I would love a cup of tea, please," said Mavis, as she settled on the small couch facing the window and laid her large black leather handbag by her feet.

After a little small talk about the weather and Billy and Mary's day in the Blue Mountains the tray of fresh tea and coffee arrived.

Billy explained to Mavis how Mary and he had met, and their subsequent mission to find out more about Violet. He also mentioned that Susan, Violet's daughter, lived in Sydney and that was why they were here, too.

Mary observed Mavis as Billy filled in the background. Mavis was clearly in her seventies or possibly even eighties, and whilst a little frail physically, perhaps, Mary determined Mavis was certainly on the ball, and was assimilating every bit of information Billy conferred on her.

"So how did you know Violet Watkins?"

"Well," said Mavis as she picked up her cup and saucer and sipped, her pinky finger extended. "Oh, that's lovely tea. It tastes so much better from a china cup, don't you think?" Looking between Billy and Mary to the view beyond as if staring into the past, she began.

"I first met Vi at nurses training in Sydney, before we were all shipped to the Far East and our first post, which was Malaya, a place called Malacca.

"My first impression was that she was a flighty young lady, somewhat air-headed. But I was proved very wrong, as she was just as dedicated as any of us. She was full of ability and application, as the rest of us soon found out. She was also rather good fun to be with," added Mavis, raising her eyebrows and smiling, as she seemed to have a picture of her in her mind's eye.

"Unfortunately, as you know, the pace of war changed things. We as a group saw less of her socially in Singapore once we were transferred there. It transpired Violet had other friends she visited." Mavis smiled and winked.

"However, Vi never let her social life get in the way of work, she was always on the ball. As things became difficult, and of course the tide of war turned, the pressure was on. As you know, we were all evacuated, well, those of us who were lucky enough to get out of Singapore unscathed, anyway. But little did we know the hell we were letting ourselves in for."

Over the next hour Mavis recanted and confirmed a lot of what Billy and Mary already knew, the desperation, fear, physical and mental torture and deprivation all the prisoners had endured.

"Muntok was awful, a number of windowless stone buildings. There were raised concrete platforms for sleeping on at the side of the hut, sloping towards the central walkway. At the far end of the room there was a small room with just a tap and a water tank, we used to splash ourselves with water to try and wash. There was a room we used for the latrine, there was no western-style toilet, if you know what I mean.

"There were men in one block and women and children in ours. In our section were Australian and British nurses alongside some Chinese or perhaps Malay nurses, VADs too."

Mary looked confused.

Mavis explained. "Sorry, Voluntary Aid Detachment nurses. There were some doctors in the men's block. A number of civilians, mostly women and children. We were eventually moved to Palembang and then back to Muntok, over time.

"We did have some bright moments, especially when Margaret Dryburgh started the choir. She had apparently been a missionary and teacher, and she had the knack of remembering music and words, and wrote them all down from memory, an amazing lady.

"It took our minds off the darn awful living conditions and diet, a small bowl of rice and thin vegetable soup twice a day." Mavis wrung her hands and took a sharp intake of breath. Almost as if she felt the hunger pangs in that moment once more. "That was, if we were lucky.

"We all learned the 'Captives' hymn', I can still remember it now, you know." Mavis cleared her throat and quietly started to sing, her voice so tuneful even at her age. As she sang, her volume rose until she stood, almost as if she was saluting her past.

Give us patience to endure
Keep our hearts serene and pure
Grant us courage, charity
Greater faith, humility
Readiness to own thy will
Be we free or captive still.

"Sorry," said Mavis as she sat and retrieved a small handkerchief from her suit sleeve. She dabbed her eyes. "It still makes me upset, even today, as I think of the good friends I left behind in that God-forsaken place!"

"I can understand," said Mary, her voice quivering. She leaned forward and touched Mavis's arm. "Yet I believe, not having endured what you have, I can never really truly comprehend your suffering."

Mavis sat erect once more, her eyes now soft, thankful for Mary's words. "It was a terrible time, but here I am. In this beautiful location, enjoying your company and hospitality."

For a few minutes, which seemed like an age, nothing was said. Billy put his hand on Mary's shoulder as a show of solidarity with her shared sentiments.

"Then, when we thought it couldn't get worse, we were taken to the 'House of the Seven Seas', or so the Japanese called it," Mavis continued, a bitterness in her voice.

"When was this?" asked Billy, trying to establish a time frame.

Mavis thought for a moment. "Early 1944, I think, yes, I'm sure ... early 1944. What ensued destroyed the souls of many of us.

"A group of us were selected at tenko. Some were

told they were going to work in a bar, but we all knew, or should I say suspected, the Japs' true intentions.

"One young Dutch girl was selected, and her mother tried to hang onto her, but the mother was beaten to the ground as they dragged the young girl away.

"To her credit Vi stepped forward and said, 'take me instead', so they did. It was an incredibly brave and selfless act by Vi to forfeit herself.

"We were transported by army truck. Bouncing along the pitted road, we clutched a few belongings we carried with us. Finally, we reached a grand-looking, former colonial house. We were shepherded into this former private home. Before long, a man, Captain Kuroki, who I remember well, even today, came to greet us. He was a softly spoken man and didn't seem to have the conviction of his words. I can't explain, really, he didn't seem like a lot of the other Japanese officers we met, he seemed kinder.

"Our photographs were taken and we were given names of flowers.

"So, officers would select us by our floral name. We protested, of course. We said this was against the Geneva Convention, but our pleas fell on deaf ears. My name was 'Tokeiso', which apparently is Japanese for 'passion flower'.

"We had been brought to a brothel, which was euphemistically called a 'comfort station'. It was for the use of their troops. In fairness, it was mostly officers we were to serve, but what did that matter? Our misery of fear and trepidation was about to get worse, as we were raped and brutally treated. It was continual, day after day, for three months, many times a day.

313

"Kuroki's men took pleasure in sadistically subjecting us to ridicule and abuse, especially one of the doctors who was supposed to give us health checks. We were given injections against venereal disease, but as well as checking our health he also took advantage of his position and raped us too.

"We heard stories of girls who became pregnant being beaten and kicked. Then if this failed to bring on a miscarriage, they were almost disembowelled to destroy the life inside them and left dreadfully scarred, physically and emotionally. It was a living hell.

"After what felt like an eternity, we were all woken up one day and given fifteen minutes to collect our belongings. They put us in an army truck. We feared the worst. We thought they were going to execute us. Some of us by then almost didn't care. But much to our surprise, we were returned to the prisoner of war camp at Palembang."

"So how did Violet cope with all this?"

"Well, that's just it. We didn't see much of her in the house. She was kept apart from us. It soon became clear she was the personal property of Kuroki. We saw her going out in the Bentley with the Japanese Rising Sun pennant blowing in the breeze at the front of the car. She was laughing and smiling. If we did get any eye contact with her, she ignored us. Are you familiar with the wartime name 'Tokyo Rose?'"

"I recall my father referring to that name," said Billy. "But I can't remember why."

"Well, 'Tokyo Rose' was the name given to an English-speaking woman who was responsible for Japanese propaganda that was broadcast over the radio airwaves. She endeavoured to demoralise the Allied troops, by suggesting their families needed them at home, and their wives might be unfaithful while they are away. She exaggerated or made up terrible military losses for the Allies and the futility of opposing the Japanese war machine."

Mavis took another sip of her now cold tea. "Violet was given the nickname of 'Tokyo Sue' by the others. Her flower name was 'Suisen' which means 'daffodil'. She was generally thought of as being a collaborator. It was felt she had not suffered like the rest of us, being the sole paramour of Captain Kuroki. Personally, I had sympathy for her. She used her good looks and guile to survive. When we returned to camp, she did not.

"I didn't set eyes on her again until over a year later when we were back in Singapore after liberation. We were waiting to be shipped home. I had stayed on a while to help with the constant flow of still sick people and returning prisoners of war into the hospital.

"I visited Raffles with a fellow nurse one day, under the escort of some doctors. As we entered the lobby, there was Violet."

"So, when was this?" questioned Billy.

"This was probably around October 1945. I didn't get to speak to her. Our eyes met briefly, after my colleague laughed at a joke one of the doctors had told, and Violet looked over. Our gazes met, but nothing was said. She was with a tall, angular-faced, British army officer.

"I wish I could meet and speak to Violet and understand what happened to her back then. But as you have informed me, due to her health, this will never be possible. Perhaps we should let bygones be bygones, but the emotional scarring is such that I cannot. Maybe Violet is blessed to have dementia, and not have to recall the horrors of war."

"Mavis, did you get married and have children after the war?" asked Mary, her brow furrowed.

"I married my job. I went on to become a matron before retiring. I felt too soiled to give myself to any man, so became absorbed by my work."

With that, pushing on the side of the chair, Mavis rose, bringing their chat to an end, her independence shining through. "I feel I must go now. I'm tired. It has been a pleasure meeting you both and I hope I have answered some of your questions and not upset you too much. Thank you for listening to the recollections of an old lady."

Billy admired this resolute character, the likes of which he could not imagine amongst the current generation, but then war can create bravery in adversity and develop character that people never show in peacetime, he thought.

"May we keep in touch?" said Mary.

"Of course, let me give you my address and telephone number."

"I am sure the journalist at the *Sydney Herald*, Felicity Mcintosh, would love to do an article on your wartime experiences but …" Billy's voice tapered off as her saw Mavis shaking her head.

"I don't think so, Billy, I would rather this just stayed between ourselves."

Descending in the lift they reached the lobby. Reception arranged for a taxi home for Mavis as they said their goodbyes. "Would you speak to Violet's daughter, Susan, if she wanted to chat?" Mary asked Mavis. "I am sure she would love to meet you."

Mavis smiled. Without answering she nestled into the rear seat of the cab, putting her hand up to wave as they headed off up Pitt Street.

Billy looked at Mary. Both had mixed emotions. Exhausted by the intensity of their meeting with Mavis, they were both elated and confused.

"Gosh! What should we tell Susan?" wondered Mary.

29

"Hi, Susan, it's Mary here."

"Oh, hi, Mary! How did your Blue Mountains visit go?" asked Susan enthusiastically.

"It was just splendid, and we had a fabulous guide called Bruce, would you believe? We resisted asking if his wife was Sheila," said Mary chuckling.

"That's great," said Susan, getting the humour.

"Susan, you know Billy wrote a letter in the *Sydney Herald*?"

"Yes. I read it today."

"Well, when we arrived back from our tour, a most amazing lady was waiting for us, and she knew your mother from the war."

"Wow! That's fantastic. Is she still there?"

"No. But we had a long chat with her."

"Oh! Really?"

Mary could sense the disappointment in Susan's voice at not being involved. "Her name is Mavis. She was very sprightly for her age, but she soon tired or we would have called you to come over. Shall we get together this evening or tomorrow, so we can share what Mavis had to tell us?"

"Sure, that would be fine. Shall I come down to the hotel in an hour or two? Danny is out and about, so it will just be me."

"Let's do that. We can chat over dinner then," said Mary apprehensively.

Susan put the receiver down and walked into her rear yard, looking up to the heavens. The sky was blue, the sun was bright but there was a cool chill in the air. A slight breeze ruffled her hair, like a harbinger of unsettling news about to arrive.

Running her fingers through her hair, she threw off her grey sweatshirt, sliding her tracksuit bottoms and underwear to the bathroom floor as she ran a long hot shower.

Rhythmically and slowly she moved her head anti-clockwise then clockwise as the therapeutic cascade from the showerhead eased her knotted shoulders and ran over her crossed arms.

Invigorated, she towelled her body dry, dried her hair and applied a little pale peach lipstick. Leaving a note for Danny, the door clicked shut behind her and she headed downtown.

Following a recommendation from the hotel concierge, Billy and Mary had secured a reservation at Alfredo's, an Italian restaurant in a historic red-brick building on Circular Quay.

They met Susan under the 'Alfredo' sign above the understated entrance, which was in the green, white and red colours of the Italian flag.

"Hi, Susan, you certainly got yourself sorted quickly to get down here so fast!" said Mary.

Susan pecked Mary and Billy on the cheek.

Greeted at the door, they were shown up the few steps into the restaurant. A soothing background of Italian classical music sung by some wonderful tenor serenaded them to their table.

Mary, Billy and Susan were soon settled into the Italian ambience around a table with a white linen cloth laid with green wine goblets and red glass water tumblers. After a sip or two of Valpolicella and a preamble of the day's Blue Mountain adventure, Mary was relaxed enough to start her story about Mavis.

Susan listened intently. She realised her anxiety had been warranted as Mary concluded her tale. Mary and Billy were aware that Susan had remained very quiet, her face had not shown any real emotion or reaction.

"Remember we only have this woman's thoughts and opinions, she may have an axe to grind and not be telling the story in a very favourable light," said Billy, endeavouring to take the tension out of the air.

Antipasti and the main courses came and went.

"It's lovely food," said Susan.

"Yes indeed," agreed Mary. "Have we upset you, my dear?"

"Mary … Billy … If I am upset, it is at what my mother and Mavis and all the other women, and men and children, had to endure. I know my mother, she is resilient and a survivor, she would have done whatever it takes to get through this terrible time.

"I witnessed this resolve in her when she lived with my stepfather. She did it for the greater good, or at least to make sure she and I had a roof above our head. I never really appreciated it at the time, in fact I was mad at her for putting up with so much from my stepfather.

"All these stories just make me very sad she never shared this with me. I could have understood better why she tolerated Ron Duncan if she had. After all, he was nothing compared to what the Japs inflicted on Mum.

"But I am sad for her, that a clearly very outgoing, happy lady was reduced to a prisoner in wartime and peace. I rather suspect it was the norm for her." Susan brushed a tear from her cheek.

"I am just bereft. I will never be able to discuss this with her, as she would not be able to explain anything to me now. But I feel I need to see her while I can. I have put it off too long. I must make plans to see her before it's too late.

"First, though, I would like to meet Mavis Walker. I have one of two questions for her."

Mary leaned across the table and put her hand on Susan's. "You're so brave and understanding, Susan, two of the things I have always loved about you. Never one to shy away from a challenge."

"On the contrary, I left my mother alone and abandoned her. I will never forgive myself," replied Susan, her face hard and determined in equal measure. "But maybe, just maybe, I can make amends, albeit belatedly. First I need to speak to Mavis Walker."

The next afternoon, following a phone call, Mary, Billy and Susan arranged to visit Mavis. At first Mavis was reluctant to see them, making all sorts of excuses, which ranged from not feeling well, to having a hairdresser's appointment, but finally here they were in Parramatta.

Susan had debated whether they should take the

river ferry to Charles Wharf, but the train seemed the more reliable option for the near twenty-mile journey west from downtown Sydney.

Standing outside the small, tin-roofed bungalow with its delightful Victorian ironwork along the eaves of the building, Billy knocked at the door and a few minutes later, Mavis appeared.

"Come in, come in," she said, turning and heading into her front parlour. She had a pot of tea already brewed, sitting beneath a colourful lemon and sky-blue striped tea cosy. Four white china cups and saucers and a plate of chocolate biscuits sat beside the teapot on the tray.

A cottage-style suite with a homely pattern of trailing wisteria, more fitting for a veranda perhaps, filled most of the small room. It clustered around a black wrought-iron fireplace, which seemed to be de rigueur in Sydney's Victorian and contemporary properties. A sole picture frame of two women sat atop the fireplace.

"You have a lovely home," said Mary. "Is that you and a sister in the photograph?"

Mavis sat in the armchair facing the front window, whilst Billy sat across in the matching chair and Susan and Mary perched on the small two-seater settee.

Mavis was studying Susan.

"Yes! That's me and a very good friend, Gladys, taken in Singapore during the war," said Mavis.

"Do you keep in touch?" asked Billy.

"No. Unfortunately Gladys did not make it home from Asia," said Mavis mournfully.

"I am sorry to hear that," replied Billy.

"So!" interrupted Mary with an air of fanfare. "This is

322

Susan, Violet's daughter."

Mavis nodded without showing any expression. Leaning forward she busied herself pouring some tea.

"Thank you for seeing me," said Susan wishing to break the somewhat awkward atmosphere. "I just wanted to meet you and if possible ask you some questions about my mother. Is that okay?"

Mavis picked up the cup and saucer, her hand shaking as she tried to sip the tea.

"Are you all right?" asked Billy.

Mavis did not answer, she just looked down and put the drink back down on the table.

Susan continued, "Can you remember much about my mother and what sort of a person she was before the war?"

Mavis seemed to be studying the carpet as though she had spotted a stain that needed dealing with.

"Mavis, are you feeling unwell?" asked Mary, reaching across to Mavis and touching her arm.

Slowly Mavis raised her head. Looking at Susan, Mavis appeared perturbed, even frightened.

"What's the matter?" said Susan, now feeling quite disconcerted.

"I'm so sorry, it's not your fault … but … well, you look so much like him," hesitated Mavis.

"Like who? My father? Did you know him?" asked Susan.

Mavis put her hand over her mouth. "It's your eyes and your mouth … I think, I think I understand now."

"Understand what?" said Susan.

"I thought I could do this, but please forgive me, just thinking about Violet and recalling all those years ago is too painful, can you leave now, please?"

Susan stood, then knelt in front of Mavis, who recoiled, fear in her eyes.

"Like who, Mavis?" said Susan, trying to hold Mavis's hand, but Mavis sat back pulling her hand away as she did so.

"Kuroki … Captain Kuroki," screamed Mavis in Susan's face.

Mary immediately rose and put her arms around Mavis.

Susan, a look of shock on her face, was stunned. She stood, turned, and steadied herself on the settee back, before heading for the front door. Billy tried to follow her.

"Leave me alone … please leave me alone!" Raising her hand, she walked through the front door. Taking a deep breath, she looked to the heavens for guidance, then sank to her knees …

30

Nothing was said as they all walked back to Parramatta station and took the train back into Sydney. Susan gazed out of the window. She felt as though she was drowning in a sea of emotion. Wild, unfocused thoughts danced around her head.

Twenty-five minutes later they approached Redfern station. Susan stood and looked at Mary and Billy. "Will you come home with me now, just for a short while? I think I need to talk. I don't want to be alone, not tonight."

Mary took one look at Billy, who nodded and said, "For sure we will Susan. It's been a traumatic time for you."

From the corner of Lawson and Gibson Street they walked the short distance to Caroline Street. A cool breeze picked up and a chill seemed to permeate their bones as they raised collars and Mary pulled Billy by the arm towards her body. All were happy to enter the sanctuary of number forty-three.

Danny was not at home. Susan made them all hot chocolate, which seemed appropriate to warm them.

There is both something comforting and incongruous about hot chocolate on a winter's evening in Sydney, Mary pondered.

Susan cupped the steaming mug as if she were drawing succour, power and inspiration from the contents. "I guess I had always wondered how my colouring was different from Mum's," she said.

Mary gave her a wistful, knowing look but said nothing.

Susan looked at her. "I did rather stand out on the Isle of Arran," she said smiling.

Mary grinned and put her arm around Susan. "I suppose you did a little, not that it ever bothered me."

"No, but it was a reason for others to tease and bully," said Susan, her eyebrows raised and lips pursed.

"I believe they were just jealous. I certainly was. You always looked so beautiful and exotic!" replied Mary.

Putting her hand on Mary's knee, Susan smiled. "You were the only one who understood me, Mary."

Taking a sip of her hot chocolate, she placed the mug on the coffee table, leaned back on her settee, feeling the leather roll of the top support her neck, and closed her eyes.

Mary and Billy looked at each other, supped their drinks and said nothing. Billy stood and picked up a photograph, of whom he presumed to be Susan's grandfather, Violet's father. It was standing on the mantelpiece, in an ornate, pewter frame.

Susan opened her eyes and looked at Billy. "My grandfather always said, 'Don't put off until tomorrow what you can achieve today.' I think the time is right for me to find my true father.

"Maybe, just maybe, he's still alive, and can answer all the questions I have, and indeed Mavis needs answers too.

"What happened to my mother on Sumatra? Why did she not have an abortion, when she knew she would suffer from the attitude of her peers and the wider world? She was always going to end up an outcast. How did she manage to survive and persuade my stepfather to take me on? Why didn't my real father make sure my mother and I were looked after and even sent to his home in Japan? So many unanswered questions."

Susan looked at Billy and Mary. She took Mary's mug and placed it beside hers on the coffee table and grasped Mary's hands.

"Mary, sweet Mary, will you please, please, help me?"

Mary, her eyes filling, nodded and hugged Susan. "Of course I will, I will do anything I possibly can to make you happy."

"Where do we start?" asked Billy.

"We must find Captain Kuroki and learn what really took place in Sumatra and after the war," said Susan excitedly. "Who knows what this can of worms will produce once opened? I don't feel like I have an option. For once in my life I need stability, to feel wanted and be a part of a real family. Perhaps I can still achieve this."

"Well," said Billy cautiously. "You must consider we may be jumping to conclusions. Captain Kuroki may not be your father. To establish the truth we may have to go to Japan."

"Gosh," said Mary. "This one-month vacation is turning into a round-the-world whirlwind."

A ray of sunshine seemed to have burst forth from the rain-cloud-filled sky of Susan's world, warming her future and blazing a trail.

*****

Mavis lay on her bed, clutching a picture of Gladys and herself taken in Singapore after the war. She had loved her so much and would do anything for her. All those years ago she had cared for her, been nursed by her though malaria and truly loved her. The love of Gladys and her tenderness pulled her through terrible times when she thought she would never survive. She just felt terribly guilty at the hurt she had caused Violet's daughter, but being reminded of Kuroki evoked horrific memories.

31

Over the next two weeks Billy, Susan and Mary worked diligently, visiting and speaking to as many people as they could who might be able to assist with their search for Captain Kuroki, or indeed for anything that could be discovered about the plight of the people in the prisoner of war camps in Sumatra.

Billy took on the research element, getting as much chronicled information as possible to help them build a true picture of the official history of Violet and her fellow prisoners' experiences, dates, movements, names of any unit or personnel moves he could lay his hands on. He trawled through reams of newspaper articles and even obituaries and reviewed books written by former prisoners of war.

It soon became clear to Billy that the Japanese not only struggled to accept their culpability for the inhumane treatment of prisoners. In many cases brought to their attention by those interned, they blatantly denied the horror they had bestowed on these people, both in the camps and throughout their World War II campaign.

It was clear that the view of what might be described as the old guard or right wingers in Japan was readily endorsed by the Japanese media. The truth was: Japan did not accept the Western view that such atrocities had occurred. Nor did they accept the reported treatment of prisoners in captivity, of women in particular, by the Japanese military.

Billy read of the Yushukan Museum, which retells history from a Japanese right-wing perspective, even suggesting that the Americans started the war. He was astonished at some of the revelations he read.

One prominent Japanese newspaper continued this line of rhetoric, commenting on the "outright lies" told by former prisoners of war, and insisting they were all well treated. All this in spite of strong protests from the South Koreans, especially, who suffered almost as badly as the Chinese. The Japanese government was reluctant to acknowledge any war crimes.

A small mention was made of "comfort stations", but there was nothing about the defiling of women by Japanese military personnel. On the contrary, various Japanese official statements said the comfort stations were staffed by willing women who were paid for their services.

In all the articles and reports Billy found, there was no mention of Australian or other Allied nationalities, other than Korean, and only an inference that Indonesian and Dutch settlers may have been affected in isolated incidents. It appeared a touchy subject that no one wanted to tackle.

Billy wondered if more information might be available in Sumatra, which he knew was part of

Indonesia these days. Then he read an article about Korean comfort women telling their story and making representations to the Japanese government. There was a movement to start a museum in Seoul in memory of those who had suffered at the hands of the Imperial Japanese Military.

All this was fuel to the fire, making the mission to find Susan's alleged father even more important on so many levels.

Susan and Mary spent their time getting to know one another better and feeling more like sisters again. Their task was to make telephone calls and speak to representatives of various army and nursing bodies to see what they could glean. Invariably, what they found out was already in the public domain, as was most of the information that Billy dug up in his delving into archives.

Most days, walking arm in arm, Susan and Mary would peruse the department stores and shops of Sydney and have picnics in the Royal Botanic Gardens. Some days they would walk out to 'The Domain', all the way to Lady Macquarie's chair.

"Did you know?" said Susan on one such walk, "Lady Macquarie was the wife of the former governor of Sydney. This chair was supposedly carved out of rock by the fledgling country's convicts."

Totally underwhelmed, Mary just said as sarcastically as she could, "Really?" and they both laughed together.

Mary and Susan loved this place where they could take in the panorama of the Harbour Bridge, the Opera House and north-west Sydney in relative peace. Time stood still for them. Each night the trio would meet back at Susan's home on Caroline Street and discuss Billy's findings.

One sunny afternoon, following a couple of fruitless phone calls to a history society and some local historians, Susan and Mary decided to take lunch sitting in their favourite spot, looking back towards Sydney and the Rocks. Mary reclined, lying on her side, her right arm propping her up. She gazed at Susan, who was sat with her arms wrapped around her knees, staring towards Sydney Harbour Bridge.

"Penny for them?" said Mary.

Susan turned her head towards Mary and smiled. "Do you think we are doing the right thing? You know, raking up the past. Perhaps we should let bygones be bygones?"

"I can understand your trepidation, Susan, but I can also feel the need for you to find your true identity."

Susan looked back across the expanse of water as a ferry and various other craft churned the waters of this grand harbour. The park was quiet. An older man jogged past, sweatband on his head, protected from the freshening breeze by his windcheater. A minute or so later he ran back past them puffing and blowing, raising his hand in greeting. Mary acknowledged him with a nod.

Susan pulled her cardigan around her, starting to collect the debris of the picnic they had brought with them. "It's getting a little cool, even Lady Macquarie has vacated her chair. I reckon we head for home, see if we have any messages from our enquiries."

By the middle of the second week of their investigations, Susan had managed to arrange an appointment with a member of the Japanese Consulate. The triumvirate of amateur investigators had figured that making representations there, asking for help in finding Captain Kuroki might be the most proactive way forward.

Wednesday morning came, and Mary and Billy went to meet Susan at the Japanese Consulate on St Martin's Place, not far from their hotel.

As they approached 52 Martin Place along the pedestrianised street they could see Susan ahead, waiting by the Cenotaph, its memorial stone guarded by the bronze army and naval figures at either end. In the lee of the tree there, they saw Susan run her hand over the side of the inscription on the stone. "Good morning, Susan, sleep well?" queried Mary.

"Yes," said Susan, "very well. Very apt, don't you think?" she said, looking back towards the Cenotaph.

Mary and Billy followed Susan's gaze to the gold letters on the stone: "Lest we forget".

"Indeed," they concurred in unison.

They approached the building that housed the Japanese Consulate on level 34. Pausing, they looked up before making their way into a large lobby.

Susan was subdued. Mary and Billy could feel her apprehension. Her fear of going in was almost palpable.

"Good morning," said Susan when they arrived at the Consulate offices, "I have a meeting with Mr Takashita."

A woman with a black bob of shining, lustrous hair, wearing a black knee-length dress, checked the diary in front of her. Smiling, she invited them to take a seat and walked off down a corridor.

Before long a middle-aged man appeared. Mary noted his highly polished black shoes. "Ms Duncan?" he asked, his hand extended, his head inclined to the right waiting for confirmation. Susan stood and he bowed. Susan automatically followed and returned his bow. "Please follow me!"

"May I bring my good friends with me, please?"

"Ah, certainly," he said in his strong Japanese, clipped accent.

They were shown into what appeared to be a meeting room. Its large oval table was surrounded by eight leather-backed chairs.

"Please take a seat. I am Kendo Takashita. How can I help you?"

Susan cleared her throat, looking at Mary for strength and reassurance. She then looked the diminutive Mr Takashita straight in the eye as he sat across the table from her.

"Do you know the word 'Suisen'?" She spelt the name out to make sure her pronunciation did not confuse Takashita.

Somewhat bemused, Takashita's forehead wrinkled in a frown. "Yes! It is a flower, you call it daffodil I believe!"

"I sent you a letter a week or more back and you kindly agreed to meet me. In that letter ..."

Takashita raised his hand to interrupt Susan. He opened a manila file on his desk, turned over some papers and held Susan's letter in his right hand. "I have read your letter regarding Captain Kuroki. Why do you want to find him?"

Again, Susan nervously cleared the back of her throat, which had become incredibly dry. Billy and Mary felt for her. "I have reason to believe Captain Kuroki may be my father."

Takashita smiled. Mary felt he was sneering

"What makes you think Captain Kuroki is your father?"

Susan proceeded to tell the story, or what she knew of it, to Takashita. He listened patiently, until she mentioned "comfort stations" and the abuse of female prisoners of war.

Suddenly, Takashita stood. His demeanour had changed, he was irate. "I would like to help you, but your story is completely wrong."

With that Mary stood, her face reddening by the second. "Wrong, wrong? You have to be joking, we have witnesses still alive, as well as many testimonies, as to the terrible treatment of prisoners of war, especially women, who were used as prostitutes by your so-called 'mighty Japanese Imperial Army'."

"Please, this isn't helping," said Billy as he tried to grab Mary's arm to make her sit and calm down. She shrugged off his efforts.

In a calm voice, Susan spoke. "I understand your beliefs, Mr Takashita, but please help me find Captain Kuroki. I need to speak to him myself. It is the least you can do, I think."

"On the contrary," said Takashita, smirking. "I cannot help you find Captain Kuroki as he is dead."

Susan pushed the chair back from the table, shocked by this revelation. "How? When?" she asked, regaining her composure.

"Thanks to your Western justice system, and unfair trial, he was executed not long after peace was declared," said Takashita, standing and closing his file.

"But, but," stuttered Susan.

"I believe our meeting is at an end," said Takashita.

Mary put her arm around Susan, who once more felt despair.

Billy spoke, quietly but firmly. "What do you know of Captain Kuroki's birthplace and any other family he had?"

Takashita narrowed his eyes, his jaw moved side to side then he looked away. He slowly put the file back onto the table and opened it. He slid a piece of paper across the table towards Billy.

"Thank you," said Billy.

Ten minutes later they stood outside 52 St Martin's Place, feeling relieved, as if they had escaped the lion's den.

"After all this, we might as well give up," said Susan.

"Boy!" said Billy. "That certainly felt hostile."

He held up an A4-size piece of paper. "But, we may have some hope!" Mary and Susan looked at him pensively. "I do believe that, if you are right and you are Kuroki's daughter, you may have a half-brother!"

Excitedly they repaired to a nearby restaurant and discussed over lunch the news Billy had referred to and their options going forward.

"What should I do?" asked Susan, knowing the answer in her heart.

"Follow your heart," said Billy.

Mary nodded.

"I must find out for sure," said Susan.

Susan looked at the names typed on the A4 paper: "Mrs Sachiko Kuroki and son Akihiko Kuroki" and an address in Nagasaki, Japan.

"I guess I always wanted to see the cherry blossom, but I can't wait for that season."

32

"What do you mean, you're not coming back home with me? That's what we planned, Billy."

"I know, my love, but I feel there is unfinished business here."

"Like what?" said Mary. She stopped brushing her hair and threw the brush towards Billy.

"Look, don't be upset, it's just, well … I feel I can help Susan more here and I want to find out more about her Mum for Gwen too."

"Susan, Gwen … What does it matter? You've made up your mind," said Mary with a disapproving snort, as she put the last of her clothes in the suitcase.

Turning, she pushed icily past Billy and into the bathroom. The door slammed shut, the lock on the door audible as it connected.

The next day, standing in the lobby with her luggage at her feet, Mary stood silently beside Billy. They had spoken little over breakfast.

He tried to put his arm around her, but Mary fended him off.

"Mary, please understand I just want to find out what happened to Violet and feel I cannot leave the story in mid-air. I'm sure I can help Susan find out more. I would much rather you stay, but I totally understand you have to go back to work. Look, if Susan doesn't want me to help, I'll come home with you, it won't take me long to pack."

Mary turned and looked at Billy. Her eyes were watering as she stepped towards him and put her arms around his neck. "I'm sorry Billy. I just … well, I think I've fallen in love with you and I don't want to be apart from you. Do you understand?" she looked up at Billy, her eyes mournful.

Billy pulled her close to him, kissing the top of her head as she nuzzled his neck. "I care a lot for you too, Mary." He squeezed her affectionately as he spoke.

"Good morning," said Susan, breaking the spell. "What's all this canoodling in public?" she jibed, winking simultaneously.

Mary wiped her eyes. Smiling, she hugged Susan.

"What's the matter?" said Susan.

"I just don't want to leave, Susan, but I have to. But the good news is Billy is staying on. He can try and help you more in your search for information about your Mum's wartime experiences. He can, he has no ties."

Ignoring Mary's dig, Billy said. "I think you may need some support through the coming weeks, and as Mary points out, I don't have to get back for any reason like work, as I'm retired."

Susan looked at Billy, having felt the sharp barb in Mary's comments. "Oh … Okay. Well, that's great," she said. "I've been thinking about what to do. I've just spoken to my Ward manager, on the way here, and she has confirmed I can have ten days' leave, but I can only have it if I take it soon, as we are understaffed at the hospital next month and beyond. So, I plan to go to Japan as soon as I can."

"Wow!" said Mary. "You're as impulsive as Billy and I were in making this trip."

"I think I will find out more if I try and track down the Kuroki family in their own country."

"But you don't even speak Japanese," said Mary.

"I guess I will find an interpreter or a guide to help me."

"What do you think, Billy?"

"I guess that is proactive and could be a good plan, but you are taking an expensive risk just flying to Japan on the off-chance of finding the Kuroki family. It's a long flight and I hear it's costly to live there. Firstly, the family may no longer be at that address and secondly even if you do find them ..." He paused.

"Yes?" prompted Susan.

"Look, I don't want to be negative, but there is always the possibility they will not want to speak to you. Perhaps I should go home with Mary," said Billy, caught in a quandary.

"What am I going to do? Wonder all my life about my father? I just might finally find my true self. Danny is all for it, he said go for it, Mum!"

Mary turned to Billy. "Would you travel with Susan to help her in Japan?"

It had crossed Billy's mind, but he had been afraid to even suggest such a course of action this morning.

"I guess I could, if you are happy for me to come too, Susan?" asked Billy.

"Suits me, it would be good to have the company."

"Sorry to disturb you, madam," said the concierge to Mary. "Your taxi is here."

Susan and Billy travelled with Mary to Kingsford-Smith airport. It was a quiet journey in the car, everyone thinking of what the future might bring. Before long they were saying their goodbyes. Susan gave Mary a big hug and both started to cry.

"It has been wonderful seeing you again, Mary, and we will meet up again. I plan to come and see Mum just as soon as I can. This time, I promise we will stay in touch."

Mary nodded, her face now quite flushed as she wiped a tear from the corner of her eye.

"I promise I will go and see your mum, Susan, as I have always done. I will tell her I have seen you and of how wonderfully well you're doing." She turned to Billy.

"Call me to let me know you've arrived home safely," said Billy as he hugged her, lifting her on to her tiptoes as he did so.

"I love you, Billy Williams! Come home soon, I am going to miss you like crazy." Mary planted a lingering kiss on his lips.

"I will be back before you know it," said Billy, holding her away from him and looking into her now reddened eyes.

Leaving Susan, Billy and Mary walked to the passport gate. She held his hand tight. He kissed her one final time, on the lips then on her cheek, feeling the warm saltiness of her tears. Their hands slid slowly apart, she turned to join the short queue. As she passed out of sight Mary waved one last time.

33

Akihiko Kuroki had returned home to Nagasaki. Now he was retired, he endeavoured to do all those things he never had time for when working. But he soon became bored of fishing, and he had never liked physical exercise.

Akihiko enjoyed painting, but somehow could not settle to get started. Sure, he bought the easel and brushes, watercolour paints and paper, but they sat in the corner of his studio untouched.

He was still disturbed by the attitude of his children. He had felt they had shown a lack of respect for him and his father and what had been sacrificed for them to be where they are today.

But something bothered him more, which he did not want to share with Miho his wife. He knew little of his father or family before his generation and feared there may be some truth in his children's comments. He felt frustrated, mad at himself that he had taken the moral high ground against his children whom he loved.

Annoyed that he was so indoctrinated, he had painted himself into a corner when it came to protecting his father. *"But isn't that pride and loyalty?"* he said to himself and he answered *"Yes, but that does not make it right."*

Akihiko decided to take the bus to the Peace Park. He alighted and entered the tranquil area, heading for the Fountain of Peace. It was already busy with school groups and foreign tourists. He strolled towards the north end of the park and the ten-metre-high Peace statue, which he remembered his mother bringing him to, as a boy.

Standing before the statue, he recalled his mother's words:

Do you know what this statue symbolises, Akihiko?

No, mother.

The statue's right hand points to the threat of nuclear weapons while the outstretched left hand symbolises eternal peace. The calm face is of divine grace, as he prays for all those killed on that sad day in 1945. The bent right leg and outstretched left leg make us think of both meditation and the will to support all those people in the world who are being badly treated.

What is a nuclear weapon, Okaasan?

When you were a small boy in 1945, remember when we came home on the train from your grandparents in Kyoto and all those people had been killed and lots of buildings destroyed? The devastation was appalling, hardly any structure survived, people wandering the streets dazed.

Yes, Okaasan.

That was caused by a nuclear bomb.

Was it a big bomb, then, Okaasan?

Very big.

But what Akihiko remembered most was his mother reminding him of the friends and neighbours who had died.

Now a black marble vault containing the names of the atomic bomb victims and survivors who had died in subsequent years was accompanied by a plaque. He read out loud the opening words of the inscription, written by Seibo Kitamura in 1995:

> After experiencing that nightmarish war,
> that blood-curdling carnage,
> that unendurable horror,
> Who could walk away without praying for peace?

Akihiko now felt guilty for his attitude as a boy. He had never wanted to come to the park with his mother. He would rather have been at home playing.

Standing before the Peace statue, he started to shake a little, moved by the immensity of it all. He steadied himself by leaning on the statue. Many of his schoolfriends, neighbours and relatives had been lost, and he felt bad and ashamed that he had survived but his best friend had not.

He looked at the sky, as if expecting, or wanting, the B29 Flying Fortress Bockscar to pass over once more and drop the 10,000-lb bomb nicknamed "Fat Man" to put him out of his misery. But all he heard in the stillness were the birds singing.

He walked the quarter of a mile or so to the Nagasaki Atomic Bomb Museum. As he entered the museum he realised he had never been in there before. He knew his children had, like all Japanese children, visited the Peace Park and museum on school tours to remind them of the horrors of war.

Akihiko found it hard to listen to first-hand testimonies from survivors, as he pressed buttons of recordings and watched short films. It became quite traumatic as he saw images of devastated trees, furniture, buildings, pottery and what looked like a bundle of clothing rags but was actually the remainder of a human being.

He paused in front of a photograph of a clock stopped at 11.02, the time of the bombing. It brought back upsetting flashbacks of the post-bomb carnage he and his mother witnessed, images that had stayed until now locked away. He found himself standing in front of a picture of his school or what was left of it. His bottom lip began to quiver and he found himself crying.

Regaining his composure, he looked around as he slid his handkerchief back into his pocket, but the few other visitors seemed not to have noticed his angst.

He thanked his good fortune that he and his mother survived. He remembered the faces of children he was at school with who were obliterated that day on 9 August 1945, and realised the anniversary of that date was rapidly approaching once again. Strangely, he could bring to mind the voice of his best friend Manabu. *He was so clever,* he recalled, *but he had just disappeared like a puff of smoke, as if he had never existed.*

Later, spending time in the library, Akihiko learned that during World War II, Hiroshima was a militarily important city. It was the 2nd Army Headquarters, which commanded the defence of southern Japan. The city was a communications hub.

He was surprised to learn that, ironically, Nagasaki was not even the first target on that fateful August day back in 1945. It was only because of cloud over Kokura that Nagasaki was bombed. This made him angry, questioning his religion. *Why*, he said to himself, *why us?*

Some of the city centre had reinforced concrete buildings. Some prefectural buildings survived. But most of Nagasaki was full of small wooden industrial buildings. Larger industrial factories lay near the outskirts but were also wooden.

Almost all the houses were made of wood with tile roofs. Akihiko reflected that it was always going to be devastated by any bombing, even though the city was spread over the surrounding hillsides and had lots of waterways.

At the time of the nuclear bomb, Hiroshima, he learned, had about 250,000 inhabitants.

Akihiko sat up straight, leaning back on his chair. He listened to the stillness of the library. Taking off his glasses, he rubbed his eyes and looked around at the students and other visitors to the library.

His mind went back to the photograph he had seen earlier that day of the clock stopped at 11.02 am. He recalled seeing newspaper pictures of radiation-affected victims.

He finally acknowledged to himself that all these years he had been conveniently blocking all this from his mind. He nodded to himself and considered perhaps his children may be right, that he should understand more about the motivations and actions of the Japanese military in the war. But more than that, he should try and embrace the fact that life had changed fifty years on.

That evening Akihiko attended a history lecture about the rise of the military influence in the tough times of the global depression of the thirties. Anyone against the decisions of the military-controlled government was considered suspicious and the secret police started to become an ever-more threatening presence, banning debates and influencing policies. Liberals were sidelined and silenced.

Akihiko was shocked by what he was hearing. Back then, within a few years, Japan became essentially a police state, run by the military. Once the war against the western Allies started, the general public was supplied with a barrage of propaganda. Always positive, never any defeats or negativity, always the mighty Japanese empire being superior! Only once the US began to constantly bomb Japanese cities did people start questioning the truth.

That night Akihiko could not sleep.

The next morning Miho had been doing some laundry. "Are you okay, Aki?" she asked. Akihiko shrugged and gave no reply. He just continued to read the morning paper.

"Aki, did you hear me?"

Aki did not reply. He stood, folded his paper, put it under his arm, and picked up his cup as he left the room.

That evening as they ate dinner in silence, Akihiko pushed the food around his bowl with his chopsticks, not eating. He looked up at Miho. "I'm sorry Miho. My mind has been in turmoil since I returned from Singapore."

Miho smiled sympathetically and nodded as if she understood totally.

"I think the children may be right. I have been too blinkered about my father and about Japan in the past."

Miho stood and came over to him. Standing behind him she put her hands on his shoulders, squeezing them in a light massage, then sat beside him at the table. Taking off his glasses, Akihiko held both her hands, their arms resting on the table. He looked into her eyes. "Have I been a good father and husband?"

"You have, Aki, yes, you have!"

"I need to find out more about my father. Why he did not come home to us, and about where and how he died. I have conveniently tried to ignore the truth, worshipping him. I loved him, you see, Miho. As tough as he was with me, I loved him!"

Miho stood and brought over two small glasses and a bottle of sake.

Pouring the rice wine, she held her glass up to Aki. "Kampai," toasted Aki. "To my father and to the truth!"

Next morning Akihiko called the museum of his father's regiment.

"Konnichiwa! I need to find out some information about the wartime service of my father, Captain Satoshi Kuroki. Can you help?"

"Certainly sir. Can you please give me his full name and rank and any other information you may have?"

"I am looking for Captain Satoshi Kuroki, I believe he served during the 1941–1945 campaign." As he spoke he perused a letter sent to his mother by his father.

Continuing his telephone conversation, he added: "According to his last letter to my mother, his commanding officer was Lieutenant General Moritake Tanabe, Commanding Officer, 25th Army, Imperial Japanese Army."

"Thank you. Please give me your address and we will make an investigation for you and send any information we may have regarding your father's whereabouts during the war. Please understand some records were destroyed during the war."

Ten days later Akihiko received a small package in a manila envelope through the mail. He walked to his study and removed the seal with an ornamental paper knife shaped like a samurai sword. He unfolded the letter.

Dear Mr Kuroki

Please find enclosed details of your father's war service with the Japanese Imperial Military.

Your father joined the 25th Army in April 1941 and served in Malaya and Singapore under Lt General Tomoyuki Yamashita, then Lt General Yaheita Saito. By 1943 his commanding officer was General Moritake Tanabe for the rest of the war.

His war record shows him involved in action in Malaya, Burma, Sumatra and Syonan-to (Singapore today).

He served with great courage and was decorated. He was injured in the conquest of Sumatra.

Captain Satoshi Kuroki was fundamental in controlling and appeasing the welfare of Japanese officers and men after the Dutch and other Western

350

forces surrendered. He was based near Palembang in Sumatra.

He served during peacetime in Palembang, Sumatra, keeping order alongside western forces from 15 August 1945 until 1946, when he was arrested.

He was transferred to Singapore and tried by the western Allies as a war criminal in 1946. He and the Japanese government strongly protested his innocence.

Whilst in custody, it was at first thought he took his own life, and we presume this is why the artefacts returned by the Americans were on file with us and sent to your family.

We have no official record of his death following his sentence to be executed. Our records merely show him as a missing person.

We suggest you contact the American authorities who may have more information.

We hope this has helped you in your quest for information about your father's war record.

It is clear from his file that he was a proud, loyal soldier.

Yours sincerely

Nakahito Suzuki

Akihiko looked out of his study window across his perfectly kept garden, containing camellias, azaleas, Japanese apricot, cydonias and, of course, cherry trees, all divided by carefully raked gravel and a smattering of moss, all purposely designed to give a restful and verdant feel whilst fitted into his small courtyard.

No matter how he tried to relax his mind, though, his thoughts came back to the words of the letter he still held in his right hand. His father had been executed. *What happened to him, what trial? For what? What were his crimes?* He had a lot more to find out.

34

"It's for you, Billy," said Susan, handing him the phone.

"Hello."

"It's me. I just called Susan to tell her I'm home safely and asking her to let you know, because the hotel said you'd checked out and I was worried. I didn't realise you would be there."

"That's great timing, Mary. I have checked out of the hotel. It was getting expensive and Susan has very kindly offered me Danny's room, as he has gone out of town on business for a week or so, so it's pretty handy, really."

There was no answer.

"Hello. Can you hear me? Are you there, Mary?"

"Yes, I am here. Yes! It is convenient that you're now living with Susan."

"Hardly living with her, Mary," said Billy, sensing Mary's disdain. "It's a temporary arrangement, it just makes sense financially and for our research. We have made plans to fly to Tokyo, in five days' time. Then we'll take the bullet train to Nagasaki. I've always wanted to go on it ever since I first heard of it."

"How long are you going for?" asked Mary.

"Susan can only get ten days' leave, so subject to what we find, and anything else that may happen, certainly no longer than that. I plan to fly home towards the end of July. It's so good to hear your voice, Mary."

"Is it?"

"You know it is. I miss you … Are you still mad at me for staying?"

"Do you really miss me, Billy? I'm out of my mind not being with you and miss touching you and feeling your arms around me. I find it very difficult to sleep at nights. I started back at work yesterday and my mind is just not there. Billy, I do hope you're coming home soon. I need you."

"How was the flight?"

"Billy, did you hear what I said? I need you to be here, with me. I miss you like crazy."

"Yes, sure I did. It seems strange without you here too. I'll be home before too long. As I said when you were here, I just want to sort things out here for both Susan and Gwen, while I have the opportunity, as I'm never likely to be back here again, am I?"

"No! I suppose not," admitted Mary dolefully. "Will you come up to Lamlash as soon as you're back?"

"Well, I'll need to straighten out a few things at home first, and then go and see Gwen, to let her know all we've found out. But don't fret, I will come and see you post haste. Have you seen Violet since you've been back?"

"No. No … I haven't had time, Billy. I'm jetlagged and have had to return to work straight away, don't forget."

"Sure, sure, I understand."

"I would love to meet Gwen. Perhaps I can come down and spend the weekend with you and we could go and see her together when you're back? I can take some time off between shifts," said Mary hopefully.

"Yes, maybe that would work."

"Well, I have to go now," said Mary. "I am rather naughtily calling from work, and my break is over, but I just had to hear your voice. Please ring and write from Japan, Billy. You have my number, don't you? I do love you. I did mean what I said."

"I know, I know, I care for you too! Yes, I have your number."

"Bye." The line went dead.

Susan was sitting on the settee, flicking through the morning newspaper. "Boy, she has the hots for you, lover boy, doesn't she?"

"She is a lovely girl, but we've only just got to know one another and … well, we'll see."

Susan smiled and returned to her reading.

Five days later, the Japan Airlines morning flight from Sydney was airborne, en route to the Land of the Rising Sun.

Billy looked across at Susan. Her eyes were closed, her head resting on a small white airline pillow against the window, oblivious to the engine thrum of the plane and the cabin staff activity dispensing welcome drinks. He admired her fine mane of black hair which caressed her shoulders as it cascaded onto her white silk blouse, flowing like the tributaries of a river, one over each breast.

Billy felt a real empathy with Susan's mixed feelings and emotions about life and her identity. Like her, he had never felt comfortable with who he was, or even his parents' relationships with him. He so hoped she would find the answers she craved.

It took just over nine and a half hours to reach Tokyo but there was only an hour difference from Sydney time. In no time at all they were on a railway platform at Tokyo station waiting to take the bullet train known as the 'JR Tokaido/Sanyo' to Fukuoka Hakata Station, where they planned to change to a normal express train to Nagasaki. This 'Shinkansen' from Tokyo to Nagasaki was a regular service which would take them over seven hours.

Tired and weary from the inactivity on the plane, Billy and Susan marvelled at the long, snub nose of the train as, like the proverbial bullet, it sped in and slowed, sliding majestically to the platform, the doors opening at the precise loading points, where they were told to stand with all the exacting organisation Billy had expected of the Japanese.

Within minutes they were on their way in their comfortable reserved seats, and a refreshments trolley soon appeared, from which they bought snacks and a hot drink.

Billy marvelled at the speed of over 250 kph he witnessed on the digital monitor above the carriage door. He was mesmerised, watching to see how fast the train was barrelling its way towards Fukuoka. He was amazed that it made not a bit of difference to the liquid in his cup. There was not a ripple. It was as if they were not moving at all.

He turned to Susan to express his delight, but she was already asleep, exhausted by the long journey maybe, but more from the rollercoaster of emotion of these past few weeks, he suspected. It did not take long for Billy to drift off, too.

It seemed no time at all when Billy, who had catnapped throughout, was disturbing Susan to change trains in Fukuoka. In a daze, they alighted and waited on the open platform. Fortunately, they only had twenty minutes to wait for their connection.

"Sorry, Billy, I haven't been much company."

Billy smiled "I didn't know you suffered from narcolepsy."

They both laughed.

The two-hour journey to Nagasaki passed quickly. Their hotel, the St Paul Nagasaki, a small, older, rather drab-looking hotel, was hard to find, even for the local cabbie. But it turned out to be just a short ride away.

Paying the taxi driver, Billy picked up both bags. "Well, the Sydney travel agent did say it had character and was well situated," he quipped as they entered the small lobby.

"Two rooms in the name of Williams," said Billy as he reached the front desk, dropping his bags to the floor to relieve the burden. He had confidently booked the hotel at a decent price with the Sydney travel agent, considering the expense of Japanese living costs. He now saw why.

"Passports yes?" said the diminutive male receptionist, who seemed flustered by the appearance of two guests.

Handing over their passports Billy was given a key.

357

"Aah! Thank you, sir, your room is number 22."

"Thank you, and the other room key?" said Billy.

"Aah! Just one room key, sorry, sir."

"But we have two rooms booked," said Billy.

The flustered receptionist rustled and shuffled a lot of paperwork in front of him. "Aaah! One room," he said, whilst showing Billy a fax from the Sydney travel agent saying room for two booked.

"No! There seems to be some mistake. We need two rooms," said Billy, getting frustrated.

"Yes, sir, very nice room with two beds."

"No! We need two rooms," stated Billy firmly, now becoming irate.

"Hotel full tonight maybe tomorrow," said the receptionist apologetically, his palms open to Billy, with a shrug of his shoulders.

"Oh, come on, Billy," said Susan, losing patience. "I'm bushed. I'm sure I can put up with sharing a room with you for a few nights."

35

Akihiko did not want to bother his mother as she had been unwell. He never called or visited her as much as he knew a good son should.

It was over five hours on the train, but Akihiko had packed an overnight bag, telling Miho he needed to see his mother and that he would be back in a day or two.

Miho understood as she always did. Where his mother was concerned, she was not always welcome or indeed considered by Akihiko. She sensed Akihiko preferred to be alone when seeing his mother.

Miho gave Akihiko a hug and watched him board the local express train to Hakata, where he planned to change to the bullet train to travel on to Kyoto at speed.

Miho's worried glance conveyed a concern for Akihiko and their relationship. She knew he had a troubled soul, which she knew would not be placated until he found out the truth about his father. She just hoped that was all that was causing his disaffection.

It was early August now. Akihiko could feel that the impending anniversary of the Nagasaki bombing would rekindle for many the memory of that awful event, fifty years before.

So now, he decided, was the time to speak to his mother in an honest and direct manner. He needed to find out more about his father. In all these years she had hardly spoken about him.

He arrived at Kyoto station and took a cab to Gion Higashi, the community where the family home of his mother and indeed her family had traditionally been for many generations. This was where Akihiko understood she had been living until she married his father and moved to Nagasaki.

The rains of this sub-tropical city were just about finished, and the humidity and heat were palpable. Akihiko loved the small-town feel of this city and was so happy his mother lived in Gion. This is where she had been for many years, it was where she felt comfortable. As he walked through the narrow streets with their plethora of telephone lines above him, he thought to himself that this old-fashioned suburb seemed to have changed little in the last fifty years. Perhaps, he mused, that is why it seemed to suit his mother's unspoken wish to hold on to an era that was long gone in cities like Nagasaki and Tokyo.

Gion was renowned for its geishas and traditional inns called ryokans, not to mention its many Shinto shrines and Buddhist temples. Akihiko loved the heritage, which Nagasaki did not have in such abundance. He could see why Kyoto was once the imperial capital of Japan, and many of the city's ancient monuments were today listed as Unesco World Heritage Sites, like the Kiyomizo-dera Buddhist temple. He enjoyed the walk up to the hill more in the winter, when the shops lining the street were quieter and the tourists were less in evidence.

Akihiko was accepting of the tourist trade. Commerce had changed, the shops mostly dealt with sales of cheap trinkets and souvenirs now. He walked on through the area which was originally developed in the middle ages, a district full of tea houses where geisha plied their trade. Traditionally they entertained men whilst serving tea, singing, playing musical instruments and reciting poetry, as well as playing games. Akihiko particularly enjoyed the traditional dances like "Nihon Buyo", a dramatic dance of precise moves. He loved the sequence with fans that the geisha used to portray at length an evocative sadness.

He had seen many beautiful girls, especially before he was married. He thought to himself how things were changing. Whilst the tradition of obtaining an invitation was still important, increasingly, the customers were tourists. This somewhat irked Akihiko, feeling it should be just for Japanese men.

Akihiko could almost hear the distinctive sound of the tall wooden sandals known as "Okobo" as they clicked on the stones signalling a geisha making her way to an assignation.

Flowers and lanterns and willow trees around traditional wooden architecture lined his journey and if you listened carefully you could hear water trickling from a bamboo fountain.

As he neared his mother's house, Akihiko knew that his mother would be astute enough to know he needed something. Indeed, his reception was likely to be cool.

He was sad that was how their relationship was. He still used the formal greeting for mother "Okaasan".

Reaching her door and taking off his shoes, he padded across the wooden floor as quietly as he could and slid aside the shoji, a light wood and paper partition between the hallway and the sparsely furnished large living room. His mother, relaxing on a large cushion, looked at him briefly, showing no emotion, and returned to reading her magazine.

Without looking up she said, "Why have you come?"

Bowing he offered, "I have come to see you, Okaasan, to make sure you are all right."

"I have not seen or heard from you, or that wife of yours, for a few months. Is it too much trouble to even ring?"

Carrying a beautiful orchid he had bought near the railway station, Akihiko did not respond. He placed the orchid on the low, dark wood table that was the centrepiece of the room. Still ignored, he said. "I know, I know." He settled himself cross-legged on the tatami mat across from her. "I have been away to Myanmar and Singapore."

His mother did not answer.

"I want to see more of you, Okaasan, and to be there for you. I know I have not seen you much recently, but I want that to change. My travels have made me realise this and I also wanted to find out more about where Dad was in the Second World War."

"How long do you plan to stay?"

"Okaasan, don't be angry, I need your help. I …"

"I didn't think you were here just to see how I was."

"Okaasan, genuinely, I have been doing a lot of thinking and want to try and understand what happened to Dad after the war! I also want to understand certain things like why we went to war, and how it affected you and Dad and indeed the whole family.

"I want to know more about how you coped after the war bringing me up. I can only remember small, insignificant things.

"I know I have not been as good a son as you or my father would have hoped, but … well, I am here to begin to put that right too!"

"You had better make some tea then, Akihiko. You can then get off your chest what is demanded by your conscience."

"Thank you, Okaasan!" said Akihiko returning to his feet and heading for the small kitchenette, with its simple two-burner stove, a small fridge, microwave and slow-cooking pot.

His mother shrugged. He gazed at her. If he ignored the scowl, she still looked as beautiful as the photographs he had of her when she was younger and with his father. A pang of guilt followed as he became very aware in that moment that she was now approaching her eighties. *Who knows how much more time we have to bond together again?* he thought.

Akihiko set the tray with an ornate matching peach-lustre teapot and tea set on the table. "I remember this tea set so well from my childhood, it has stood the test of time well," he said.

"It was a wedding gift.

"If you genuinely want to try and understand, Akihiko, I must start by telling you a little background as to how your father and I met."

"Please, mother."

"I was born in Kyoto and I met your father when he came one evening to a tea house where I was a young 'Maiko', learning to be a geisha.

"Satoshi appeared regularly, and it was clear he was fond of me. He loved the bright red colour of my kimono and how it hung loosely at the back to accentuate the nape of my neck. My white make-up on my face and the nape of my neck was always perfectly applied by my dresser. It was all done, of course, before I dressed. It left two or sometimes three stripes of bare skin exposed.

"My kimono was bright and colourful, with an elaborately tied 'obi' on my back, which hung down to my ankles. I had long since learned to take very small steps and I wore traditional okobo wooden shoes, which, at almost four inches off the ground, were difficult to walk in. Anyway,–as I progressed, my hairstyle changed and your father loved this, but it just showed I was becoming more experienced and developing.

"It was not easy as maikos. We had to sleep on pillows with holes in to preserve the very structured hair styling. Sometimes instead, we put a support under our neck. It was very uncomfortable, a labour of love, but we were proud of our tradition.

"Satoshi waited outside the tea house and followed me one night as I shuffled home. The rest is history.

Your father swept me off my feet, he was a very handsome and gentle man. I loved him.

"My father was not happy," she added with a frown. "He took me aside and said he forbade me to see your father Satoshi. I was devastated. My mother was very sympathetic, she told me in confidence to be patient. She said 'Sach Chan', follow your heart!

"Satoshi would not give up and we used to meet in secret. Our first real date was when your father took me to watch a Sumo wrestling bout, not very romantic perhaps to you. But I was thrilled, watching these fine figures of Japanese manhood, trying to throw each other out of the ring.

"Eventually Satoshi came to my father in uniform in 1941. He was so handsome! I listened in from another room with my mother. We eavesdropped as your father begged my father to allow him to marry me. He said soon he would be going overseas to fight for the Emperor and to have such a wonderful lady as his wife would help him be a truly great warrior for Japan. Reluctantly my father agreed to our marriage. It was an uncertain time for all.

"In Japan, you know, the crane is the symbol of longevity and good luck, happiness and eternal youth because it was thought to have a life span of a thousand years. Cranes are also monogamous and therefore often used for wedding décor.

"When we were married shortly afterwards, your father and I moved to Nagasaki and my parents gave us a folding screen to protect my modesty when undressing. It had four beautifully embroidered folding panels all depicting cranes in different poses. It was just one of our wedding presents; we had beautiful gifts from Satoshi's parents too. The screen still stands in my bedroom.

"I missed your father so much. He didn't come home on leave much. Then when he did come home the last time, in early 1945, he was injured. His leg had been damaged in battle, and he told me he had been posted to a safe area and had been there a long time and not to worry.

"I was relieved, of course, but he told me no more than that. He was a passionate man and after his last leave I found out I was pregnant with a brother or sister for you, but Satoshi never knew as he did not return."

Akihiko was astonished. "So, do I have a sibling, mother?"

"No! I am sorry, Akihiko. With the shock of everything that went on with the bomb, the invasion and indeed the loss of your father, I was not myself and I believe the stress led to me miscarrying. It was perhaps a blessing, I struggled to feed just the two of us.

"In August that year almost fifty years ago, nuclear bombs fell on Hiroshima and Nagasaki. I had not been well for a few weeks, we had not been eating well as supplies were rationed. But my morning sickness and general malaise were a blessing in disguise. I was so ill my parents begged me to go back to them. So, you see, I had taken you to Kyoto to stay with my parents as they helped me to convalesce. It was fate we were not killed in Nagasaki.

"You and I had been visiting my parents and we were on the train back to Nagasaki on 9 August. We were frightened because of the bombing of Hiroshima, three days before. I wanted to come home and collect some belongings and return to my parents where I felt we might be safer. By the time we arrived in Nagasaki the second bomb had been dropped, destroying a swathe of Nagasaki, killing and injuring many.

"When we arrived, the station was largely destroyed. We actually walked through what was left of the station, as our train had stopped up the line and we had followed the track into the city. We picked our way through the streets, your school was gone, our home was miraculously unscathed, but Japan was not.

"Less than a week later on 15 August, Emperor Hirohito announced Japan's surrender. I recall he gave three major reasons for surrender: Tokyo's defences would not be complete before the American invasion of Japan, the sacred Ise Shrine would be lost to the Americans, and atomic weapons deployed by the Americans would lead to the death of the entire Japanese race.

"We were stunned, bereft beyond belief. All that infallible propaganda of the previous years gone, and now we were vulnerable, scared and alone.

"Our Emperor Hirohito asked us to 'endure the unendurable and suffer what is not sufferable'.

"When we had recovered our senses and contained our emotions, survival instincts kicked in. I thought positively. At least peace is here, and your father will be home, but that never happened."

"What do you know of Father's death, Okaasan?"

"I was sent an official letter saying he had died an honorable death serving the Emperor."

"Do you know how or where?"

"No! It mattered not, he was not coming back. So, I had to look after you, you became my only reason for living.

"We returned to my parents for a short while after I lost the baby, but then eventually came back to Nagasaki and with help from Satoshi's parents lived our lives. It was hard, especially when the Americans and other Western troops controlled our city."

"What did you do?"

Sachiko Huroki's eyes filled with tears, spilling over onto her cheeks. She stood. "I did what I had to, Aki, to survive. I became a modern-day geisha."

"Why are you so upset, Okaasan? You did what you had to."

"There were few Japanese men around and even less money. So, my main customers were American GIs. I dressed conservatively and tried to follow the convention of my teachings, but the soldiers just drank and wanted fun. My parents disowned me, treated me as a pariah. It was as if I was dead to them."

Akihiko nodded. He felt sick, his face became wan, then flushed. He had no words.

Sachiko wore a painful expression. "We survived, Akihiko, that's all that matters. We survived. I must rest now." She turned away from him and walked from the room.

A few minutes later she returned carrying a small lacquered wooden box. Sitting by Akihiko she said. "A few of your father's belongings were returned to me."

Akihiko studied his mother as she gently opened the box and sifted through the contents taking items and briefly perusing them, before laying them on the table in front of him. As she did so, Akihiko tried to imagine her as a young geisha. Sachiko still possessed a beauty, her skin seemed like porcelain, small wisps of grey hair had appeared at her temples, adding a certain elegance to her later years. Her dark brown eyes were still keen and clear.

Akihiko could imagine how his father had been spellbound and beguiled by his mother's features. Even without the make-up and elegant kimono and hairstyles, she was attractive. Her eyebrows were longer now, she no longer needed to pluck them as she did as a geisha, but her beauty was still indisputable.

Sachiko held a few sheets of paper and read them to herself, as if for the first time. Before her lay some photographs and amazingly some artefacts, which included a Seiko wristwatch, its silver casing with a little accumulated patina, especially on the winder. The white watch face, adorned with a red anchor and with the second hand at the bottom, seemed in good shape. There were also a pair of glasses with one arm broken off and missing and, lastly, a book of poems entitled *Ichiaku no Suna*, A Handful of Sand, by Takuboku Ishikawa.

Akihiko opened the book. As he did so, a lock of blonde hair slid out and floated to the floor. He retrieved the hair and looked at his mother, who seemed not to notice, distracted by the papers in her hands. She stood again and left the room.

He shuffled the three photographs on the table, spreading them out so they sat side by side. First, a picture of his father in uniform and his mother in full ceremonial kimono. He wondered if this was their wedding day.

Second, a group photograph of his father with other military officers, presumably from a similar time.

Then, a picture on a large verandah featuring four officers, which included his father standing, and two ladies sitting around a table, a bottle of wine and glasses ready to drink. To Akihiko, one of the ladies looked positively Western and the other oriental.

Returning his attention to the rest of the artefacts in front of him, Akihiko picked up the book of poems again. Turning it over and over in his hands, his eyes misted as he flicked through the pages of traditional Tanka-style poetry, each offering a five-line, thirty-one-syllable poem that has historically been the basic form of Japanese poetry.

He wondered which one was his father's favourite, and if he read the poems before he went into battle. As he flicked through the pages his eyes settled on one poem and these words kept running over and over in his mind:

> *Like to a stone*
> *That rolls down a hill,*
> *I have come to this day*

He held up the lock of blonde hair and surveyed the photographs once more and wondered. As he looked up his mother was standing in the entrance to the room. She was giving him that all-knowing look that appeared to echo his thoughts.

36

Susan and Billy had not so much slept as been in a comatose state.

Billy was first to wake. He found the two beds were low to the ground, more like futons. For Billy, it seemed a long way down, he had to roll off the bed onto his knees before pushing himself up. It was becoming clear to Billy that a lot of things in Japan are not built for tall people.

He looked over at Susan as she lay on the bed nearest the en-suite bathroom, her back towards him. The room had been warm, she had thrown the duvet off. Her diminutive figure lay in the foetal position wearing a short-sleeved grey T-shirt with "Sydney Pride" emblazoned on it. It failed to cover her black briefs. Billy felt like a giant in her presence.

Tiptoeing quietly on the cherry wood floor, he stole past her.

An overhead rainfall shower relaxed his tight muscles as it cascaded onto his weary body. Towelling himself down, he looked across at the toilet which had an array of buttons like a television remote control.

He sat on the toilet and ran through the buttons checking out their functions. One heated the toilet seat, which amused him. If only he had had that as a small boy in winter at home, or even better in the outside privy at his grandparents. Suddenly he was given a real shock as he pressed a button and felt a jet of water assault his undercarriage. He jumped up dripping from the nether regions and laughed quietly to himself.

Dressing as silently as he could, he left a note on the desk and carefully opened the door, trying not to wake Susan. He took one last look at her doll-like form, deep in slumber, and headed down for breakfast.

When he returned to the room, Susan had a towel wrapped around her and she was drying her hair in front of a mirror which sat above the dressing table.

"I didn't want to wake you, you looked so peaceful sleeping." Said Billy

"I was dead to the world. Thanks for letting me sleep in. Have you eaten?"

"Well, I gave it a go, but these Japanese breakfasts are … well, they're Japanese."

Susan laughed. "I see."

"Maybe we can find somewhere when we head out for you to have breakfast, or should I say brunch?" he corrected himself as he looked at his watch, seeing it was approaching midday.

"So, what is the plan, Billy?"

"First of all, I will get another room and then I figure we can check the local telephone directories, and if that fails head to the local council offices and find out if there is some sort of Nagasaki residents register."

"Why don't you head down to reception and see if they have a directory, while I get dressed and straighten myself up?" said Susan.

"Sure," said Billy as he disappeared once more.

"Good morning! I wonder if you have a telephone directory?" asked Billy at the reception desk. The mature male receptionist turned, opened a drawer and handed a slim book to Billy. Without speaking the receptionist returned to his form filling behind the reception desk.

Sitting in the small, sparsely furnished lobby, Billy opened the directory only to find, unsurprisingly, that it was in Japanese script. Purposely avoiding the older receptionist, Billy approached the desk once more. "Excuse me," he said, attracting the attention of a young woman. "I wonder if you can help me? I am having trouble understanding this directory. I am looking for a Mr Akihiko Kuroki. Could you help me see if he is in this directory, please?"

Smiling, she went through the directory but found no Kuroki family names. "Sorry, sir. No luck." She smiled and frowned at the same time.

"How else can I find someone?"

"Do you know where they live?" said the young lady.

"We have a name and an address in Nagasaki, but of course we are not sure if we will find who we are looking for there. The address may be old."

"Sir! Nagasaki is a big place, almost half a million people," replied the receptionist with a half-smile, half-laugh and a toss of her head. "So good job you have an address. Good place to start!"

"I guess we were a little optimistic. We didn't really think this one out," chuckled Billy.

"You could also place an advertisement in the press, a national paper like the *Asahi Shimbum*, just in case the people you are looking for have moved. You need to put the names and any other information you have. Many people in Japan have the same or very similar names, so more details will help with your search."

"That is a great idea. But it may take us a lot of time. We don't have long. I suppose we'll try and find this address and if they are not there, perhaps the people living there now will know them."

Billy produced a piece of folded paper from his pocket and showed the receptionist.

"Sure. That's not too far, you could take the train." She looked at Billy and hesitated. "Or maybe I can order you a cab. Take this hotel card, though, so you can ask anyone how to get back here. Is that okay?"

"Excellent," replied Billy. "Ah! I will also need an additional room for our stay."

An hour later their taxi rolled slowly up to their destination address. Susan and Billy arrived in front of a characterful house in the suburb of Iki-Shi.

"It looks like a sort of two-tiered temple with the red tiled roof and wide eaves," said Billy.

"It's imposing and stands out as an older property. Most of them here appear to be more modern as this looks a relatively new area."

An acacia tree softened the front aspect of the intriguing building. A heavily laden telegraph pole looked like it would break under the weight of the cables it bore down towards the oceanfront as the road fell away.

Susan looked at Billy and took his hand as they approached the house. Billy knocked at the door. For a moment, they thought there was no one in.

Miho had heard the door and wondered who it might be. Busy taking off her make-up. she wiped her hands and walked with the cloth to the door. As she opened it she was very surprised to see such a tall white man and a petite lady beside him.

"Hello," said Susan, clearing her throat. As she tried to talk, the words seemed to dry and pile up in her mouth.

Billy was immediately entranced as he observed this diminutive figure looking serene in her kimono, framed by the doorway.

"My name is Susan Duncan and this is Billy Williams. Do you speak English? Do Akihiko Kuroki and Sachiko Kuroki live here?"

Miho viewed them a little bemused, still coming to terms with westerners at her door. "Akihiko Kuroki is my husband. But he is not here. He is visiting his mother in Kyoto," said Miho in perfect English.

"Oh! When will he return?" said Billy.

"I am expecting him this evening. Why do you want to see him?"

"It's a very long story," said Susan. "May we come in and explain a little?"

There was a slight pause, before Miho said, "Please come up."

Stepping up into the home and taking off their shoes n the entrance they were shown down the long, wooden-floored hallway, which appeared to skirt the outside of the house. A sliding door was slightly open, allowing a glimpse of a small Japanese garden beyond. Another sliding screened door with translucent paper panels opened into a large room covered in tatami mats and zabutons, flat cushions for people to sit on.

A central low, wooden table held a teapot and small beakers. Against one of the walls was a large dark wood cabinet.

"Please," said Miho as she motioned for them to sit.

Billy watched Susan sit and followed suit. He kneeled down, then tucked the square zabuton beneath him. His long legs awkwardly folded, he sat back with his hands propping him up. Susan had easily sat down and now perched cross-legged comfortable in the environment as if it was second nature.

"Can I offer you some tea?" asked Miho.

"Yes, please," said Billy and Susan in unison.

Billy was surprised at the minimalism of the furniture and decoration. There was a distinct lack of anything in the room and no windows to the outside as such, just the screens. One was open like a sliding door to the outside, making the garden feel like an extension to the room. Billy found it very relaxing, as if you were in a conservatory.

Susan was impressed by the diffused light, which gave the room a sense of harmony, with the paper shoji screen opening to the garden sanctuary. A small pond was evident to them and the sound of water trickled into it from a bamboo half pipe, calming the mind.

Before long Miho returned, knelt, and placed on the table the small porcelain tea set. The porcelain was so fine you could practically see through its pretty floral design. Miho proceeded to pour them all some tea.

Susan studied Miho. She wore a bright red kimono with a gold leaf pattern. It had long, flowing sleeves and her wide, elaborate obi ties in the front brought the whole costume together. But she wore no white make-up to show off her traditional hairstyle. With her white socks and Japanese sandals, she looked so beautiful.

Miho looked up, as she presented first Billy, then Susan with a tea cup.

"I was due to go to a birthday party of a dear friend shortly, but she has been taken ill, so please excuse my appearance. I do not usually dress as formally at home."

"I think you look beautiful," said Susan.

"Very elegant," chimed in Billy.

Miho bowed, embarrassed by their compliments. "So! You tell me you have a long story!" she prompted.

"Yes. We have brought you and your husband a small gift," said Billy as he handed Miho a gift-wrapped cake, which the hotel receptionist had both suggested, then procured for Billy, advising it would be an appropriate present when visiting someone's home.

Miho smiled and nodded, taking the gift and placing it on the table alongside the tea-set.

Susan cleared her throat and put her teacup and saucer on the table. She opened her handbag and took out a photograph, which she handed to Miho.

Miho perused the picture, then looked up at Susan. "Who is this?"

"This is Violet, my mother. I believe my father, who I never knew, is also Akihiko's father."

Miho looked at Susan and Billy and back at the photograph. "But how can this be? Satoshi Kuroki died after the long struggle to free Asia from the yolk of Western oppression in 1945 and he was married to Sachiko Kuroki."

Susan nodded. "I know it's hard to understand, it took a while for me to comprehend how this could be.

"I was brought up in Scotland in the United Kingdom by my mother and a stepfather, before I left home and eventually moved to Australia. Then, a month or so back, Billy here, and my best friend from childhood turned up and …"

Suddenly Susan was interrupted by a voice from the genkan area of the home.

"Tadaimi."

Susan, Miho and Billy sat in silence for what seemed like ages.

"Tadaimi, Miho," called Akihiko.

As he entered the tea room, he was surprised to see two guests enjoying tea with his wife. Standing and bowing, Miho said in welcome, "Okaeri Nasai, Akihiko."

Akihiko looked at the guests then at Miho for an explanation.

"Gomennasai, Akihiko … we have visitors from Australia and Great Britain."

Billy stood awkwardly, first putting out his hand, but then bowing in unison with Susan towards Akihiko.

"I am Susan Watkins, this is my friend Billy Williams. We are so pleased to meet you."

Akihiko looked confused and a little annoyed. Billy could see this slightly built and balding man looked both tired and perplexed.

"Husband, Susan and Billy believe that … Well. they have a photograph," said Miho and she bent to the table picking up the snap of Violet. "This is Susan's mother."

Still bemused, Akihiko studied the photograph, then looked at Susan before returning his gaze to the snapshot. Akihiko put down his overnight bag and Miho instantly picked it up and left the room.

"Forgive me, I am a little confused as to who you are and why you are here to see us," said Akihiko.

Billy took over. "Susan's mother, Violet Watkins, was in a prisoner of war camp on Sumatra during the war. We believe your father knew Violet rather intimately." He knew as soon as he said it he had phrased it badly.

A flash of anger flew across Akihiko's face and his brow furrowed. "You come into my house and insult me. How dare you?"

"I think you may be my half-brother, Akihiko," said Susan.

"Preposterous," countered Akihiko. "You must leave now."

Billy tried to intervene. "I know this must be a shock to you but …"

"Please leave at once," said Akihiko gesturing with his extended arm towards the front door.

Miho returned to see Susan and Billy being shepherded to their shoes and out of the building.

Susan turned. "Please do not be angry. Please consider that we have a lot more to tell you, how it happened and how …"

"Kyuusoku … leave my house."

As they were hurried on their way, Susan turned and bowed and gave Akihiko the hotel card.

"We are at this hotel, for a few more days. Please contact us."

With that, Akihiko turned his back. Miho bowed to Billy and Susan, an apologetic, almost frightened look on her face. She closed the door screen.

Akihiko looked out over his beloved garden, then to the sky. Calming down, he breathed deeply and headed to the west of the house and to the altar to his ancestors. He knelt, lighting two candles, which he placed on the altar, he banged a gong and chanted prayers and incantations for guidance from the jade image of Buddha that looked down on him.

Now more at one with the world and himself, he washed and returned to Miho who had prepared a light meal. They ate in silence. That night they went to bed without further discussion about the visitors, or his visit to his mother in Kyoto.

Akihiko lay awake, sleep escaping him. As the sun rose, daylight crept up the shoji enclosure illuminating the bedroom with a pool of light.

Miho awoke, sensing a light breeze. Sitting up in bed she saw Akihiko cross-legged, looking through the open door across his treasured garden.

She walked over and knelt behind him to massage his shoulders. She saw the sepia photograph in his hands and realised he was crying.

37

Susan and Billy had made the best of the rest of their day, visiting the Peace Park.

Neither of them referred much to their visit to the Kurokis' home, choosing to immerse themselves in Nagasaki culture and history, like true tourists.

"This must be Urakami Cathedral," said Billy, consulting the guide book he had purchased before they left Sydney.

"I'm surprised it's so ... well ... plain," said Susan as she looked up at the red-brick building with its stained-glass windows.

"I read in a leaflet in the hotel room that this had been at the centre of the atomic bombing, and therefore completely destroyed and rebuilt, so I guess that was the material at hand. I wonder what the old cathedral looked like."

"What's in there, I wonder?" said Susan, heading towards a small outbuilding beside the church.

Billy followed her, and they peered through the door. "Looks like a few artefacts. From the original church maybe?" he said, more a question than a statement.

"All the signs are in Japanese, which doesn't help us much," said Susan, a little disappointed.

Returning to the grounds of the cathedral, Susan's attention was drawn to a statue of an angel. The angel had a blackened face looking towards the sky. She paused and looked at the sky herself. *Very apt*, she thought, taking out her camera and taking a snap of it.

Moving on, they walked towards the large harbour, before taking a short, steep uphill climb. Stopping briefly to rest, they turned around and surveyed the harbour from an impressive vantage point.

"Wow," said Billy. "This is some harbour, much bigger than I thought. Now you can see its full extent, you can appreciate how important it must have been during the war to the Japanese navy."

As they climbed higher they reached the area known as Glover Gardens. "This is supposed to be a hilltop open-air museum," said Susan as she consulted the tourist leaflet she had picked up down in the harbour area. "Apparently, these mansions are from the Meiji period, and they belonged to former Western residents of Nagasaki," she said, reading on.

"Gosh, Billy," she said as she stood in front of one of the houses. "Look at the beautiful panoramic views of the bay they had from here. I can only think they were very rich people and lived a very privileged existence. These lovely landscaped gardens with their ponds full of koi carp are so serene. Do you think they were there in those days?"

"Maybe," said Billy. "This chap, Thomas Blake Glover, must have done well for himself," he added as they entered the former Glover's Mansion, typical of the many bungalows built by the British abroad. "It says here," he said, picking up an information sheet, "that he helped modernise Japan in the nineteenth century, and, get this, he was probably the inspiration for Puccini's Madame Butterfly."

Glover's house was situated lower on the hill than some of the houses, but in a great location, making it perfect for views over the bay from an elevated but flat space.

"Given my understanding of Japan," Billy went on, "as a closed society to the west in the nineteenth century, old Tom Glover must have ingratiated himself to the Japanese and been very special to be allowed to build here and trade with them.

"Wow! 1863 was when this was erected. Wonder if it's changed much over the years?" Reading more, he said. "Nagasaki was one of the few international trading ports in Japan. Foreign traders flocked to the city and a number of western-style houses were built on a hill overlooking Nagasaki and the harbour."

Susan was lost in thought. The views from the top of the hill they had climbed, the black-faced angel, the cathedral and Peace Park all melded into one. She felt they added some perspective to their journey here and took her back to the time her mother and Billy's father had lived through.

"Penny for them ...?" interrupted Billy.

"I was just thinking, Billy. I've been pent up with so many emotions over the years and hurting for what Mum suffered. But these people suffered too, war is evil whichever side you're on. I believe politicians and governments of the day have a lot to answer for."

"True, but that's why the war should not have been allowed to start, so the Japs and the other enemies of the Allies brought all this on themselves."

"Maybe … But what of me and Akihiko and his mother, we were all innocent parties but have all suffered too."

Billy looked back at the house. "Can you imagine Madame Butterfly floating from room to room in there and then three little maids from school arriving?" he asked with a smile.

Susan seated herself on the grassy lawn, her legs stretched out in front of her, resting back on her arms, her canary-yellow cotton dress spread like a fan on the grass. She took in the immediate gardens and tropical plants A brief smell of some exotic plant tickled her nose and made her eyes water a little, leading to a sneeze.

"Bless you," said Billy as she sneezed again.

"Thank you." she replied as Billy sat beside her.

"So, Susan, Mr and Mrs Kuroki don't want to know. We might as well head for home soon, don't you think? Was your half-brother what you expected? If he is your half-brother, that is."

"His reaction was no shock, that's for sure. But I've been thinking. Why don't we try and find his mother Sachiko Kuroki? We have nothing to lose, not now we're here.

"I would love to see Kyoto. I read about it before we came. There are loads of geishas still in the old part of the city. And it has lots of beautiful temples and a castle."

"A castle? Surely not. I can't imagine it's anything like Caernarfon or Harlech. I'm not sure we will learn any more or even find Mrs Kuroki. However, like you say, we have come all this way, and the geishas certainly sound interesting," said Billy with a wink.

That evening, Billy slept well. He showered and knocked on Susan's door.

Almost immediately Susan opened the door, fully dressed.

"Couldn't you sleep? I thought you would still be resting," said a surprised Billy.

"I slept okay. When I'm awake I have to get up. I've been thinking ..."

"That's sounds dangerous," teased Billy.

"Perhaps we should just leave everything in the past. We have obviously upset Akihiko Kuroki and we may not even be right with our assumptions."

"I see your point, but we do know from testimonies of Mavis and historical notes that what happened to your Mum is true. I thought it was more about you finding your father, or at least establishing more about him, should I say."

"Maybe." said Susan. "I think we should catch the train to Kyoto and at least be a tourist for another day or two before heading home. What do you say?"

"Sounds fine to me," said Billy. "But can we have breakfast first?"

Susan smiled. "You and your stomach."

Failing to cope with the strange-looking foods on the Japanese buffet, Susan settled for a black coffee. As she stirred it, Billy returned to the table with a strange concoction on his plate, consisting of Japanese noodles and a bread roll alongside western breakfast cereal. She started to laugh. Billy smirked, "What?"

Then her facial expression changed as she looked beyond Billy towards the entrance to the restaurant.

Billy turned to follow her gaze. Akihiko Kuroki, dressed smartly in a suit, was talking with the Maître d', who was pointing towards their table.

"Ohaiyo gozaimasu … Good morning," said Akihiko as he bowed. "May I join you?"

Lost for words, Billy extended his arm opening his palm to indicate for Akihiko to pull up a chair.

"Can we get you some coffee?" said Susan.

"Very kind, but no, thank you. I have come to apologise. I am ashamed of how I reacted yesterday, I was upset and irrational."

"We understand," said Susan as she looked at Billy, who nodded in agreement.

"It was a big shock, we're sure. For us to just turn up on your doorstep and make what many would consider such a wild claim," said Billy apologetically.

"If you would permit me, I would like to show you something, and perhaps explain a little of my life. Perhaps you will allow me to share my feelings and beliefs with you when you have finished breakfast."

Billy wiped his mouth with his napkin and Susan stood. "We're ready now, aren't we, Billy?" stated Susan.

"Why, yes, certainly," said Billy as he took a slurp of tea from his cup and forlornly looked at his barely touched breakfast plate. He followed Susan and Akihiko out of the restaurant.

As they approached the door to the street, Akihiko stopped and turned to Billy and Susan. "It is of course very hot and humid today, as usual. There may be

386

thunderstorms. Do you have some rainwear?" Susan produced a small, folded-up raincoat from her bag. "Very good!"

Nothing was said on the short walk to the Peace Park. As they entered from the south, Akihiko stopped. "This is the Fountain of Peace."

They stood in front of a splendid fountain and plaque. Ahead of them they could see a large statue and without dallying, Akihiko walked towards it.

"This was not far from the centre of the nuclear explosion in 1945," said Akihiko. "My mother used to bring me here regularly as a child." As they walked down the paved avenue to the statue they were silent. Standing in front of the statue, Akihiko bowed. Susan and Billy followed suit.

"The statue's right-hand points to the threat of nuclear weapons, while the extended left hand symbolises eternal peace. Look at the graceful face with its eyes closed. It is offering a prayer, so that souls of those who died may rest in peace. The folded right leg and extended left leg signify both meditation and the initiative to stand up and give hope to the people of the world.

"Do you see the black marble vault in front of the statue? It contains the names of the atomic bomb victims and survivors who died in subsequent years, many of them my friends and family."

"I am so sorry," said Susan.

Billy put his arm around Susan and nodded his agreement.

Akihiko bowed again as he turned towards them, Susan could see he had tears in his eyes. The sun disappeared behind a cloud and the sky darkened. Addressing Billy and Susan, Akihiko said, "For years I have been blinkered by this experience in my childhood. I was lucky enough to avoid its terrible blight. I had been visiting my grandparents with my mother in Kyoto. They were kimono manufacturers. I used to love visiting them and seeing all the beautifully dressed ladies.

"On that terrible day back in 1945, we arrived at the railway station, or should I say we alighted from the train a good way from the centre of the city, as the station had been devastated.

"As we made our way towards our home we had to walk many miles and we witnessed terrible sights. The fierce nuclear blast had created a wind of evil, heat rays reached several thousand degrees and deadly radiation generated by the explosion crushed, burned and killed everything in sight and reduced this entire area to an apocalyptic devastation."

Akihiko paused. His voice cracked as he choked back his emotions. "All that remained was a barren wasteland of tree stumps and derelict buildings, a land strewn with rubble. A third of Nagasaki City prefectures were destroyed and 150,000 people killed or injured. We never thought it would be rebuilt. I have felt guilty ever since, just for surviving.

"I have blamed the Americans, and indeed the British and all the Allies, for the devastation they brought on my country and its people. But I have realised very late in my life that we the Japanese were as much to blame."

Akihiko walked a few steps to a park bench and invited Susan and Billy to sit with him. He reached inside his jacket pocket and took out the sepia photograph his mother had given him a day or so before. He studied it and gave it to Susan.

"My father is the one standing on the left behind the lady who ..."

Susan looked up, interrupting him. "That is my mother Violet. She looks happy."

Billy took the photograph and looked at Susan then at Akihiko. "Did your father give you this?"

"My mother showed it to me, just the other day. I had never seen it before. It was sent with other personal belongings when my father did not return from the war.

"I have one other item with me," said Akihiko as he reached into his jacket pocket once more, producing his father's book of poetry.

As he opened the book he retrieved and held out in his open hand a lock of fair hair.

Susan looked at it with trepidation, and with her eyes asked for Akihiko's permission to take the hair in her hands. As she took it, then smelled it, she looked at Akihiko. "Now do you think we may be brother and sister, Akihiko?"

Akihiko looked lost, he was so forlorn, like the small child that his mother used to bring to the Peace Park. "When you showed me the photograph of your mother yesterday I recognised her as the lady in this picture, but of course that does not prove anything."

"There may be one way to find out for sure," interceded Billy. Now he had Akihiko and Susan's undivided attention. "I was reading an article earlier in the year that said they can now test your DNA by taking a strand of your hair and/or some blood. It's not cheap but it would prove once and for all if what you are thinking is true, that you may well be brother and sister."

"That's true. I read an article about it too," said Susan. "It's like a genetic fingerprint, used to determine whether two individuals are parent and child or indeed related. I think they check the blood group and enzymes or something, but it's worth a go, I think."

"I have heard of this," said Akihiko. He looked at Susan.

"Shall we?" asked Susan.

Akihiko nodded and put his hand on her shoulder. "We have nothing to lose and everything to gain."

38

Gwen was sitting on a sunlounger on her verandah, enjoying the warmth of the August sun. She had felt tired of late and was fed up of the constant indigestion she suffered. It had become far worse recently, disturbing her sleep every night. She had taken to sitting propped up in bed.

Gwen had dozed off in the sunshine. Sunglasses askew on her face, Gwen awoke suddenly from a frightening dream she was having. Her heart was beating fast, her lilac short-sleeved top stained with dribble. Gwen often had this same recurring dream.

She was always running through the jungle, trying to escape her Japanese pursuers. Thrashing through undergrowth, perspiring like crazy in her frantic flight, her head pounding in the heat of the sun.

Relieved to be awake and safe from her fear, she felt thirsty. Grunting out loud in response to her stiff body and its aches and pains she moved slowly to extricate herself from her sunbed repose.

Pink faced, she shuffled over the smooth slated paving area and returned inside the house, thankful for the respite from the sun's heat. As she stretched upwards to try and relieve the stiffness of her back, she saw a cobweb in the corner of the room by the ceiling. It floated free like a parachute's silk descending to earth. She made a mental note to remove it later.

As she approached the kitchen she heard the clatter of the letter box, so she continued into the hallway to retrieve the morning mail. As she stooped to pick it up, she felt her back catch once more. She winced as she held it with her free hand. She glanced at the envelopes: a reminder for her council tax, a couple of pieces of junk mail and a thin envelope with Par Avion and the familiar stamps of Australia.

Returning to the kitchen she boiled the kettle, having tucked the airmail letter into her pinafore pocket. Cutting herself a scone and smearing butter sparingly, she added a large blob of her favourite Bonne Maman raspberry jam, one of her weaknesses.

It had been harder to get around these last few months. Her joints seemed to be ever stiffer. Probably arthritis, she had decided. She was relieved summer made the days longer and warmer, albeit that four-seasons-in-one-day weather still punctuated the summer occasionally.

She shuffled to her rocking chair in front of the open patio doors. Placing her plated scone and her steaming hot cup of tea onto the table she sat back into her chair, put on her glasses dangling from the chain around her neck and opened the airmail letter.

Dear Gwen,
How are you? I hope you are keeping well.

It's cool here in Sydney today, there was even a little ice on the car windscreen this morning. But the day has warmed nicely and I look forward to spring.

You will never guess what has just happened. I have lots to tell you!

It is such a small world. I have just met Tom's son, Billy Williams. Yes, the very same, he was in Sydney. It was sad to hear Tom had died as per your last letter, and I was so pleased Billy had been to meet you. Then, lo and behold, here he is in Sydney.

Also, he has found Violet's daughter Susan and made contact with her.

I couldn't believe it when I was having a cup of tea and reading my daily copy of the Sydney Herald. There it was, an appeal for anyone who knew Violet Watkins to get in touch. Well, I just had to go.

When I met Billy at the Renaissance Hotel, he was accompanied, indeed sharing a room, with a rather pleasant, caring lady called Mary Anderson. I believe he was in a relationship with this lady. Apparently, she lived in Scotland, on the Isle of Arran. He is a lovely chap, Gwen, he reminds me so much of Tom.

Apparently, Violet is living in a nursing home in Scotland. She has Alzheimer's. She suffered as much as anyone did under the Japanese. I hope if there is one blessing of dementia, it is that she is free from those awful wartime memories.

Who knows what would have happened if Tom had known Violet's full story? He could have rescued her from the sad life she apparently led after the war in a loveless relationship.

I have to tell you, Gwen, I also met Vi's daughter, Susan. I had quite a shock, in fact it quite unnerved me She is the image of Captain Kuroki. I do believe she must be his child, which must have been terrible for Violet to deal with over the years. How can you love a child who was the result of rape? It must explain why Vi never returned to Sydney.

I feel even more sorry for Violet now.

Please send the photographs and letters Gladys wrote, as you promised. I miss her so much. Thanks for looking after them for me, I am ready to see them now. I loved you too in a caring way, Gwen, but Gladys made me feel special, which no man could ever do.

I admire you, Gwen, for not telling Tom about the disgusting way the Japanese treated us or indeed about Violet's fraternisation, it would have broken him. War makes us do the strangest things, Gwen.

I must continue to live with myself and those difficult memories, but not for much longer, my dear Gwen. I must tell you I have stage four bowel cancer and the prognosis is not good.

I am not afraid, I am ready. So please don't fret for me.

Look after yourself, old stick

See you in the next life,

Lots of love, Mavis XXX

Gwen was horrified as the words jumped off the page Her heart raced, her breathing became erratic. She sa with tears in her eyes. She was angry that Mavis wa:

suffering, especially as she had known nothing of Mavis being in ill health. She felt helpless.

She was not surprised. That was how Mavis was, stoic, always the strong one. It had been Mavis who had mothered and looked after Gwen during those dreadful years of war and Gwen knew she owed her life to Mavis, who was always tender towards her and nursed her through great bouts of sickness and malaria.

Yet now she could not shake the guilt she felt for the way she had felt jealous of Violet. Nor could she come to terms with her failing to tell Tom the whole truth about the time on Java. She could not imagine the shame Violet must have felt having an illegitimate child of the enemy. Gwen felt ashamed.

Gwen reached for her teacup and saucer, took a sip and tried to calm herself. I should have made camomile, she mused. Stretching over for her scone, she took a mouthful, leaving crumbs around her mouth, some dropping on the floor.

Before she could savour the taste of the raspberry jam, a hammer blow hit her chest and she gasped out loud. The plate and scone toppled onto the floor, as if in slow motion. She rocked forward, holding her chest, her eyes rolled into the top of her head and she fell across the coffee table, scattering the cup and saucer.

Weak and dazed, and with a massive effort, it took what seemed like ages for her to crawl out onto her patio. She tried to shout for help, but no sound came, her speech had gone. She felt the sea breeze one last time as it ruffled her grey hair.

The last thing she saw was the well-kept flower border of her garden. The daffodils had flowered and gone, but alongside them the forget-me-nots, five-petalled, blue blooms with yellow centres, danced in the wind.

39

Akihiko and Miho spent a pleasant evening with Billy and Susan. They talked of their lives and their hopes and fears for their children, and by the end of the evening they had agreed to find out how they could take the DNA test to put each other's mind at rest, and to confirm or otherwise whether they truly were brother and sister.

"A toast," said Akihiko, "to our parents, whoever they are, and to peace and, of course, to a safe journey home for you both tomorrow."

"Thank you," responded Billy. "May I also add friendship? That whatever happens with the DNA test, we keep in touch."

"Here, here," agreed Susan.

"Kampai," offered Akihiko, raising his glass.

"Cheers," said Susan.

"Iechyd da!" threw in Billy, not wanting his Welsh heritage forgotten.

The next morning Billy was first up as usual but was soon joined by Susan at breakfast.

"Gosh, I'd better shake a leg and pack my bag." said Susan as she donned her brown teardrop-shaped glasses and realising the time. My flight is at 1 pm and the time will soon go. What time is your flight to the UK?"

"Same, 1 pm like you. I have to change in Tokyo. In fact, I may have to overnight there for a connection tomorrow, but I will come with you to see you off."

It was later than they thought, so they decided to grab something to eat at the airport after Susan had checked in. Billy also offloaded his case at check-in, so they were free of encumbrances.

Over a drink they reflected on their visit.

"I have had a great time meeting you, Susan, it has been an honour and a pleasure."

"Thank you, Billy, likewise."

"I'm going to miss you. What do you think your plans will be?"

"It's been a blast and it's been great meeting you and wonderful seeing Mary after all these years. I bet she'll be over the moon to have you back home." Billy blushed. "I guess I'll go back to work and we'll get these DNA tests done and see what the future holds.

"What about you, Billy? Do I hear the sound of wedding bells?" said Susan mischievously.

Billy pulled his head back from the neck and raised his brows. "Not sure, I've been there and done that and as they say, got the T-shirt."

"How do you feel about Mary? You know she is besotted with you and hopelessly in love."

Billy turned a little red in the cheeks. "My, it's warm in here," he jested, fanning himself with his napkin. "

do care for her, she is a lovely girl. I'll see where things go when we get back, it's quite early days."

"Don't hurt her, Billy."

"I have no intention of hurting Mary," said Billy, starting to get a little tetchy. "I'll get home and then go up to Scotland for a weekend to catch up as soon as I can and when Mary is free, too, of course."

Looking at her small gold-faced Tissot wristwatch, Susan adjusted the white leather strap and said "We need to head towards the departure gate. We'll be boarding soon."

Sure enough, the All Nippon Airways flight to Tokyo was on time and had started to board business class and families with children.

Susan turned to Billy and held out her hand. Billy took her hand, pulled her closer and kissed her on the top of the head, he then lowered his frame and with his right hand held her chin and kissed her lightly on the lips.

"Sayonara, Suisen."

Susan's eyes filled with emotion. "Sayonara, my friend, safe travels."

Clutching her small carry-on bag, she turned away towards the boarding-pass desk, then looked back and waved before disappearing down the tunnel to her plane.

To her surprise, ten minutes later, Billy plonked himself beside her.

"What are you doing here?" said Susan, fearing he had changed his mind and was coming back to Sydney.

"I made sure we were on the same flight to Tokyo, I said I would see you off. I just wanted to do it twice."

She gave him a playful punch on the shoulder, smiled and pulled out her magazine to read. In true fashion she was asleep, almost before the plane took off.

There was a stopover in Tokyo for Susan, too, as they waited for their flight connections, so they shared a few drinks in the bar.

"Will you ever marry, Susan?"

"No! I am quite happy, I'm hoping Danny has grandchildren to keep me busy!"

Time soon went and Billy waved Susan off for the final time. He decided not to pay the exorbitant hotel prices in Tokyo and put his head down on his cabin luggage until his early morning flight back to Heathrow.

After an uneventful flight, Billy arrived back in the United Kingdom. He was very tired from the long journey but was so happy to pay off the taxi cab and reach his Shropshire home and finally be able to sleep in his own bed, almost thirty-six hours after leaving Nagasaki.

He entered the kitchen through the side door and dropped his luggage on the floor. The house had a musty, enclosed smell to it, but it was comforting, it was home.

For just a moment he pondered calling Mary but then decided to do so the next day after a good night's sleep, maybe he would also call Gwen to report his findings after updating Mary and finding out how Violet was.

He entered his hallway and walked onto a carpet of mail. He kicked it into a pile and bent his aching, tall body to gather it up. He could see at a glance that it was mostly marketing correspondence. He left it on the bottom step of the stairs as he wearily climbed the wooden hill towards rest. He fell onto the bed without undressing and into a deep slumber where he witnessed a kaleidoscopic plethora of disturbing events.

He awoke thinking he had slept for days, but it was the early hours of the morning. His eyes opened but could not register his location. His mind was in a fog-like state, but finally his brain cleared and told him he was home. He had been chased by a pack of ravenous fierce dogs in his dream, so was relieved to wake. Dazed, he raised himself off the bed, shuffling his way to the bathroom. Barely awake he came back to his bedroom, took off his trousers, sweater and shirt, draping them on the bathtub chair in the corner of the room.

He pulled back the sheets and slept for twelve more hours. Dozing, he started to run his adventure through his mind. He wondered about many facets of his overall journey and the people he had met since his father's funeral.

He contemplated how much he had to tell Gwen.

He wondered what the future held for himself and Mary.

A plethora of other characters he had met en route sailed on the ocean of his mind. He wondered how memories differed or were confused by all the old war veterans. After all, memory is a fickle thing.

Billy woke with a start. Someone was knocking at the door. He grabbed his dressing gown hanging on the bedroom door and, barefoot, descended the stairs to the front door.

"Good morning, sir, had a lie in, have we?" said the postman, holding out a padded envelope and a small book for him to sign.

Taking the envelope, Billy signed, not bothering to counter the postman's allusions. He walked to the kitchen, filled the kettle and made himself a strong black coffee.

Ripping apart the A6-sized package, he produced a folded letter and foraged for any other contents, but there was none. On the heading was Parry, Thomas and Morgan, Solicitors, 4 Bank Place, Porthmadog.

Dear Mr Williams
We have been asked to contact you and inform you of the passing of Ms Gwen Powell of Awel y Mor, Ralph Street, Borth-y-Gest.
A reading of Ms Powell's last will and testament is planned for midday on the 20 September and your attendance is requested by the late Ms Powell.
We look forward to hearing from you.
Yours sincerely
Lloyd Morgan LLB

Billy's hand started to tremble. He was visibly shaken by this very sad news. Then his thoughts bounced to the word "will". An innate fear of wills being read after his father's will was understandable. It reminded him to contact his father's lawyer to confirm he had fulfilled his father's wishes. He wondered what more was to be thrown at him.

Billy immediately rang the lawyers and confirmed his attendance. He learned that Gwen's passing was recent and that the funeral had already taken place. Other than that, they chose to offer nothing more than their condolences.

Following a hot shower that failed to rejuvenate his tired body, he decided he must call Mary. Sitting in his navy-blue dressing gown, he dialled the number.

"Hello, Mary, it's Billy."

"Hello! Sorry, Billy who? Hello, who is calling?"

"Sorry, Mrs Anderson, I thought you were Mary. It's Billy Williams from Shrewsbury, I think Mary has possibly told you about me."

"Och, the mysterious Billy Williams, is it? Hold on."

"Maryeeeee." He heard the shrill voice of Mrs Anderson calling her daughter. "I think the wandering Sassenach may have returned and is calling you!"

A few seconds elapsed.

"Hello, Billy. Where are you?"

"I'm at home, Mary, arrived back late yesterday."

"I've been worried to death. You haven't been in touch for over two weeks, not a phone call, a card, a letter."

"I'm sorry Mary, it's been intense, I haven't had a chance. Listen, I have lots to tell you, but I have some sad news ... Gwen has passed away."

"Oh, I'm so sorry to hear that, Billy."

"Look, Mary, I have to go to a reading of her last will and testament on 20 September, which is only next week. I wonder ..."

"I'm sure I can get leave," said Mary, anticipating his question. "Perhaps only a few days, though. I can't wait to see you, Billy. I have missed you sooooo much!"

"Yes. I've missed you too, Mary."

19 September soon arrived. Billy had frantically been trying to get his house ship-shape, tidying and cleaning. The garden was pristine in his eyes, almost as good as his father would have liked it.

Billy took the railway station steps two by two as he made sure he arrived on the platform at Shrewsbury station in time for the arrival of the Crewe train. It was just after 6 pm and the station was busy with those who commuted to Telford, Wolverhampton and other stations down the line.

As everyone disembarked on platform 4, he saw the tall, elegant figure of Mary walking towards him. His heart skipped, it finally dawned on him how much she had changed his life for the better. There was nothing like being loved.

Mary wore a charcoal grey, pleated skirt and white blouse and she had a cerise cardigan draped over one arm, carrying her small travel case in the other hand. As soon as she saw him, her pace quickened to a canter, dodging between her fellow passengers. As they met Mary set down her valise and Billy embraced her, kissing her like they had been apart for far too long. He held her tight as if he would never let her go.

A big cheer went up, and a wolf whistle or two which failed to embarrass them. With their lips still locked Mary raised her right hand to the crowd, as if in triumph as well as in acknowledgement of the now applauding phalanx of rail passengers.

Billy held her at arm's length. "Boy, I've missed you!"

"Are those beautiful red roses for me, Billy?"

He realised the bunch of roses he had for her was still in his hand wrapped around her waist. "I'm afraid they are outshone by your beauty, dear Mary!"

"Billy, they're gorgeous, and flattery will get you everywhere."

That evening they exchanged tales of what had been happening since they were apart. Mary was astounded to hear of their Japan experiences and so happy for Susan.

Mary had been to see Violet, but felt she was deteriorating, and hoped she would not suffer much longer.

After a romantic supper of Chinese takeaway washed down with a crisp Chablis, they ascended the stairs hand in hand. "This seems very strange," said Billy as they entered his bedroom, formerly his parents' room.

Next morning, when Billy awoke, Mary was resting on her elbow beside him, admiring his strong body and soft facial features that she had so fallen in love with.

"Come on, sleepy head, you have an appointment."

She slid out of bed and turned in the doorway, her attractive silk-nightdress-clad form framed by the ambient light behind.

"I love you, Mary Anderson," said Billy, glowing.

It took the usual two hours' drive to arrive in Porthmadog.

Billy parked by the side of some tennis courts, a block or so away from Bank Place. Mary straightened his tie and they walked together to the solicitors' office.

Billy and Mary were shown into a small back office with a large desk. A couple of scratched and worn bottle-green filing cabinets filled the right corner of the room. Everything in the office had seen better days, including Lloyd Morgan.

"Now this is a simple will and testament. As you may know, Ms Powell had no living relatives. This will was only made in the last few months. Perhaps Ms Powell had a premonition or just wanted to finally be prepared for her passing, as many fail to do, and they die intestate causing all sorts of problems for those left behind ... Anyway," Lloyd Morgan cleared his throat and began to read.

To whom it may concern.

I, Gwen Daisy Powell, being in sound mind, wish to leave my painting of the fox on Moel y Gest to my dear friend Mair Morris, who always admired it, and as a token of my thanks for her friendship all these years. Please forward the package I have left with you to Mavis Walker in Sydney upon my death.

I would like to leave all of my bank account proceeds after funeral and legal costs to the Royal British Legion.

Finally, I wish for Mr William James Williams of 1 Caradoc View, Shrewsbury to be the beneficiary of Awel y Mor, Ralph Street, Borth-y-Gest, my home.

I also wish for the same Billy Williams, as I know him, to take care of my personal belongings and chattels and do what he cares to with them. All except the ring, the band of gold which I bequeath specifically to him.

Billy and Mary were flabbergasted. They had been expecting others to be at the reading, Billy had certainly not expected to be the recipient of such a bequest.

Mr Morgan concluded the proceedings by handing Billy an envelope, which contained a set of house keys, the deeds to Awel y Mor, a gold ring and a sealed letter, which, Mr Morgan explained, he was instructed to give to Billy in the event of Gwen's death and specifically she insisted it was to be opened by Billy whilst sitting overlooking the estuary on the seat at the end of Ralph Street, the seat which they had shared on their walks.

Still stunned, Billy and Mary returned to the car and drove to Awel y Mor, parking right outside, as he had done the very first time earlier that year. As Billy opened the door, he felt like he was intruding on Gwen's privacy. He could not get his head around the fact that he now owned the property.

He gazed at Gwen's empty chair and surveyed the kitchen whilst looking towards the view beyond the patio doors. The Matterhorn impostor, Cnicht, resplendent in the afternoon sunshine, was surrounded by clear skies, but for a wisp of cloud appearing like a puff of smoke from the peak.

Mary put her arm through Billy's. "You still have the letter to open," she reminded him.

Closing the door, they turned left out of the low picket gate and walked the short distance to the estuary viewpoint he was familiar with. Sitting on the green slatted bench, he held the letter in his trembling hands. He scanned the horizon towards Portmeirion and the Cob causeway on the left, built by William Maddocks to create the harbour at Porthmadog that bears his name.

Gwen had told him it was all done to export Maddocks' slate.

Formidable Harlech Castle, built by Edward I but once home to Owain Glyndwr, was basking in sunshine to his right. With trepidation he slid his finger under the seal of the envelope.

Dear Billy

I have always loved you and I hope in time you can forgive me for my lack of honesty.

I cannot tell you how good it felt to have you in my home, which is now yours.

You are the image of your father, he was a strong, kind man. More than that, your mother was a saint.

I was not truthful with you regarding your father and our liaisons. Yes, we met in Singapore and yes, I first courted Jimmy. However, after the war, Tom and I found one another again. Your mother was now on the scene and she was indeed pregnant, but lost her child, she miscarried.

She just could not handle her loss, going into fits of depression. Your father was very tolerant and understanding, but he had to get away and talk to someone. That someone was me.

The letter to Violet, whom he still held a torch for was full of hope, but the reply was heartbreaking for your father. But it was a blessing for me because loved him.

Yes, I did love Jimmy, but in many ways because knew I could not have Tom as he was besotted with Violet. It made me want Tom more. It's funny how life turns out. I am ashamed knowing what I know now.

What I didn't tell you is that we had an affair, not just a fling, a loving relationship. I loved Tom and always have from the moment I set eyes on him. I became pregnant rather quickly, but I knew I couldn't keep the baby, not whilst I was living with my grandparents. The scandal would have been too much for them to bear, with me being unmarried, in a small chapel community.

So, for nine months, I moved to Shrewsbury, telling my grandparents I was on a nursing secondment. After you were born, you and I lived in a mother and baby's home and Tom came to visit us.

I begged your father to marry me and leave your mother. I have felt terrible all my life for putting your father through this. It was he who lived the lie with your mother.

I knew you would have to be adopted, and that is where your mother came in. Tom and I concocted a story that I (an old friend) had become pregnant with a man who had left me in the lurch and was unable to keep you because of my grandparents and their chapel upbringing and society's view of children born out of wedlock, especially here in Wales.

Your mother had no hesitation and wanted to bring you up and that is what happened. No authorities were involved. It was the best, we felt, for everyone.

Never a day passed when I didn't think of you. I did come and visit you in the early years but then your mother found this difficult, so I stopped coming. But I always celebrated your birthday, Billy, I just could not be part of your day-to-day life for your mother and father's sake.

Please forgive me.

All my love

Your birth mother, Gwen

Billy was trembling. He could not say anything. His eyes were full and tears started to roll down his cheeks. He was assaulted by a million emotions.

How wonderful his mother had been to adopt him, yet she knew nothing or at least she may have not known anything.

His father had been … well, he did not know how to feel about his father.

As for Gwen, why had she just not told him the truth? He would have understood, he could have held her, they could have had some time together and … well, it didn't matter now, he thought, they are all gone!

He handed Mary the letter. As she read, she too became consumed by emotion and they held each other on that bench of truth, their minds in turmoil just like the whirlpools in the windswept estuary beyond.

After what seemed an eon they strolled arm in arm back to the house that was now his. It seemed strange as the key turned in the door that he was now entering the home of his biological mother.

As always, he walked straight through to the patio doors and out onto the verandah beyond. He surveyed the vista of mountains and sea, Mary slightly behind him.

"It is beautiful here," she said.

He turned to her. "As are you, Mary." He took her hand and knelt before her and looked up into her eyes. Her face, mind and body he knew were his, his and his.

"Mary. Will you do me the honour of becoming my wife?"

40

The phone was ringing.

"Hello."

"Mary? Is that you? It's Susan!"

"Hi, Susan, great to hear from you, how are things?"

"Brilliant, Mary. So, are you visiting Billy?"

"Well, not quite. I have some news, Susan, hot off the press. Billy has asked me to marry him and I have accepted!"

"That is wonderful news. Is it going to be a family wedding, as I would like to come with Danny and maybe my brother Akihiko would like to come too!"

"Your brother?" said an excited and inquisitive Mary

"Yes indeed! The DNA tests we did have confirmed we have the same father."

"Oh! That's terrific, I'm so happy for you, Susan. Yes of course we would love to see you all here! Wait! Here is Billy, you can tell him yourself!"

"Hi, Susan. What's happening?"

"Billy, I am so excited. I have great news, Akihiko and I are siblings, the DNA results have come back positive with a 98 per cent chance Satoshi is our father.

"I want to thank you and Mary so much for helping me finally feel as though I belong to someone, that I am part of a family. I would love to talk to my mother about this, but … well, I guess that ship has sailed."

"How is Akihiko feeling?" asked Billy.

"Terrific! He's very excited, he seems to have embraced this whole sea change of thinking and understanding. He wants to visit Danny and me in Sydney with his wife Miho and his two grown-up children. I'm so happy.

"We've both come to terms with the fact that we cannot live in the past or be responsible for our parents' or indeed previous generations' actions, but we can understand and forgive. Although we have vowed that together we will find out what happened to our father and where he is buried."

"Well, that is wonderful, Susan and, if I may, I will pass you back to your best friend, who is chomping at the bit to speak to you. Sayonara."

"Susan, at the end of the day let's focus on the positives, your new family with Akihiko and our wedding!" said Mary. "We would love it if you and Danny could come to the wedding. We plan to hold it in Lamlash, this Christmas. Please say you'll come."

"How can I refuse? I get to see you finally happy in love, and I must see Mum too, as, sad as it might be to see her unwell, I just need to hold her."

*****

Akihiko felt like he had been reborn, free of the yolk of his own narrowmindedness. His son and daughter

413

regularly called round to visit and everyone seemed more relaxed.

One day after a sumptuous dinner cooked by Miho aided and abetted by Cho, Akihiko turned to his son and daughter. "Children, it is so good to see you both again and to hear of your lives. The joy it brings to you in turn brings us contentment."

"It is indeed good to see you relaxed and happy, papasan," sighed Kin.

Akihiko took off his glasses and rubbed his eyes with his finger-tips as if clearing his mind.

"I have been speaking to the Japanese government departments regarding your grandfather. They put me in touch with a western organisation that has details of all the War Crimes Trials after the Second World War. As you both know, I wanted to finally find out what happened to him and I believe I now know."

Standing, he walked to the small desk and retrieved an envelope out of which he drew a piece of paper Returning to his seat at the dinner table and replacing his glasses, he cleared his throat and read:

In response to your request for details of your father's final days we now confirm the following:
Between 24 July and 6 September Captain Satoshi Kuroki was put on trial by the War Crimes Investigation Commission which was based at the Goodwood Hotel Singapore. Captain Satoshi Kuroki was tried along with other Japanese Army personnel at Anson Road in Singapore.
He was eventually convicted of ill-treatment of prisoners of war and allowing the brutal treatment of

them by his men including the violation of women against their will resulting in physical and mental suffering at and in the vicinity of Palembang, Sumatra Netherlands Dutch East Indies between 27 July 1944 and 25 June 1945 but not limited to these dates.

After the verdict of guilty he was sentenced to death by hanging followed by cremation.

His ashes are interred with other Japanese soldiers at the Japanese Cemetery Park at 825B Chuan Hoe Avenue, Singapore.

There are a number of memorial pillars in this cemetery. Of these, we believe the one for 135 war criminals is the likely final resting place of Captain Satoshi Kuroki.

With that Akihiko looked up at his children. "So my father was branded a war criminal by the West, yet I am led to believe the memorial paid for by the Japanese government describes them as martyrs.

"All I can say is he was my father and your grandfather, it is because of him we are here today."

Cho and Kin stood and hugged their father.

*****

At Christmas, Mary and Billy picked up Susan and Danny at Glasgow airport. It had been a tiring journey, but mother and son were both excited to be there.

Susan kept leaning forward between the seats of the car and saying, "I just cannot believe I'm back here, Susan, it's truly like a dream."

"We're so thrilled to have you both here."

"Is everything on course for the wedding?" said Susan.

"Indeed it is. It's only going to be a small gathering, just ourselves and my mother, who is still ticking along, and a couple of girls from the hospital."

"Yes! Only forty-eight hours of freedom to go," chimed in Billy sarcastically, receiving a slap on the arm from Mary in the passenger seat whilst the others laughed.

At that moment "Mary's Boy Child" came on the radio.

"That could be an omen," said Susan.

Mary turned. "Now that would be a miracle, giving birth at my age, but if you see three wise men and a gathering of shepherds, be sure to let me know." The whole of the car seemed to vibrate with mirth.

*****

A crisp December day greeted the happy couple as they emerged from the Gothic-style red sandstone church sitting sentinel over waveletted Lamlash Bay with Holy Isle in the distance.

The peal of nine bells rang out the joys of the day and confetti was dispensed liberally over the deliriously happy Billy and Mary. Some of the confetti was picked up by the wind and flew high up towards Goat Fell behind them, taking the message of love to the heavens.

The local photographer, a good friend of Mary, took photographs of the small gathering and Susan hugged Mary.

Mary looked divine in her ivory cap-sleeved wedding dress with its sweetheart collar embellished with beading, sequins and crystals and its body-hugging style descending in exquisite embroidered lace to its sweeping train.

"I am so happy for you, Mary, your dress looks fabulous and you look like a fairytale bride."

"Thank you, Susan, I am euphoric. Billy is the man of my dreams and, boy, did I have to wait a long time to find him."

"Congratulations. So, the honeymoon starts Monday, then," said Danny, patting Billy on the back.

"Indeed."

"Mum would like to go and see her mother before we fly back. It would be terrific if Mary, and of course you, were to take us. Is that possible?"

"Of course." said Billy. "We are pretty well ready and packed, so no problem, let's head off tomorrow morning, but not too early," he said with a wry smile. "I think there's some celebrating to do first," he said winking.

Next morning, all a little worse for wear, they boarded the ferry over to Ardrossan. The sky brooded, a chill was in the air, even the seagulls sounded colder in their calls.

The cool winter wind of the upper deck made their eyes water and after a few minutes they descended to get a steaming hot coffee and warm up in the ship's restaurant.

Before long they were driving into the grounds of the care home where Violet lived. Susan could feel her heart beating fast.

Danny put his arm around his mother as they walked across the car park. Entering the double doors, Mary said hello to the reception staff and signed the visitors book on behalf of them all.

"Good morning, Miss Anderson."

Mary smiled, not bothering to correct them. "Is Violet in her room? How has she been?"

"Yes. She's in her room and has been okay, perhaps a little off her food lately, but generally fine."

Susan felt a little sick. If she could have run out of the building she would have, she felt so guilty. She felt sure if she could, her mother would admonish her, even disown her.

Mary knocked on Violet's door and let herself in. As usual Violet sat in her chair facing the garden. Her hair was in a bun, her mauve warm cardigan pulled around her white plain blouse and black pleated skirt. Her slippers were mauve with a flower motif matching her cardigan.

Mary moved in front of her whilst the others stood behind.

"Hello, Violet, it's Mary. Sorry I haven't been to see you for so long. But today I have a big surprise. I have brought some people to see you." Mary motioned Danny and Susan forward whilst Billy held back.

Danny held Violet's hand between both of his and Violet seemed to look through him. "Hello, Grandma, I'm Danny."

Then Susan knelt before her mother, taking her other hand. "Mum, it's me, Susan. Mum, I'm your daughter, do you remember me? It's been such a long time. I went to Australia to nurse and this is your grandson Danny."

418

Danny patted his grandmother's hand and said "Hi, Gran."

Violet continued to look towards the garden.

Then Susan spotted the photograph of her mother with her as a small child. Standing, she fetched the picture from Violet's bedside cabinet.

"Look, Mum, this is you with me, when I was little."

Still no response, but she proceeded to tell Violet what had happened over the last years since she had seen her mother. Of the unfortunate death of Danny's father and of the wonderful knowledge that she now knew that she had a family in Japan. She said she had a brother, Akihiko Kuroki.

"Do you remember, Mum? Do you recall the war and meeting Captain Satoshi Kuroki?"

Violet looked down at the picture and then at Susan.

"Mum, do you remember?"

"Susan …" said Violet, looking at the picture.

"Yes, yes, Mum. It's Susan, your daughter, this little girl was me," she said, pointing to the photograph.

"Susan," repeated Violet.

"Yes, Mum," said Susan, embracing Violet. "I'm so sorry to have been away for so long."

"I'm hungry."

"Sure, Mum, what do you fancy to eat? Let's go and find something."

Mary reached for the wheelchair, folded in the corner of the room, and together they put Violet into it. Walking along the corridor to the small dining room they asked the staff for some tea and biscuits, and they kindly obliged, adding some homemade cake.

"It's so good to meet you, Gran, after all these years," added Danny.

Violet did not reply or acknowledge Danny. She grabbed a piece of the fruit cake, and ate hurriedly, crumbs tumbling onto her black skirt and the photograph which was still on her lap. She then looked up and smiled at them all, before sipping her tea.

Mary reintroduced Billy and told Violet all about the wedding. But Violet's eyes started to close. They decided to take her back to her room. Sitting Violet on the side of the bed, then letting her lie back, they covered her with a crocheted, multi-coloured blanket. Violet was still clutching the photograph.

Danny patted his grandmother's shoulder. "Goodbye, Gran, I'm so glad I've met you."

Mary and Billy left the room with Danny, leaving Susan alone with her mother.

Violet lay on her back, her breathing rhythmic and peaceful but shallow.

"I do so love you, Mum, I wish I had known about..." Susan felt a lump in her throat. "Well, about all you went through in life, in that awful prison camp and putting up with my stepfather, all to give me a chance and a better life.

"I'm so proud of you, Mum. I have made a good life for myself and I'm so privileged to have a lovely boy in Danny. I am sure I would have forgiven Captain Kurok too if I had met him, because between you and him you gave me life."

Susan kissed her mum once more. She didn't want to leave, but this did not feel like her mum any more. It was as if Violet's soul had departed.

420

"I am so sorry for not being there for you, Mum, but please know, I do love you and always have and it is only these last few months that I have realised that, not only do I love you, but I admire you for being such a wonderful and strong and selfless woman."

Susan kissed her mother on the forehead, savouring her familiar scent, a lily of the valley talcum powder, that she had always used. She felt her mum's grey hair tickle her nose and the touch of her skin on her lips. "Goodbye, Mum, sleep well."

Later that day Violet awoke perspiring. Her mind had been racing furiously, but nothing made sense. She let the blanket slip off the bed to the floor. She looked towards the sodden garden as the wind lashed the rain against the window.

She looked at the photograph again, smiled and said "Suisen" before falling asleep one last time.

Mary had barely arrived back in Lamlash and was preparing a small afternoon tea when the phone rang.

"Oh no!" Mary put her hand to her mouth. "Yes, I see, of course, her daughter is here now. I am so, so sorry, Susan," said Mary with a pained look on her face, "apparently your Mum died not long after we visited her."

Susan took the receiver. "Hello. No, of course, I understand. I will come back right away. Oh! I see. No, please don't move her. Yes. I understand you have to let the authorities know and the funeral director. Could you take care of that, please, but don't let Mum's body go until I arrive. Thank you."

Mary hugged Susan as she sobbed and convulsed, full of guilt and grief.

"Why didn't I stay with her and help her combat my father and deal with life? I would have learned about what happened to her and understood."

"But maybe you wouldn't," said Mary. "That generation didn't really talk about personal things and certainly didn't share any bad experiences like what happened in the war!"

"I've let her down."

"No, you haven't," countered Mary. "She would have been happy that you were making a life for yourself, one she never had the chance to have."

Two hours later they were back at the nursing home, laying out Violet with the assistance of the staff in charge.

"I suppose we will have a small service and have Mum cremated," said Susan, almost without emotion, as if she was on autopilot.

"Actually," said the nursing home manager, "your mother left instructions when she first came here. Shall I get them?"

"Yes. Yes, please," said Susan as she looked in surprise at Mary.

When they had finished, Mrs Gillespie took Susan and Mary into the small day room they set aside for private conversations. A picture of daffodils swaying in a field leading up to some hills beyond adorned one wall. A photograph of a picturesque stream in a glen was on another.

"So, Mrs Gillespie, what did my mother say she wanted?"

"Please call me Moira," she said as she opened the green cardboard folder on her lap. Mary sat holding

Susan's hand in hers on the settee facing Moira Gillespie, who sat prim and proper in her dark blue shift dress, her white bare legs together above some plain black flat shoes.

Opening the file, Moira read from a document which had been dictated and signed by Violet a number of years ago:

My last will and testament.

Please contact my daughter Susan Duncan in the event of my passing. I believe she is in Sydney, Australia. Her good friend Mary Anderson of Lamlash can be my executor in Susan's absence.

I leave all my worldly goods to my daughter Susan Duncan and should she have passed on, to any offspring from her relationships. I specifically ask she take care of the treasured photograph in the oak wooden frame of her as a child alongside me.

I wish to be cremated and my ashes spread in Sydney Harbour, a place so dear to me and my family growing up.

Signed Violet Duncan née Watkins

Countersigned David Mackenzie, Mackenzie and Mackenzie Solicitors, Ardrossan

Witness: Moira Gillespie

A short ceremony was held two weeks later at Lamlash Church. Danny had flown back to Sydney, but Susan stayed on, living with Mrs Anderson and remembering her time on Arran. Mary and Billy returned from their honeymoon for the funeral and the small congregation included former neighbours and friends, who came to pay their respects.

Mrs Macgregor held Susan's hand and said Violet was a lovely lady, reassuring Susan her mother was in a better place now.

*****

It was January and Summer had come to Sydney. Armed with a casket of her mother's ashes Susan took the early evening ferry with Danny to Manly, a journey Violet had told Susan she had made many times to a favourite uncle she used to see at weekends.

Leaving the dock, they walked to the beach and wandered around to the point, relaxing and looking back towards Manly before returning for the ferry home having taken Violet for one last walk.

Violet, even when Susan was a young child, talked about death as nothing to worry about. She always told Susan that we all return to the elements when we die and to never be afraid of death as it means our life has run its course and a new horizon beckons.

Susan was too young at that time to understand, but as the ferry churned its way across the harbour Susan felt calm, as if her mother was reminding her of her words and had her hand on her shoulder.

Susan and Danny stood at the stern of the boat looking at the Grand Harbour Bridge, then at the Opera House and marvelled at this beautiful iconic panorama that was a joy to behold. Susan removed the top of the urn and gradually tipped the ashes and they scattered with the breeze and settled on the water in the lee of the

424

boat. "Good-bye, Mum, until we meet again. I love you!"

Placing the urn back in her raffia shopping bag, Susan put on her sunglasses to mask her grief, looked at the setting sun and accepted her mother was back home and truly at rest.

That evening Susan sat on her small wrought-iron balcony, the breeze wafting around her warm body. A ceiling fan in the bedroom behind her circled, creaking as it spun, as if it was off kilter and about to come off and whizz around the room.

Later, she came in and lay down on the bed. She looked at the photograph her mother had bequeathed to her that meant so much to her. She reached for it, studying it and trying to remember the day it was taken and how much she loved her mother, but all she could recall was the way her mother was so badly treated by her stepfather.

Susan felt one of the clips was a little loose on the back. As she started to try and secure it, she took off the other clips, and took off the back of the frame. As she did so another small photograph fell out and floated to the carpet below, landing face down. She lay the frame and picture of her mum on the bed and picked up the picture from the floor, seeing that it had some writing on it.

Grabbing her glasses from the bedside table, Susan focused on the elaborate curls of the script.

My Dearest Violet
I will always love you, please don't forget me.
Look after Suisen and tell her one day I love her too!

425

Forever in my heart
Satoshi X

Slowly, Susan turned over the picture and saw her mother smiling adoringly at a Japanese officer who was returning that affection, seen quite clearly in his eyes. In that moment Susan realised her mother had found a forbidden love and had paid the price throughout her life.

Satoshi and Violet had suffered so that Suisen could flourish. She now knew she was truly Akihiko's sister and felt wonderful!

*****

Back in Borth-y-Gest, Billy and Mary sat beside one another cuddled up on the settee in the cosy lounge of Awel y Mor, the log burner warming them against the cool winter evening outside.

Life had changed significantly for them both. Billy had well and truly immersed himself in his Welsh heritage. He had rented out his childhood home in Shrewsbury and had been taking Welsh classes out on the Lleyn peninsula at Nant Gwytheryn. He now had a good understanding of Welsh and an improving command of pronunciation, using place names and signs. He knew how to greet people, he could count to one hundred, knew most colours, all the days of the week, everyday phrases and, of course, like every good person from the British Isles, he could talk about the weather.

Mary had moved her life down to Borth-y-Gest. She had feared what would happen to her mother, as she could not leave her and, lo and behold, her prayers were answered as her brother and his partner decided to return to Lamlash and look after their mother, so all was well with the world, especially as Mary had managed to transfer to Bangor Hospital. Although it was strange at first she was now used to the new environment and enjoying the drive to work, especially as she had reduced her hours to three shifts a week.

"We had a letter from Susan this morning," said Mary reaching into her handbag. She unfolded the letter, adjusted her glasses and read:

Dear Mary and Billy
Hope all is good in your new life. Everyone is well here. Danny and I are planning another vacation to meet our new extended family at Akihiko's in Japan.

Mary paused, then resumed, "Get this, she also says that Akihiko has researched the meanings of the flower names for her Mum Violet. Apparently in Japanese culture 'Suisen' means respect, joy and happiness. Gwen was 'Kuchinashi' meaning secret love and Mavis was 'Tokeiso'." Mary paused again.

Billy looked up. "And Mavis was what?"

"Well, for want of a better phrase," said Mary, raising her eyebrows, "The symbolism of the passion flower Tokeiso is fondness of the same sex."

"That is uncanny, very apt and fateful," commented Billy.

"I wonder if Mavis Walker is still alive in Australia. Perhaps Susan could contact her again and tell her Gwen has passed away. She may be able to tell us more about Gwen," mused Mary as she took a sip of the red wine which gave her a warm glow.

Just then the old dog Billy had been introduced to by Gwen earlier that year tottered by the window, followed a minute or two later by his master, who stopped under the street light, lit a cigarette, which momentarily illuminated his craggy, bewhiskered, pale face, then full of determination he shuffled on.

"Well, you just never know how long people will last and what they overcome in life. The human spirit is very resilient," said Billy philosophically. "We must never forget the sacrifice people have made for us to live as we do, in freedom and peace. One thing does puzzle me still, though."

"What's that?" questioned Mary.

"I wonder what happened to Gwen's wartime diary."

Mary thought for a moment and looked at Billy. She held his right hand and touched the gold ring adorning his finger.

"I wonder what the significance of this ring was Billy."

Billy took the ring off and studied it. "I have no idea, perhaps it was Gwen's mother's?"

"May I?" said Mary. Taking the ring Mary studied the gold band before holding it up to the light. "There seems to be a small inscription inside the ring, Billy."

"Really? Let me look." Billy was amazed. "You're right."

Leaving the room, Billy fetched a small magnifying glass. As he held the ring under the light, he turned it to read the script out loud: "*Diolch am ein mab.*"

"What does that mean?" asked Mary.

Billy looked at Mary, his eyes filling with tears. Mary held his hand between hers.

His voice cracking, Billy replied, "It means thank you for my son."

Acknowledgements

I am so blessed by the encouragement of my lovely wife Dianne and the support of my family and friends.

Big shout out to Deb Renshaw for her invaluable editing, proofreading and advice. Also to Rich Evans Design for his superb work on the book cover.

Special thanks to Vic Pugh, for his insight into life in Singapore before the Japanese invasion and as a prisoner of war of the Japanese after the fall of Singapore, as well as his experiences and emotions on coming home.

A massive thank you to the fabulous author Fiona Mcintosh for her constant support and inspiration.

Finally, I would like to thank cancer so much for visiting me and making me focus on achieving my ambition of writing a novel in a time frame which was unknown!

Although this book is a work of fiction and its story and characters are imaginary, I am indebted to Betty Jeffrey for *White Coolies*; Nicola Tyler for *Sisters in Arms* M.R.D. Foot for *S.O.E.: The Special Operations Executive* and Jan Ruff-O'Herne for *Fifty Years of Silence*.

I would also like to acknowledge Hedd Wyn Rudyard Kipling, Seibo Kitamura and Takuboku Ishikawa for their extracts quoted in the text.

Printed in Great Britain
by Amazon